The only witness to Benedict Absalom's death was Pierre-Luc Ponelle, the simple-minded son of a village shop-keeper. Directly opposite Pierre-Luc was the cliff known locally as Le Mur. A body was poised on the edge. Pierre-Luc heard a despairing shout, then it plunged down the wall. He raised his binoculars and saw the palm-fronds being shaken by the passage of a retreating figure.

He could not see the thorns that cut through the man's clothes and ripped into his face, nor the broken fingers that scrabbled vainly for support. But he did see the landslide of loosened boulders that struck the tumbling body like bullets, before bounding on into the valley. The desperate hands stopped reaching, the torso arced back, gained speed as it fell away from the cliff-face, then crashed into the rocky ledge.

Pierre-Luc watched for a few more minutes. By the time he had wandered back into the village, he had almost forgotten what he had seen.

SHADOWS
IN THE
SUN

Kate Denver

CORGI BOOKS

SHADOWS IN THE SUN
A CORGI BOOK 0 552 13457 0

First publication in Great Britain

PRINTING HISTORY
Corgi edition published 1991

This book is set in 10/11pt Plantin by County Typesetters,
Margate, Kent

Corgi Books are published by Transworld Publishers Ltd.,
61–63 Uxbridge Road, Ealing, London W5 5SA, in Australia by
Transworld Publishers (Australia) Pty. Ltd., 15–23 Helles
Avenue, Moorebank, NSW 2170, and in New Zealand by
Transworld Publishers (N.Z.) Ltd., Cnr Moselle and
Waipareira Avenues, Henderson, Auckland.

Printed and bound in Great Britain by
Cox & Wyman Ltd, Reading, Berks.

To Nicola Scholefield, with love

PART ONE

1

The only witness to Benedict Absalom's death was Pierre-Luc Ponelle, the simple-minded son of a village shop-keeper.

At thirty, he was a huge, shambling man who spent his days rocking back and forth on a bench outside his mother's shop, or wandering alone in the Massif des Maures, that wild range of hills and valleys behind the Riviera resorts of St-Tropez and Ste-Maxime.

His single vice was *voyeurism*. Lovers taking advantage of the solitude had occasionally been disturbed by the sight of Pierre-Luc standing silently in the distance, watching them through his binoculars. His mother had given them to him so he could watch birds, but he preferred to focus on human beings.

Otherwise, he was harmless, gentle, with a permanent smile pasted on his loose-lipped mouth. He rarely spoke to anyone except his mother, and sometimes she was driven to explain, defensively: 'The truth is, you know, he understands more than we think.' No one believed her, but few people argued with Georgette Ponelle.

On this humid September afternoon, as rain-clouds hovered above the Mediterranean, Pierre-Luc was sitting on a rock looking over a narrow valley that ran east-west through the Massif. The binoculars were hanging from a leather strap around his neck.

During the summer, he had watched from the same rock as forest fires roared over the opposite hillside. Now he faced a landscape stripped of undergrowth, its nakedness broken by blackened tree-stumps.

Only two areas of colour survived.

One was the green grass of the lawns and terraces surrounding Ben Absalom's sprawling villa, which was set into the hill, its privacy ensured by a fence of high, iron railings tipped with gilded arrow-heads. Fire-fighters had held back the flames at the edge of the property.

The second was Amyas Mahr's small, pink-washed house, a kilometre away from the villa, which had been protected by its position at the base of a shallow gorge.

Directly opposite Pierre-Luc, below the villa, was the cliff known locally as Le Mur, a wall of rock which fell some fifty feet to a wide ledge, then on into the valley. A few briars and other thorny bushes struggled to survive on its face, rooted in clefts and crevices. A narrow, little-used path wound around the top, where a great palm-tree, which had miraculously survived the fires, was silhouetted against the skyline.

The rock was one of Pierre-Luc's favourite resting-places. From it he could see anyone who walked on the hillside, cars on the road that ran through the valley bottom, and seagulls which drifted in from the coast.

His eyes followed the flight of some gulls which were wheeling above him and he turned away from the valley to gaze up, unblinking, until their widening circles took them out of sight.

When he looked back, there was movement above Le Mur. A body was poised on the edge. He heard a despairing shout, then it plunged down the wall.

He raised his binoculars and saw, behind it, the palm-fronds being shaken by the passage of a retreating figure.

As he watched, there was no more expression on his face than there had been when he was looking at the seagulls.

He could not see the thorns that cut through the falling man's clothes and ripped into his face, nor the broken fingers that scrabbled vainly for support. But he did see the landslide of loosened boulders that struck the tumbling body like bullets, before bounding on into the valley.

The desperate hands stopped reaching, the torso arced back, gained speed as it fell away from the cliff-face, then crashed onto the rocky ledge, where it was to lie, undiscovered, for two hours.

Pierre-Luc watched for a few more minutes. There were still cars on the road, but the seagulls had gone and there was no further movement on the opposite hillside. By the time he had wandered back into the village, and taken up his position on the bench, he had almost forgotten what he had seen.

The knocking was urgent, punctuated by sharp peals of the door-bell.

Bare-footed, Joanna Absalom hurried through the tile-floored hall, and looked up at the tall young man who stood on the terrace. Her surprise turned to apprehension. 'Nicholas? You shouldn't be here!'

'There's been an accident, Jo. We need an ambulance . . .'

She indicated the telephone, saw his hand shaking as he pressed its buttons. She clutched his arm. 'What's happened? Is it Ben?'

When he hung up, she had already thrust her feet into espadrilles that lay near the door, and was running towards the iron-barred gates. He caught up with her and five minutes later they were standing, looking down at the pathetic shape sprawled on the ledge.

He would never forget the desolation in her voice as she said, 'He's dead, isn't he?'

The next day, *Nice Matin* headlined the news in a florid, hurriedly-written story on its front page.

BENEDICT ABSALOM IS DEAD!

Yesterday the British painter Benedict Absalom fell to

his death from a precipice below his home near the village of La Belette.

M. Absalom, 51, was taking his regular afternoon walk when he met with the tragic accident.

One of the world's major portraitists and landscape-painters, his work is represented in art galleries throughout Europe and the U.S. He was popular even among those who know nothing about art, from his appearances on television. These, sadly, were curtailed in recent years due to the onset of severe arthritis, which virtually ended his career.

He and his wife have made their home in Provence for many years, though he spent much of his time abroad, painting international figures in all fields of endeavour.

The body was discovered by his friend, Nicholas Garnier, 27. M. Garnier, an actor and writer, recently returned from the United States to join his father, popular Côte d'Azur personality Peter Garnier, in conducting his Michelin-starred restaurant, Le Lion d'Or, in La Belette.

The young man said last night, 'Ben Absalom will be a sad loss to the world of art.'

Tributes to the dead man are pouring in to the family's villa.

Among those who mourn him is art connoisseur M. Amyas Mahr, a neighbour of the Absaloms.

He said: 'I am shocked and horrified by Ben's death. He was my closest friend.'

Mme Absalom has been too distraught to comment.

M. Absalom's actress daughter, Lisa, 23, who lives in London, was unavailable. It is believed that she is filming a television series in Portugal.

In the weeks after Benedict Absalom's death, it was to emerge that there were several errors of fact in *Nice Matin's* report.

2

' . . . The untimely death that has robbed the world of a matchless talent . . .' The vicar's words throbbed with reverence.

Lisa Absalom watched him with distaste. He was leaning forward, fingers interlaced in front of his chest. Behind the small eyes that roved over the congregation there was, she guessed, a mental computer greedily storing away the faces of the mighty, his captive audience. It included a minor member of the Royal Family, whose portrait by Benedict Absalom hung in the Tate Gallery, two theatrical knights, a duke, politicians, stars of film and television, industrialists, best-selling authors. He could never have anticipated their collective appearance in his village church, nor the television cameras and microphones that were recording his eulogy for posterity.

She turned a few degrees to her right, widening her focus to study the gathering in the opposite pews. Some of the faces she knew personally; others she recognized from pictures in newspapers; still others she saw as curious double-images, the flesh and blood features superimposed on Ben's portraits of them.

She became aware of being watched by a man, short, dark-haired, with a coarse, flattened nose and fleshy lips. A stranger to her, he was wearing jeans and a washed-out denim jacket over a t-shirt.

Her glance swept over him and she caught the eye of a woman sitting next to the aisle. For a moment, their stares locked, then the woman lifted her chin in an ostentatious effort to control emotion, and patted away a tear.

Lisa remembered her. She had been dining with Ben in Le Gavroche one night and Lisa, on her way out with her former husband, had passed their table without acknowledging them. The thought of her mother, Joanna, alone in the villa in France, while Ben enjoyed his mistresses in London, had made her bitterly angry. She was sure that there were other women in the congregation who were also mourning their lost lover.

' . . . But with all his fame and fortune, Benedict Absalom never lost touch with the village which took him and his beloved mother to their hearts . . .'

(She thought: He came back once in thirty-five years. And then only because he was flattered to be asked to open your summer fête.)

' . . . A big man in every sense: generous with his talent and with his friendship . . .'

(Especially his friendship with women.)

Who was this saintly Benedict Absalom, whose memorial service had attracted the rich and famous to the Sussex village from which he had departed at the first opportunity? Who was being described by a stranger in phrases which bore no relation to the foster-father she had known?

'A man of integrity, honest and open in all his dealings, uncompromising in his search for perfection in his art . . .'

A string of adjectives formed in her mind: flamboyant, arrogant, magnetic, shrewd, even brave, according to legend. But honest? Open? She knew that the outgoing, larger-than-life personality was a carapace under which another man lurked: amoral, secretive, domineering, egocentric.

A hand touched her elbow, and Joanna whispered: 'The grieving daughter is not supposed to glare at the congregation.'

'I don't know how much longer I can stand this charade.'

14

'You're an actress. So act.'

Joanna was sitting straight-backed, her dark eyes fixed on the vicar. She was wearing a tentlike black dress which Lisa knew she'd had for at least ten years. A straw trilby that had probably belonged to Ben, around which she had tied a black chiffon scarf, perched on her short, curly, brown hair. Each garment, in itself, was without style, but on her slim figure they took on elegance and dignity.

Despite her apparent serenity, Lisa guessed that she was hating every moment of the service, knowing she was a centre of attention, aware of the curiosity and speculation: So that's the widow . . . wasn't able to keep up with him when he became successful . . . lives in a village in France . . . no wonder he turned to other women . . .

(You're wrong, every one of you! She kept up with him until she couldn't take his life-style any longer. She's the only woman who could have endured marriage to him, and he couldn't do without her. He always came back.)

The end of the service took her by surprise, and she realized that the congregation was waiting for the chief mourners to lead the way from the church.

She and Jo processed along the aisle. The vicar was waiting in the sunshine outside, surrounded by press photographers and tv cameramen. He murmured condolences as he looked beyond Jo to make sure he did not miss any of the celebrities, then focused on Lisa, who was one of them: 'Miss Absalom, if we could only have met at a happier time! My wife and daughter have never missed an episode of *Families*. If I only had the time . . . but I understand your performance is delightful.'

'Thank you.'

'My wife would never forgive me if I didn't ask . . . Your father was once kind enough to open our annual fête. Is it possible that you might be persuaded . . .?'

'I'm afraid not,' she said briskly. 'I never open fêtes. If you'll excuse me . . .'

She smiled inwardly as she walked on. Clearly the vicar

15

didn't read the tabloids or he would hardly see Lisa Absalom as a suitable person to open the church fête.

Jo was talking to a thin, grey man who was carrying a briefcase. As Lisa joined them, he said, 'Until tomorrow, Mrs Absalom,' and went towards the row of waiting cars.

'Ben's lawyer,' Jo said. 'Do let's try to get away . . .' She broke off as a new arrival touched her arm. 'Anthony, I believe I have to thank you for arranging the service.'

He kissed her on both cheeks. 'Joanna, it's been too long. I assure you, this was a labour of love. And it looks as though the whole world's come to pay tribute. He will be sadly missed. Lisa, it's been years. You're even prettier off the box.'

'Hello, Anthony. Still ripping off impoverished artists?'

Anthony Henriques was Ben's agent in London, the owner of a Bond Street art-gallery. A willowy, elegant man in his forties, with mouse-brown hair that fell in an artistic fringe to his eyebrows, he had once attempted to entice Lisa into his bed. She had laughed at him, and they had disliked each other ever since. He turned back to Jo. 'She's always been a waspish child. Darling, this is no time for business, but we must meet. Your place or mine?'

'I'll come to the gallery. Tomorrow morning?'

He allowed himself to be swept aside by a man dressed almost entirely in black suede: wide-brimmed hat, jacket, trousers, the whole relieved by a ruffled shirt open to the waist. There was a glint of gold chains in the mat of black hair that covered his chest. The wide-mouthed, deeply-lined face had green-shadowed eyelids and a touch of colour had been stroked onto the sagging cheeks. From the middle of the stalls, Lisa thought, he might have some sexual attraction. Close up, he looked like a pantomime dame.

He made no pretence of offering commiseration. After the briefest greeting, he said, 'Like to talk to you about old Ben's pictures, Mrs Absalom.' The voice was thick, adenoidal, Birmingham-born.

16

Joanna looked at him blankly.

'I'll take anything you've got, finished or unfinished. Pay you top price.' He stopped, not from delicacy, but because he realized that she had not recognized him. 'You know me, love! I'm Dominic Partridge. Me and Ben were doing business.'

'I have no idea what you're talking about, Mr Partridge,' she said icily.

'He didn't tell you about my collection?' His voice was shrill with disbelief. 'I prob'ly got the best private collection of Absaloms in the world. I'm negotiating now with some guy in Switzerland who wants to sell a couple.'

'I don't handle the sale of my husband's work.' Jo took Lisa's arm and they went towards the cars.

Ignoring the cameramen who walked backwards in front of them, they did not notice the man in jeans who was trying to attract their attention.

As they reached the lych-gate, Lisa said, 'I know Partridge is a has-been, but didn't you recognize him? He was a pop-singer in the sixties and he still turns up on the box from time to time.'

'Of course I did. I just didn't care for him. He used to do a semi-striptease on stage and little girls had orgasms. Ben told me about him, too. Now he's no longer top of the pops he's going in for culture and he thinks that collecting Absaloms will improve his image.'

'Did they meet? I wouldn't have thought he's Ben's type.'

'Amyas Mahr introduced them.'

'That old crook! Are he and Ona still living in La Belette?'

'Yes.'

'Do you see much of them?'

'As much as one must in a small community. They came to the villa the day after Ben's death. Ona brought me a cake she had baked. Amyas was impossible. He actually cried. You'd have thought he and Ben had been bosom

17

friends, instead of having disliked each other for years.'

Lisa's scarlet soft-top Beetle was parked behind the hired car that had brought Jo directly from Heathrow to the church. 'Pay the driver off and come with me,' she said. 'You're staying at the flat.'

'Won't I bc a nuisance?'

'Don't be ridiculous! I've been longing to see you.'

'Let me transfer my suitcase. I don't suppose I can pay him in French francs, can I? I didn't have time to change any money at the airport.'

'Let me.' Lisa paid the driver. Then she said, 'You wouldn't have come if I hadn't phoned yesterday, would you?'

'No. I remember Ben in my own way. I don't need a clergyman to tell me about him. I'm glad I did come, though. I didn't know you were back from Portugal until your call.'

'I couldn't have borne that service by myself.'

'You could have opted out.'

'I thought of it. Then I imagined what the media would have made of it. "Famous artist's family ignore his memorial." "Actress daughter refuses to pay last respects."'

'Would that have happened?'

'I'm getting to be an expert on predicting their reactions.' She hesitated. 'I suppose there was some guilt mixed up in it, too. Maybe I could have been less – intolerant.'

They had pulled away from the churchyard and were negotiating the village's picturesque main street, with its Georgian houses and a few nineteenth-century shop-fronts. Several people turned to watch the cars, pointing out the celebrities.

As they were stopped by traffic-lights at the end of the High Street, Jo felt the impact of staring eyes and heard a woman say to her friend, 'There's that girl who's in *Families . . .*'

18

The lights changed and the little car shot forward as Lisa stamped on the accelerator.

'How can you stand this attention all the time?' Jo said. 'Ben loved it, but I used to hate it when we lived in England.'

Lisa shrugged. 'It was fun at first. I suppose everyone deals with it differently. The lucky ones can ignore it. Some get angry. I try to pretend it's an extension of my job, and that I'm on-stage as soon as I go out of my front door.'

'I would find that intolerable.'

'I do now. It's been harder since the divorce. I had the Press camping on my doorstep for days.'

'I read some of the reports. They made me feel sick . . .' She stopped, and said, 'Take the next turn to the left, just past that red-brick house.'

'Is it a short cut?'

'No, I want to show you something.'

They turned into a country road which narrowed into a lane. After half a mile, they came to a group of cottages and two large houses, surrounded by well-trimmed hedges, with gravel drives and smooth lawns.

'Stop here.'

Lisa pulled up outside a white-washed, two-up, two-down cottage which had originally been built for a farm-labourer's family. An extension had been added, there were carriage lamps on each side of the front door, and a lion's head knocker. A corn-dolly pheasant surmounted the new thatch and the grass verge outside its hedge of variegated privet was neatly mown. On the centre of its wrought-iron gate a slice of varnished tree-trunk, the bark intact, announced in black letters that this was Primrose Cottage.

'Who lives there?'

'God knows. Yuppies, from the look of it. But Ben was brought up in that cottage. In those days, there was a kitchen and a living-room with a black-leaded coal stove

19

downstairs, two tiny bedrooms and a bathroom the size of a postage-stamp on top. An old-fashioned bath and a loo with a wooden seat. There were apple trees in the garden. Nettles and weeds choked the grass, the wooden fence was broken – and no one ever mowed the verge.' She paused. 'It was nicer then.'

Lisa was trying to absorb a new vision of Ben's childhood. 'Were they that poor?'

'He lived with his mother, Anna. And yes, she was poor.'

'The Czech peasant? I remember he used to make fun of her. It always rather embarrassed me.'

'Me, too. Especially having known Anna.'

'Otherwise, he hardly ever mentioned her. I find it hard to see him in a tumbledown cottage in the country. He was such a citified person.'

Jo nodded. 'He was never really happy away from the centre of the action. That's why he found the last few years so difficult.'

'I didn't even know he had died until I got back yesterday. I feel wretched that you've been alone.'

'You hadn't seen any newspapers?'

'We were on location north of the Algarve, working from morning until late at night. Didn't see a paper or talk about anything except what we'd be doing the next day.'

'And you had to come home to this. I'm sorry, love. I couldn't think of any easy way to break the news, not knowing where you were.'

'There was a pile of mail in the flat. The first letter I opened was from Anthony, telling me about the memorial service. The second was yours. But I still don't understand exactly what happened. You just said he had slipped and fallen over the cliff. Can you bear to talk about it?'

'I think so. It doesn't hurt so much any more. It's unreal, rather like describing a nightmare. He went out for a walk as he often did, because he was determined to stay mobile for as long as possible. Sometimes I went with him,

20

sometimes he preferred to be by himself. This day, I stayed behind to start a *coq au vin* for supper. There'd been heavy rain and the path was muddy. It happened near the phoenix tree. He must have fallen, and couldn't stop himself from sliding over the edge of Le Mur. His walking stick was still lying under the tree.' She stopped as her voice broke, then she said, 'After all, it does still hurt. Would you mind if we didn't talk about it any more?'

They finished the journey into London in silence.

Lisa's flat was in a mansion block overlooking Hampstead Heath. It had large rooms, furnished in high-tech overlaid with litter: white chairs of plastic-covered steel mesh, cushioned in black; chrome-framed glass coffee-tables; metal uprights bearing glass shelves. The flooring was dimpled white vinyl, the curtains swags of white muslin, long enough to fall into pools on the floor. She had thrown bright Persian prayer-rugs onto the vinyl, tied back the curtains with scarlet ribbon, piled books on the shelves and set vases of flowers on the tables.

For the first time that day, Jo smiled. 'This reminds me of your room at home when you were fourteen. You redecorated it and said you didn't want anything that wasn't white or black. But within a month you'd brought back all the bits and pieces you'd banished to the shed: toys, books, shells, posters, the pottery you'd made at school, the green glass bottles from Biot . . .'

'Simon decorated this. Until he left, I wasn't allowed to add even a bunch of flowers. Bleak was beautiful, according to him. I've been trying to cosy it up ever since.'

'We haven't talked about your divorce . . .'

She shrugged. 'We will. How long can you stay?'

'A few days. I have to see the solicitor tomorrow, then Henriques. I must find out how I stand financially. Are you working now?'

Lisa didn't answer the question. 'A drink? Vodka and something?'

'Tonic or bitter lemon. Whatever you have.'

Watching her as she poured the drinks, Jo thought that one of her strengths as a tv actress must be that she looked like a real person. Her light-brown, silky hair hung loose to her shoulders, framing a face that was alive and normally full of humour, but now she seemed tired and there were dark circles under her heavily-lashed eyes. Her middle european parentage had bequeathed her the high, flat cheek-bones and firm jawline. Her mouth was wide, her smooth skin lightly tanned. Slightly below medium height, she carried herself so gracefully that she looked taller.

As she handed Jo a glass, she said abruptly: 'You asked if I was working. No, I'm not. I've been fired.'

'I can't believe it! Why?'

'We've finished the current seri   They're writing my character out of the next one.'

'Did they give any reason?'

'I suppose it was inevitable. *Families* makes the ratings because it's good, clean entertainment. It goes out at 6.30, prime time for family viewing. My character, Bridget, was whiter than white. Everyone adored her: a virgin at twenty-one, in love with good, clean, Henry, who never laid a hand on her. It was about as true to life as *Conan the Barbarian*.' She sighed. 'When the tabloids discovered that Bridget was divorcing her real-life husband, that was bad enough. But when that real-life husband was arrested for having sex with a fifteen-year-old boy and given a prison sentence, that was it.'

She moved restlessly around the room. 'I went to see him, you know. Photographers were lying in wait for pictures of me going into gaol. Simon said I wasn't to come again. One newspaper managed to dig up old – friends of his. One or two talked about his past. It wasn't all that lurid, he'd always been discreet, but they speculated on what sort of a woman would have married that sort of man. Not our Bridget, that's for sure. They had to let her survive the series, but next year she – and I – will have

22

been killed off.' She looked at Jo defiantly. 'I'm still fond of Simon, you know. He's a good friend.'

Jo nodded. 'I liked him, but I find it hard to forgive him for what happened. What will you do now?'

'There'll be other jobs. I've had a couple of offers, but I've turned them down. I've made enough out of the series to exist without working for a while, and I want to – to get myself together again.'

After a moment's silence, Jo said hesitantly, 'I suppose you wouldn't consider coming home with me?'

Lisa's face lightened. 'You've read my mind. I was going to ask you if I could.'

'I can think of nothing I'd like more.'

'Do you realize it's nearly eight years since I've seen La Belette?'

'It hasn't changed. I used to long for you to come back, but I knew it was no good asking. You never forgave Ben, did you?'

'Never.' Her face was bleak. 'Whenever my life goes wrong, I can trace it back to him. What he did to Nick Garnier and me was unforgivable.'

'You were only just sixteen. The situation would have changed even without Ben.'

'Maybe. But it would have been *our* decision. Ben forced me to come here, so Nick went to America and turned into a drunken slob. I married Simon . . . oh, hell, it's over now. And Ben's dead. No point in talking about it.'

'Suppose you were to meet Nick again. He'd have changed. Isn't it possible . . .?'

'Never!' The denial was so vehement that Jo looked at her in surprise.'

'But if . . .'

'Let's drop it, darling.' Her voice was steely. 'There are things you don't know about Nick. If you did, you'd understand why I don't want to have anything to do with him, ever again.'

23

3

Two weeks before Ben Absalom fell to his death, Nicholas Garnier came home to La Belette, and felt as though he had stepped into a time-capsule.

His father met him at Nice Airport and they drove west along the Corniche. During the eight years he had been away, villas and apartment blocks had proliferated, the traffic was heavier than it had been, and the ports had filled with yachts. Port Grimaud, the 'medieval fishing-port' which had been manufactured in the early sixties, had still been somewhat unsettled; now it looked as though it had been tucked into the bay for centuries, and its houses, with their private moorings, advertised their owners' wealth.

They turned inland. He was pleased to see that Cotolin, the nearest town to La Belette, had changed less than the resorts, and remained a working environment. Its twin industries of cork, harvested from the cork-oaks that grew throughout the area, and pipe-manufacturing, from the local briars, survived. But even here, villas had mushroomed on its outskirts and new souvenir shops and bars had appeared.

La Belette, on the other hand, had not increased by a single building. The road which wound through the hills passed it without a sideways glance. There was the same shabby PTT, with its yellow post-van parked outside, and the fly-blown general shop. As they drew level with it, Nick leant out of the car and waved to Georgette Ponelle, its Corsican owner. She was leaning against the door, a cigarette, as always, hanging from the corner of her mouth. Her impossibly black hair was piled into a towering beehive. Pierre-Luc was sitting on a bench beside the door, his body rocking as he stared vacantly ahead. Georgette was chatting with a blue-overalled workman from the timber-yard which was on the edge of the village and gave employment to many of the local men. She looked towards the car. When she recognized Nick, her arms became windmills, and the brown, creased face split into a smile.

'Does she still write poetry?' Nick asked his father.

'More – and worse – than ever. She is also working on a novel about Napoleon's younger days.'

'Does she read it to you?'

'Another instalment every time I go into the shop. It's distressingly full of his – or her – sexual fantasies.'

'Who was Monsieur Ponelle?' Nick said idly. 'I presume there was one.'

'God knows. She doesn't mention him. She and Pierre-Luc have been alone ever since we came to La Belette.'

'Pierre-Luc looks just the same.'

'He spends most of his time in the hills. Never speaks. He sometimes frightens tourists who come on him unexpectedly, and the local girls are wary of him.'

The Lion d'Or was beyond the shop. The vines covering the pergola over its terrace were thicker, but the white plastic chairs and tables under their Cinzano umbrellas were arranged as they always had been. He could see through the open door what might have been the same groups of locals who had been standing at the bar the day he left. Behind it was the restaurant, which attracted a very different class of customer.

'How's business?' he said.

'Flourishing. Ben Absalom brings his famous friends and during the season people come from all over hoping to catch a glimpse of them.' Peter looked speculatively at his son. 'I expect you'll attract a few more.'

'That's the sort of thing I've come home to avoid.

Ben loves the attention, I suppose?'

'What do you think? And the other person who makes the most of it is Amyas Mahr.'

'Hanging onto Ben's coat-tails?'

'Hardly that. Ben swats him like an over-sized fly if he takes liberties. But Amyas can talk about his good friends, Ben Absalom and the late Pablo Picasso – at the mention of whose name his eyes tend to mist over – and this impresses the silly people who believe he's the expert on modern art that he claims. They buy him meals and if Ben happens to be around, Amyas greets him . . . "My dear boy, great to see you! Joanna well, I hope?" Ben puts up with that, and Amyas knows better than to pursue it any further. It's enough to convince his pals.'

Nick laughed. 'What a charlatan he is! How's Ona?'

'Down-trodden as always.'

'D'you think she believes his stories about having been Picasso's great chum?'

'Who knows what Ona believes? He rarely gives her a chance to speak.'

They turned into a drive that led up to a small château with pepper-pot towers at each corner. Peter had bought it twenty years earlier, when his family *parfumerie* in Grasse had been taken over by a Hamburg-based multi-national.

In his late thirties, with a wife and a young son, he had cast around for something to occupy his time. The village's only restaurant, the Lion d'Or, was owned by Jean-Louis Mazeau, a superb chef, but a poor businessman. The bar at the front of the building was well patronized by the largely peasant community, but there was no passing tourist trade and the restaurant attracted few customers, despite its low prices.

Jean-Louis and his young wife, Marie, cooked because they loved cooking, and they ate because they loved eating. And they put on weight because they could not bear to waste the good food for which there had been insufficient demand.

They made their pâtés and quiches, and other dishes bequeathed to them by Jean-Louis' mother, who had been brought up in Strasbourg – goose in wine sauce thickened with blood and spices, jugged hare, roast pork seasoned with sage and rosemary and served with quetsche plums. They counted a day successful if they served half-a-dozen meals.

Peter Garnier was the first person fully to appreciate their genius, but he soon realized that it was only a matter of time before they would be forced to sell up.

He bought the business and appointed Jean-Louis partner, manager and chef. It was a successful arrangement from the start. The Mazeaus lived above the bar and cooked happily from morning until night, on a generous share of the profits, but with no financial responsibilities.

Peter had a wide circle of friends throughout Europe and America and enticed many of them to La Belette for a free introductory meal.

He persuaded Jean-Louis to produce only one menu each day, a limited choice within it. For this, he announced, they would charge five hundred francs a head – excluding wine and service.

'No-one will pay such a price!' Marie wailed.

'Wait and see.'

They waited, and they saw. Peter's friends came back again and again, and told *their* friends about the restaurant. Its fame spread, and it became a tradition for celebrities visiting Cannes for the annual Film Festival to drive along the coast for at least one meal at the Lion d'Or. In high season, patrons wrote from New York or London weeks in advance to book their tables.

The Mazeaus lost much of their excess weight because there were no longer any left-overs to be eaten up.

At the same time, Peter insisted that the bar must remain unchanged, the domain of the local farmers and *ouvriers*.

Nick remembered him saying that the Lion d'Or

typified the two faces of the village. On the one hand, there were the rural people who had maintained their peasant way of life for generations, working their tiny farms and vineyards, grazing their sheep, indifferent to the outside world. On the other, the wealthy visitors who spilled in from all over Europe, frequently to visit Benedict Absalom, who had moved into the village a few years after the Garniers.

The locals went into the bar from the terrace, drank a quick *fine* in the mornings, or more leisurely beers at mid-day. The restaurant patrons parked their BMWs and Porsches behind the building, and entered the restaurant through a side door. On the whole, the two factions tolerated each other, but should a group from foreign parts invade the bar, few were sufficiently strong-minded to endure for long the silent stares which greeted them.

Nick's American-born mother had contracted multiple sclerosis and died two years after they moved to La Belette. Peter assuaged his grief by taking a more active part in running the restaurant, and Nick came to regard it as his second home, spending almost as much time with Jean-Louis and Marie as with his father. They taught him to cook and when he was twelve he made his first rum-soaked Alsatian *kugelhopf* which, on high days and holidays, was served to friends in the restaurant, accompanied by glasses of sugared and spiced wine. He suffered his first hang-over after such a feast on Bastille Day the year he entered his teens.

Now he was home, after nearly eight years during which he had travelled the length and breadth of the United States, enjoyed happy times and endured deep depressions, spent a night in gaol, and worked at a dozen different jobs, ranging from assistant stage-manager in a summer theatre to short-order cook and journalist. These had culminated in twin successes: first in Hollywood, as an actor in a hugely acclaimed motion picture, then as the author of a book about the dark side of the film world

28

which reached the best-seller lists. After its publication he had found himself being fêted by the very people he had exposed. Finally, disgusted by sycophants, bored with his own notoriety, he had fled back to the Provençal village in which he had been brought up. Only his publishers knew where he had gone, and he had sworn them to secrecy.

For nearly two weeks he relaxed in the tranquility of La Belette. He occupied himself helping out in the Lion d'Or, and renewed acquaintance with local people who cared nothing for his success in America, hadn't seen his film nor read his book.

His first and only encounter with Ben Absalom took place in the Lion d'Or a few days after his return.

He had entered the bar-restaurant through the kitchen, and set down the basket of *langoustines* he had collected from the port. He made a brisk, pinching pass at Marie's ample bottom, and nodded casually to the pretty waitress, Claudette Dorsey. She was wearing a brown dress, high-necked and, at first sight, discreet enough to satisfy even Marie's fiercely conservative standards. But seventeen-year-old Claudette could inject sensuality into a nun's habit by the swing of her buttocks, her voluptuous breasts, the sullen pout of her full lips and, in the case of this brown dress, the slit in its skirt high enough to reveal provocative glimpses of bare, rounded thighs.

Her instant pursuit of Nick had made him wary, since Marie had intimated that she had a reputation among the local men as an easy lay – this despite the fact that her stern, puritanical father, a timber-yard worker, believed that she was still pure as an unborn baby.

'She's shameless, that one,' Marie had said. 'A man-eater.'

'How long has she lived here?'

'André Dorsey is a widower. He sent her to school in Nice and she lived with her aunt there for years. When she left school, she told André that she wanted to be a dancer and go on the stage. Well, the fuss there was! He thinks show-business is another word for vice and corruption, so he brought her straight home. She's been back for about six months – and hates it.'

'Has she worked here ever since?'

'No. She was helping Joanna Absalom at the Villa Mimosa, but she was given notice a few weeks ago. Why, I do not know – but I could make a guess.'

Nick raised his eyebrows questioningly, but she shook her head. 'I do not gossip about my friends. Anyhow, she came crying to Peter, saying she wanted work. He is the kindest man in the world, and we were short of a waitress, so he took her on. It will not be for long if I have anything to do with it. She is a disrupting influence.' She kneaded her pastry with vigour, and said again, 'Be careful of her, Nick. She will go after you because of what she thinks you might do for her – apart from your other attractions, of course. She still wants to go on the stage and she's desperate to get away from her father.' She paused. 'I have to say, André would not be the easiest person to live with.'

'I hardly remember him. Big chap, never smiles, right?'

'Never smiles. Doesn't talk much. Doesn't drink or smoke. Disapproves of almost everything. A hard man.'

Nick, who did not find Claudette attractive, had treated her with implacable formality after that and been relieved when she had lately shown signs of giving up the chase.

He turned towards the swing doors that led into the restaurant, but before he reached them, Jean-Louis appeared and said, without preamble, 'Ben Absalom's in there.'

'So?'

'So if I were you, I'd go out the way you came in.'

'Hell, I have to see him some time. Might as well be now.'

'He's been drinking.'

Nick's eyebrows lifted. 'Ben never used to drink.'

'Have a look at his hands and you'll see why he's taken to it.'

'Peter told me about his arthritis.'

'He can be aggressive.'

'I'll keep the bar between us.'

Jean-Louis, a small man with a rosy face and a grey tonsure around his shining pink scalp, wiped his hands nervously on his apron, and followed Nick through the crowded restaurant and the arch which led into the bar. At one end of the scrubbed wooden counter were three stoneware terrines of the pâtés for which the restaurant was famous, a jar of *cornichons* and a dish of green tomatoes.

The young barman, Lucien, was dealing with other customers, but keeping a wary eye on the stool on which Ben Absalom sat. M. Absalom was generous with his tips, but demanded instant service.

The brooding expression on Ben's face forbade any attempts at casual conversation. Nick watched him for a moment. In his fifties, he was still a spectacularly handsome man. His thick hair had turned prematurely grey years ago, and his square, Slav face, with its high cheekbones and piercing blue eyes, had hardly aged. But the joints of his left hand, which was curved around the stem of his brandy glass, were swollen and blue. The right, the hand with which he painted, was a claw. The fingers were twisted, some top joints almost at right-angles to the second, and the thumb was curved back. Jean-Louis whispered, 'He's in constant pain. He can't hold a brush. It's a tragedy.'

A second man was standing at the bar, reaching occasionally to pick out a *cornichon* with a pair of olive-wood tongs. Over six feet tall, he had curly, grey-black hair and a full beard that looked like wire wool. He was wearing blue cotton work-pants and a check shirt, both of which were stretched over his great belly. His glance flicked from Nick to Absalom. His small, bright, black eyes sparkled with malicious anticipation. 'Nick! Ça va?'

31

'Hi, Amyas.'

Absalom looked up. He frowned, then, as Nick walked towards him, all expression was wiped from his face.

'Hello, Ben.'

The other man ignored his outstretched hand. 'I heard you were here. How long are you staying?'

'Indefinitely.'

'You've got a bloody nerve, coming back after what you did to my daughter.' He lifted his glass, and drained it.

Nick's voice was steady. 'Ben, we haven't seen each other for a long time. I've come back because this is my home. For Christ's sake, let's forget the past.'

'Let's not!' His voice had risen. The words were slurred. Nick was uncomfortably aware that silence had fallen in the bar and that several diners were watching them from the restaurant.

Ben lowered himself painfully off the stool, reached for his walking-stick, and leant forward. 'Why don't you go back to your junkie friends? You're polluting the place!'

'You're drunk, Ben.' Nick rounded the end of the bar and stood over him, taller, fitter, more than twenty years younger. He said softly, 'You're disturbing the patrons.'

'Fuck the patrons!'

Nick beckoned to Jean-Louis. They each took one of his arms and turned him towards the door. He struggled for only a moment, then, head high, walked between them, stumbling occasionally. The local taxi was standing outside. He snapped an order through the window. The driver, who was dozing behind the wheel, jumped out, opened the passenger door, and they drove off.

The other two men went back into the bar, where Amyas Mahr still stood, smiling to himself.

'He hasn't changed,' Jean-Louis said.

Nick shrugged indifferently. 'It was too much to hope for. Once a shit . . . I'm not going to let him bother me.'

Several days later, Nick stood on the cliff below the

Absaloms' sprawling white villa. Behind it, the Massif des Maures rose in folds, covered in the blackened stumps of cork-oaks. His father had written to him about the forest fires. The villa, and Amyas Mahr's house, had been saved by hundreds of fire-fighters and by helicopters fitted with great scoops, which had dumped gallons of lake water on the buildings. Since then heavy rain had brought rivers of khaki-coloured mud, now unimpeded by undergrowth, down the hills.

Having spent the morning shopping for the restaurant in St-Tropez, Nick had walked out from the village, seeking solitude to contemplate his uncertain future. Would it really be possible, now that Lisa Absalom was lost to him, to recapture the peace and happiness he had once known in La Belette? Or had Ben shattered it beyond repair?

When he reached the place which he and Lisa had regarded as their own, memories flooded back – and Ben was a part of them all.

Four metres from the cliff-edge, the phoenix tree stood, thick-stemmed, with its magnificent crown of fronds, some of them fifteen feet long, arching down towards the ground.

It was Ben who had identified the tree as *phoenix canariensis*, a date-palm native to North Africa, which had no right to be growing wild in France. Its name, he had explained, was derived from the Greek *phoinex*, which meant both phoenix and palm-tree.

Nick and Lisa had been enthralled by his stories about the fabulous bird which had given the tree its name. To keep them quiet while he painted them, he would embroider the legend of how, when it was ready to die, the phoenix made itself a nest of spices, sang its own dirge and, with its wings, created a spark which set the nest alight. It would settle in the flames, burn itself alive and then, miraculously, be reborn from its own ashes.

After that, they had always called their palm the phoenix tree.

33

In those days, the children had regarded Ben as their fount of knowledge, their sympathetic friend and confidant, a glamorous figure whose presence enhanced the excitement and intensity of their lives.

As Nick grew older, and the scales of innocence began to fall from his eyes, a strain crept into the friendship. More than once, Ben complained of his insolence in daring to challenge opinions he would once have accepted without question. There were times, too, when Nick suspected that Ben resented his monopoly of Lisa's company. When he was at the villa, between painting trips, he would keep them apart as much as he could, and eventually they began to look forward to his departures.

Lisa was not yet sixteen when the phoenix tree witnessed the event that finally destroyed the relationship and changed the course of their lives: Ben came upon them lying, half hidden by the fronds, making love. Looking at the place, even after so long, Nick cringed inwardly as he remembered the man's savage fury, Lisa's tears, his own stammering excuses. Ben immediately took Lisa with him to London, where she would go to school. Nick, lonely and ashamed, agreed to his father's suggestion that he should go to college in the United States, the birth-place of his own mother and of Peter's mother.

He had seen Lisa only once since then, a painful occasion that had put paid to any possibility of resuming their friendship.

That was a memory he did not want to pursue. He walked to the edge of the cliff and looked across the valley, where the last fold of hills sloped towards the coast. Apart from some charred tree-trunks, there were fewer traces of the fire there. It had been fiercest on the south-facing slopes behind and below him and the road which ran through the valley must have acted as a fire-break. A stream of cars was scurrying along it like busy ants, making, in the one direction, for St-Tropez, Cannes, Nice,

Monte Carlo; in the other for Toulon, Marseilles and the Spanish border. He and Lisa used to sit on the cliff, betting on the number of cars that would pass in ten minutes. Now there were so many, moving so fast, that it would be almost impossible to count them.

His focus shifted to the steep slope below him, and another memory surfaced, of himself challenging Lisa, aged twelve, to climb with him to the rocky ledge half way down the cliff.

Never one to allow him to get the better of her, she had started off, stretching from one foot-hold to the next, clutching bushes that grew out from the face. At a point where there was a vertical slab of rock, she had stuck with one foot jammed in a crevice, clinging to an exposed root. He was not tall enough to reach her from above or below and had been forced to leave her while he raced for help to the Absalom's villa. His own father and Ben had been furious with him.

At that point in memory, he looked down at the ledge towards which they had climbed, and at first he did not register what he was seeing. Then, horrified, he realized that a man's body was sprawled there, legs splayed, his head twisted at an unnatural angle, his face hidden. The rock below him was stained red.

Without pausing to think, he slithered over the edge and down the cliff-face, ripping his shirt on briars, lacerating his hands as he scrabbled for holds.

He reached the body and saw who it was. The unmistakable shock of grey hair was soaked in blood, the deformed fingers were broken and raw, from clawing at the rocks.

Sick and breathless, Nick scrambled back up the cliff and dashed to the villa.

He took the stone steps that led up onto the terrace two at a time, and banged on the front door.

* * *

The cremation service was interrupted by the constant flare of flash-bulbs and clicking of cameras. Ben Absalom's death was a media event, made more titillating by the fact that Nicholas Garnier, the hero of a younger generation, had found the body.

4

'I have to tell you, Mrs Absalom, that your late husband's funds in this country will barely cover the taxes and death duties.'

Ben's accountant, a round-faced, portly man with wispy hair and a habit of clicking his tongue before he spoke, had made no attempt to break the news gently and at first she did not understand its implication.

She turned to the grey solicitor. 'The flat in Islington . . .'

'It was sold two years ago. Didn't he tell you?'

'I thought it was let.'

He spoke slowly and carefully, as to a child. 'Your husband's expenses when he came to London were heavy. His hotel suite alone cost five hundred a night. He entertained a great deal. And the fact that his illness has prevented him from working meant that no money has come in. He has refused television engagements . . .'

'He hated people to see how crippled he was.'

' . . . There was also the regular monthly transfer, which he recently increased, in line with inflation – and against my advice – to eight hundred pounds.'

'What transfer was that?'

'For the past – what? Nineteen years, I believe, he has been regularly transferring money into an account in the National Westminster Bank, Swiss Cottage. I assumed you knew about it.'

'Whose account?'

'A Mrs Alicia Freeman. A relative, perhaps? Over the years, it has been a considerable drain.'

Numbly, she said, 'A relative. Yes, of course.'

'Naturally, the payments ceased on his death, since there have been no funds available. I have advised the bank. Mrs Freeman has not been in touch. If you wish to continue . . .?'

'No,' she said. 'No, I don't.'

They talked for an hour about Ben's affairs. She took little in, beyond the fact that both men had warned him, personally and by letter, of the gravity of his financial situation.

Abruptly, she stood up. 'Thank you,' she said. 'I'll let you know what I plan to do, Mr . . .' His name had gone from her mind.

'One moment . . .' He handed her an envelope. 'This is a letter for Miss Absalom. Your husband left it with me some years ago, to be held until his death.'

Lisa's name was typewritten. She glanced at it, then put it in her hand-bag, too absorbed in her own problems to be more than momentarily curious.

In effect, apart from a few thousand pounds in the joint account she and Ben had kept in France, she was broke.

Half an hour later, she was moving slowly up Bond Street towards the Henriques Gallery, unaware of the people who stepped out of her way, or apologized politely as she bumped into them.

During the long walk from the Strand, her thoughts had become increasingly chaotic. Years ago, when she had shared with Ben the secret in her own life that she had never revealed before – or since – he had said 'From now on, my darling, we will hide nothing from each other. A bargain?'

His reaction had released her from the loneliness of a guilt that had haunted her since she was five years old, so she had nodded eagerly, and she had kept the bargain, even after she discovered that he'd had no intention of taking it seriously.

38

Six months after their wedding, he had hidden his first extramarital affair from her. She had found out about it, cried, and reminded him of what he had said. Apparently overwhelmed by contrition, he promised there would be no more secrets, no more affairs. Within a year, the promise had been shattered.

Slowly and painfully , she had adjusted to the knowledge that he was incapable of being faithful to one woman. Eventually, still loving him, she had broken the barriers of jealousy and resentment, and emerged into calm resignation. She had never made a scene again, and had discovered that his entanglements rarely lasted longer than a few months.

But it seemed that parts of his life had been hidden more deeply than she had ever suspected. For nearly twenty years he had been maintaining a woman named Alicia Freeman and without telling her, he had sold the London flat. He had never hinted that he was in financial difficulties.

She was brought back to the present by the sight of a crowd gathered around the Henriques Gallery's showwindow. She looked over the heads and saw, propped against black velvet curtains, the first painting Ben had ever done of Nick Garnier and Lisa.

Always obsessed by faces, he had used a huge canvas, which he had filled with the two heads, each three times life-size. The children had been about seven and ten then. Now they looked into Bond Street, seeming to float in mid-air, without background or torsos.

They were beautiful. Lisa's hair was drawn up into a little muffin on top of her head, held by a red comb. Her brown eyes were slanted towards Nicholas, and she looked as though she was about to break into laughter. Her skin had the bloom and shadings of a peach. The boy's face was thin, with high cheekbones and a wide mouth, already giving promise of strength. His eyes, under the dark, tumbled hair, were a curious, smoky grey, with a black line around the irises.

The picture's impact was so strong that passers-by seemed to be momentarily transfixed by it. There was nothing else behind the plate glass, apart from a discreet gold card on which, in black type, were the words:

BENEDICT ABSALOM
Portrait of L. & N.

La Belette, 1972.

From the collection of Dominic Partridge, Esq.

She remembered hearing that Partridge had bought it at auction. He had paid a quarter of a million for it, and Ben had been furious – with the seller, a German collector, rather than the buyer.

'You know what I got for that? Fifteen hundred bloody pounds!' he said. 'Look at the profit that bastard's made, and I won't see a penny of it.'

His anger had been softened later when Amyas Mahr had informed him that Partridge wanted to meet him.

'I have told him, dear boy, that the picture should be the foundation of an Absalom collection,' Mahr said. 'I am his adviser, you understand. He has a great deal of loose money, but very little taste or knowledge. I have a feeling that you and I might do rather well out of him.'

Subsequently, Ben had been invited to spend a weekend on Partridge's yacht, from which he had returned, heavy-eyed, hung-over, but flattered into good temper.

Buoyantly, he had told her, 'I'll work again, you know, even if I have to strap a brush to my wrist. I could sell this imbecile a design for a kitchen sink and he'd think it was great art as long as it had my name on it.'

He had actually attempted to paint, using strips of plaster to attach the long handle of a brush to his forearm, shutting himself into his studio as he experimented.

One day Jo had taken him a cup of coffee and found

him sitting at his table, staring at his twisted hands, with tears running down his cheeks.

He had said nothing, simply gesturing towards his easel. The canvas might have been attacked by an infant. The brush-strokes were wavering and uncertain, the colours spreading into each other, forming muddy patches.

He had never touched a brush again, but, with Amyas Mahr acting as agent, he had sold Partridge two pictures which had been hanging on the walls of the *salon* in the villa. One was an early portrait of Joanna, which had been her favourite. The other was a landscape which belonged to a later period.

It was said that Mahr was earning a substantial commission from the former pop-star by searching out other collectors who owned Ben's work, and persuading them to sell. The first time he achieved such a coup, he had reported it gleefully, and been unprepared for the anger with which the news had been received.

Later Ben said to Jo: 'He expected me to be pleased because he got as much in commission as I was originally paid!' He had spread his deformed hands and looked at them bitterly. 'It's so bloody unfair! Just when my stuff's fetching top prices, this has to happen. Everyone's cashing in on the market, except me.'

Henriques was waiting for her at the door of the gallery. He gestured towards the window. 'My little tribute to Ben. I hope you approve. Dom keeps it on the yacht, but he had it flown up from St-Trop.'

He led her into his office, a small room with an eighteenth-century marquetry table which he used as a desk, and several armchairs upholstered in grey velvet. A magnificent Lurçat tapestry hung on one wall, and the only other decoration was an easel which stood opposite it, bearing, at the moment, a bizarre painting of what appeared to be bird-droppings by an American artist of whom she had never heard.

'He's the current rage in New York, darling. But he

41

won't last. Unlike Ben. Did you know that one of the early landscapes was sold in Frankfurt the other day for nearly half a million?'

After what she had just learnt from the lawyer, she fully understood Ben's resentment for the first time. It was hard that most of his work had been sold before its value had soared, to fetch prices at auction equalled by few other modern painters.

'Coffee? A drink?' Henriques said.

'No, thank you. Anthony, do you have any unsold pictures?'

'I haven't had an Absalom in the gallery for years. That's what I wanted to see you about. Partridge was on to me after the service yesterday. He'll take whatever you have. Moneywise, the sky's the limit.'

'There isn't anything.'

He looked at her with disbelief. 'Ben wrote that he was painting again.'

'He couldn't even hold a brush. Are you *sure* everything's been sold?'

'That isn't something I'd make a mistake about. I wish I had a gallery full of them.' He leant forward. 'I could sell anything, Jo; sketches, unfinished work . . .'

'There's nothing. You've had all the sketches from stock. He hadn't started anything new.'

'Buried in the studio? Your attic? Something you might have overlooked.'

'Nothing.'

'Note-books?'

She shook her head. She had no intention of telling him about Ben's note-books, because they were more like diaries, studded with vicious caricatures and personal comments on his sitters. Studying them since his death, she had found that they revealed a side of his personality which she wanted to forget. She had already burned most of them.

As she left, Henriques followed her to the door. His last

words were: 'Remember, my dear, if you come across anything, anything at all . . .'

It was one o'clock when she got back to the flat. Lisa came from the kitchen, holding a ham sandwich in one hand, a glass of white wine in the other. She was wearing jeans and a scarlet shirt, belted around her slim waist.

Looking at her mother's tired face, she wasted no time on small-talk. 'Sit down before you fall down. Drink?'

'I could do with one.'

Lisa poured her a hefty vodka and added tonic. 'Rough morning?'

'Sort of. Ben was broke. And Lord knows what other debts there might be.'

'That's impossible!'

'It's true.' She took a mouthful of vodka, choking a little as it reached the back of her throat. Then, as though trying to make sense of it herself, she repeated everything she had learnt, including the fact that for eighteen years her husband had apparently been maintaining a mistress in Swiss Cottage.

'The lawyer suggested she must have been a relative. But Ben was an only child, and as far as I know he had no relations in this country,' she said bleakly.

'So what happens now?'

'About the Freeman woman? Nothing. I don't want to see her. I don't want to know anything about her. She must have realized that there won't be any more money.'

'I meant, how are *you* going to live?'

'I've been thinking about it all the way home. I believe I can manage, with some changes in life-style. I have enough money in France to tide me over for a few months. Fortunately, the villa is mine. I don't want to sell it, though eventually I might have to.'

'No! You love that house, and so do I. Jo, I've made a lot of money out of tv. You shall have whatever you need.'

'Thanks, darling, but no thanks.' She paused, then

43

went on slowly. 'Even before I came over, I was trying to work out what I'd do. Not because I realized then that I'd be short of money, but I need something to fill my time. I've thought of selling off some of the land for building, then farming the rest. I could grow flowers and vegetables, maybe raise geese and chickens for the market. I could take paying guests, too. God knows, the place is big enough.'

'Wouldn't you hate having strangers around all the time?'

'After he moved down permanently, Ben filled the house with people. Until the last years, when he was in such pain, he couldn't stand being without company for more than a few weeks. No paying guest could be more difficult than some of his friends.'

'I can imagine. But it will be hard work.'

'I'm pretty tough.' She lifted herself out of the low, steel-mesh chair and reached for her hand-bag. 'I nearly forgot, the lawyer gave me a letter for you. Ben had left it with him.'

Lisa took the brown foolscap envelope, with its typed inscription, turned it over, then tore it open. Inside, there were two sheets of note-paper, covered with Ben's small, untidy hand-writing. Automatically, she looked first at the signature, his characteristic, scrawled initials, B.A., which appeared in the bottom right-hand corner of all his paintings. She shivered. It was a communication from the dead and she found herself reluctant to start reading.

But Joanna was watching her, waiting.

The letter began, 'My darling Lisa, What I have to say will be a surprise to you – not an unpleasant one, I hope . . .'

By the time she reached the second page, she was oblivious to anything but the astonishing words. She reached the signature, turned back to the beginning, and read it again.

Finally, she looked up, and said, dazedly: 'He was my father.'

'Well, of course. Since you were three . . .'

'No! My *real* father. I was his daughter, by some woman in Czechoslovakia.' She thrust the letter at Jo. 'Read it for yourself.'

' . . . When you see this – I hope not for many years – I will be gone and it will no longer matter who knows. You might have wondered why Jo and I never adopted you officially. In fact, the adoption was unnecessary. You are my natural daughter.

'Your mother was a young woman named Eva – the rest doesn't matter – with whom I had an affair when I took my own mother back to her home in Czechoslovakia in 1965. I did not realize you had been born until I went back three years later. She was, tragically, shot when the Russian tanks entered Prague to put an end to the new liberalism. As you already know, I managed to escape with you.

'When we reached England, I decided that I did not wish to tell Joanna the truth. It could have created difficulties. She might even have decided to leave me. I needed her – as I still do – so I could not let that happen. She is, as you know, a woman of great reserve, and a depth of feeling that she is often unwilling to reveal, for reasons of her own. We have been married for many years, and I still cannot tell how she would react to this news.

'It was easy enough to pass you off as the child of dissident parents who had both been killed during that Prague Spring. Jo and I decided to keep you with us, because she could not have children.

'When you read this, there won't be any further need for secrecy. I want you to know that I have always loved you, and hope that eventually you will understand that my decisions on your behalf were for the best. The fact that we grew apart was no fault of mine.'

Grim-faced, Jo handed the letter back. 'I need another drink.' She poured herself a second vodka, and this time she did not choke on it.

45

'Do you believe it?' Lisa said.

'Oh, yes. I already knew Ben's habits with women. When he arrived back from Prague with you, I wondered. It was uncharacteristic of him to be so – altruistic. Then, after you'd been with us for a few weeks, his behaviour seemed less important. I only wanted to keep you, so I put anything else out of my mind.'

Lisa was standing by the window. Her profile, silhouetted by the spring sunshine, was hard. 'If he thought I'd be pleased to know he was my father, he was wrong,' she said. 'He was a selfish, arrogant bastard! I hate this letter! All he cared about was himself, always. He needed you, so he lied and lied, because the truth might affect his own comfort. He didn't give a damn how we'd feel when we read it.'

Holding her drink, Jo walked to the window and looked out over the trees of Hampstead Heath. 'He *was* selfish, but that was only one side of him. He was generous and understanding. When we were married, he gave me a whole new life. Sometimes things weren't easy, but I never stopped being grateful to him. I never will.' Her voice softened. 'And it was a privilege to be close to an artist with such talent.'

'I have never thought talent was an excuse for behaving like a shit.'

'He didn't always . . .' She stopped as the telephone rang.

Lisa went into the hall to answer it. When she came back, she said, 'Some newspaper. They want to interview you about your life with Ben. I said you weren't here. They're going to ring back.'

'I won't talk to them.' The exhaustion, briefly banished by the shock of the letter, had returned, and her voice was unsteady. 'Would you mind if we went home tomorrow? Could you be ready in time? I'd planned to stay for a few days, but all this has been rather much. I feel like a rabbit that needs the safety of its burrow.'

'I'll be ready.' Lisa's eyes were still on the letter. 'It's going to take some getting used to, Ben having been my father. When we were angry with each other, I used to tell myself that I didn't have to care, because he had no rights over me, that we'd only come together in the same family by accident. Now . . . it's odd. Things are starting to seem important that never meant anything before. Ben's mother . . . the Czech peasant he used to make fun of . . . she was my grandmother. I asked him once about my parents, and he said there wasn't anything he could tell me, because he hardly knew them. Another lie! Who *was* my mother?'

'I learnt never to ask him any questions about women. That way, our lives were a lot easier.'

'And what about this Alicia Freeman? Where did she fit into his life – and mine?'

'I don't know. Lisa . . . maybe it's best to leave the past buried.'

'But there's so much I'd like to know. It's a curious feeling, finding out that you aren't the person you thought you were. Who the hell *am* I? Jo, how much do you know about Ben's background?'

'Please, love, if you want to ask questions later, do. But I've had about enough for today.'

Looking at her strained face, Lisa said, 'I'm sorry. Would you like to rest? It's all been sort of shattering, hasn't it?'

'Sort of. No, I don't want to rest. You have to pack, and I'll organize our flight, then we'll clean the flat so you don't have to come back to a mess, and we'll go somewhere cheerful for dinner . . .'

And tomorrow I can go home and get on with my own life, she thought. Am I doing the right thing, taking her with me without telling her that Nick is there? But if I did, she wouldn't come, and she can't know how he's changed. Shouldn't they be given another chance? Or is this a rationalization because I don't want to face

47

being back in that house without Ben?

The nightmare she had not suffered for years woke her at three o'clock the next morning. Shivering, gasping for breath, she jerked upright as a light was switched on in the passage. There was a shadow in the doorway and Lisa's voice said sharply: 'What's the matter?'

For a moment, she couldn't speak, still feeling herself crouching in the cell from which there was no escape. 'Did I call out? It was a bad dream. I'm sorry if I woke you.'

Lisa sat on the edge of her bed. 'I wasn't asleep. My mind's like boiling soup . . . all sorts of things keep bubbling to the surface. I'm going to make myself a cup of hot chocolate. Want one?'

Afraid that sleep would drop her back into the nightmare, she nodded.

They went into the sleek, modern kitchen, with its pine cupboards, strip lighting and window-sills packed with pots of herbs and geraniums. Jo relaxed. After all, she had escaped from her prison.

As she put a saucepan of milk on the white ceramic hob to warm, Lisa said: 'You screamed. Was it an awful dream?'

'It's one I used to have regularly when I was a child, but this was the first time for years. It's as though, now Ben's dead . . . well, never mind.' She shivered again, and drew her dressing-gown around her. 'What were your thoughts about?'

'Ben. You. Me. The woman who was my real mother. My grandmother. Her husband, my grandfather. I don't know anything about him, either.'

Jo drank her chocolate and warmed her hands on the mug. Then she said: 'Ben used to have a box of photographs. What happened to his stuff from the flat?'

'I suppose he got rid of it . . . I didn't know he'd sold the flat. But a parcel did come from him once. Could be a box, I've never looked at it. It arrived by carrier with a note telling – telling, not asking – me to look after it. I'd forgotten all about it.'

'Could you find it?'

'I think so. Don't you want to go back to bed?'

'No. Do you?'

'I'll never sleep now. What photographs are they?'

'If your box is the one I think it is, they're of Anna's family. Ben had it when he came back from Prague with you after her death. It was the only thing of hers he managed to bring out. There's a particular picture I want you to see.'

Lisa left the room, and returned with a parcel wrapped in brown paper, tied with string. She opened it, and they saw an old shoe-box, filled with photographs. Some had faded and turned brown with age.

Jo looked through them and separated one, more recent than the others, which was near the top of the pile.

It showed two women and a man, standing in what appeared to be a courtyard, under a tree, with the corner of a house in the background. One of the women was elderly, squarely-built, with strong features and light eyes. She was wearing a head-scarf, a black apron over her flowered skirt, thick black stockings and sturdy laced shoes. The other was much younger, slim, pretty, with fair hair tied back in a pony-tail. She was wearing a sixties mini-skirt and open-neck blouse, and was smiling. The man who stood between them, his arms around their shoulders, was Ben. Jo turned it over and glanced at some writing on the back, then handed it to Lisa.

'That's your grandmother,' she said. 'And I believe that girl was your mother.'

Lisa stared at it. 'When was it taken?'

'Before you were born, when Ben took Anna home to Czechoslovakia in 1965.'

'What makes you think she's the one?'

'Before she went home, Anna used to talk to me. She loved showing me her photographs. I knew them all.

49

When Ben brought them back after her death, I went through them, and found this, which I hadn't seen before. I asked him who the girl was – not trying to check up on him, it was idle curiosity – and he told me she was the daughter of old family friends. Anna had been living with her in Prague. Then he put the box away. I haven't seen it since. In fact, I haven't thought about it for years.

'Your mother's name was Eva. Turn the photograph over.'

Lisa looked at the words written in spiky lettering on the back. 'Anna. Ben. Eva.' She put it on the table in front of her, and studied it. After a few moments, she looked up. 'I'd still like to know more about her, because I'd be finding out about myself, but, do you know, she doesn't mean a damn thing to me! It's a relief. I was wondering just now if I was going to have some emotional crisis about the picture of a dead woman. But you're my mother, love. Were, are, and always will be.'

The rigid, almost obsessive self-control Jo had practised since she was a child, came to her rescue, and she was able to return Lisa's smile.

'I can't tell you much more about Eva,' she said. 'But if you like, I can fill you in on your grandparents' lives.'

She leant her elbows on the kitchen table and, as she talked, was transported back in her mind to the cottage in Sussex where, newly-married, she had spent hours listening to Anna Absalom's reminiscences.

At first, Anna had been suspicious of her son's wife, but Jo had soon realized that much of her reserve stemmed from shyness. She was also lonely. She had little in common with other women in the village and would sit alone, day after day, in front of the black-leaded coal-stove, embroidering tablecloths and napkins and pillow-cases which she would never use. She had fallen out of the habit of making friends.

Jo had visited her regularly, and encouraged her to talk, and gradually her reserve had broken down. Her thick, cold-reddened hands would lie motionless in her lap, the needle and thread suspended between finger and thumb as she remembered her own country and the young English journalist who became Ben's father.

PART TWO

1

Anna's first sight of Martin Absalom in the summer of 1936 was a figure crouched over the handle-bars of his bicycle as it swooped down the steep hill that led past her father's farm.

She was convoying a flock of geese across the road, and leaped to safety in the ditch that bordered it. The geese, on the other hand, continued their stately procession towards a pond on the other side.

There was no way the cyclist could stop. The flock, suddenly aware of the monster descending on them, were more angry than frightened. Instead of getting out of the way, several of them stood their ground, flapped their wings, stretched their necks towards him, and hissed.

He tried to swerve between them, but one huge bird moved at the wrong time, into his path, and he was on it. He went over the handle-bars; goose and bicycle flew into the air, then fell in a hopeless tangle on top of him. He lay on the hard-baked yellow ground, draped in the bicycle and a mass of feathers. Geese pecked his legs viciously. Anna ran towards him, shouting angrily as she shooed the flock. He was trying to struggle free, but the bird he had hit was heavy and the bike seemed to have twisted itself around them both like barbed wire.

She pulled the goose off by its neck and examined it. It was dead. Shaking it accusingly, she directed a stream of words at him as he stood up, battered and shaken.

When she stopped, he said, 'Oh, My God! I'm terribly sorry. I'll pay for it . . .' Unthinkingly, he spoke in English.

Her face changed. She said: 'You are Mis-ter Ab-sa-lom?'

They peered at each other. She saw a tall, lanky young man with aquiline features and fair hair, his skin flushed by the wind of his descent. He found himself staring at a girl as fair as himself who looked about twenty. Her hair was pulled into two plaits. Of medium height, big-breasted, with sturdy legs, she had blue eyes, high, flat cheek-bones and a square jaw. Her features were too strong for conventional beauty, but she was not unattractive.

'You're Anna! Tommy told me about you.' Calmer now, he was able to speak in slow, but fluent Czech. She nodded, then said severely, 'You were riding too fast.'

'I know. But it was a straight hill . . . a lovely day. You must tell me how much . . .'

She smiled suddenly. 'It doesn't matter. We were expecting you, and we were going to kill a goose in your honour. You have saved us the trouble. Now I take you to my parents.'

His saddle-bags had flown into the road. He picked them up, then inspected the bicycle. Anna said, 'There is a man in our village who will mend it. Leave it here and I will tell him to collect it.'

'Will it be safe?'

'Safe?' She understood. 'You mean someone might steal it? We have no thieves here, Mis-ter Ab-sa-lom.'

'Martin.'

Her brother, Tomas, was his assistant in the Prague news-agency called European News Features, but he appeared little older than herself. She said, 'If you wish,' and reached up to pull away a feather that had tucked itself behind his ear.

As they walked towards the farmhouse, she studied him out of the corners of her eyes, remembering the letter Tomas had written to announce his arrival: 'You will like Martin. He badly needs a holiday after a difficult time he has had with a woman here, so I suggested he might stay at the farm for a few weeks. It would be nice if Anna could be home to keep him company and show him something of the countryside. He has been in Prague for nearly a year and we have become good friends.'

Curious about Tomas's boss, she had arranged to take a vacation from her job in a dress-shop in Bratislava, and come home.

The Flekovsky farmhouse was a short walk down a rough track beyond the pond. It was an L-shaped building with a flagged courtyard set into the L. Anna led Martin through wide wooden gates into the yard, where hens were pecking between the flags. There was a spreading tree in the centre and, against the walls, stacks of straw next to a pile of firewood. Four pink pigs were penned in a corner.

Her parents were standing in the doorway. Where Anna was wearing a loose dress in flowered cotton, her mother had dressed formally for the guest in a long black skirt, with a white apron, a heavily embroidered waistcoat over her white blouse, and the black head-scarf which she put on as soon as she got up in the morning, and did not take off until she went to bed.

Anna's father, Jan, was small and dark, with a gentle, gnomelike face. Their greetings were nervous, but as soon as they learned that Martin spoke their language, they relaxed.

Anna showed him into a big, light guest-room with a carved bed covered in a down quilt, then conducted him to the kitchen, the centre of the family's life.

As they passed through the parlour, which was used only on formal occasions, she paused to straighten one of the fresh, embroidered antimacassars that were set on the back and arms of every chair. Embroidered cloths covered every table.

He looked around curiously. 'You seem to do a lot of sewing,' he remarked.

'That is how we spend our winters. There isn't much

57

outside work to be done, so the women sew. Every girl has a trousseau of hand-embroidered linens when she marries.'

'You, too?'

'Of course. I have several drawers full, and glass and china which my mother has collected for me.'

The entire household had gathered to welcome the guest and Anna introduced them one by one: her orphaned cousin, Josef, a little, wizened man who, she whispered, believed that he was in touch with the inhabitants of the planet Venus; her grandmother, a dark, silent old woman who was rocking beside a huge porcelain stove; her grandfather, who suffered from emphysema and breathed like a steam-engine; assorted aunts and uncles, and a vast woman, as round as she was tall, whom Anna described as 'our kitchen-maker', who cooked for the family.

Jan produced a bottle of slivovice, the ubiquitous plum-brandy of Middle Europe. 'You will find this stronger than that commercial rubbish,' he said proudly. 'I make it myself from my own plums. It is not legal, you understand, but it is very good. It is kept for our special guests.'

Anna watched with amusement as Martin gasped at the trail of fire that seemed to run into his stomach. Fighting for breath, he waved his glass in the air and Jan, assuming it was an invitation, refilled it.

'You have not drunk slivovice before?' she asked.

'Many times – but nothing as good as this. Tomas introduced me to it.'

'Please tell us about our son,' Jan said. 'He is not a good correspondent. He is well? He works hard, I hope? His wife and children are happy?'

As they settled around the long kitchen table, Martin answered their questions.

He told them how, when he had arrived in Prague the previous year, to take over as Prague correspondent of the London-based European News Features service, Tommy had been there to greet him.

58

They all laughed when he said, 'He told me his name was Tomas Flekovsky, but that I would find it easier to adopt the name my predecessor had given him: Tommy Flek. That's how everyone in Prague knows him now.'

'It suits him,' Anna said.

'I couldn't have managed without him. This is my first overseas post and he showed me around, and kept me company and taught me how everything works.

'My apartment is above the office and that first afternoon he produced a bottle of slivovice. After two drinks, it seemed that he was an old friend – and that's what he is now. My best friend.'

He told them how, after another two drinks, Tommy had said, 'No work today, Martin. Instead, I show you the town.'

They had wandered through Prague's winding streets, many spanned by arches. Some were so narrow that the eaves of houses opposite each other almost touched. Occasionally through a gap, he had seen clusters of domes and pinnacles rising above the roof-tops. He recognized Gothic architecture, Renaissance, Romanesque, Baroque, existing in higgledy-piggledy harmony. They had walked by the River Vltava that ran through the city. Studded with islands, it was a quarter-mile wide at some points. Martin had seen it all through a rosy haze of plum brandy.

'Tommy has taught me Czech, too,' he said. 'As well as his ordinary work, he gives me a lesson every day.'

Anna's mother intervened shyly: 'Tell us about his wife, Blanka, and the two little ones.'

'She is well, and Tommy asked me to give you love from her and the children.'

'Blanka does not like the country,' Anna said sadly. 'We are six hours by train from Prague, but we might as well be six thousand, as far as she is concerned.'

It was the beginning of a momentous holiday for them both.

When his bicycle had been mended, she took him out

every day to explore the surrounding countryside. They looked up at the turreted castles that were set on hilltops, explored tiny Lutheran churches, sometimes paused at an inn for a beer, served by women in traditional costumes.

And they talked. Anna was a receptive audience, wide-eyed and attentive, questioning him eagerly about his life in Prague, helpful when he occasionally sought for a word in her language. He was a man unlike any she had met: friendly as a puppy, cheerful, articulate, intelligent, but never patronizing when he saw that she was less know-ledgeable than he. By the end of the first week, she was already falling in love with him. Later, she was surprised to learn from her mother that her feelings had been clear to everyone.

He told her how he and Tommy would often go after work to one of the beer-halls with which the city was amply provided, and that their favourite was U Kalicha, a haunt of writers, artists, students and philosophers. Secretly, she was proud that her brother kept such company.

Many years later Martins's son, Benedict, was to visit U Kalicha with an older, sadder Tommy Flek, and find it patronized largely by tourists, with waiters serving sophisticated food. It was, Tommy said unhappily, very different from the place where he and Martin had been so happy.

In the thirties, they loved the tavern's relaxed, smoke-filled atmosphere, the pervading smell of stale beer, the arguments that were constantly breaking out about everything from politics to women.

'That's where we held the dumpling contest,' he said, as he and Anna were riding along an overgrown path by a narrow, tumbling stream. 'Did Tommy write about it?'

She shook her head. 'Tell me!'

It was then that she heard, for the first time, about Bruno, who was to play a frightening role in their futures, and that of her brother.

Martin had acquired a passion for one of the great Czech

culinary achievements, dumplings, which might be based on dough made from potatoes or bread or flour or cream cheese or semolina. They would be served with meat, in soup, as a snack, as a dessert filled with sour cherries, plum jam or apricots. His capacity for them created awe and amusement among his new friends, until one evening, several months after his arrival, a post-graduate student of political philosophy, named Bruno, challenged him to a contest.

Bruno was only five feet five, but weighed over two hundred pounds. He was proud of his huge appetite and had expressed resentment at a suggestion that, compared with the tall, skinny Englishman, he was a novice in the dumpling-eating stakes.

'So, Martin, I show you who is the better man!' he shouted. 'Tomorrow, Franz will provide us with all the dumplings we can eat, and we will see who calls a halt first!'

For no reason Martin could put his finger on, since he hardly knew the man, Bruno was one of the few people he had met in Prague whom he did not like. Recklessly downing his third mug of Pilsner, ignoring Tommy Flek's anxious protests, he said: 'I'll take the challenge! I'll beat you, Bruno, by God, for the honour of Old England!'

The loser, it was decided, would buy beer for the winner throughout the following week.

After they left the tavern, Martin and Tommy discussed the contest, of which Tommy strongly disapproved. 'It is not good to make a pig of yourself, Martin, if you will forgive me for saying so. That Bruno is already a pig. You should not place yourself on his level.'

Martin laughed. 'It's only a bit of fun. Who is Bruno, anyway? I've never really talked to him.'

'I don't know him well, either. I believe he comes from Germany. He arrived in Prague a couple of years ago, to study at the University. He goes often to Berlin. Sometimes we do not see him for weeks at a time.'

* * *

By the next night, news of the contest had spread and U Kalicha was packed with eager spectators. The two young men were conducted ceremoniously to a bare wooden table marked with the circles of hundreds of wet beer-mugs. They sat, facing each other, with plates in front of them. The crowd which had gathered around them parted to allow Franz, bearing two steaming platters, to reach the table.

Against his will, disapproving of the whole peformance, Tommy had been persuaded to act as starter and umpire. The tavern fell silent as he raised his handkerchief, said 'Begin!' and dropped it.

Martin began to stuff dumplings into his mouth, scarcely bothering to chew them, forgetting, in his excitement, that speed was not part of the competition.

A man stood behind each contestant, counting aloud as the dumplings disappeared. Martin was soon running two or three ahead of Bruno.

On he went – six, seven, ten, twelve. His supporters were chanting the count. At first, the spheres of poached dough went down easily, little more than a mouthful each, but by the time he reached fifteen, they seemed to have swelled, and he had to slow so that one would settle in his stomach before he started on the next. They grew heavier, too: souffles turned into cannon-balls. First his belly, then his chest, began to feel like an overflowing garbage-can. The eighteenth dumpling stuck in his gullet and he had to wash it down with beer. When he reached twenty, he paused and, for the first time, looked across at Bruno.

The fat young man's invigilator was snapping numbers with metronomic regularity: eighteen . . . nineteen . . . twenty. Bruno himself appeared as fresh and hungry as he had been when he started, eating steadily, chewing each dumpling several times before swallowing it.

As Martin watched, he began to feel sick. Behind him, Tommy, caught up in the battle, whispered: 'Come on, my friend, remember Old England!'

Twenty-one, twenty-two . . . Martin clapped a hand to his mouth and made a dash for the lavatory.

When he returned, pale and shaking, Bruno was still eating stolidly: twenty-nine, thirty . . .

'Now I stop,' he announced. 'It is enough. I must leave some room for my supper.'

Martin raised his hands in a gesture of submission, and the contest was over.

Bruno was not a sporting winner and spent the rest of the evening gloating, mocking Martin's pallid face, his frequent departures to the men's room. Later the mockery became increasingly vicious as Bruno downed one beer after another. In some mysterious way, politics were introduced, and he began to shout that Martin's defeat was a symbol of what would eventually be the fate of Great Britain when the Third Reich's glorious Fuehrer became the rightful leader of Europe.

Anna's face wrinkled with distaste. 'I do not like the sound of that man,' she said firmly. 'Have you seen him since?'

There was a long silence, then he said. 'Yes. Once. I'll tell you about it some day. Maybe.'

No pleas would persuade him to say any more.

As the days passed, the one flaw in their relationship, as far as Anna was concerned, was his physical restraint.

Although she was still a virgin, she had been brought up on a farm and knew all about the mating process, at least among animals. Now she decided it was time she had first-hand experience, and that Martin was the man above all others whom she wanted to initiate her into its mysteries.

Sometimes, when they were alone, she would reach out to him, moving so their bodies were close together. She was hurt and bewildered when he did not respond. He had kissed her once or twice during their cycling expeditions, but when she responded eagerly, something always seemed to hold him back.

One night, she took matters into her own hands and

went to his room. He was lying in bed, reading, when she knocked and opened the door. She was wearing a flimsy cotton night-gown. He dropped his book and sat upright, staring at her.

She took a deep breath, and said: 'Martin, I wish to ask something. Do you like me?'

'God, yes! You know I do!'

'Then why do you not want to make love with me? I am not attractive?'

'Of course you are, and I want you, Anna. But . . .'

'But what?'

'In Prague, there was a woman. It turned out badly . . .'

She nodded. 'Tomas wrote of her. So now you're frightened, no? You were hurt, and you don't want it to happen again.'

'I suppose so.' He seemed to come to a decision. 'I'd like to tell you about it. Maybe, when you've heard, you won't be – interested any more.'

'Then I will tell you so. Move over.'

He edged towards the wall and she slid into the bed beside him. He put his arm around her shoulders and told her about Magda, and it was like a catharsis as the words poured out.

A few months ago, he had found himself suffering a restlessness which had nothing to do with his work. He'd had one or two minor affairs since arriving in Prague, but they had ended, and now there was no woman in whom he was interested.

He had begun to look more carefully at the girls in U Kalicha. Most of the female students and artists were already spoken for by his friends, so his eyes moved on to the prostitutes who wandered in and out of the taverns, hoping to find customers.

Many of them were young and attractive, but one was outstanding: a tall, slender girl named Magda, who, ignoring the current fashion for short hair waved close to the head, wore hers loose and reaching to her waist. She was dark, with an almond slant to her eyes. It was said that she was a White Russian, with a Mongolian mother. She lived in a luxurious apartment, where she was allegedly maintained by a rich and jealous man. He seemed to be often away, and then she would sometimes choose another lucky man to accompany her home.

One night, in the tavern, Martin tore a sheet out of his reporter's note-book, and wrote on it: 'May I come with you?'

He watched a waiter give it to her, and gesture towards him. She assessed him for a long moment, then nodded lazily.

That was the beginning of a month which took him into a private, erotic world that bore no relation to the realities of his life in Prague. Skilled, uninhibited, she was, he decided, the woman of whom he had always dreamed.

He often wondered about the man who was paying her rent, but she refused to answer questions and would contribute no information about herself.

He became increasingly obsessed by her. He even managed to convince himself that she was in love with him, as he knew he was with her.

His jealousy of the man he thought of as his rival increased, but Magda refused to discuss him until, one evening, when she was lying on her bed, smoking one of the black Balkan cigarettes she affected, she said casually, 'My friend comes back next week. You and I cannot see each other any more.'

His love-making after that took on a kind of desperation, and he felt he could not get enough of her. Most of his waking hours were spent thinking of ways to keep her with him, and finally he realized there was only one possibility: he would have to marry her. To hell with her past, once she belonged to him, only the future would matter.

The day after he had come to this decision, he hurried to her apartment just before dark, clutching a bottle of champagne.

There was no time to talk before they fell on the bed, then they relaxed among the cushions, still entwined.

After a while, her eyes closed. He felt himself, too, drifting off to sleep. Later, he would tell her his plans for their future.

He was awakened by sounds outside on the landing, then the turning of a key, and the door that led into the big room opened. He heard footsteps, soft on the thick carpeting. Still half-believing he was asleep, he opened his eyes, and saw Bruno at the end of the bed. Two other men stood behind him. They were all staring down at himself and Magda. Bruno's face was the colour of mashed potatoes, and puffy with anger. His small eyes were like dagger points.

Martin rolled off the bed, making an undignified scramble for his clothes, which lay in a heap on the floor.

As he pulled on his trousers, Magda woke up. For an instant, her lovely face was frightened, then it relaxed into impassivity. She sat up, making no attempt to cover herself.

'The last three times I've been away, I have heard rumours,' Bruno said. 'This time, you were watched.' He turned to Martin. 'I must ask you, Old England, to leave my apartment.'

Martin had been too befuddled by sleep to understand the implications of the men's arrival. 'Your apartment?'

'My apartment. My woman. I see you have been using them both. But no longer. Out!'

'She's not your woman any longer,' he said furiously. 'She's mine. I'm going to marry her.'

There was a moment when time seemed to stand still, then the last reaction he could have expected: Magda laughed.

She said, 'I do not marry anyone, especially not you.

You are a nice boy, but you have no money.' She slid off the bed and reached for her robe. 'We have had fun, but it's over. Bruno is home.'

Without a word, he turned to the door. He had almost reached it when he heard Bruno's soft voice. 'A moment, please.'

He looked round. One of the other men had a light cane in his right hand, the second was holding Magda so she faced Bruno. Before Martin could move, Bruno had taken the cane and slashed her viciously across the cheek. Her head jerked to the side, but she made no sound, though tears welled out of her eyes.

Martin started forward, but Bruno's men grabbed him, and one twisted his arm up behind his back.

'That is a warning of what will happen to her – *her*, not you, you understand – if you ever come near her again,' Bruno said. 'Now you can go.'

The two men pushed him through the door, and closed it behind him.

After three days of torment, when he did not eat, drank steadily and refused to leave his apartment, he told Tommy the whole story.

When he had finished, Tommy said, 'She's gone to Germany with him. I've been making inquiries about him, Martin. He's no normal student. That was only his excuse for being here. He has been working for the Nazis.'

'You mean he's a spy?'

'Perhaps that is a word too melodramatic. He is more an – an assessor.'

'Assessing what, for God's sake?'

Tommy's shoulders lifted. 'The mood of the people. How we think of Germany. What the reaction might be if Herr Hitler decided that Czechoslovakia could provide the *lebensraum* he wants. Now Bruno has done his work, and he has gone back to Berlin, with Magda.'

For the next two weeks, he carried out his tasks apathetically. His days and nights were grey and lonely.

He ate almost nothing, and lost an alarming amount of weight. He luxuriated in his misery.

Then one evening, Tommy came to the apartment, bearing the inevitable bottle of slivovice. They drank together, talking little, until Tommy took a deep breath, and said: 'You are making a fool of yourself, Martin. She wasn't worth it. She was a whore. Almost every man you know had her before you did, whenever Bruno was away.'

Martin poured himself another drink. 'I know you're right, but, God, life isn't the same without her.'

Tommy sighed. 'So you become sorry for yourself.' His smile removed any offence. 'My friend, I have had an idea. Do you realize that you have been in Prague for nearly a year, without a holiday? Why don't you go away for a while? Come back to a new start.'

'I don't know. What the hell would I do, by myself?'

'I have an idea for that, too. My family lives near Bratislava. You could cycle down. The countryside is very beautiful. We have a farm outside a little village, and my mother and father would be honoured if you would visit them.'

'So here I am,' he ended. 'I made a bloody fool of myself over Magda. And you're right, it hurt more than I could have imagined. Maybe I'd be no good for you, Anna.'

'I still think you would,' she said calmly. 'Now I don't only hate that Bruno, I hate her, too, for what she has done to you.' She turned her body towards him and her heavy breasts pressed against his chest as she put her arms around him. 'I can make you forget her, Martin.'

And, indeed, she did.

The day came for him to leave and, after an emotional farewell to her family and to the kitchen-maker, he and Anna started off to cycle to Bratislava, where he would put his bike on the train for the five-and-a-half hour journey to Prague.

It was a silent ride. It seemed that they had nothing left

68

to say to each other, and he had made no commitment for the future.

As his train arrived, he kissed her and at last she heard the words she had been waiting for: 'Come to Prague! Come soon!'

Three months later, they were married in the Lutheran church near the farm. Tommy was Martin's best man.

The ceremony was preceded by a party that continued, on and off, for three days. Everyone danced in the village streets, accompanied by three musicians. The kitchen-maker, sweating profusely over great cauldrons of savory stew and dumplings, claimed at the end of the party that her weight had dropped by ten pounds and her husband would no longer find her attractive. Jan brought out several dozen bottles of his slivovice, which had been laid down for just such an occasion.

Martin got very drunk. To Anna's chagrin, he fell instantly into a deep slumber after they had been conducted, with much ribaldry, to the bedroom they could now officially share.

They returned to Prague the following morning.

Before the wedding, Jan Flekovsky had presented them with a thick envelope of money. This, he said, was Anna's dowry, five hundred English pounds, and he apologized that it was not more generous.

'I can't possibly take it!' Martin protested.

Jan said quietly, 'This is our custom. I don't doubt that you will always look after my Anna. It is in case you and she are ever in need of something extra.'

In Prague, Martin handed the untouched envelope to her, and told her to use the money as she liked. She tucked it away under the pile of embroidered linens in her cupboard, never guessing how grateful she would be for it a few years hence.

Their son, Benedict, was born ten months after their wedding.

2

One night early in 1938, as Martin and Tommy were playing chess, while Anna sewed, Tommy said, 'Remember Bruno, Martin?'

'How could I forget?'

'I wouldn't be surprised if we were to find him back here in some high position when the Germans take us over.'

Martin's hand hovered over his knight. '*When*? Not if? Are you as pessimistic as that?'

Tommy nodded. 'I don't think there's any hope for us. They'll over-run Europe. Austria first, then Czechoslovakia. Poland. Hungary. Yugoslavia. Rumania. To the west, Belgium, Holland, France . . .'

'It'll never come to that. *We* wouldn't allow it!'

'You mean Old England? Alone?'

'If necessary. But what I really mean is the whole civilized world.'

Anna, with total confidence in her husband's judgement, remained unworried by the situation.

In March 1938, German troops streamed into Austria and the country was proclaimed a province of the German Reich.

Martin went to Vienna to assess the situation. He saw old Jewish men and women on their hands and knees in the streets, being made to scrub away anti-Nazi slogans, kicked and beaten by louts wearing swastika badges. He saw beautiful houses belonging to rich Jews being raided and their possessions carried away. He saw children weeping as their parents were dragged from their homes.

When he returned to Prague, he wrote a bitter denunciation of the Nazis.

'And that's what could happen here, too,' he told Anna and Tommy. 'Just thank God you're not Jews.'

There was a moment's pause, then Tommy said: 'But we do have Jewish blood. Our grandmother, whom you have met, is a Jew from Russia. She came to Czechoslovakia with her parents to escape the pogroms in Kiev. Our father is half-Jewish. We are only a quarter, but for *them*, it will be enough.'

'Who knows this?'

'In the village, I suppose, many people must have guessed.'

Anna and Ben were both fair-haired, with blue eyes. 'There's no way they could tell . . .' Martin began, then he and Anna both looked at Tommy: small, dark, with bruiselike shadows under his eyes and a nose that was large in proportion to his face.

'I am an obvious candidate, no?' He tried to smile, then shrugged. 'We can only wait and see.'

For the first time, Anna felt a pang of apprehension.

One day in August, Tommy said, 'When they come, Martin, you must get out with Anna and Ben as quickly as you can.'

'They wouldn't touch an English journalist and his family – anyhow, nobody knows about Anna's background.'

'They know everything. They have traced families back for generations, looking for Jewish blood. And your anti-Nazi writing has come to their attention already. You will have made enemies.'

Throughout September the crisis escalated until, on 30 September, Czech president Benes, denied support by the Western Governments, had no alternative but to submit to

71

Hitler's demands, and the Germans took virtual control of the country.

On the surface, life did not change too much in Prague at first, except that Nazi uniforms were suddenly everywhere, and people became increasingly reluctant to be seen with their Jewish friends.

One evening, wanting to check the barometer of public opinion, Martin decided to go to U Kalicha.

It was November, and snow was falling outside the apartment. As he put on his overcoat, he said, 'Come on, Tommy. We'll have a couple of beers.'

Not looking at him, Tommy shook his head. 'No, you go. Take Anna. She hasn't been out for days. I'll stay with Ben until you come back.'

Dressed in snow, the Old Town was a study in black and white under the gas-lamps which still lit many of the narrow streets. Anna and Martin walked arm in arm. There were few people about and their breath steamed.

Suddenly, Martin said: 'It's months since Tommy came to U Kalicha. He always seems to find an excuse . . .'

'He's afraid,' Anna said softly. 'He worries all the time about what's going to happen.'

The tavern was crowded. Looking around, Martin spotted a group of Czech friends, and they joined them. Newly sensitive, Anna began to recognize their fear, too, and a difference in the general atmosphere. In the past, everyone had talked at the top of their voices; now they scarcely spoke above a whisper. Some glanced constantly from side to side to see who was within earshot.

Martin had just ordered his second beer when a gust of cold air swept into the tavern. Half a dozen men, in civilian clothes, but wearing swastika badges on their shirts, stood in the doorway.

A hush fell as heads turned towards them, then they swaggered to the centre of the room. They helped one of their number up onto a table. He stood with legs spread, hands on his hips, staring arrogantly around the silent room. His small eyes fell on Martin, and widened.

Anna heard Martin's horrified whisper: 'My God! It's Bruno!'

Bruno began to speak. His voice became steadily louder, and there was an undertone of hysteria as he shouted the praises of the German Chancellor who had rescued Czechoslovakia from the machinations of her enemies, Britain and France. The country's future lay with National Socialism. But to achieve the greatness that was their right, the Jews must be destroyed. 'We call on you all!' he screamed. 'Give us their names and we will see that Czechoslovakia is made clean again!'

Sickened, Martin and Anna looked around, awaiting the protests, but there were none. Most of the drinkers were staring down into their glasses, tight-lipped, but silent.

Bruno's face reddened and sweat began to bead his forehead as he ranted on.

Still, nobody spoke, nobody moved.

Finally, Martin could stand it no longer. He pushed back his chair, pulled Anna to her feet, and said clearly, 'I will not listen to these obscenities!' They went towards the door.

Bruno's voice faltered, stopped, and for a moment it was as though all movement in the tavern had been frozen. There was no sound except the Absaloms' footsteps, loud in the silence. As they reached the door, they heard a shout: 'Jew-lover!' Martin turned, to see Bruno's fat, quivering forefinger pointing at him. 'Many of you know this English Jew-lover! So do I. What you might not know is that he is married to one of them! Look at her! He employs one of them, too . . . he *is* one of them! Their fate will be his . . .'

Martin opened the heavy door, followed Anna out, then slammed it behind them. Outside, the snow was falling more heavily, but the air was clean and the hysterical voice was muffled.

Anna clung to him as they stood for a moment,

shivering, huddling in their coats. As they turned towards home, they heard the tavern door open again, and looked round. From inside, Bruno's voice still echoed, but a procession of men and women was coming quietly through the doorway. Some turned left, some right, and disappeared in the darkness. Several people stopped, and shook Martin's hand.

Within minutes the place had emptied. Then members of the staff came out, coatless, still in their black trousers and waistcoats, and they, too, hurried away.

The next day, Martin, Anna and Ben prepared to leave Prague for London.

3

They crossed the border from Bratislava into Vienna, where they spent two nervous hours awaiting the train which would carry them into Switzerland. But they were not stopped, and two days later, they arrived in England.

They had begged Tommy to come with them, but he refused.

'If I were to leave, it might attract attention to our family,' he said. 'I don't think Bruno will trouble me. You made a fool of him, Martin. You're the one he'll be after. It is necessary for you to make sure you and Anna and Ben are safe.'

'I'm frightened for you, Tomas,' Anna said.

He took her hand. 'I'll be okay. Some day, maybe, I'll join you in London.'

They moved into a small apartment near enough to the Covent Garden market for the smell of rotting fruit and vegetables to pervade the rooms. It was on the first floor of a depressing, red-brick block in a bleak street. They had taken it as a temporary measure because it was close to Fleet Street, until they could find somewhere in the country, within commuting distance.

London frightened Anna. It was too big and she found that her English, of which she had been proud, was barely adequate even for the day-to-day communication with tradesmen. Settling back into his work, Martin was away for long hours, leaving her alone with Ben.

Although she sometimes had reddened eyes when he came home, she never complained. She set to and turned the dreary furnished apartment into a home, brightening it with embroidered cloths and the glass and china her mother had collected for her.

Some weeks after their arrival, they received a letter from Tommy. It said, as usual, that all was well, and Anna was not to worry about the family. He had sent Blanka and his two little boys to stay on the farm for a while. He was resigning from the Agency, he added, because it was not the same without Martin.

Martin accepted the letter at face-value, but Anna, reading it a second time, found it worrying. Why had Tommy felt it necessary to send his wife and children to the farm? Blanka did not like the country and did not get on with their parents. And his resignation was a shock, especially as he made no mention of future plans.

There was no news for several weeks, then one Saturday morning, a letter arrived from Anna's father.

While Martin sat Ben in his high chair in the kitchen and fed him his cereal and pureed apples, she took it into the sitting-room.

Ten minutes later, Martin found her there. She was standing by the window, her face pale and tight. Wordlessly, she handed him the letter, which was much longer than Jan's normal communication. He began to read:

'My dear daughter, Anna,
   Your mother and I send you greetings and we hope you and your husband and son are in good health.
   I am afraid I have some bad news for you.
   Tomas has come home. When he arrived, we were horrified by the look of him. He didn't weigh much more than a hundred pounds, and his eyes were like black holes in his head. It seems that for weeks he had been strong, and had not allowed himself to be ill, but when he got here, he collapsed.'

As Martin read on, Anna was trying to take in the full

76

horror of what had happened to her brother.

Several days after she and Martin had left Prague, Bruno had come to the office with two other men. He had been looking for Martin, was furious when he discovered that he had gone, and insulted and abused Tommy.

A few nights later, when Tommy was riding home on his bicycle, he noticed that a car was following. It pulled level, and the men in it began shouting at him: 'Filthy Jew!' 'Stinking caftan-wearer!' People in the street turned to look, and one or two of them joined the shouting.

The same thing happened the following evening, and every evening during the next three weeks, until Tommy was terrified to go out. Then one night the men in the car bumped his bicycle up onto the pavement. As he fell, he saw Bruno sitting in the back.

He had said nothing to anyone because he did not want the story to get back to London and worry his sister. Frightened for his family, he had insisted that Blanka and the children should go to the farm.

He had resigned from his job, hoping that might end the persecution, but the torments continued. Stones were thrown through the windows of his apartment; oil was spread on his front step so he would slip.

Then came the final attack. He was returning from a shopping expedition when the same car blocked his way in a dark, narrow alley. Bruno and three big men got out. They pulled him off his bicycle and beat him up, breaking his nose and two ribs.

They left him lying in the gutter. He had not been found for an hour, then two passers-by took him to hospital.

He was in a dilemma: running out of money, but terrified the same thing might happen if he looked for another job; afraid to stay in Prague; worried that if he went back to the farm, he could endanger his family. He had a superstitious feeling that Bruno's vindictiveness would follow him anywhere.

Discharged from the hospital, he stayed in his apartment, seeing no one, not answering the door, eating nothing.

He knew that German troops were closing in on Prague, that every day his position became more dangerous. Ill and almost starving, he had finally decided to seek refuge with his parents.

Jan's letter ended:

'Now, I am pleased to say, he is mending. So far, we have been free of persecution by the Nazis in this remote village. But Tomas sends a particular message to Martin: on no account is he to return to Czechoslovakia. The man Bruno would certainly have him killed.

One other thing: Tomas says Bruno's woman, Magda, has played him false. She went to Berlin with him, got everything she could out of him, then left him for a Nazi Colonel. Bruno vents his bitterness and anger on everyone else.

I leave you now, dear Anna, with all our love to you and Martin and our grandson. You must not worry about your brother.

I pray that one day we will all be reunited.

Your affectionate father,
Jan.'

4

When Britain declared war on Germany in September, 1939, Martin and Anna had just moved into their cottage in the Sussex village of Hinley. Though in need of renovation, it was picturesque, cheap and not too far from London.

As the war swung into its first phase, Martin was appointed the agency's chief war correspondent.

Inevitably, he was away a great deal, and during the long, lonely evenings, Anna embroidered table-cloths and napkins, pillow cases and antimacassars, which she tucked away in a drawer – 'For our daughter,' she told him.

She desperately wanted another child, and he was not unwilling, but although they made love regularly and with the same passion as they had when they were first married, she did not become pregnant.

A few letters from her family had got through after the one from Jan. Tomas had written that he was improving every day and had settled back on the farm to work with his father. He had even managed a touch of humour: 'The one thing that is bothering Jan is that if the German troops should come here, they will steal his slivovice. So the other night he and I went into the orchard with wheelbarrows full of bottles. We buried them a foot deep under the corner plum-tree and he says they will not be dug up until we celebrate the coming of peace.'

After her first stunned tears following Jan's letter, Anna had settled into a kind of stoic resignation, revealing her distress only in pallor and lack of appetite.

Ben was her greatest comfort, and she clung to him

desperately. He was her main contact with other human beings when Martin was away.

After they arrived in Hinley, various people had called and offered a polite welcome, but soon discovered that they had little in common with this shy Czech woman who spoke a strange, often incomprehensible English.

On 31 May 1940, Martin was killed.

The British evacuation of France was under way and he had joined one of the small boats that were sailing from the South of England to bring the troops off the Dunkirk beaches.

Anna was never to learn anything about his last hours, for the boat, a 35-foot motor-launch, was lost with all on board.

Because of Ben, she had to maintain some semblance of normal life, and her neighbours rallied round. So many kindly women arrived at her door with sympathy and gifts of cakes and casseroles cooked from their meagre rations, that sometimes she longed to be left alone. But having to talk English to them forced her to make an effort so that she did not sink into total despair. She was so successful at hiding her feelings that some of the visitors whispered that she was hard and insensitive.

At night, she gave way, not only to her longing for Martin, but to her fear of the future. She had to face the fact that she and her son were alone in a country that would always be strange to her. There was no way she could return to Czechoslovakia, she had no contact with her family, no idea what had happened to them.

Ben's future was her major problem. Martin had often said that he wanted the boy to go as a boarder to his old school in Surrey, and she was determined to see that his wishes were carried out. Reviewing her financial situation, she realized that with his insurance she could probably manage from day to day. Fortunately, she still had her dowry intact. Five hundred pounds should pay for several years at school for Ben, and give her time to earn what she could for the future.

She had seen that people put notices about lost dogs and cats and items for sale in the local newsagent's window, so she advertised the household linens she had worked for the daughter she would never have. Within a couple of days, everything had been sold and she added the money to her education fund.

She advertised again, this time offering herself as a house-cleaner. As a foreign-born widow with a young child to bring up, she was exempt from war work, so she was free to take any job. Her one stipulation was that Ben must be allowed to accompany her.

Soon she was working full-time, moving from house to house, dusting, scrubbing floors, polishing furniture. In the evenings, she cooked supper for a retired Admiral and his wife, then washed up. She started work at eight o'clock each morning and did not finish until nine at night.

For a couple of years, Ben was happy enough to trail around with her, and be allowed to polish a mahogany table or sweep a floor.

When he was six, she sent him to the village school, and his attitude began to change. It was borne upon him that he was different from many of the other local children. One small girl said, 'Your mum does talk funny. She can't be very well educated.' Another, whom he invited to play with him, sniffed: 'No, thanks. Your mother's my mother's servant.'

That night, he said to Anna, 'You clean my house. Are you my servant?'

Not understanding what had prompted the question, she smiled. 'Of course I am! I work always for you, my darling.'

After that there was a subtle change in their relationship as he began to emulate the women for whom she worked, and issued orders, rather than requests. She noticed but, in her humility, admired his arrogance as a sign of his

81

increasing strength of character. There is no doubt that he was a spoiled and over-indulged child, but he already possessed considerable charm and good looks. Women found him enchanting.

The first indication that there was a darker side to his character was when Anna went one day to the drawer where she kept, buried under her clothes, her horde of bank-notes.

She knew at once that it had been disturbed. The neat piles were disarranged, and when she reached under them, one package of notes was no longer secured by its rubber band. She took them out and counted them. Ten pounds were missing.

That night, she faced Ben with her discovery, and he made no attempt to deny the theft.

'I took them. You said we share everything. So they're mine, too, aren't they?'

'But why did you not ask me?'

'You wouldn't have given them to me.'

His logic was unassailable. And his honesty, which anyone less devoted might have realized was calculated with remarkable sophistication for a six-year-old, saved him from her anger. She didn't even ask him what he had done with the money, assuming it had been used to buy sweets from those of his friends who were willing to give up their ration.

In fact, he was spending the proceeds of his theft on art supplies. To Anna, his passion for drawing was no more than a useful means of keeping him occupied. She was prepared to provide the basic essentials, but even at that early age, he wanted more. He scoured the village newsagents, and bought water-colours, tubes of gouache, inks, brushes and a few expensive oil-paints.

The first people to recognize his precocious talent were his school-fellows, and he was to discover that it could buy the respect and admiration he craved even from children who regarded him as their social inferior.

One day, during the morning break, he was sitting on a wall at school, sketch-pad on his lap, drawing a picture of another boy who was idly kicking a ball around the playground.

Someone called him to play football, and he left the pad on the wall. His subject picked it up, and shouted: 'Hey, this is me!'

The likeness was extraordinary. Suddenly, Ben was surrounded by little boys and girls demanding: 'Do me next!'

After that, he spent much of his spare time drawing their portraits, which they took home and showed their parents.

Anna learned about his activities from the mother of one of his subjects, something of an amateur artist herself, who told her that he had a remarkable talent, which must be encouraged.

At first, she did not understand. All children liked to draw pictures. She certainly wouldn't want to encourage Ben to think that he could make a career out of it. He would go on from school to Oxford, as Martin had, and take up the kind of profession his father would have recommended, though she wasn't too clear what that might have been.

But when her seven-year-old was invited to attend a fund-raising function in the village hall, and draw portraits of members of the public, who would pay for them – proceeds to go to war-charities – she began to take him more seriously.

Watching people queue for his attention, she overheard one woman say: 'Clever child, that. Extraordinary, with his humble background. His mother's our char, some sort of Middle European peasant.'

Being devoid of social pride, she found nothing offensive in the contemptuous description. Her son, on the other hand, was outraged and humiliated.

5

Ben was eleven when he went to his father's old school. At first, he hated it, for his education at Hinley's village school had left him far behind his contemporaries.

Once again, his ability to draw came to his rescue. Although art did not play a major part in the curriculum, the master in charge of arts and crafts had taught in a London art-school, and was delighted to find a boy of considerable talent in his class. Not only did he encourage Ben to spend all the time he could drawing and painting, but he gave up much of his spare time to tutor him on other subjects so he could catch up.

After a couple of terms, he had settled down, and was even enjoying himself. He was a good athlete and, again due to his willingness to draw their portraits, popular with staff and pupils.

During talks after lights-out, when the boys compared notes about their parents, he emphasized the hero's death of his father, the famous war-correspondent. It was generally assumed that his mother was just a mother, like everyone else's. Since at that stage his one desire was to conform, he kept dark the fact that she was a foreigner and earned her living cleaning other people's houses.

Then came Founders's Day, when parents gathered at the school to watch a cricket-match, discuss their sons' progress with the staff and take tea on the lawn.

Anna received a formal invitation from the headmaster, and was delighted to accept. Ben was not pleased. Although her English had vastly improved, she was still unmistakably foreign.

When the day arrived he waited anxiously, with a crowd of his friends, at the school gates.

Most parents came in their own cars, but Anna climbed out of the local bus that had brought her from the station.

His instant reaction was that no one must know she belonged to him. But she saw him, and waved. He heard smothered giggles from the boys, and one remarked: 'She must think she's going to a fancy-dress ball!'

For Anna, determined to do him honour, had put on her folk costume, which had been packed away in moth-balls since she arrived in England. Her black skirt was almost ankle-length, with a wide band of embroidery around the hem. Over it was a starched white apron; above, a white blouse with huge, gathered sleeves, and over that, a black waistcoat, thickly embroidered with multi-coloured flowers. He hair was hidden by a kerchief which was tied under her chin.

Instead of embracing her, Ben backed off and hissed: 'Why did you wear *that*?'

'It is my best. We wear such a costume only on special occasions.'

'Mother, you're in England! Nobody wears anything like that.' He was almost crying. 'It looks stupid! And it smells of moth-balls.'

She looked around at the other mothers, and understood her gaffe. They were all in neat floral summer dresses and straw hats, with a uniformity that made them almost indistinguishable.

'I am sorry,' she said quietly. 'I didn't understand. I'll go home now.'

But even Ben could not allow that, although he was tempted. The best he could do was keep her as far as possible away from his friends.

She never went to another Founder's Day.

6

The sun was coming up over Hampstead Heath. Wrinkled skin covered the dregs of hot chocolate in the two cups, Joanna's voice was cracking with exhaustion.

Lisa had been staring down at the table. As Jo said, 'She never went back to the school again . . .' she looked up and, for the first time, Jo saw a reflection of Ben in her eyes: the Ben who had frightened her sometimes with his hostility to anyone who he thought might have wronged him.

'I said he was a shit! Nothing you've told me has changed my mind. How could he behave like that to his mother?'

'He was a child. He had no idea what he was doing to her. And in spite of it, she still adored him. You haven't heard all the story.'

'So tell me something that will change my mind.'

Jo was stiff in every muscle, and her elbows were sore from leaning on the table. She stood up and stretched. 'We'd better get moving. We'll have to go in a couple of hours.'

But the long pre-dawn talk had focused her mind on the past and as they were washing their breakfast plates, she found herself returning compulsively to Anna's story: 'You know, it took her a long time to come to terms with the fact that Ben was making money from painting. She said to me once, "He stands there, Joanna, in front of his easel, all day, making pictures, isn't it?" And I said yes, it was. She shook her head and muttered, "My God, I wouldn't feel that I was doing a day's work!" I told Ben because I thought he'd laugh, but he was furious. He couldn't stand her belittling him.'

'Wasn't she lonely when he left home?'

'Yes. He hardly ever went back after he started school, even spent the holidays with friends. Although he eventually made jokes about it, I don't think he ever got over the humiliation of his mother having been a char. But she'd saved her money, and when he left school, she was able to afford to give him a year at an art college in Chelsea. He moved permanently to London.

'He'd already decided to concentrate on portraits. He use to go into Hyde Park and draw anyone who took his fancy – tramps, duchesses, shop-girls, old, young. He had no inhibitions about asking people to pose for him, and he was so good-looking, with such charm, that they rarely refused. He'd make a series of quick sketches, then go back to his studio, which was off the King's Road, and work up the paintings.'

Jo hung up the damp tea-towel. She stood, looking out of the window again, over the Heath's sun-drenched trees, but she was seeing the pictures she had loved, which had now all gone. 'He didn't want anyone to be distracted from the faces. That's why he filled his canvases with them – no backgrounds, no bodies, just faces.

'A gallery in Chelsea gave him a show, and it was a wild success. The critics raved about him. He seemed to have raised portraiture to a new level, painting faces that were expressive, and recognizable, but at the same time you could see planes and angles which revealed the bone-structure, and even their minds. The show sold out. And he was only nineteen!'

'The Infant Phenomenon.'

'Don't sneer. The Tate bought his picture of "The Sleeping Tramp", and the National Portrait Gallery bought two others. He made a big thing of painting only faces that interested him, so an Absalom portrait gave the sitter immense *cachet*.'

'Presumably he made sure the faces that interested him belonged to people who could afford his prices.'

'He said there was no reason why the rich shouldn't have character, but he painted poor people, too, if they took his fancy. Later on, he used the same technique in his landscapes: he never painted pretty scenes. Detritus on a beach, a burned-out car by the roadside . . . he saw beauty and colour where other people only saw decay.'

'I remember one he did of the phoenix tree's trunk . . .' Lisa paused, then said crossly, 'Oh, God, nostalgia time again! We'll never get away at this rate.'

The telephone rang as they were on their way out to the taxi that was waiting to take them to the airport.

Jo was nearest, so she picked it up.

'I don't want to talk to anyone. Say I've left,' Lisa called.

A man's voice said: 'I want to speak to Mrs Absalom.'

'I'm not sure whether she's here,' Jo said cautiously. 'What is it about?'

'Is that Miss Absalom?'

'No.'

'Then you gotta be her mother, right?'

'Please tell me what you want.'

'Can't over the telephone. It's a proposition . . .'

She wondered whether it could be the ex-pop singer, Dominic Partridge, but his Birmingham accent had been unmistakable.

So this one had to be from a newspaper. She remembered there had been a call the previous night and Lisa had told them to ring back. 'I'm sorry, but I'm not interested,' she said.

'Hang on . . .'

She replaced the receiver and ran down to join Lisa. Two hours later, they were air-borne, on their way to Nice.

PART THREE

1

'So what are you planning to do with the rest of your life?'

Nick and his father were sitting on their terrace, sharing a bottle of Bandol. The day was cloudy, with a promise of more of the rain which would make this the wettest autumn within living memory. But it was still warm, and below them, grassy slopes, dotted with grey-green olive trees and graceful clumps of pampas, stretched down to the little river which bordered the property. Neither man nor machine blemished the landscape, and Peter's abrupt question was a rude interruption to Nick's enjoyment of its tranquillity. It was one he had avoided facing since he had returned to La Belette.

He stood up, poured himself another glass of wine, and began to pace restlessly. After a moment, he shrugged and said, 'Christ knows. Do I have to do anything?'

Peter watched him, frowning. In eight years, he had changed dramatically. From a boy whose eyes were bright and mischievous, who spent his time devising amusement for himself and Lisa Absalom – often with unfortunate consequences – and was interested in everything from geology to cooking, he had become a tired, cynical man, apparently happy to sit for hours doing nothing. He seemed to enjoy helping the Mazeaus at the Lion d'Or, but Peter suspected that he was spending too much time in the bar. Since the destruction of his anonymity after Ben's death two weeks ago, there were always celebrity-hunting visitors eager to buy him a drink. He had given up trying to avoid them.

'Do you see yourself vegetating here for ever?'

'Trying to get rid of me?'

'Far from it! But for God's sake, you're nearly twenty-seven. You're facing a hell of a long time stretched out in a chair staring at the view.'

Nick looked down at him affectionately. At fifty-five, Peter was showing his years. Tall and lanky, he was slightly stooped, and his hair, though still dark, was thinning. Deep lines cut into his forehead and ran from his nose to the corners of his mouth. But there was a gentleness in his expression that won the friendship of men and women of all ages and Nick knew that his generosity and genuine interest in people had made him one of La Belette's most popular inhabitants. The only person in the village for whom he had ever been heard to admit dislike was Ben Absalom. And that was partly because he had been hopelessly in love with Joanna for years.

'The view will pall in time, I expect,' he said.

'Then what?'

'Honestly, I don't know. A couple of times in America, I thought I'd found my future, but it never worked out. Either I got bored, or my employers got bored with me.'

'What about movie-acting?'

'No way! It took one movie to cure me of that. Hours of tedium and repetition. Dreadful people.'

'Writing? Have I told you I thought your book was great?'

'Several times. You're prejudiced, but thanks. I suppose writing is a possibility. But what about? I'm not interested in fiction. *Road-Runners* was a gift. I was writing about myself, and the people I knew. Dirk Chavez, particularly.'

Peter nodded. 'Interesting man. But some of it made painful reading.'

'The final thing that screwed up my relationship with America was when the media suggested that we'd had a homosexual relationship.'

'So you wrote the book.' Peter laughed. 'Which proved your heterosexuality was beyond question.'

'I hope so. I really did enjoy working in that cottage on Cape Cod. Hardly saw a soul for six months. The publishers have come up with a few suggestions for another biography, but always about people I haven't known, who don't particularly interest me.' He put his glass down. 'I guess something will turn up. I think I'll go for a walk along the river. Want to come?'

'No, thanks. Jo said she might call from London and let me know when she'd be back. Could be any time now.' He hesitated, then said, 'Had any news of Lisa?'

'No. And won't. That's been finished for years, as you well know. Anyhow, she's married.'

'No, she isn't,' Peter said quietly.

'You wrote . . .'

'She was divorced earlier this year.'

Nick had to make an effort to keep his tone casual. 'That didn't last long. Any idea what happened?'

'It seems that the man she married was gay.'

'Jesus . . . the poor kid! She didn't know?'

'Obviously not. According to Jo, she'd been away, and met him on the aircraft coming home. They were married a few weeks later.'

Nick cleared his throat. 'Where was she coming home from?'

'I don't know. She had just finished a tv series and been away for a holiday. A few weeks later, she telephoned Jo from London and said she was married. As you might expect, Ben was furious. He and Jo flew to London to see her. Jo liked the man. She had no idea he was a homosexual, but Ben suspected it. I suppose he understood faces and body language better than most people. Jo didn't say much when they got back, but apparently he and Lisa had an almighty row.' He paused. 'It was their last, as it turned out.'

'I'm going for that walk.' Nick jumped down from the

terrace and strode towards the river, where once he and Lisa had splashed among the stones, building dams, playing Pooh-sticks from the little bridge, fishing with rods made of twigs and string.

Peter went inside, so he would be near the telephone if Joanna rang.

When Nick returned, a black Peugeot was parked in front of the house. His father was standing on the terrace, talking to two men. All three turned towards him. One of the strangers was tall, thin, neatly-dressed, with a still, dark face, and expressionless eyes. The other was square, bull-headed, needed a shave.

'This is my son,' Peter said. 'Nick, these gentlemen are from the police. Commissaire Molinard, Inspecteur Demazin. They want to ask you some questions.'

'What about?'

Demazin stepped forward, 'About your discovery of M. Benedict Absalom's body, m'sieu.'

'I've already told the police about that. What else is there to say?'

'Some circumstances have arisen that require explanation. We must ask you to account for your actions throughout the day of the . . .' He paused for just long enough to emphasize the word. ' . . . accident.'

'Why the hell should I? What is this?'

The thin man spoke for the first time. 'Routine questioning, m'sieu,' he said smoothly. 'Nothing to worry about.'

In English, Peter said, 'Tell them, for God's sake!'

'I don't see why . . .' He shrugged. 'Okay. In the morning, I went into the market in St-Tropez to buy some vegetables for Marie Mazeau at the Lion d'Or. I stopped for a coffee at Senequier's, on the Port, and ran into a man I knew . . .'

'His name, please.' Demazin was taking notes.

'Wilbur Block. He's a film-studio executive in Los

Angeles. His yacht, the *Shaman*, was tied up in Cannes and he was in St-Tropez for the day. I had a drink with him. He asked me to lunch, but I had to get back. Arrived at the restaurant about one, helped Jean-Louis in the bar for a while, then when the rush was over I had lunch with the Mazeaus, and gave them a hand clearing up. I needed fresh air and exercise, so I went for a walk to look at some of the places where I used to play when I was a kid. You know the rest.'

Molinard said, 'Did you see anyone during your walk? Monsieur or Madame Absalom, for instance?'

'How could I? He was already lying at the bottom of the cliff. The doctor said he'd been dead for about two hours. Madame Absalom was in the house.'

'Did anyone see you?'

'I've no idea. Are you going to tell me what this is all about?'

'It has been reported that you and M. Absalom were overheard having an argument in the Lion d'Or a few days before the accident.'

'Absalom was drunk, and I asked him to leave. Then Jean-Louis and I escorted him out. I never saw him again after that – not alive. That's the only time I've seen him in eight years. I've been out of the country . . .'

'We know about that.' Demazin thrust his heavy head forward. 'And that in the United States you were not unknown to the police.'

Molinard nodded. 'You spent at least one night in gaol. I read your book, m'sieu.'

Realizing that he was being baited, not understanding why, Nick kept his voice low. 'Then you will also know that there were no charges.'

'Your lack of respect for law and order, even as a child, is well-known in this village.'

He tried to keep a rein on rising temper. 'When I was thirteen, I borrowed a car to go joy-riding for an hour. What else? Oh, yes, I organized a bicycle race through the

95

village when I was about twelve. That makes me a criminal?'

'You damaged the car, which belonged to M. Absalom. You rode your bicycle through the market-place, destroying several stalls.'

'For which I paid in full,' Peter snapped. 'I paid for the damage to the car, too.'

'That is beside the point.' Molinard turned back to Nick. 'Children sometimes believe they can get away with murder, M'sieu. You are no longer a child.'

'*Murder!*'

The Commissaire switched to English: 'I use a figure of speech. The English exaggeration: to get away with murder. Meaning, to commit a misdemeanour and go unpunished.' He moved towards the steps that led down to the drive and said formally, 'I thank you for your cooperation. We will talk again.'

When they had gone, Nick sank into a chair and looked up at his father. 'Ben slipped and fell, didn't he? There hasn't been any suspicion that it wasn't an accient.'

Peter shrugged. 'Not that I've heard. But Ben was a celebrity. Maybe the *flics* are hoping to get themselves into the news by drumming up a mystery.'

'And suggesting he was murdered? Ridiculous! Who'd want to murder Ben? You know, even after the episode in the bar, I found I didn't dislike him any more. I was sorry for him. Those hands . . . Jesus!'

'Arthritis hadn't improved his temper. He'd antagonized a lot of people.'

'You don't chuck someone over a cliff because you dislike him. *Had* to be an accident.' Nick frowned. 'Something must have made them suspicious, though.'

Peter stood up. 'I'm going to try to find out. Serge Berenger might know something.'

'Who's he?'

'Our local cop. He's been here for about five years. Nice chap.'

As he was on his way to the telephone, an ancient Deux Chevaux came rattling towards the house. 'Oh, Lord, it's the Mahrs,' he said. 'I'll bet they want to know why the police were here. Amyas can't bear to be left out of anything.'

Amyas Mahr emerged from the car like a surfacing whale and came towards them. The passenger door had jammed and Ona, small, frail, her grey hair lank and wild, had to struggle to open it without his help.

His great voice, with its slight, unidentifiable accent, boomed over the peaceful landscape. 'Peter, my friend! Nicholas! Well met! But sad times, sad times! Our beloved Ben gone, poor Joanna bereft, and now the police. They were here, I noticed, so you'll have heard?'

Peter led Ona to a chair. 'A glass of wine?' She nodded gratefully. He poured for her and for Amyas. Only then did he say, 'Heard what?'

'The dreadful news, my dear: it seems that after Ben died they discovered bloodstains under the palm tree, several metres from the edge of the cliff. They said nothing about it at first, but they've been investigating. Now they think he was killed there and pushed over the edge.' Peter and Nicholas stared at him. 'They didn't tell you? Why were they here, then?' The sharp, black eyes peered inquisitively at them and his great beard seemed to quiver with curiosity.

'Some idiot had told them Ben and I had a row in the Lion d'Or,' Nick said shortly. 'They asked me . . .' He stopped. 'It wasn't you, was it, Amyas? You were in the bar that day.'

'My dear boy, how can you think such a thing! Of course it wasn't. At least twenty people overheard your – conversation with Ben.' Amyas finished his wine. 'What a sad welcome home for Joanna this will be. She went to a memorial service, didn't she? I must say, I was surprised that none of his old friends from here were invited.'

Nick remembered that he had never liked Amyas.

'Shame, wasn't it?' he said maliciously. 'Especially when you think of the people who *were* there. Did you see the list in *The Times* this morning? Everyone who is anyone.'

Looking regretfully at his empty glass, Amyas heaved his vast bulk out of the chair. 'A vulgar crush, from the sound of it. Ona, we're going. Just came to pay our respects, Peter. Let us exchange news if we learn anything more . . .'

Ona pattered behind him to the car and it wasn't until they had driven off that Nick realized she had not uttered a word.

His father was standing, untouched glass in his hand. 'This is dreadful! When we talked about it, I didn't really believe . . . it was a sort of fantasy. My God, what is this going to do to Jo . . .?'

2

As Lisa took her seat in the aircraft, she was aware of recognition from other passengers, of heads turning to look at her. Still on show, she thought, but for how long? No more *Families*, no more Bridget. Give 'em a few months and, to the public, Lisa Absalom will be hardly a memory. She laughed suddenly, and Jo looked at her inquiringly.

'I was wondering how long it will be before I'm featured in one of those "Whatever happened to . . ." newspaper stories.'

'Are you going to miss the attention? I warn you, La Belette is very matter-of-fact about celebrities.'

'Not at all. It'll be lovely to be able to go out without worrying whether there are paparazzi under every bush.'

'Did you hate them?'

'Yes, but they were only doing their jobs.'

It was easy to see why she attracted public attention, Jo thought. She radiated a kind of aura that was as much to do with a generous, out-going personality as her beauty, though she had a body that would look spectacular in a potato-sack. Now, she was wearing a short tan and blue check skirt and a big, loose tan jersey which only seemed to emphasize her tiny waist and the small, high breasts that never felt the constriction of a bra. Her only jewellery was gold hoop ear-rings. A folded, blue chiffon scarf, knotted under one ear, held back her hair.

When they were settled she said, 'How about the next instalment of the family serial? We haven't got to me yet.'

'Egotist!' She thought for a moment. 'Well, let's skip to

1965, when you came into our lives. Ben was at the height of his success, we were living in the maisonette in Islington. He'd had the whole place redecorated when we moved in. It cost the earth, but he wanted to make a splash. When it was finished, it was in all the glossies, *House and Garden, Vogue, Harper's* . . .'

In those early years of their marriage, the young Absaloms were in demand for every party, were seen regularly in London's expensive restaurants, at first nights in the West End, Ascot, Covent Garden, at concerts and private views. Every exhibition of Ben's work was a sell-out. They were a spectacular couple; Ben, handsome, talented, gregarious; Joanna, a shy, remote beauty.

'I tried to like that sort of life, because Ben did,' she said. 'He made me buy clothes from Hartnell and Michael and Cavanagh, and spent a fortune on them. Before he took over, I'd stocked my wardrobe from Oxfam and jumble sales. Our money flowed out like the Thames in flood. We had a cook and a maid, and when we weren't dining out, we had parties at home. The guests were household names, they all seemed to know each other and were so self-assured that I felt like a frightened mouse. I wasn't part of their world, and I couldn't pretend I was. Ben could, and after a while he didn't have to pretend. He *was* part of it. Then he started to appear on tv, in chat-shows and as an art-critic. He was recognized everywhere. When I wasn't with him, there was always some other woman to keep him company.'

A stewardess came around with champagne, and she fell silent, her eyes looking back into the past.

'Didn't you mind the women?' Lisa said.

'I minded. But I learned to live with it. He needed attention and flattery. Maybe it was a result of his humiliations as a child.

'It was better when I decided that I had to make a life for myself. I took various courses, art history, quilting, cooking, pottery, anything to fill the time.

'I went down to Hinley to see his mother as often as I could. It was peaceful there, just Anna, sitting in front of her coal-fire, sewing, with those thick, red fingers turning out the most delicate embroidery.'

She smiled reminiscently. 'Once Ben insisted that she should come up to London and spend a week-end with us. He said it was to give her a break, but he really wanted to show her what a success he was.

'She hated every minute. On Saturday night, he had invited a crowd of friends in to impress her, faces whom she would have seen on tv, in films or on the news. Only she never watched tv and all she saw were noisy people who drank too much and called everyone darling. She had one glass of champagne, and sat in a corner looking disapproving. She went to bed at nine o'clock.

'The next time I went to Hinley, she said that she had decided to go back to Czechoslovakia. She'd never felt at home in England, she was in her fifties, and she wanted to see her family. Her parents were dead, and Tommy Flek was running the farm. She'd had letters from him after the war, but they were short and unsatisfactory. What she'd seen of our life in London had made her realize how far away from her Ben had grown. She said, "He has now you, Joanna, he is rich and successful and he doesn't need me any longer. I'm going home." The Communists were in control in Czechoslovakia, but she said she didn't care who ruled the country, she wasn't interested in politics.'

'How did Ben react?'

'At first he tried to talk her out of it, but not very seriously. Then he said he'd take her back. I think he was curious to see his birth-place. He had no difficulty getting a visa, the Czechs were flattered that a man with his reputation wanted to visit them.'

'And that was when he met the woman who was my mother?'

'Yes, that was when he met Eva . . .'

101

3

Tommy Flek was waiting for them at the Praha-Ruzyne Airport.

Ben saw a small man with thin, white hair and bent shoulders, his face creased from long hours out of doors in all weathers, his features unmistakably semitic. He was wearing a shabby sports jacket cut in the style of the forties, an open-neck shirt and grey, shapeless trousers. He was clutching a bunch of red roses and anxiously scanning the arrivals. His eyes passed over Anna and Ben, then returned. A smile removed years from his appearance, which could have been that of a seventy-year-old, rather than a man in his fifties.

Wordlessly, he and Anna embraced, then held each other apart, studying the effect of the years. Simultaneously, they burst into a stream of words, totally incomprehensible to Ben. When he was a little boy, Anna had tried to talk to him in her own language, but as he grew older, and became ashamed of her foreignness, he had refused to listen to anything but English and had forgotten the few words of Slovak he had picked up.

There were tears in Tommy's eyes when he turned to clasp his hand. He said: 'Martin's son! And so like! Bigger, and more fair. But indeed, Anna, it is Martin, risen again!' He picked up her suitcase and led the way towards the entrance. 'Tonight, we stay in Prague. I have booked rooms at a hotel which is recommended for foreign visitors. Tomorrow, we take the train to home . . .'

They were crossing the concourse when a flash-bulb went off. Half-a-dozen men and women were hurrying towards them, some carrying cameras. Ben glanced at Tommy and was startled by the fear on his face. Then they were surrounded, and questions in English of varying fluency were being shot at him. '*Pan* Absalom, why have you come to Prague?' 'Where are you staying?' 'Will you be painting any of our notable citizens?'

And to Anna: 'Why have you not come back before to your homeland?' 'How long do you plan to stay?' 'What changes do you notice?'

Anna clutched Tommy's hand as, bewildered, they shrank away from the barrage. Smiling, Ben stepped forward and fielded the questions with practised ease: he had brought his mother home after nearly thirty years; she was returning to the family farm near Bratislava; no, he would not be undertaking any portrait commissions, for him, this was a holiday, an opportunity to visit the land of his birth; neither he nor his mother had so far had time to see any more of Prague than this excellent air-terminal. He made jokes, charmed the reporters, posed for the photographers.

Then came the first of what he suspected would be a series of loaded questions: 'What is your opinion of the capitalist politician Profumo, and his association with the woman Kristina Keeler?' Ben's smile didn't waver. 'I'm a painter,' he said gently. 'This happened two years ago and I have no interest in the behaviour of politicians. But I do believe that a representative of the Soviet Government was also involved with Miss Keeler.' There was a brief silence, then a woman's indignant voice. 'That is not so! It is a lie put about by the capitalist press.'

Ben shrugged. 'I wouldn't presume to question your greater knowledge.' He picked up his suitcase and took his mother's arm. 'And now, if you will forgive me . . .'

Their hotel was on the wide avenue called Wenceslas Square, which was dominated by an equestrian statue of the city's patron saint, Prince Wenceslas.

Ben's room, with an adjoining bathroom– there was no

103

hot water in the hand-basin, and no soap – was a shabby version of any bedroom in any international hotel. It was comfortable enough, but there were stains on the bed-cover, worn patches on the red plush upholstery of the chairs.

The room overlooked the street, and he went to the window. For a moment, he couldn't identify what made this cityscape different from other capitals. Then he realized that there was almost no traffic. Instead of the constant stream of cars and buses in Knightsbridge or the Champs Élysées, a few stray vehicles moved up and down at a stately pace. It was a grey afternoon, with a drizzle, and pedestrians shuffled along the pavements, heads down, enveloped in plastic rain-coats, a drab outlook, without colour or animation.

He knocked at the door which connected his room with Anna's, and went in. She and Tommy were sitting uncomfortably on the edge of the bed, not talking.

'What's the matter?' he said. 'Don't tell me you've had a disagreement already? How does it feel to be home, Mother?'

'It is very nice. Prague is very nice,' she said loudly.

'Not exciting, though. All I can see are grey people in grey macs, carrying grey briefcases. They look pretty downtrodden. Surely it wasn't always like this, Tommy?'

Again the fearful look widened Tommy's eyes as, without speaking, he put a finger to his lips.

Ben looked around. 'You don't mean . . .? Here? Surely not!'

Tommy nodded. His voice, too, was louder than normal. 'Shall we go for a walk? I wish to show you your father's Prague . . . the old building of European News Features where we worked, and the great river Vltava. You will see how beautiful our city is. Anna?'

Looking suddenly weary, she said, 'I believe I stay here and rest for a little while. In the aeroplane, it was only two hours, but it seems that I have come thousands of miles.'

Tommy did not speak as they went down to the entrance hall in the old, creaking lift, and relaxed only when they were out in the street. He took a deep breath, 'Now we can talk! You think I was foolish in there?'

It was still drizzling, and Ben buttoned his expensive vicuna overcoat. 'Isn't it possible you over-reacted? They'd hardly bug all the hotel rooms in Prague, would they?'

'Not all, but there are only a few where foreigners are permitted to stay. There is a story about an English couple who were here for a trade conference. When they were alone in their bedroom, with the door closed, he said to his wife, "I do not like these puffy eiderdowns they put on the beds. I prefer good English blankets." When they returned after dinner, the bed had been remade with blankets.'

Ben laughed. 'I've heard the story before. I suppose you could say that was real service.'

Tommy had no answering smile. 'It is necessary that you are always careful what you say. Even in the dining-room, if you wish to talk without being overheard, you choose a table which is not near a pillar, and you say nothing in front of the waiters. They are all paid to report to the authorities, who want to know everything about every visitor.'

'They won't have a great deal to report about us, I'm afraid. What time are we leaving tomorrow?'

'As early as possible.' He shivered. 'I do not like to be in Prague now. It is – uncomfortable. Eyes watching. Ears listening. Not like it was when your father lived here.'

'You were good friends, my mother says.'

'The best. And this is just what we did on his first day. We walked for a long, long way, and talked. After that, we used to go often together to drink beer at U Kalicha.' He paused, and said hopefully: 'Would you care for a beer, Ben?'

'I'd love one.'

'Then we go to U Kalicha. I haven't been there since Martin left.' He sighed. 'Many times I miss those days. We had fun. Under our present régime, life is not so amusing.'

Dusk was falling when they arrived at the beer-hall. A dozen men had tankards in front of them, but the atmosphere was subdued, voices were quiet. It had little of the cheerful, fusty beer-hall atmosphere Ben had expected. Tommy looked disappointed. 'I heard that it had been rebuilt for tourists, at State expense. They've spoiled it.' He glanced around and his eyes fell on three men who were talking together. Suddenly, Ben felt his arm grasped and heard him whisper urgently: 'We cannot stay. Come!'

'Why? Let's have a beer first . . .'

'No, no! Not here. Quickly!'

As Ben turned to the door, he became aware that one of the men was looking at him: a fat, bald man with a thick neck that bulged over his collar. His small eyes narrowed and there was in them a look compounded of shock and recognition.

When he reached the street, Tommy was already a few yards away, huddled into his coat, walking quickly.

Ben caught him up. 'What was all that about?'

Tommy's face was pale and drawn in the dusk, his voice little more than a whisper. 'I saw a man in there . . . someone I thought I knew. It was – a surprise.' Then, almost to himself, he said, 'It couldn't have been. I was wrong . . .'

'Who do you think it was?'

'A man called Bruno. Your father knew him.'

'The Nazi? My mother told me once about my father and him, and some woman . . . Magda? Wasn't he the reason why we had to leave Prague in a hurry?'

Tommy nodded. As they turned a corner, out of sight of the tavern, he breathed deeply and his voice became stronger. 'The last I heard of him, he was working for the

106

Nazis. He had an important post in the government here. That was early in the war. Then, nothing. I've thought of him sometimes and I have to confess to you, I've hoped that he was punished for what he did.'

'I remember . . . didn't he persecute you after we left?'

'For weeks. He drove me out of Prague, and for a long time after I went back to the farm, I used to have nightmares that he was coming after me.'

'You never saw him again?'

'No. And that was so long ago . . . there are many fat men with faces like pigs, no? That could not have been him. There was just a resemblance. Let's forget it, and we find another beer-hall.'

Later, as they were on their way back to the hotel, he said: 'Please, do not tell Anna about the man we saw. I'm sure I was wrong, and she should not be reminded of Bruno.'

Ben was pleased to be leaving Prague the next morning. Later, he was to tell Jo that he could not be sure whether his unease was because there was a genuine atmosphere of fear and distrust, or had been inspired by Tommy's nervousness.

His spirits were not lifted when he awoke early in a curious red gloom. He opened his curtains and found that the window had been covered by a huge red banner that stretched across the front of the hotel.

'It is the Soviet flag, because it is Red Army Day, when we spontaneously celebrate the victories of the glorious Soviet military,' Tommy told him ironically as they waited outside the hotel for a taxi to take them to the station. 'This afternoon, there will be a march to the Old Town Square, where there will be speeches and patriotic songs. Be happy you are not here then, because the speeches will be broadcast from loud-speakers on lamp-posts throughout the city. There was one directly outside your room.'

107

'Is it a military parade?'

'Not only soldiers. Everyone must join in. I was here once before on this day. Shops and offices were closed. Thousands of people shuffled along, no one looked happy. But it was noticed if you did not join in, and you were reported for disloyalty to our masters.'

The train journey was tedious, the seats uncomfortable. At Bratislava, they had to wait for two hours for their connection to Piestany. Ben, long unaccustomed to anything but luxury travel, made little attempt to hide his irritation, and Tommy became increasingly distressed, apologizing at every delay.

As they sat on Bratislava's hard waiting-room benches, Ben took out his sketch-book, and forgot his ill temper. It was an astonishing room. A dusty crystal chandelier hung from the ceiling, and the walls were decorated with sombre oil-paintings of workers in fields and factories. The floor was unswept and spattered with crumbs. But for him, there was magic in the faces of the peasant men and women who waited impassively on the benches. None were young, and most looked tired. The women were wearing full black skirts, shabby coats, black boots and black headscarves. Many had great bundles wrapped in sheets beside them. When their train-time approached, they hoisted the bundles onto their backs and went out, bent under the weight. Some chewed sandwiches as they waited. Nobody spoke.

Ben made half-a-dozen rapid sketches before someone noticed what he was doing. An old woman with fierce eyes and a seamed face came to stand in front of him, and spoke angrily.

Nervously, Tommy said: 'She wants to know why you are staring at her. She does not like it, Ben. She says, what are you writing about her in that book.'

Ben smiled, and handed her his sketch-book. After a suspicious pause, she took it, and her anger faded. Roaring with laughter, she pointed at his drawing of herself, and showed it around. People began to chatter excitedly as they recognized their own portraits.

When she brought it back, she pulled out a few coins from a capacious pocket in her skirt, and offered them to him.

Tommy said, 'She wants to know if she can buy the drawing so she can show it to her grandchildren.'

Her face fell as she saw him shake his head, and she was about to turn away when he said to Tommy: 'Tell her to go back to her seat and I will make another drawing and give it to her.'

He was to tell Joanna that it was his school-days all over again. Reserve and suspicion faded as the people waited eagerly for him to draw them. By the time their train was due, he had sketched most of the faces twice, once for himself, a second time on a separate sheet which he tore from the book's spiral binding and handed to the subject.

When he stood up to leave, there was a chorus of farewells, and the first old woman rose and made a solemn little speech.

Tommy translated: 'She says to thank you, that you have made the hours pass quickly and your kindness will never be forgotten. Many years ago her younger daughter married an Englishman, Mr John Robertson, and went to live in Manchester. She asks that if you are ever in Manchester, you will tell *Pani* Robertson that her mother is well. She would like to go to England and see her, but she is not allowed to leave this country. Would you also tell her daughter that it is now nearly ten years since she has had a letter from her, and she would like to know how many more grandchildren she has.'

On the surface, it appeared that Anna's village had not changed since Martin had described it when he had ridden in on his bicycle thirty years before. Geese still made their stately way from the fields to the pond, the hill, down which he had swooped to disaster, was still surfaced with hard-packed yellow earth, the same tree spread its branches over the farm's courtyard, though there were no longer any pigs in the pen.

Inside the house, it was different. There was none of the bustle Anna remembered. The furnishings remained the same, in their old positions, but the antimacassars on the backs of the chairs were grubby, there was dust on the heavy oak tables, the stone floors were unswept. In the kitchen, the sink was cracked, the wooden draining boards encrusted with slime. Where once the kitchen-maker had stirred her cauldrons of goulash for the wedding-guests, there were blackened iron saucepans that had started to rust. There was overall an atmosphere of old age and neglect.

Anna stood at the door which connected the kitchen with the back hall and they all listened to the silence. Ben's mouth turned down with distaste as he surveyed his ancestral home.

After a moment Anna said: 'Where is everyone, Tomas? I know Blanka has gone . . . I have not said how sorry I was . . . but the children? Josef? Is there no one?'

'The children left with Blanka,' he said heavily. 'She never liked it here, and she did not get on with our mother. After the war, she took them to Bratislava. I haven't seen them for years, because she said it was not good for them to be separated from her when they were little, and now they're grown-up, they are not interested to come here, though I have asked them. I wrote you that our grandmother died during the war, and later our parents. Josef is still here, but he spends most of his time in his room, talking with his friends from Venus.'

She tried to smile. 'At least that is something that hasn't changed. There's no one else?'

'I have two – lodgers. Andreas Magal and his wife. You remember them?'

'Lodgers? Andreas and Irena? But they are rich! They

110

had their own house in the village! Why would they live here?'

He sighed. 'My dear, there is so much you don't understand about what has happened . . .'

'Then you must tell us everything,' she said briskly. 'But first, we always welcome our guests with a drink, no?'

His face brightened. 'As Martin was welcomed! And see what I have . . .'

He opened a cupboard and brought out an unlabelled bottle. Anna gave an exclamation of pleasure. 'Our father's?'

'One of the last three bottles.' He turned to Ben. 'Your grandfather, Jan, made this slivovice out of plums from our own trees before the war. He buried it to prevent the Nazis from stealing it, but they bulldozed our fields and many bottles were broken. He dug up what were left, and since then I have kept them hidden in the loft, waiting for this very moment!'

They toasted each other in the thimble-sized glasses. Ben choked on the fiery liquor, and Tommy laughed delightedly. 'It is like watching Martin all over again.'

They sat at the long kitchen table as he filled in the lost years.

'When the Russians came after the war, and gave us a Communist government, our land became part of a collective, and now I work in the chicken-houses they have built over the orchard. But we were known to be hard-working and sober, and they could find no excuse to deprive us of everything. They left us the house, and a bit of garden. We were lucky. They don't like people who own big houses in which few people live.

'The Magals weren't so lucky. Andreas had money which he had inherited from his parents. His father had been a capitalist, with his own engineering company, and that made Andreas unpopular. After their daughter, Eva, left home to work in Prague, there were only the two of

111

them in that house with many rooms. It was requisitioned for farmworkers and they were offered two rooms in an apartment in Piestany.

'Our parents had died by then, and I was afraid the same thing would happen to Josef and me, so I invited them to come and live here instead.'

Anna looked disapprovingly around the grubby kithen. 'Does Irena never clean the place?'

'She works in the kitchen of a hotel in Piestany all week. At week-ends, she is too tired to do much.'

'Now I am home, things will improve,' Anna said. 'Is there no longer danger that the house will be requisitioned?'

'The bureaucrats have the power to do anything they want. But I live quietly. I don't complain. As far as they know, I am a good Communist.' He smiled wryly. 'At least now there is no longer any risk in having Jewish blood.'

That night, after Tommy had gone to bed, Ben said to Anna: 'You could come back to England with me, you know.'

She shook her head. 'I stay here. This is my real home and Tomas needs me. We need each other. How long will you stay with us?'

He looked around the drab room. 'Not too long. To tell you the truth, Mother, I am *not* at home here. A week, to see you settled. Okay?'

'What you like.' Suddenly, there were tears in her eyes. 'You will come again, to see me? And bring Joanna?'

'Of course. When I can.' But they both knew he had no intention of coming back.

As it turned out, his week extended into more than a month, because a few days after their arrival, Eva Magal came home from Prague to see her parents.

4

As they drank their coffee, having eaten what they could of the airline lunch, Lisa said, 'I wonder whether any of those people Ben drew in the waiting-room discovered how valuable the pictures became, and cashed in on them?'

'I hope not. I'd like to think that they – or their grandchildren – still have them, and remember Ben's generosity.'

'I've seen reproductions of the paintings he did of Tommy and Anna, of course.'

'The best one of Tommy was bought by the Museum of Modern Art in New York. There was this extraordinary contrast: the thin, intelligent old face and the hands of a labourer. It was one of the few times Ben painted hands in a portrait.'

'You never met Tommy, did you? But when you talk about him, it seems that you must have known him well.'

'I've always felt I did, from listening to Anna.'

'Didn't Ben mention Eva at all?'

'Only as a casual acquaintance. When he came home, he simply said that he'd stayed longer than he planned because he didn't want to waste an opportunity to see more of Czechoslovakia. He must have been with her all that time.'

'Did you hear much from Anna and Tommy after that?'

Jo sighed. 'I'm not going to enjoy this part, but you might as well have the lot. After Ben came home, he was quieter than usual for a while, but as far as I know, he had no further contact with Eva. We settled down and everything went back to normal – or as "normal" as Ben's life ever was. He was more and more in the public eye, appearing on tv and radio, giving interviews, painting, painting, painting. I missed Anna dreadfully. She'd sold the cottage and I had no escape from London. We had letters from her, and at first, they were cheerful. She told us she had enjoyed putting the house back in order, and she sent us translations of newspaper stories that had appeared in Prague about Ben. I think she rather liked seeing her own name in them. She got on well with the Magals, especially Eva, who was a successful radio journalist in Prague, but often came down to visit her mother and father.

'Not long after Ben left, the trouble started. Officials from the local housing organization turned up unexpectedly at the farm and went from room to room, asking questions about who lived there, making notes about the accommodation. Tommy and Anna couldn't understand it, and no explanation was given.

'Finally, a notice came that the house was being requisitioned. They were given only two weeks to vacate it, and there was no appeal.

'Tommy was distraught. He was told that there would be some compensation and he had been allocated a room in a run-down house in the village. As if that could make up for losing his family home! No provision was made for Anna, because she had a British passport. Almost worst of all, poor harmless Josef was removed to a lunatic asylum.

'Eva Magalova had a two-room flat in Prague – she was fortunate, because there was a shortage of accommodation and in many cases whole families had to live in a single room. Her parents had decided to move to Piestany and stay with a relative, so she offered to take Anna in.'

'I'm surprised Anna didn't come back to England.'

'I wrote and asked her to, but she refused. I think she really was happy to be back with her own people.' Jo paused, as another thought came to her. 'Of course! *You*

114

were the reason she stayed! Ben's child. She must have known by then that Eva was pregnant, and she wouldn't leave her.'

'But she never told Ben?'

'Never. Maybe Eva wouldn't let her; maybe she was thinking of me. There were long gaps between her letters after that. We didn't worry too much, because she wasn't a good letter-writer at the best of times, and she'd said she was perfectly comfortable and enjoyed being with Eva.

'But then she wrote with terrible news: Tommy had committed suicide.'

Lisa gasped. 'Because he'd lost the farm?'

'That, and because he had discovered that Bruno had been the cause of his persecution. Before he died – he hanged himself from a branch of a tree in the farm courtyard – he wrote to Anna, and she sent a translation of the letter on to us.

'He had continued to worry about the identity of the man he and Ben saw in U Kalicha that night. Though he didn't say anything at the time, he had made inquiries from friends in Prague, and discovered that somehow Bruno had survived the change from Nazism to Communism – not only survived, but flourished. He had surfaced again during the fifties. It seems that he had buried his Nazi past so effectively, and embraced the new régime with such enthusiasm, that he was accepted as a true believer. He had a good job in one of the ministries and the ear of high officials in the Party.

'He had spotted Tommy in U Kalicha. For a moment, he had thought Ben was Martin. The next day, when the newspaper reports about Ben appeared, all his old hatreds had revived. Martin was out of reach, but there was still Tommy, whom he regarded as a kind of extension of Martin.'

'How could Tommy have found out all this?'

'Bruno went to the village after he'd pulled strings to have the farmhouse requisitioned. He visited Tommy and gloated over what he'd done. He made no attempt to hide the fact that he was as anti-semitic as he had ever been, and he laughed, just as he had after his thugs had beaten Tommy up in Prague more than twenty-five years before. His final revenge for Martin's affair with Magda, and what he believed had been Tommy's connivance, was that the next day, he had Tommy fired from his job.

'A week later, Tommy was dead. He'd lost his wife and children, his parents and his farm. His sister was gone, and now he had no job. There was nothing left to make him want to live. He wrote it all in the letter to Anna.'

'And Bruno got away scot-free, I suppose.'

'No. What happened to him was the one good thing that came out of it. Tommy still had friends among newspaper-men in Prague. Before he died, he wrote to one of them, telling the whole story, from the first days he and Martin had known Bruno. He was able to give chapter and verse of his Nazi activities . . . details of his involvement in the setting-up of concentration camps in Germany, which Tommy had learned after the war from a Czech Jew who had survived. At that stage, he had assumed that Bruno was already dead, which was one reason why he'd been so shocked to see him in U Kalicha.

'It was a good story, especially in view of Tommy's suicide, and it was picked up by newspapers in other countries. Bruno was arrested and tried as a war-criminal. The day he was due to be sentenced, he had a heart-attack, and died.' She stopped for a moment. 'Anna said writing that letter was the only vindictive action of Tommy's entire life.'

'I don't suppose he ever knew Martin's grandchild was on the way. I wonder if it would have given him some incentive to carry on?'

'Maybe. Anna was devastated by his death, but I imagine your birth helped her to get over it.'

'So tell me what happened in 1968, when Ben fetched me out.'

'I know less about that than the earlier years, which Anna described endlessly. When Ben came back to England with you, he didn't want to discuss it. It must have been a traumatic experience for him, seeing his friends machine-gunned. Didn't he ever talk to you?'

Lisa shook her head. 'When Nick and I were kids, we tried to get him to tell us about it. Nick, particularly, was intrigued by the excitement and what a hero Ben had been, rescuing me. But he always brushed us off, made excuses, went into stories about the phoenix instead.'

Jo peered out of the window at the cloud layer below the aircraft. 'How long before we land, d'you think?'

Lisa glanced at her watch. 'Half an hour or so.'

'That's time enough. You don't remember anything about the escape from Prague?'

'I was three years old. In my memory, it's as though I began my life in London, with you and Ben.'

'In May, 1968, we had a letter from Anna. The writing was shaky, and she said she hadn't been well, but was now better. Ben was about to leave for the United States to carry out a portrait commission . . . a Texas oil millionaire, I believe.

'It was the time when Czechoslovakia's political climate was changing. The people were fed up with the restrictions and domination of Moscow. The country's writers, journalists and students were leading a reform movement. A Slovak, Alexander Dubcek, became First Secretary of the Czech Communist Party, and said his aim was to encourage "socialism with a human face," combining the best features of Communism with Western-style democracy. It all led up to what people called the "Prague Spring," when there was a tremendous feeling of unity and optimism bubbling throughout the country. For the first time since 1948, there was freedom of the press and radio, and the hard-line Communists in the Government were being replaced by liberals. Maybe, if Tommy Flek

117

had lived, he'd have found that some of the fun had been restored to life.

'It didn't last, though. In August, we had a letter from Anna, a few scrawled lines which didn't make much sense. Clearly, she wasn't well, although all she said was that she had been to see her doctor for some minor internal problem. I tried to telephone her, but I couldn't get through.

'During the previous couple of weeks the whole edifice of liberalism Dubcek built up had started to collapse. The Soviets had been appalled at the speed of the reforms and were determined to restore their authority.

'When Ben got back from America, I persuaded him that he must go to Prague and at least try to see his mother. Preferably bring her to England. She was ill, and the political situation was explosive.

'He wasn't too happy about leaving his work, but he finally agreed. He arrived in Prague on August the twenty-first, the day the Soviet tanks rolled in and Dubcek and his supporters were arrested.

'I learnt about what happened then mostly from the papers, which carried stories about Ben's heroism in rescuing the baby daughter of two young liberals who had been among the twenty Praguers killed by the Russians.

'It seemed that he had gone to Eva's apartment, to find that his mother had died of cancer two days earlier. Eva had married recently and she and her husband were in the thick of the conflict, because they were both working for a radio station which was moving its headquarters around the city, trying to broadcast uncensored news of the Russian invasion.

'It wasn't nearly as bloody an occupation as it had been in Budapest twelve years earlier, when the Hungarians had risen, but it was bad enough.

'I remember reading that an eleven-year-old boy was murdered as he tried to push a Czech flag down the gun barrel of a Soviet tank, and a group of young men set some

Soviet vehicles alight with Molotov cocktails outside the Prague Radio building.

'From the little Ben told me, Eva and her husband seem to have been killed in a gun battle near their apartment. She was carrying you. According to the papers, Ben was caught in the middle of it and risked his life to pick you up out of your dead mother's arms.

'He made for the offices of an American newsagency in the Old Town . . . the centre of the fighting was in the New Town, in and around Wenceslas Square . . . where he knew one of the correspondents from 1965.' She stopped briefly. 'Perhaps he had met him through Eva. He explained what had happened, and that he intended to take you back to England. Your grandparents had long since died and there were no other relations, so as far as he knew, you were alone in the world. Strangely, no one questioned him. I suppose the country was in such turmoil that the fate of one small child was not important.

'Ben's American friend organized a car for him and he drove down to Bratislava, and across the border into Austria. In Vienna, he picked up a flight to London. It was the long way round, but he wanted to avoid awkward questions at the airport in Prague.

'The newspaperman had been intrigued by his story, and sent it out on the wires: artist's heroic rescue of Czech orphan. By the time Ben got home, it was in all the papers. Reporters met him at the airport, but he refused to give any interviews. It was unlike him, but everyone realized that it had been a horrendous experience.

'Anna's death affected him, too. Although he resented his childhood and had left home as soon as possible, he'd always known she was there, and that even when she criticized his way of life, she adored him unquestioningly. He needed that kind of adoration . . .' She stopped, and inhaled deeply. 'At least now you know something about your roots, and that Ben wanted you enough to risk his life for you.'

'There were never any inquiries about me from Prague?'

'Never. At first I used to worry about it, because as soon as I saw you, I wanted to keep you more than anything in the world. We'd discovered about a year after our marriage that I couldn't have children and we'd already talked about adopting.'

'You didn't adopt me officially, though.'

'I used to beg Ben to do it, but he always refused. He said it would involve too much red tape. As the years passed, people simply accepted that you were our adopted daughter, and there was no contact with anyone from Czechoslovakia, so I stopped worrying. Now we know why he didn't want to start any inquiries.'

A stewardess's voice interrupted, to inform the passengers that they would be landing in Nice in fifteen minutes.

Lisa stretched and ran a hand through her hair. 'Somehow I feel a lot closer to Anna and Tommy Flek than I do to Eva, or even Ben. I still can't understand why he never told me he was my father. I mean, after a few years, would it have made any difference to you?'

'Probably not. But at the least, I suppose telling me would have created an emotional upheaval which might have affected his ability to work.'

'Shaw wrote that a true artist will let his wife starve, his children go barefoot, his mother drudge for his living at seventy, sooner than work at anything but his art. Who does that remind you of?'

'Oh, yes! God knows, Ben played hard, but nothing was allowed to interfere with his painting. When arthritis began to cripple his fingers, he still tried to work. He didn't stop until the pain made it impossible.'

As the 'Fasten seat-belts, extinguish cigarettes' lights flashed, Lisa said thoughtfully, 'It's curious that I seem to have learnt more about him since he died than I ever knew when he was alive. It's almost as though he's that phoenix, coming back to life from the ashes.'

5

They collected Jo's little Renault from a garage in Nice.

Amused, Lisa said: 'This is a change. Ben never owned anything so modest.'

'He sold his Ferrari when he realized he wouldn't be able to drive any longer. He said it was because we didn't need two cars, not that he needed the money.'

They made good time to La Belette, because the summer traffic jams that made the coast road a nightmare had ended. The village was quiet, with the Lion d'Or deserted, the Mazeaus catching their breath before the evening rush. They passed the Garnier's mini-château, with its pepper-pot towers, and turned up the road that led towards the Massif.

The villa was stark white against emerald grass, more startling than Lisa remembered now that it was surrounded by landscape blackened by the summer fires.

She left the car to unlock the iron gates, and stood looking up at it, unmindful of the steady rain soaking her hair and clothes. Mimosa and olive trees dotted a green plateau behind the vast, sprawling house, which was surrounded by terraces on which bright geraniums spilled from terracotta urns. A high stone wall curved out from one end, giving privacy to the swimming-pool where she and Nick had spent hours as children. There were extensions which were unfamiliar to her, but she recognized the house's core, the living-room with big windows shaded by yellow and white striped awnings. Fringed yellow sun-umbrellas, groups of tables and chairs, and massed pot-plants stood on its flat, terraced roof. It was a house made for sunshine and people. Now, deserted, under grey, dripping skies, its splendour was forlorn.

Jo drove through the gates and they closed automatically behind her.

'It looks bigger than it did,' Lisa said.

'Ben kept adding bits. It was one of the ways he amused himself when he couldn't paint any longer. I'm afraid that's where a lot of the money went.'

'It's beautiful, but how on earth do you manage it?'

'We used to have village women to help, but we let them go. Ben made the excuse that he hated having outsiders around the house. I thought it was because of his condition, but again it must have been one of his economies. In the end one girl, Claudette Dorsey, came in a couple of times a week, but he made me get rid of her, too.'

'We're going to be like a couple of goldfish dropped into an Olympic pool.'

'We can close half of it off until I decide what I'm going to do. Would you believe, ten bedrooms, and often they were all in use.'

'He never grew out of his need to have people constantly around him?'

'He began to slow down a couple of years ago, when the pain had become bad. That was when he began to drink. Before that, friends seemed to give him confidence that although he was semi-crippled, he could still dominate a crowd. During the last year he went to London a couple of times, but that was all. He stayed at the Connaught.' She smiled wryly. 'I thought he could afford it because the flat was let. I had no idea how little money there was, but even so I used to have nightmares about the amount we spent.' She edged the car through an archway at the side of the house and pulled up outside a yellow-painted door.

They carried their suitcases into a huge area with three walls made almost entirely of glass, that was combined kitchen and living-room. A bar separated the work area, which was stocked with every conceivable kitchen gadget. The centre-piece was a refectory table which could seat twenty. Sofas and chairs upholstered in green and yellow chintz were arranged informally in two groups, one around a big stone fire-place, the other facing French windows with a view across the valley. The floor was yellow and white ceramic tiles on which sea-grass mats were scattered. An open staircase rose to a landing which led out onto the flat roof.

There were shelves between the windows, filled with books, and occasional tables bearing knick-knacks, many of which Lisa recognized. She picked up a small brown glass hedgehog and held it against the light. 'I always thought this looked like solidified whisky. And you've never had the nose mended. Remember when Nick dropped it and it chipped? He was so upset he cried for an hour.'

'What you probably never knew was that it had been Anna's. She brought it from Czechoslovakia when she came over with Martin, and gave it to me before she left.'

Lisa was looking around the walls, which were decorated with Provençal plates in sharp primary colours. 'There are no pictures. Not one!'

'They've all been sold. The last two went to Dominic Partridge.'

'I remember them all. The one of you, your hair tied back with a red ribbon, faced the windows. There was a landscape, *Le Mur*, grey rock, with the phoenix tree at the top on the left, opposite that wrinkled face of an old gypsy with a scarf around his head. I miss them.'

Jo picked up her suitcase. 'They've been gone for a long time. I don't brood about them. You can sleep in your old room. It hasn't been changed, and it was the only one we kept free of guests.'

But Lisa had moved to the French windows and was looking out at the rain-sodden terrace. She turned suddenly. 'Did Ben commit suicide?'

Jo stiffened, and for a moment her face was agonized, then she said softly: 'I've wondered, of course. He couldn't paint. He must have known how little money was left . . .' She turned away abruptly. 'I can't bear to think about it.'

Lisa crossed the floor and put her arms around her. 'I'm an idiot! Ben would never have killed himself. He was too fond of life. It was an accident, like they say.'

'Yes. Now let's get you settled.' After clinging to her briefly, Jo, as always, regained control of her emotions with almost unnatural swiftness.

A door-bell peeled, startling in the silent house.

The telephone, connected with a speaker at the gates, hung beside the bar. She picked it up and said, 'Peter? Is it you?' Her face changed. 'Who? . . . But I've only just arrived from London . . . Of course. If you must.' She pressed the button that released the gate-lock, and turned. 'It's the police. They want to talk to me.'

6

The postman had finished the glass of wine which he could count on being offered by Peter Garnier at the end of his afternoon deliveries, and his yellow van was disappearing towards the village.

'One for you.' Peter handed Nicholas an airmail envelope. 'The rest is junk. I'd been hoping for a card from Jo, saying when she'd be back. I've been trying to phone her all morning to warn her about the police, but there's been no answer from Lisa's flat.'

Nick was not listening. 'I'll be damned!' he said. 'This is from Jared Cowan.'

'Jared Cowan?'

'Head of Cowan and Es`k`clund, who published *Road-runners*. He wants me to do a book about Ben Absalom. He says, " . . . you knew Absalom, from what you told me, better than most people. In view of his fame, the prices his work is fetching, his glitzy life-style, unusual background, and his untimely death, we think he's a great subject. The Guggenheim is planning a retrospective. We could coincide publication of the biography. How do you feel about this?"'

'How *do* you feel?'

'I don't know. I haven't had time to think.' He frowned. 'It's a possibility, though. I'm in the right place. Everyone who knew Ben well during the last years is here. Jo. You. Amyas and Ona. London's a couple of hours away for checking on his early life. Jo must have any papers or diaries he left.' For the first time since he had returned home, his eyes had come alive with interest.

'I just might do it! What do you think?'

Peter said slowly, 'Someone's going to do a biography of him sooner or later. It might as well be you. But isn't there a chance your own relationship with Ben might colour what you write? You haven't exactly been friends during recent years.'

'No, but apart from that one meeting the other night, I think there's been enough distance between us for me to be able to see him objectively. He used to talk a lot about his work, too, while I was sitting for him. D'you think Jo will be a problem? Maybe she'll realize it's better for me to write about him than a stranger.'

'Maybe.' The telephone rang, and as he went to answer it, he added, 'This could be her now . . .'

Nick was still studying Cowan's letter when he returned, and said sharply. 'I'm going to the villa. Jo's home, and the police are there. They've said they simply want to talk to her, but I don't like it. They've refused to let Lisa stay with her.'

'Lisa?'

Peter was already on his way out. 'Apparently they came back together.' He stopped. 'Will you come?'

There was a pause, then Nick shook his head. 'She won't want to see me.'

'How do you know until you meet? But if that's how you feel . . .'

'Does she know I'm here?' His voice was strained.

'She didn't mention you. She was pretty upset.'

'If she doesn't know, don't tell her.'

'Why not? You'll have to meet eventually.'

'I'd like it to be on my own terms. Not now, when she's got other things on her mind. Surely they can't think Jo had anything to do with Ben's death?'

'The whole thing's absurd!' Gravel spat out under the car's wheels as Peter accelerated down the drive.

'They say they're *police judiciare*. They arrived just after

126

we got in from Nice. Jo's in the little sitting-room with one of them, and the other is standing at the door, like a guard. Peter, what's been going on here? Ben slipped in the mud and fell over the cliff, didn't he?' Lisa's face was drawn, and her voice fell almost to a whisper. 'The only other thing it could have been was suicide.'

They were sitting side by side on the sofa near the French windows. It was still raining, and the outlook was bleak.

Peter covered her hand with his and said, 'I have to tell you something. They came to see us – me – yesterday. They've found bloodstains on a rock under the phoenix tree and they think that Ben was attacked.'

She stared at him speechlessly for a moment. 'Someone *killed* him? My God, not Jo . . .?'

'Of course not. It will be routine questioning, maybe to find out if she saw any strangers around that day.'

'A tramp? But I still can't believe it was anything but an accident.'

Although her long hair was tangled from being pushed about by nervous fingers, and her face was innocent of make-up, he thought that she was even more attractive in maturity than she had been when she left La Belette eight years ago. In the present situation there was no display of the self-conscious emotion an actress might have felt obliged to project, and her determined control reminded him of Jo's. He spared a thought for the bitter ending of her friendship with his son. Ben Absalom had been wrong to separate them.

Commissaire Molinard said, 'It has been reported, Madame, that you and your husband were given to angry arguments. There was one a few weeks before his death. Will you explain what it was about?'

They were in the sitting-room which she and Ben had used when they were alone, but it no longer felt like theirs. Molinard had turned it into an interrogation room.

127

Jo was sitting opposite him, on the edge of a cane armchair, the light falling on her face. She knew that the bull-like Demazin was standing outside the closed door.

Now that the first shock of their arrival had passed, her still face gave no hint of her bewilderment.

When Molinard had informed her that he wanted to question her about her husband's death she had said, 'I don't understand. Why should there be questions?'

'Perhaps you already know, Madame.'

'I haven't the faintest idea what you're talking about.'

'Later, I will explain. For the moment, I must ask for your co-operation.'

Now she said quietly, 'We were not "given" to arguments. I can only remember one in recent years, and it was soon over. Who told you?'

'You were overheard.'

She thought, by Claudette, of course, who couldn't take her eyes off Ben. Never were rooms so thoroughly cleaned as the ones he happened to be in. Who blamed me when he said she had to go.

'The argument was unimportant.'

'Nevertheless . . .'

'He wanted to ask some friends to spend a few weeks with us. I was against it.'

'Why?'

'He wasn't strong enough to cope with visitors.' And because they included a Viennese woman he had met last time he was in London, and I couldn't face the humiliation of watching him start yet another affair in my own house.

'Your opposition angered your husband?'

'Yes. But his anger didn't last long.'

'On the day of his death, did you have another argument?'

'No.'

'But I understand that you usually accompanied him on his walks. This time you say you did not. Why?'

'He often preferred to be alone.'

128

'Surely he needed your help?'

'He could manage quite well with his stick. His hands were the worst. He insisted on walking every day to keep himself mobile.'

'Weren't you worried when he didn't return?'

'Sometimes he'd walk down into the village, have a drink in the Lion d'Or, then take a taxi back. He'd be away for a couple of hours.' She allowed herself the unusual luxury of a flash of anger. 'You must tell me why you're asking me all these questions!'

'Because your husband's death was not an accident, Madame. Nor could it have been suicide.'

It was dark before Molinard left, informing her that he would be back the following morning for a second interview.

Jo answered Peter's questions steadily. 'I'm not under arrest. I have been invited to help the police with their inquiries.' She raised an eyebrow ironically. 'I am "requested" not to leave La Belette, and the Commissaire hopes that by tomorrow I might have recalled something that might be helpful in their investigations. He talks like something out of a *crimi*.'

'I can't believe this is happening!' Lisa said.

'Neither can I. So I'm pretending it's a dream.'

'They're making a terrible mistake!' Peter said. 'Jo, I'm going to call Maître Gonnet . . .'

Gonnet, the *avocat* who looked after the business affairs of the Absaloms and Peter Garnier, was shocked to hear about the police suspicions, but pointed out that if they were right, and Ben's death had not been an accident, they would be interrogating everyone connected with him. Mme Absalom must not think she had been singled out. He would, of course, be at her service if required.

'He pointed out that he's not a criminal lawyer,' Peter said. 'I had a feeling that he won't be too happy to be associated with this affair.'

129

What he did not pass on was Gonnet's final remark: 'That Molinard is one who will do anything to secure a conviction. We must hope that Madame Absalom can prove her whereabouts at the time her husband was killed.'

Seeing the lines of exhaustion on Jo's face, Peter left after refusing Lisa's offer of a drink, saying he would also come back the following day, though he suspected that by then Molinard would probably have turned his attention elsewhere.

He was less successful in hiding his concern when Lisa walked down to his car with him. Pleading the need to take a shower and unpack, Jo had gone to her room.

'Even to hint that she was involved in Ben's death is absurd!' he said angrily. 'He neglected her, flaunted his affairs with other women, but she loved him and she was totally loyal. Years ago, I would have asked her to leave him, but I knew she never would. Once she talked about her "gratitude" to him. For what? I never understood.' Under stress his French accent, which was rarely detectable, strengthened.

'Nor I. She never talks about her childhood, but I've always assumed that it wasn't happy, and that he rescued her from it. Peter, is there anyone here who might have wanted to kill him?'

'I cannot begin to guess. He was well enough liked by the locals and they enjoyed the *cachet* he and his friends added to La Belette.' He paused. 'There were exceptions, of course. Georgette Ponelle, for one.'

'But she always adored him!'

'Not after what happened to Pierre-Luc. You didn't hear about it?' She shook her head.

'It was five years ago. Pierre-Luc likes to watch couples making love up in the hills. Everyone knows about it, though Georgette still insists he's bird-watching. Mostly he uses binoculars, but sometimes he goes too close.

'On this occasion, Ben had a crowd of guests in the villa,

a pretty wild lot. I saw them in the Lion d'Or. They were young and weren't finding La Belette lively enough.

'Ben was working and he left them to themselves for much of the time. He just liked to know they were around when he needed company. Jo had had enough of them, and one day she'd driven into Cannes to shop. Several of them came into the village and started baiting poor Pierre-Luc as he was sitting on his bench. Georgette ordered them away.

'Later, Pierre-Luc wandered off towards the Massif, and they found him again, and took him back to the villa. They gave him brandy. When he was thoroughly drunk, they got tired of the fun and sent him on his way.

'He staggered up into the hills around dusk and came on a couple lying on a rug near their car. This time, instead of just watching, his natural instincts must have surfaced. He went up to them and exposed himself.

'The man was a rugby player from Toulouse, who had come to see his girl-friend. He grabbed Pierre-Luc, marched him down into the village and handed him over to the police. There was a new young officer on duty, who wasn't familiar with the local people. Pierre-Luc was put into a cold, damp cell for the night. Georgette was frantic with worry when he didn't come home and spent hours in the hills, searching for him.

'Fortunately, Serge Berenger was on duty the next morning and he persuaded the couple that it would be less embarrassing for them if they did not insist on prosecuting. Pierre-Luc eventually told Georgette enough about his "friends" at the villa, who had given him nice drinks, to make her realize what had happened. She was humiliated, because she always tries so hard to make people believe that he isn't sub-normal, only a little slow.

'She went storming up to complain to Ben, who only laughed, and offered her some money in compensation. She was insulted, and refused to serve him or his friends in her shop again. She's stuck to it. The ban doesn't extend to Jo. Georgette's fond of her, like everyone else.

'That wasn't the end of the episode. Pierre-Luc got pneumonia, and nearly died, and she swore that it was because of his imprisonment. She put all the blame on Ben.'

After a moment, Lisa said slowly, 'If Pierre-Luc had been drinking again . . . couldn't he be dangerous?'

'I wouldn't think so. What he had shown was sexual frustration, not violence. Anyhow, Georgette makes very sure he drinks nothing stronger than Perrier.'

'But he has always walked around in the hills . . .'

'It would be tempting to hang the blame – if there is any blame – for Ben's death on someone like him,' Peter said. 'But that I cannot believe, either. He's a poor, feeble-minded wretch who wouldn't kill an ant if he could help it.'

'Georgette had a grudge against Ben.'

'It happened five years ago. She hadn't spoken to Ben since. Why should she suddenly have attacked him?'

'Then it was a tramp – a stranger.'

'After we'd talked to Molinard yesterday I called Berenger. He said they'd made exhaustive inquiries, and they'd established that there had been no tramps, gypsies or strangers in the vicinity of La Belette that day.'

'Why would anyone else attack him?'

'Why indeed? There had to be a reason.' He sighed. 'There were many things about Ben I didn't understand, after knowing him for nearly twenty years. One saw his surface: the celebrity who loved luxury and high living and women and parties and had to be the centre of attention. But I always felt that there were depths, that he was a man who kept his secrets.'

'You can say that again . . .'

He was surprised by the bitterness in her voice.

She and Jo talked little that evening, each thinking her own thoughts. It was as though the shock of Molinard's

132

revelation had been too much for them to take in.

At eight o'clock, Lisa made them each an omelette, but Jo hardly touched hers and an hour later she excused herself and went to bed.

Without her, the villa's rooms were like echoing caverns. Lisa switched on extra lights, and thought that to anyone looking up from the valley it must look as cheerful as a cruise liner on a dark ocean.

She went to the French windows that led onto the terrace, remembering Peter's words. Already, two of Ben's secrets had been revealed. Were there others . . . including one which might have caused his death? I didn't know him, either, and he was my father, she thought. The only certain thing is that Jo had nothing to do with it.

Rain was falling again, glittering like crystal threads on the light from the room. Beyond the terrace, everything was dark, the only sound a steady dripping from the branches of the trees. As she stood, breathing the fresh, damp air, the years suddenly telescoped, and the scene was transformed. She was a child again . . .

7

The terraces were a blaze of lights, reflected in the pool, thrown up into the trees. There was movement as groups of people drifted in and out of the house, from the buffet set out on the long table, to the bar attended by a white-coated waiter borrowed from the Lion d'Or for the night.

Lisa, aged ten, was sitting sedately on the edge of the pool with Nick. They were drinking iced cokes, their feet in the warm water, eyes and ears absorbing the scene. Occasionally they giggled at a moment of adult foolishness, and each knew that the other was storing it up to reproduce later in one of their private performances.

It had been a productive party. First they had overheard Ben and the woman named Miranda, talking softly as they stood close together on the lawn, unaware of the two small figures hidden behind a lime-tree.

As the evening progressed, and drink had flowed, and voices had slurred, and façades cracked, there had been other delicious moments.

Later, Lisa would play the part of the Englishwoman with the long, contemptuous Modigliani face and ear-rings which reached to her shoulders, who owned a gallery in London. Nick would become the short, fat, rich Australian telling her how he and his wife had 'done' every major art-gallery in Europe. 'And now Beryl and me can tell at the front door how long it's going to take us to get through. Take the Prado. I said to Beryl, right, you go one way and I'll go the other. Twenty minutes, we'll meet back here. That ought to do it.'

The party had been given to celebrate Jo's birthday, but

the guests, apart from Peter Garnier and the Mahrs, were Ben's friends, a mixed bag of Riviera residents, yacht-owners and some who had flown in from London.

Amyas and Ona Mahr were there at Jo's insistence, and his great, bearded presence clearly irritated Ben, who had never made any secret of his contempt for Amyas's claims to expertise on modern art. Ona was wearing a grey dress that matched her personality and few people even noticed the small woman with the yellowish skin and straight, basin-cut hair. She sat meekly on a chair to which Amyas had directed her when they arrived and, as far as the children could tell, the only people who had talked to her were Jo and Peter.

Amyas, on the other hand, was always good for a few quotable lines, and he had cornered Miranda, who was looking less than fascinated.

'I well remember the first time Pablo came to the Madoura pottery at Vallauris,' he boomed. 'A fine day, a beautiful day, and I was little more than a boy, working with the clay. He watched me, and he was fascinated and took up some clay. We worked together, and I showed him the principle of the wheel. You might say that I, myself, was responsible for the superb ceramics we were to see later.'

'I didn't realize you were a potter.' Miranda looked at her watch. The children knew that she had a rendezvous to keep.

'Alas, God gave with one hand, and took away with the other. When the Master entered the lists, who could compete? I never threw a pot again. I was happy simply to watch a genius. But I had my reward: he presented me with one of his early paintings.'

With sudden respect, Miranda said, 'It must be worth a bit now.'

'A fortune! It should be in a bank, but I cannot bear to part with it. When I am feeling low, I refresh myself simply by looking at it.'

Lisa nudged Nick. 'Ben doesn't believe he has any painting. I heard him telling Jo Amyas made it up.'

'Another drink, my dear?' Amyas stood up, a flamboyant figure in scarlet trousers topped by a loose, collarless smock made of blue and gold brocade. On anyone else, the combination would have been ridiculous. With his huge size and great, bearded head, it was awe-inspiring.

But Miranda was not sufficiently impressed to wait for his return with her drink. As soon as he turned his back, she hurried towards the rear of the house, where a door led directly into Ben's studio. She was a pretty, graceful woman in her early thirties, the wife of a successful attorney from Los Angeles. Out of the court-room, he was a dull man with little conversation. Even the children had noticed that since their arrival she had spent more time at Ben's side than her husband's.

'Come on, let's do a play,' Lisa said. 'It's boring out here now.'

They made their way to their 'stage', a natural amphitheatre surrounded by grassy banks, well away from the house. Lights strung through the tree branches lit it softly, and they took up their positions.

'What'll we start with?' Nick said.

'Miranda and Ben, then we can go on to the others.'

For years, they had amused themselves re-enacting scenes from the life around them, creating stories peopled sometimes by real, sometimes by imagined characters, sharing the parts between them. Ben's tales of the phoenix were a rich source. He and Jo were a sympathetic audience on occasions, but it didn't really matter to the children whether there was an audience, or not. Their satisfaction was in the acting.

Nick stood centre stage and Lisa some yards away. As their conversation, accurately reflecting that of Ben and Miranda, progressed, she moved step by step closer to him as Miranda had.

'I had never thought,' she said softly, 'that this could

happen to me. To be here, in this wonderful place, with Benedict Absalom.'

Nick's voice was deep and caressing, unmistakably the timbre of Ben's. 'The good fortune is mine. A beautiful woman, with a beautiful name. Ah, Miranda . . .'

'Ben . . .'

'Miranda, talking to you is not enough! I need you . . . all of you. We must be alone.'

'How can we?'

'In an hour. My studio. It's out of bounds to our guests. We won't be disturbed.'

'Oh, God, how can I wait . . .' Lisa's voice cracked as she could no longer control her laughter, and she reverted to herself. 'Aren't they *silly!*'

They hadn't seen the man who was watching them from the side of their stage. Nor had they heard the intake of breath when Miranda's husband began to understand what he was hearing.

The party broke up in disarray just after midnight. Even those who did not witness the scene had soon heard the details: how Ben and Miranda had been caught *in flagrante delicto* in the studio; how her husband, a small man, had attempted to attack Ben and been flung out; how he and his wife had packed their bags; how they had departed in the early hours of the morning, bound for the airport. Several other guests had followed them. Those who had been invited to stay over held meetings in each other's rooms and delightedly discussed the scandal. The only people who were not aware of what had happened were the Garniers, for Peter had taken Nick home before the row erupted.

Joanna behaved with stoic dignity, smiling pleasantly as she said goodbye to the last stayers after breakfast, showing neither anger nor distress.

The angry husband had told Ben how he learned of the tryst. When Nick arrived at the villa in mid-morning the

137

next day, and asked for Lisa, he found himself standing with her in front of an infuriated man who bore little resemblance to their much-loved friend. By the time Ben ran out of searing words, both children were crying. Lisa was sent to her room and Nick was told that he was no longer welcome at the villa.

The episode caused the first crack in their devotion to Ben, though his ban on Nick's presence lasted no longer than his next departure for London. Jo allowed the resumption of the children's friendship and by the time Ben returned, he had forgotten his anger.

The past faded and Lisa was alone again, watching the rain. There had been other husbands who must have hated Ben. Was it possible that one of them had finally returned to attack the man who had cuckolded him? Or a woman, used and then discarded? But no strangers had been seen in the area, according to Berenger and, remembering how scarcely a sneeze went unrecorded in La Belette, she had to believe him.

She went into the kitchen and made herself a cup of coffee. As she drank it, the worry that she had denied both to Peter and herself, forced its way to the surface of her mind. Was it possible that Jo might finally have been tried too far? Could a new Miranda have appeared on the scene, and an argument flared? Could Jo have walked with him to Le Mur and continued it? Perhaps Ben had raised his hand against her and, in defending herself, she had caused him to fall and slip over the edge.

But if it had happened like that, Jo would instantly have told the truth. She had never lied in her life. Hang on to that, Lisa told herself, and realized that Peter had been right: already distrust and suspicion were souring her thoughts. If Ben's death was not an accident, there was a reason for it that had nothing to do with Jo. Someone *needed* to kill him, and it seems that no one knew him well enough to understand why.

8

The next morning Molinard and Demazin arrived at the villa at nine o'clock. Once again, Jo's presence was requested in the sitting-room, and Demazin took up his position at the door.

Unwillingly, Lisa offered them coffee, but they refused. Jo, she thought, was like a prisoner on her way to the gallows as, head high, she followed the Commissaire.

Left alone, Lisa called Peter. 'There's not much point in you coming up,' she said. 'I've been shut out, and they won't say how long they're likely to be. Peter, what are we to do?'

'Why don't you and Jo meet me at the Lion d'Or for lunch?' he said. 'It might do her good to get out, and we can talk then.'

With time to kill, too restless to settle down to household chores or a book, she went outside. The rain had stopped and in the sky a blurred yellow circle veiled by clouds indicated that the Riviera sun still existed. The ground was saturated and the grass squelched under her espadrilles, soaking their rope soles. She unlocked the gates and stood for a moment, looking across the burned land that was now a sea of khaki mud. Over the valley, the last line of hills before the coastal plain was etched like paper cut-outs against the grey sky.

Almost unconsciously, she turned along the path that led to Le Mur. Where it had been shaded by cork-oaks and lime-trees before the fires, now only the bizarre shapes of blackened, leafless tree-trunks rose from the mud.

But the phoenix tree stood as it always had, arching

fronds creating the hiding-place where she and Nick had first explored each other's bodies.

She walked to the edge of the cliff, where Ben had fallen. It was at least five metres from the palm, and the police claimed to have found blood-stains on a stone at the base of the tree, near Ben's discarded walking-stick. She saw that there was no way he could have slipped and hit his head there, then slid or rolled over the cliff. If anything, the ground rose slightly between the tree and the edge.

She looked down. He had been lying on the ledge when he was found – by whom? She hadn't thought to ask.

The voice was such an uncanny continuation of her thoughts that at first she could not separate the two.

'He must have gone over a few feet to the right. As soon as I reached him, I knew he was dead.'

She whirled around. Nick Garnier was standing beside the tree.

She blinked, wondering if he was a phantom conjured up by her imagination. Then she said: 'What are you doing here?'

'Looking for you. I knew you'd come eventually. It's a good place to meet.'

'No place is a good place for us to meet,' she said flatly.

'It was inevitable. I thought we should get it over, and try to come to terms with the fact that we're both in La Belette and it won't be possible to avoid each other.'

'Nobody told me you were here. If I'd known, I wouldn't have come back.'

He was taller and broader than she remembered, and there was no boyishness in the hard planes of his face, but the thick dark hair, ruffled by the wind, was unchanged, and the grey eyes, narrowed under the well-marked brows, were those Ben had painted a dozen times.

'You haven't changed,' he remarked. 'And you're dressed the same . . .' He stopped, but she knew what he was thinking. On that last day, under the phoenix tree, she

140

had been wearing jeans and an oversized white sweat-shirt, as she was today. As they lay together, she had pulled off her shirt and he had unzipped her jeans, then his, and she had felt his lips on her breasts and the hardness of his penis as he entered her. It wasn't the first occasion, that had been as painful as it had been exciting. Now they were at ease, relaxed with each other, and it had seemed to be better each time.

They had not dressed immediately it was over, but stayed together, entwined, naked, until that dreadful moment when Nick had gasped, flung himself away from her and grabbed for something to cover himself. She had looked up into Ben's suffused face, heard him whisper: 'You little whore! Get dressed! I can't bear to look at you!'

She had seen Nick only once since then, and that occasion remained the most painful and humiliating memory of all. Even its fleeting passage through her mind was enough to make her mouth tighten and her eyes harden into chips of ice.

In a way, the reminder was a help. Now that the first shock of the meeting had faded, she found herself able to regard him with the objectivity of a stranger. The man she had seen in Los Angeles had, in fact, been a stranger.

'How long have you been back?' Her tone was that of a new acquaintance making polite conversation.

'A few weeks. Are you staying long?'

He walked by her side towards the villa.

'Until Ben's death is cleared up. Those fools seem to think Jo killed him.'

'I'm sure it won't be long before they realize they're wrong. How is she coping?'

'I suppose, as well as can be expected, but it was a horrible shock, finding out that it wasn't an accident. She's talking to the Commissaire now. When are you leaving?'

'I'm here indefinitely. Maybe for good.'

'How nice,' she said politely.

She turned her head, to meet his amused eyes. She had forgotten that Nick had always had the ability to recognize when she was playing a part.

His punctilious civility was a mockery of her own. 'And nice for me, meeting old friends after all this time.'

She erased any interest from her voice. 'I thought you were living permanently in America.'

'Few things are permanent in this life.'

She lengthened her stride until she was trotting in her eagerness to escape him. Then she almost slipped in the mud as he gripped her arm and swung her round to face him.

'This is pretty childish,' he said. 'In a minute, you're going to say you won't speak to me, and when we see each other, as we inevitably will, we'll cross the street so we don't have to meet. There are things I want to say to you. May I come in for a few minutes?'

They had reached the gates, and she stopped. 'No. We'll talk here. What do you want to say?'

He sighed. 'Okay. First, I'm sorry for what happened in L.A. And that's the only time I'll mention it. Second, I'd like to do anything I can to help Jo.'

Unrelenting, she said, 'I'm sure no help will be needed. No one could suspect her for long.'

'The police want someone they can charge, and so far, Jo's all they have. Did you know that I found Ben's body?'

'Not until you told me just now.'

'I've been in their sights, too. I had a row with him in the Lion d'Or a couple of days before it happened.'

'What about?'

'He told me I had no right to come back. It seems I pollute the village.'

'Did you see him the day he died?'

'Not until he was lying on the ledge. I told them what I'd been doing before that. They're probably checking it out. And before you ask: I did not push him.'

She looked down at her feet. Her espadrilles were

soaked through, the canvas dark and stained with mud. 'I have to go up and change,' she said abruptly. 'Your father's asked us to lunch. Will you be there?'

'If I am, would you call it off?'

'No.' She met his eyes for the first time. 'Jo needs all the support she can get.'

He smiled, and she caught her breath. Nick's smile . . . white teeth against the sun-tan, the face alight . . . had often got him out of trouble as a child. Did he know the effect it had, she wondered? Then, resentfully: of course he did, and used it deliberately to the best effect. Maybe, after all, she'd cancel the lunch . . .

But with a murmured 'See you later,' he was walking back towards the village.

'I ran into Lisa this morning.' His voice was deliberately casual.

'Did she have any news?'

Nick knew that Peter's concern for Jo dominated his every waking moment. Last night, when he had fallen asleep around one o'clock, his father was still pacing up and down on the terrace below.

'Molinard was still there.'

'I called earlier. She told me not to come. Christ, I feel so bloody helpless! They haven't charged Jo, but Berenger told me last night that Molinard's convinced she was responsible for Ben's death. It's monstrous!' He took a deep breath, then seemed to realize what Nick had told him: 'So you met Lisa. How was it?'

'She wasn't overwhelmed with delight to see me, but it looks as though she's prepared to be polite. It's the best I could hope for. She's turned into a tough cookie, seems to be on-stage all the time. Whatever we had as kids, it's over.'

'Something more happened between you after you left here,' Peter said. 'Want to tell me?'

143

'No. But I'm joining you for lunch. Hope you don't mind.'

'I don't. What about Lisa?'

'She'll put up with me as long as she's worried about Jo.'

Having been fussed over by the Mazeaus, Lisa was waiting for them at Peter's table. His progress was interrupted by frequent pauses to greet friends, and Nick, as usual, was the focus for strangers' recognition. A party of English tourists had recognized Lisa, too, and one man had turned his chair so that he could have an uninterrupted view of her while he ate.

'Where's Jo?' Peter said.

'She couldn't come. They're still talking. I don't know what's going on. All I hear are their voices, I can't make out words. Whenever I go near the door, Demazin stands in the way. And in our own house!'

'Aren't they taking a lunch break?'

'I made them some sandwiches and coffee, really to have an excuse to go in. Jo said to thank you for the invitation. She seemed quite calm.'

'No thumb-screws?' Nick said lightly, but neither Lisa nor Peter smiled.

A pretty waitress came towards them. Lisa watched her seductive hip-swinging as she walked through the restaurant, and did not miss the way she allowed her breasts to brush Nick's shoulder when she leant over to take their orders, her intimate smile when he glanced up from the menu.

'Who's that?' she said. 'I haven't seen her before.'

Peter said, 'Her name's Claudette Dorsey. She worked briefly for Jo. I hired her because we were desperate after Simone left to get married. A mistake, I'm afraid. She's not very efficient and the Mazeaus don't like her. But I was sorry for her. She needed the job.'

Nick wondered whether his father knew Claudette's reputation, and guessed that he did not. Although he would listen with patience and sympathy to anyone in trouble, he was not a receptive audience for tittle-tattle.

For half an hour, they paid Jean-Louis the compliment of concentrating on his cooking. None of them had been hungry, but their appetites were revived by a plate of *crudités* – matchsticks of crisp fresh vegetables which they dipped in a garlic and cucumber mayonnaise. They followed it with fish quenelles in a light shrimp sauce, a green salad, and cheese. No one could eat a dessert, which distressed Marie so much that she emerged from the kitchen to demand what was wrong with the food.

It was not until coffee had been poured that Lisa said abruptly, 'We must find a way to convince Molinard that Jo had nothing to do with Ben's death.'

'They're turning the village upside down,' Nick said. 'He and his fat friend were bullying Georgette yesterday. She was angry because they kept asking her about Pierre-Luc.'

Peter nodded. 'They're upsetting everyone. Nobody wants to believe one of us killed him, so now they're closing ranks and refusing to answer questions. You know, a situation like this changes people. The ripples spread. There's suspicion. Distrust. I only hope it can be resolved quickly, or I have a feeling the village won't ever be the same.'

'And it'll all be due to Ben,' Lisa said. 'He's influencing our lives even after he's dead. I sometimes wonder if we'll ever escape him.'

Again, Peter wondered at her bitterness.

'Lisa, did Jo talk much about what he was up to before he died?' Nick said. 'The people he'd seen, who had been staying with them?'

She shook her head. 'Nothing significant. I don't think they'd had any guests for some time. But we did find out a few things in London . . .' She hesitated, then said, 'I'm going to tell you what they were. Maybe talking about it might give us an idea. Something out of his past . . .'

They were still sitting, finishing a second pot of coffee, with glasses of brandy, an hour later. The restaurant had emptied, the tables had been reset for dinner, and the Mazeaus had retired to their apartment.

Lisa summed up: '. . . So that's it. I'm Ben's illegitimate daughter, and he was broke when he died, partly because he'd been paying a monthly allowance to some woman named Alicia Freeman, presumably one of his ex-mistresses, for nearly twenty years.'

The men had listened in silence and now Peter said, 'Are you telling us that Jo's been left with nothing?'

'Damn all. She has some money here but it won't last long. She won't take anything from me, either. She's thinking of turning the villa into a guest-house.'

He was appalled. 'Jo to be a servant to tourists?'

'She pointed out that she'd been a servant to Ben's friends for a long time.'

'It's unthinkable!'

'Ben was even more of a bastard than I'd thought,' Nick said. 'But I don't see how anything you've told us can help in the present circumstances. It'd be interesting to know more about the Freeman woman, though she seems to have lost, not gained, by his death. Anyhow, we don't even know whether they had any personal contact in recent years. Was Jo very shocked by all this?'

'Less than another woman might have been. Life with Ben toughened her. Toughened us both.' She smiled wryly. 'Finding out that he was my father hasn't changed me, except that now I'll know who to blame for some of my less pleasant characteristics. None of this has got us any further, has it? Is there anyone here who had cause to hate him?'

'Nick and I have thought about that. As I told you yesterday, there are certainly some who didn't care for him.' Peter raised an eyebrow. 'That included me, by the way.'

'And me, I suppose,' Nick said. 'But let's assume that

'neither of us did it. There's Amyas, of course.'

'They've never been friends,' Lisa said. 'It was always Jo who insisted that we should occasionally invite them to the villa, simply because they were neighbours . . . though he and Ben did recently have some business dealings.'

'What kind of business dealings?'

'Amyas introduced Ben to a former pop-singer named Dominic Partridge, who's been collecting his work. Presumably Amyas makes a commission on pictures he finds for him.'

'Ben could have pointed him in the direction of possible sellers, so it would hardly have been in Amyas's interest to cause anything to happen to him.'

Lisa looked thoughtful. 'I remember once someone reported to Amyas that Ben had said he was a charlatan who didn't know a damn thing about art. He threatened to sue for slander. Jo had to cool things down by apologizing on Ben's behalf. He wouldn't do it himself. That was a long time ago, though.'

'Amyas is a bit of a mystery, isn't he?' Nick said. 'When we were kids we accepted him and Ona as part of the landscape, but I realize now that I know hardly anything about them. Isn't he supposed to be a Hungarian, or something?'

'I don't know any more than you do,' Peter said. 'He appears to be the great extrovert, but I can't remember ever hearing him talk about his background, except for some vague references to lost family fortunes, which forced him to make his own way in the world.'

Almost as though drawn by their focus on him, heavy footsteps echoed in the empty bar, and Amyas appeared in the archway.

He surged towards them: 'I heard you were here. Couldn't miss the opportunity to greet my lovely Lisa after so long.'

Her face disappeared into his beard as he enveloped her

147

in a smothering hug. When she emerged, he looked around, large yellow teeth showing amid the tangle of wiry hair. 'So here you are, together again! But without Joanna. My dears, I've heard that the police are with her. Do they actually suspect her? Scandalous! As if she could hurt a fly, let alone Ben. She adored him.' Not waiting to be invited, he drew up a chair and sat down. 'The *flics* are only chasing publicity. Ben fell, and didn't have the strength to save himself. It will all blow over.'

Peter said, 'I suppose you've been questioned by the police, like the rest of us?'

'Indeed. To my poor Ona's distress. But of course they quickly realized that we could have had no connection with the case. Ben was my greatest friend.'

'That's bullshit, Amyas,' Nick said. 'Everyone knows you disliked each other.'

The button eyes, sunk in fleshy folds, became slits. 'How wrong you are, dear boy. Our friendship did not depend on constant contact. We had our own lives to live, but Ben and I had a great deal in common.' He leant back and the bentwood chair creaked ominously. He turned to Lisa. 'I understand you met Dominic Partridge at the memorial service. One day, with my help, that man will own the world's greatest private collection of Absaloms. I am hoping to persuade your mother to allow me to go through the studio. Partridge will buy any relic of Ben's life and work – his brushes, smocks, easel, sketches, notebooks. He'll pay anything. He's considering setting up a gallery devoted to the great man.' He smiled. 'In the meantime, I will be working on my Absalom memoire.'

'Your Absalom what?' Lisa said.

'Who better to write about him after our long acquaintance, and my experience? A personal reminiscence of Benedict Absalom, with notes on his work.'

Lisa was not sure whether to laugh or be angry.

Then Nick said casually: 'Ever thought of writing your own autobiography, Amyas? It should be fascinating.

How you made it to the top in the art world. Where you came from originally . . . Hungary, was it?'

Amyas heaved himself up. 'A sad childhood, my boy, which I prefer not to remember. But one day, perhaps, one day. At the moment, I must concentrate on poor Ben. Such a pleasure to have seen you all.' He waved a fat hand, and left.

'That was pretty sharp, wasn't it?' Nick said. 'As soon as his past was mentioned . . .'

Lisa was not listening. 'Amyas to write about Ben? It's impossible!' she said. 'Jo wouldn't allow it.'

'Someone's going to do it,' Nick said. 'Ben was too important a painter to be ignored after his death.'

'Maybe. But anyone rather than Amyas!'

Peter's housekeeper, Mme Fronval, had left a message for Nick on a pad that hung by the telephone. A M. Jared Cowan had called from England and would like him to ring back as soon as possible.

When he rejoined his father, Nick said: 'Jared has asked me to meet him in London tomorrow. He wanted to find out if I was interested in his idea and I said I was. He thinks we should talk.'

'Why not ask him here to stay for a few days?'

'He's due back in New York at the end of the week and he's busy seeing London agents and authors. If I fly over, he'll fit me in between meetings. But I don't like running out on you.'

'Go to London. There isn't much more we can do for Jo at the moment. So you've made up your mind about the book?'

'More or less. Especially after what Lisa told us about Ben's background. It's more interesting than I'd realized.'

Hesitantly, Peter said: 'I don't want to interfere, but it might be wise to talk to Jo before you sign any contract.'

'Of course. Inevitably, she'll be involved. Lisa, too. But

149

you heard what she said, anyone would be more acceptable than Amyas.'

'You wouldn't be thinking of doing a – what do they call it? – a hatchet job?'

'An honest job. Up to a point, Jo would have a say in what should be left out. There's a lot of good stuff she couldn't possibly object to: the way he brought Lisa out of Czechoslovakia, his relationship with his mother, his father's time in Prague, his progress as a painter. Come to think of it, I might stay over in London for an extra day or so and check the newspaper files. I'll need photocopies of published profiles of him and critics' reviews.'

Already his mind was running ahead. Ben had been a complex personality. If he could somehow piece together the jigsaw of his character from people who had known him at different periods of his life, maybe facts would emerge which would also help to throw light on his death.

PART FOUR

1

Commissaire Molinard was finding it increasingly difficult to hide his irritation.

He disliked Joanna Absalom for several reasons, of which the first was simply that she was English, and all English women made him remember his former wife, Elizabeth.

The second was this house of which she was the mistress. Its informality offended him. A French woman of her age and status would be surrounded by antiques and mahogany, stiff family portraits and porcelain, brocades and bibelots. In such dignified surroundings he would have felt at ease. This light, casual room, with its deeply-cushioned cane furniture, its clutter of books, the half-finished patchwork quilt flung over the back of the sofa, the vases of wilting flowers she hadn't bothered to replace, offended him. It was no place to conduct an interrogation. Unfortunately, he had not sufficient evidence to order her into twenty-four hour preventive detention, *garde à vue*, when he could have questioned her on his own ground.

The third reason was that he had no doubt she had killed her husband, but so far he could see no way to prove it.

Henri Molinard, whose father had been an undistinguished member of the police force in Marseilles, had never thought of following any other profession and with a University degree in psychology, he had been confident that he was destined for better things than his parent.

He had met the woman who would become his wife during a visit to London, when he was attending a language school to improve his English. She was one of his tutors, a self-confident academic with a Cambridge degree who could talk intelligently about literature, music, art and the sciences.

She had taken an interest in him and he, in his turn, was impressed by her erudition and social ease. Believing that she would help to further his ambitions, he had asked her to marry him after they had known each other for two months. She accepted promptly.

When he took her back to Cotolin, she had been dismayed to find herself in a small provincial town where her circle of friends was restricted to other policemen and their wives.

She stood it for two years, then departed.

Before she left, she had said: 'I made two mistakes, Henri. The first was listening to your Maurice Chevalier accent rather than what you were saying. The second was believing that all Frenchmen are good in bed. Your conversation and your love-making are equally uninteresting.'

He had never forgiven her for that. He had never remarried.

Another factor contributing to his determination to convict Benedict Absalom's killer was the need for a boost to his career.

Although his devotion to duty was legendary in Cotolin, his promotion had not been as fast as he believed he deserved.

Now, at forty, he had applied for a transfer to the *police judiciare* in Marseilles, and a spectacular success in a murder investigation should clinch his next step up the ladder.

He had promised himself that by the time he had finished with her, the woman who faced him, apparently relaxed, her hands clasped loosely in her lap, would have been proven guilty beyond doubt.

She reminded him of Elizabeth in many ways: her cool

dignity, the self-control with which she fielded his repetitive questions, the expressionless face which gave no hint of what she thought of him.

He had questioned her for hours and now she was wearily repeating what she had already said a dozen times: 'My husband had arthritis. Walking was difficult for him, but he insisted on going out every afternoon. When he slipped in the mud, he must have tried to struggle to his feet, not realizing how near he was to the edge of the cliff.'

'You do not seem to have understood, Madame. We know that was not so. He was attacked as he stood near the palm-tree. There were blood-stains on a rock, and his walking-stick was lying beside it. Then he was dragged to the edge.'

'I was in the house. I only knew what had happened when Nicholas Garnier came to tell me. I can think of no one who would want to kill my husband. It was an accident.'

He leant forward. 'You are not being helpful. I believe there is a great deal you have not told me about your husband's life, his friends, your relationship with him, his last days. What are you hiding, Madame?'

'I have told you everything.'

'We will go over it again . . .'

He hoped she would protest, show some sign that her control was weakening, but she simply closed her eyes for a moment, then nodded.

By late afternoon, he had reluctantly concluded that questioning would not break her. But there were other avenues of investigation. It might take time, but eventually he would find the motive he needed.

At seven o'clock, he rose. 'That is enough for the moment, Madame.' He added, with heavy irony, 'I thank you for your help. If you recall any further information which might bear on your husband's death, I will be available at any time.'

'I loved my husband. I've told you everything I can.'

'Something in his past, your own . . .' A memory came to him and he added reflectively, in his excellent English: 'Time present and time past/ Are both perhaps present in time future,/ And time future contained in time past.'

He was pleased to see that, for the first time, she was disconcerted. 'Surely that's . . . ?'

'Eliot.'

'You know his poetry?'

'I studied in London. Reading the poets was part of my English course. I have always believed it helped me to understand the British character.'

Later, Jo was to wonder why the words had sounded like a threat.

Two hours later her body in the bed she had once shared with Ben was a child's foetal curve. The night was warm and humid, but a blanket was shelter, and she had drawn it up over her head. She was lying as she had been accustomed to lie as a child, shutting out a world she did not understand.

The Commissaire's pale, sharp eyes had seemed to bore into her brain. Though he remained unfailingly polite, she knew instinctively that he was her enemy, rather than simply her adversary in the game of question-and-answer.

She had told him about Ben's work, his travels, his friends and sitters – naming eminent names which he must have recognized, but noted down without comment. She explained why Ben had divided his life between France and London. She told him about Lisa's arrival from Prague as a child, but saw no reason to divulge what they had discovered about her parentage. She listed her own relationships in the village and described her long friendship with Peter Garnier, contemptuously refuting his innuendos about its form.

At mid-day, Lisa had brought them a buttered *baguette* split horizontally and filled with ham. They had shared it, but the breaking of bread together had done nothing to dispel his cold animosity.

As the afternoon wore on, she no longer had to think before she spoke, since she was mechanically repeating her own words.

She had begun to wonder about him. Did he have a wife? Family? What did he do when he wasn't interrogating suspects? Listen to music? Work in his garden? Take his children to the beach? There was a remoteness in his personality that made it difficult to imagine him exhibiting any tender emotion.

Above all, she wondered why he disliked her so much.

Sometimes she saw the muscles in his jaw tighten when she refused to give the answers he required. She could sense his anger, though he never raised his voice. With increasing horror, though she did not allow it to show on her face, she came to understand that he had decided she had murdered Ben and that he was a man who would do almost anything to avoid admitting he was wrong.

When she had finally emerged, she wanted only to be alone. For Lisa's sake she had been reassuring, pretending confidence that all would be well.

But her exhaustion was difficult to hide, and she had gone to her room early.

After turning her light off, she drew her knees up and buried her head under the blanket, praying for sleep.

Molinard clearly intended to dig into her past. If he were inadvertently to uncover the secret she had kept for forty years from everyone except Ben, her last hope of convincing him that she was not guilty would be gone.

As important in her own eyes, would be the effect of its revelation on Lisa. Discussing Ben's deceptions at the Greek restaurant in Hampstead, she had said: 'I think you're the only person I know who is totally honest. Which makes you the one steady, shining light in a dark world.' She had laughed, mocking her descent into theatricality.

Jo had tried to laugh, too, but a cold hand seemed to squeeze her heart.

Now, as she huddled under the blanket, she drifted back in time to the house near Baker Street when she had sat, aged five, thumb in her mouth, her head aching, her short legs dangling from the chair as other policemen had shot questions at her.

She had been brought from her room, where she had been listening to unfamiliar noises from downstairs: strange voices, sirens, the clatter of heavy boots. When she was tired of sitting on her bed by herself, she had tried to open the door, but it was locked. There was a strong smell of burning, rather like when her mother cooked roast beef on Sundays, but not so nice. Earlier, her brother Markie had been screaming. There had been a fire in the grate . . . why did her head hurt?

Then her step-father, Carl, had come for her. His normally pink face was grey. Their own father had died when Joanna was a baby and she and Markie both hated Carl, whom Mummy had married a year ago. He had a loud voice and a short temper and was quick with a punishing hand when the children irritated him.

There were three men in the drawing-room, and they made her sit down. One stood in front of her. He had a bald head and a thick grey moustache. The other two were younger and in between asking her questions, they walked up and down. To her child's eye, they were giants. They frightened her, and she would not speak to them, but sat, sucking her thumb and clutching a ragged teddy-bear. Markie had only allowed her to keep the bear for her own because it was dirty and there were bald patches in its yellow fur. Earlier she had been angry with Markie, but now, with the large men trying to persuade her to talk about him, she wished he was there, too. She hadn't seen him since she had gone into the little sitting-room.

After a while, a woman replaced the men. She was wearing a black skirt and jacket over a white blouse and carried a hat with a black and white chequered band around it. Her voice was soft and patient, though she pronounced some words in a peculiar way: 'coom' for come and 'loove' for love.

'Coom on, loove, let's have a little talk,' she said. 'My name's Thelma. What's yours?'

'Joanna.'

'That's pretty. Do people call you Jo?'

'Mummy does.'

'We'll be talking to your Mummy. D'you know where she is?'

'She went out.'

'And left you – and your brother – all by yourselves?'

'Carl's here. And so is Sandra.'

'Sandra's your nanny?'

'She's the au pair, Mummy says.'

'D'you like her?'

'She's all right.'

'And what about your brother, Mark. Do you like him?'

She hesitated, then said, 'Sometimes.'

'Sometimes not? Why don't you like him?'

'He took my little grey elephant. He takes all my toys.'

'Tell me about it. What happened when he took your elephant?'

'He hit me, too. He often hits me. I cried. Then I went downstairs and he was in the little sitting-room. There was a big fire. Then . . .' She blinked. 'I fell over and hit my head. It hurts. Carl was angry with me and Sandra was crying. And then those men came.'

'You had a fight with Mark, didn't you?'

'He took my elephant. Where is it?'

'I'm afraid it was all burnt up in the fire. You have fights with Mark quite often, don't you?'

'I want my elephant. Mummy gave it to *me*.'

'I told you it was burnt. Don't you remember?'

Some sense warned her that this woman was not as friendly as she pretended to be, and the thumb went back into her mouth.

'I want Mummy,' she said.

Later her mother came. But she was different. Her hair was wild, tears were pouring down her face, making shiny streaks in her make-up. Carl had his arm around her. They stared at Jo as though they had never seen her before, then her mother said: 'You killed your brother! You killed Mark!'

And Carl said, 'I told you something would happen, the way they fought. She's a vicious little savage. Pushed him into the fire. By the time I got there . . .' His body shuddered, and her mother turned to him.

Joanna slipped off the chair, went to them and tugged her mother's skirt. 'Mummy! Markie took my elephant!'

Her mother looked down at her through the tears, then pushed her hand away. She and Carl went out, leaving her alone with the woman in black.

It was a long time before she fully understood what she had done.

During the weeks after Mark's death, strangers came to the house and asked her more questions, and shook their heads at her. And he never came back. He had been burned up, like her elephant, and they kept asking her about how he had fallen into the fire. At first she couldn't remember, but they talked about it so often that finally she agreed that she had been angry and had given him a push. He had fallen, and screamed, and there had been flames.

She had cried for Markie then, and that night, curled up in bed, she had cried more loudly, hoping that Mummy would hear. But Carl came instead, and leant over the bed and told her to shut up. 'Your mother can't even bear to look at you.'

She had known that Mummy loved Markie best, because he had told her so. He was three years older than her, with beautiful, curly fair hair and blue eyes. He got more presents than she did, but even so, he took her things and often broke them. Then she would fly at him and beat him with her fists and have to be hauled off by Carl or Sandra and smacked. But he could be nice sometimes, and now she missed him.

A week after his death, Sandra was replaced by another au pair, only this time, because she was older, it seemed that she was to be called Nanny. She was a large woman with a colourless face and hair dragged back so tightly that from the front it looked as though she was bald.

Jo didn't see much of her mother and step-father after that, and when she did, they hurried past her with hardly a sideways glance. Sometimes she heard her mother crying in her bedroom, but when she tried to go in, the door was always locked.

Her guilt burgeoned. She had hurt Markie and made her mother unhappy. Because of this, everyone hated her.

The new nanny was strict and unloving. Once, when Jo told her, 'I'm nearly six. I can bath myself now,' the woman said shortly, 'You'll do as I say. My job's to see that you're clean.'

Jo stamped her foot and shouted, 'I don't want you! I don't like you!' and Nanny picked her up and slapped her face. 'You don't get away with your tantrums now, young lady!' Then she pushed her into the wardrobe and locked the door 'You can come out when you're ready to apologize. And you'll go back every time you show that evil temper. That's what killed your poor little brother!'

After that, she began consciously to control her temper. The next time she wanted to run at Nanny and hit her, she stopped herself. She became unnaturally obedient and only spoke when she was spoken to. She began to bite her finger-nails. She rarely left the house, because no other children wanted to play with her. Carl had told her that one day when she was alone in the small back garden, tossing a ball against the wall. She looked around, to see him leaning against the door, watching her. Then he said, 'You know why you aren't allowed to see Sharon or Margaret now, don't you? It's because of what you did to your brother.' He beckoned her and she went slowly towards him, nibbling on a finger-nail. He leant down and said softly: 'Tell me what you did to Mark, Joanna.' She shook her head, and felt his fingers digging into her shoulder. 'Tell me!'

'I pushed him into the fire,' she whispered.

'Right. You lost your temper, and you pushed him into the fire.'

Six months later, her mother was killed in a car-crash. She and Carl had been to a dinner-party in Highgate and he had been driving when the accident occurred.

Nanny broke the news to Joanna. For once, she was gentle, and Jo clung to her gratefully.

Again, the house was invaded by strangers who talked to her, then to each other.

She overheard some of their conversations, and for the rest of her life snatches would return to her: *He was drunk, of course . . . inherited everything . . . a rich woman . . .* And the one phrase, loud and clear: *The child will have to go into care.*

She never saw Carl again.

At first, terrified and bewildered, she was sent to foster-parents. They were kind enough, but they had a son named Arthur who was about Markie's age and disliked the strange children they brought into the house.

Later she realized that the social workers had been obliged to tell the couple what she had done, and they must have passed it on to Arthur. One day he came up and whispered: 'I know all about you. You're a murderer, you are. You killed your brother. If you aren't good, you'll be sent to prison.' She clamped her mouth shut and said nothing, but that night she dreamed for the first time of being shut in a cell by herself.

She loved to read and to draw because they were solitary occupations in which she could lose herself. One day her foster-father bought her a roll of lining paper and a set of felt pens in different colours. Arthur had no interest in drawing, but, as Markie had, he resented the fact that she had received a gift. One afternoon she returned to her room to find the roll ripped into small pieces. The pens had been used to scrawl multi-coloured doodles on the wall.

For the first time since Nanny had told her what her rage had done to Markie, she lost her temper, and flew at him, shrieking, stabbing at him with one of the pens. His mother came in and dragged her away.

Arthur said: 'I'm scared of her, Mummy! Look what she's done to her room, and she tried to kill me, like her brother.' The foster-parents reported that she was uncontrollable and a danger to others, so she was sent to the children's home where she was to live for the next twelve years. Night after night, in a dormitory, she huddled under her blankets, praying that she would never lose her temper again, and would never be sent to prison.

At first, the staff in the Home kept a constant watch on her, but far from being a problem, she was docile and reserved. Even under the severest provocation, she never lost her temper with her peers and if fights broke out in the playground, she fled.

At eight, she was sent to a local school, where she was an above-average student, and worked her way up through the educational system. Each night, she returned to the Home. It was her only security. She felt safe there. No one mentioned what she had done to her brother.

At eighteen, she had to leave, though she begged to be allowed to stay.

She had done a course in shorthand and typing, but having become thoroughly institutionalized, the thought of working with strangers outside terrified her.

When the day of departure arrived, she walked out with her one suitcase and twenty pounds in her purse, given to her by the Social Services to tide her over until she found a job. Her farewells took only a few minutes, because her reticence and the tight control over her emotions that had become a habit had prevented her from making any close relationships. She had heard herself described as secretive and sly, and she knew no one would miss her.

The Home was in North London and, clinging to its familiarity, she went to a newsagent's shop nearby, where people put up cards offering accommodation.

That afternoon, she moved into a lodging-house which catered mainly for students. Her room was on the fourth floor, with a window looking out onto a dull street. But it was comfortable enough, with a shilling-in-the-slot gas heater and cooker, and only cost three pounds a week.

She was never to feel as lonely again as she did the first night. At whatever hour she had been awake in the Home, there had been sounds: restless sleepers, low-voiced conversations, someone tip-toeing to the lavatory. Here the silence was almost unbroken, and she knew none of the people leading their private lives behind the closed doors.

The next morning, renewed by sleep and the prospect of a fine day, she made herself a cup of coffee on her gas-ring, and gathered her courage to look for a job.

The bathroom was on the floor below her room, and she made her way cautiously down the stairs. The house was coming to life. From one room she heard music, from another voices, from a third came the smell of bacon frying.

She decided that clean hair might help her confidence. As she was leaning over the basin her head foaming with shampoo, there was a bang on the door. A voice shouted: 'For God's sake, you've been in there for more than twenty minutes! I've got a class at nine.'

She rinsed her hair hurriedly, twisted a towel around it, clutched her dressing-gown, and opened the door.

A man in a maroon dressing-gown was waiting outside. He glared at her, then his expression changed. 'Hey, you're new, aren't you? Sorry I yelled.'

'It's all right. I'm sorry I was so long.'

'We have a bath-roster. Twenty minutes each. You'll have to go onto it. I'm Jeff Chambers. What's your name?'

'Joanna Stewart.' Giving her name, she felt the familiar apprehension: would someone, some day, recognize it as that of the child who had killed her brother?

'When did you move in?'

'Last night.'

He was about twenty, with light brown hair and a mobile, clown's face: round eyes under peaked eyebrows, a large nose and a mouth that turned up at the corners even when he was not smiling. His ears stuck out almost at right-angles to his head.

Jo's experience of men was limited. There had been boys at the Home, but she had avoided them as much as possible. When she was fifteen, a youth named Barry, with acne-pitted skin and permanently dirty finger-nails, had cornered her as she was walking through a deserted alleyway on her way from school. He had pushed her against a fence, kissed her and fumbled at her breasts, parting her legs with his knee. Revolted by his sour breath and wet lips, she had dropped her school-books, grabbed his hair with one hand, and raked his face with her finger-nails. With a muted howl, he had let her go, put his hand to his face and looked unbelievingly at the blood. She had picked up her books and marched on. Not a word had been spoken.

The story of their encounter was circulated throughout the Home and, for a while, some of the boys had regarded her as a challenge. She was already tall and well-built, and most of them were weedy. She treated their approaches with cold contempt. After a while, they were discouraged, called her a stuck-up bitch, and left her alone.

This young man bore no resemblance to any of them. His sunny smile was friendly and infectious. Before retiring into the bathroom, he invited her to his room for coffee that evening.

165

She had a frustrating day walking the length of Oxford Street and Bond Street, going in to every employment agency she saw. She was interviewed, filled in forms, did typing tests, but returned to her room with no more than vague promises that if anything came up, she would be contacted.

At eight o'clock, she knocked at Jeff's door. He opened it, and she saw half a dozen men and girls sitting around on chairs, the bed and the floor. If he had not had a firm grip on her arm, she would have gone away.

In fact, she enjoyed herself. Jeff and his friends were art-students, talkative, intelligent, with wide interests. They discussed books, the theatre, music and, most of all, painting. She found that she could keep up with the book-talk, because in her solitude at the Home she had read everything she could lay her hands on and had visited the public library two or three times a week. For the rest, she was ignorant, but she vowed to herself that she would correct that, and listened with genuine interest. Nobody seemed to mind that she didn't say much, and nobody patronized her.

During the next few weeks, she saw Jeff almost every day, and they dropped into the habit of sharing their evening meal when he was at home. She would provide the food and he the wine, for he was rarely without a glass in his hand, and refilled it frequently.

While his words occasionally slurred, he did not get offensively drunk. She began cautiously to wonder if it might be possible, at last, for her to have found a real friend.

But she did not have a job, and her money was running out. She could go on the dole, but she hated the idea. All her life, she had been maintained by the State, and now she wanted to earn her own living.

One evening Jeff dropped in and, as they drank coffee, he said casually: 'Are you self-conscious about your body?'

She blinked. 'I – I don't know.'

'Because our life-class model is pregnant and she doesn't want to pose any more. Why don't you have a go?'

'Without clothes? I couldn't.'

'Why not? You've got a terrific figure. Anyhow, models aren't people to us, they're just shapes with shadows and highlights and flesh-tones. You'd get paid by the hour and all you'd have to do is sit still. Think about it.'

His casualness was the key to her decision. She had heard the students discussing their life-classes and, indeed, there had been nothing overtly sexual in their analyses of the women they had been painting.

She had never thought much about her own body, though her mirror told her that it was slim and well-proportioned. What she had hated in the Home was the endless, lewd discussion among the girls about the body's function as a sex object, and how to increase its allure to one or other of the unattractive youths in Boys' Wing. Without having had any experience – apart from Barry's fumbling attack – she knew, from listening to their talk, what sexual intercourse entailed, and nothing she heard had aroused her enthusiasm.

She occasionally allowed herself sexual fantasies about male movie stars or, perhaps, a handsome man she had passed in the street, but they lived in a world so far removed from her own that it was inconceivable she could ever come into contact with them. Still, she enjoyed her dreams and would return to the real world with tingling skin and a pleasurable sensation in what Nanny had called her private parts.

Thinking of her thin purse, and the telephone that never rang with a job-offer, she told Jeff the following morning that she would take up his suggestion, at least for one day.

That evening, he said he had fixed it with the college, and she was expected the next morning, a two-hour sitting for his class.

The fact of going behind a screen, taking off her clothes,

167

then facing a dozen male and female students, nude, was far worse than the anticipation. Also, it had not occurred to her to take a dressing-gown with her. As she sidled, naked, from her shelter, her hands unconsciously took up the classic position, one spread over her pubic hair, the other shielding her breasts. She did not look up from the floor.

There was a moment's silence, then she heard Jeff's casual voice: 'That's great! Can you hold it like that? Everybody, this is Jo.'

She heard murmured greetings, and a girl said, 'Could you come forward a couple of steps, keeping the same pose?'

She moved and, for the first time, dared to flick her eyes upwards. She was standing in a circle of easels, the focus of twelve pairs of eyes. Some were narrowed, others roved over her body, but Jeff had been right: to them she seemed to be an image to be transferred to paper or canvas, not a woman. She began to feel more at ease.

By the end of the session, she was stiff from maintaining the pose, but had lost her nervousness. A couple of the students congratulated her on her ability to keep still, and invited her to join them for a sandwich.

In the afternoon, she posed again, this time sitting on a dais, and the professional painter who was taking the class, a minor artist named Manfred Syler, grasped her bare shoulders and manipulated her until he was satisfied with her position. He might have been touching a wooden lay-figure. Again, her years of sitting still as a mouse, so that she would not attract attention, stood her in good stead.

When she was asked to return the following day, she agreed.

That evening, Jeff brought a bottle of champagne to her room. 'To celebrate your job,' he said. For the first time, he kissed her as they said goodnight. Apart from surprise, the kiss did not arouse her emotions. She liked Jeff, but he did not attract her physically.

The next morning, her class was interrupted by the arrival of Syler and a stranger. Suddenly self-conscious, she reached for her dressing-gown, but Syler said sharply, 'Keep your pose.'

The students had stopped painting, and were staring at the stranger. He was in her direct line of vision, a tall, well-built young man who appeared to be in his early twenties, with fair, tumbled hair. His features were regular, well-defined, and she thought that he was only just saved from being too good-looking by cheekbones that were high and flat, and a wide, generous mouth. She noticed that he walked with a cat-like grace and that the girl students didn't take their eyes off him.

He and Syler wandered around the room, looking at the paintings. It appeared from their conversation that he was a former student, revisiting old haunts. Once, her eyes met his, and she was unnerved by the intensity of his gaze. She had to resist reaching again for her dressing-gown.

Jeff joined her as she was leaving the studio. 'Who was that man with Syler?' she asked.

'You didn't recognize him? That was Benedict Absalom.'

'The painter?' She recognized his name from newspapers. He had recently had an exhibition of portraits which was a sell-out even before it opened. The Tate Gallery had bought one.

'He's quite a guy. Give old Syler half a chance and he'll rabbit on for hours about him. Child prodigy, brilliant student, unique talent, and all that. Also, he must be making a small fortune.' His clown's face was envious.

She refused his invitation to coffee that evening, wanting to mend the split seam of a blouse she had bought from a charity shop the previous day. She was sitting on her bed, sewing, when he knocked at her door. He was holding a bottle of red wine and his face was flushed.

She refused a drink. He poured himself another glass of wine, drank deeply and set it on her bedside table.

Without warning, he pulled her sewing away and pushed her back on the bed. Then he straddled her and pressed her shoulders into the mattress. 'Jesus, you're beautiful!' he said thickly, and put his mouth on hers.

She wrenched herself away. 'Stop it! Jeff, stop that!'

'No. I've been wanting you for two days . . . ever since I saw . . . since you took your clothes off. Your body . . . unbelievable. Christ, it's been hell . . . looking at you . . .' Dropping his weight on her, he began to tear at her dress.

Almost smothered, she gasped, 'You're drunk! Get off me.' He took no notice. She felt buttons give way and then he dragged her bra up so it was around her neck. His mouth went down onto her flesh, and now he was fumbling at his trousers and she could feel his hardness.

Even when she had driven Barry off, she had been in control of herself. Now she became a wild woman. Jeff was wiry and strong, and tried to keep her pinioned as she fought silently, thrashing from side to side, turning her body into a weapon. She smashed her head into his Adam's apple and heard him gasp. The shock made him loosen his grip on one of her arms and she flung it back, ready to hit his face. Her eyes were misted with rage.

Her hand landed on cold metal and she grasped her scissors. With a thin scream, she raised them and stabbed the points against the side of his neck.

At that moment, he twisted to one side, still choking from the blow against his throat, and they ripped into his shirt. He slithered onto the floor and lay there, all aggression gone.

She stood over him. The scissors were poised to plunge into his body. He opened his mouth to scream. In that moment, she realized what she was about to do and dropped the scissors.

A terrified child looked out of his eyes as, slowly, he got to his feet. They stood, staring at each other, and he whispered. 'You would have done it, too, wouldn't you?'

'Get out of my room.'

She cried herself to sleep, not so much for the ending of her first relationship, but because she had lost control of herself. It must never happen again. The vision of Markie's burning body rose in her mind, the sound of his screams was in her ears.

She didn't go to the college the next morning. Jeff's reaction to seeing her naked had set off his attack. So much for the female body being no more than a series of shadows and highlights. She wondered how many other students were tempted to react as he did.

She would have to find another job. She would have to find somewhere else to live, too. She couldn't stay where she was, with the constant embarrassment of running into Jeff.

She didn't get up until she knew he would have left the house, and was still in her dressing-gown when there was a knock on her door.

After a frozen moment, she said: 'Who is it?'

'Benedict Absalom.'

Later she was to realize that it was typical of his self-confidence – arrogance? – that it simply did not occur to him that she would not know who he was.

She opened the door.

'Hi,' he said. 'I want to talk to you. May I come in?'

Looking at him with wide, startled eyes, she clutched the edges of her old towelling robe and stood aside.

He glanced around the shabby, high-ceilinged room, the gas-fire, the unmade bed, the brown curtain that hid a sink and cooker, the two worn arm-chairs, on one of which lay her half-mended blouse. Moving past her, he strolled across to the dusty window, leant against the frame and said, 'Why aren't you working this morning? I went to find you. They said you hadn't turned up, and gave me this address.'

'I didn't feel well.'

'You don't look ill.'

'I'm better now.'

'Good. I want you to model for me.'

'No! I'm not doing that any more.'

'Don't be silly. What's brought this on?' He saw her mouth tremble and his face became concerned. 'Has something upset you? Tell me about it. Can we have a cup of coffee?'

She nodded, thankful to be able to turn her back as she measured out the instant coffee and waited for the kettle to boil.

When she emerged from behind the curtain she was calm as she handed him a mug. 'There's no milk. I haven't been out this morning.'

'Don't take it. Nor sugar.'

For several minutes, they sat in opposite chairs in silence, studying each other. Jo saw that his mouth revealed white, even teeth, his fair hair was thick and springy and his blue eyes were fringed by golden-brown lashes. His concentration on her was so intense that it was like being touched.

Much later, in bed one night, he was to tell her what he had seen: 'The face I'd always dreamed of painting. Exciting. Sensitive. A face that kept its secrets. Calm, but a suggestion of strong emotions hidden under the surface. I liked the unfashionable way your hair curls, its rich-mouse colour. And the shape of your nose, and that sensuous lower lip. And your general air of a woman waiting for me to bring you to life.'

'What's made you unhappy?' he said gently.

'Nothing.'

'You're lying. Tell me.'

She had known him for about ten minutes, but his sympathy opened the flood-gates. She found herself telling him about her introduction to the life-class and, with cold anger, what had happened the previous night. She left out

172

only her attempt to stab Jeff with the scissors, which still lay on the floor where she had dropped them. 'I'm not going back. I don't ever want to be stared at again by people like him,' she ended.

'Or me? I stared at you yesterday. Only it was your face I was interested in.'

'My face?'

'I want to paint your portrait, not your body. As far as I'm concerned, you can wear as many layers of clothes as you like.'

'But why?'

He waved a hand impatiently. 'Because I like faces and yours is something special. How about it? I want to start tomorrow. A pound an hour. I've got a studio in Chelsea, you'd have to come there.'

'I couldn't . . .'

'Please!'

'Well . . . when?'

'Tomorrow. Nine o'clock..'

She nodded.

'That's settled. What are you doing for the rest of the day.'

'I have to find somewhere else to live.'

'You don't need to worry about that, either. My studio's got a bed in it, and there's a small kitchen with a bath in the corner. You can move in there for a while.'

'But what about you?'

'My flat's underneath the studio. Now I'll help you pack.'

A week later, he made love to her for the first time, in the studio, and his magic was such that it did not occur to her to wonder how many models had previously been his willing bed-mates.

There was pain when he entered her, and some blood on the bed-cover, but all she remembered afterwards was the ecstasy: the seeking tongue between her lips, the gentle rise and fall of his weight, increasing to a frenzy. Nothing reminded her of the inept onslaughts of Barry and Jeff.

For her, it was the beginning of an idyll. Most days, he worked on her portrait, sometimes breaking off to rush her to the bed as though he could not wait another moment. When he did not feel like working, they would drive into the West End in his recently-acquired MG, bought with some of the proceeds from his exhibition, and visit art-galleries. Determined to improve her knowledge, she looked carefully at the pictures and stored away his comments. His judgement of painting was fair and objective, his exposition lucid. His descriptions of living painters, on the other hand, were prejudiced and frequently malicious. She realized early on that he was not generous to his competitors. At night, when he did not have one of his many social engagements, he came to her, or took her down to his own flat. During his absences, she waited in a kind of limbo for his return.

When they had been together for two weeks, he said, 'Let's go shopping. I'm going to buy you some clothes.'

'I've got some clothes.'

'What you wear aren't clothes, they're coverings.'

'I can't afford . . .'

'I can.'

He appeared to enjoy the shopping expeditions even more than she did. He signed cheques for amounts which appalled her, and steered her to fashion houses in Mayfair, where the sales-women were called *vendeuses* and came in black dresses and grey hair and carefully cultivated accents. Ben charmed the most superior with a mixture of flattery and deference.

Dazed by what was happening to her, she lived in the present, wanting only to please him, accepting without resentment his determination to transform her from her shy awkward self into a spectacular woman.

When she eventually met Anna Absalom, she was to realize that it was all part of his revolt against the humiliations of his impoverished past, and the mother of whose appearance he had been so ashamed.

Day after day, they shopped: Harrod's for satin underwear; Hardy Amies for a soft wool suit that cost an amount which would have paid the rent of her North London room for more than a year; the Queen's milliner, Aage Thaarup, for a hat. 'Why on earth are we doing this. I don't like hats,' she whispered. But he said calmly, 'You'll be coming to Ascot with me. Girls all wear hats to Ascot.'

They went to Norman Hartnell's salon in Bruton Street and bought a pale pink satin evening dress with shoe-string straps, and a matching chiffon jacket entirely covered in beads and sequins. As she was trying it on, under protest, because she could not visualize herself ever wearing such a garment, a thick-set, exquisitely-tailored man whom she recognized from photographs as the Queen's couturier, came from behind a velvet curtain, hands outstretched to grasp Ben's.

She heard him say, 'Benedict, dear boy, they told me you were here. Had to renew acquaintance. Adore my picture. It's transformed the drawing-room: a lovely butch note amid the camp.'

When Jo emerged from the dressing-room, he walked around her, and nodded. 'She will do you credit. You'll be able to take her anywhere.' A manicured forefinger poked her in the ribs. 'Always remember, dear, shoulders back, tummy in. Think of yourself as an I, not an S.'

'How did you meet him?' she asked afterwards.

'He came to my private view and bought a painting of an old tramp I'd seen in Hyde Park. He invited me to his house in Windsor for the hanging ceremony.' He laughed. 'I had to go to the loo while I was there. There was a rose floating in the lavatory bowl.'

'What on earth did you do?'

'Picked it out, peed, put it back. What else?'

A rose in the loo. This, she thought, was a world which she could never have imagined herself entering. And it was little more than a month since she had left the Home.

But her happiness was not wholly unalloyed, for there was always the shadow of what she had done to Markie and the fear that Ben might somehow find out.

A more immediate worry was his promise that soon he would introduce her to his friends, the West End glitterati whom he had so far only described to her. The prospect of meeting them terrified her.

Her formal entry into his world took place at a private view of the work of a new young painter in a smart gallery in Bond Street, and it was not as painful as she had anticipated. Her close attention to his instruction during their West End perambulations paid off and her occasional comments were received with tolerance. Ben, who knew everyone, gave her confidence by staying at her side.

She was wearing a sleek tube in turquoise silk with a plunging neckline and long, tight sleeves. To go with it, he had bought her a necklace of Mexican turquoises, with matching drop ear-rings.

She overheard an outsider's opinion of her transformation as she stood, unobserved, behind two men who were more absorbed in their gossip than the paintings.

'Have you seen Absalom's latest discovery?'

'Sensational. Lucky bastard. Where does he find them?'

'God knows. I've never seen this one before. Seems he discarded Dottie Marchant a few weeks ago.'

'She makes Dottie look like a Surbiton *hausfrau* . . .'

Jo moved away, her feelings a mixture of amusement and embarrassment, with a touch of jealousy: who was Dottie Marchant?

When she asked Ben later, he shrugged, and said: 'A nice enough girl. Father's in the House of Lords.'

'Is she pretty?'

'Reasonably, in an English rose way. Used to ring me up three times a day. Always questions: what are you doing? Where have you been? Who did you meet? What did you

176

talk about? When am I seeing you? Drove me crazy.'

It was an implicit warning Jo was always to remember.

Her portrait was finished after they had been together for nearly two months. By then, she was hopelessly in love with him, but was by no means sure of the strength of his feelings for her. Sometimes his attitude was less that of a lover than of the owner of a decorative and expensive object that enhanced his own image.

She learnt that many women had preceded her in his life. She met some of them and endured, with no trace of triumph, their envious, assessing eyes. They all seemed to be older and more polished than she was, at home in a world in which she still felt herself out of place.

One evening, after they had made love and were lying on his bed, sharing a vodka-and-tonic, Ben said casually: 'I was at the gallery today when your friend Jeff dropped in.'

Her body stiffened. 'He wasn't my friend.'

'So I gathered. You missed something out when you told me about that night he tried to rape you: he claims you stabbed him with a pair of scissors.'

She rolled off the bed and picked up her clothes, without looking at him. 'I had the scissors, but I didn't stab him. You had no right to discuss me. I'm going to get dressed.'

'Wait a minute!' She turned. 'He was looking at your picture in Henriques' office and recognized you. I overheard them talking. He tried to make a joke of it. Why didn't you tell me? I've always thought there was a volcano under that icy exterior.'

'I don't want to talk about it. I might have killed him.'

'Any girl would have lost her temper under the circumstances.'

'Not the way I did. I *wanted* to kill him.'

'That's okay. He deserved it . . .'

She swung around and said, desperately: 'Listen! Years

177

ago I lost my temper and I did kill someone . . .' She was unable to go on and stood, with eyes closed. Then she felt Ben's arms around her, drawing her towards the bed, heard his voice saying, as he had before: 'Tell me about it.'

So, for the first time in her life, she spilled out the whole story. She told him about her mother and her step-father, Carl, and how Markie had enjoyed tormenting her until she would fly at him, and about that last day when he had taken her toy elephant.

'. . . My mother had brought him a train set from Hamleys, and she brought me this little soft grey elephant with big ears and a long trunk and a red ribbon around its neck. When he got tired of playing trains, he took it away from me. I cried, then after a while I went downstairs to look for him. I heard him in the little sitting-room. I must have been so angry that I didn't know what I was doing. I only wanted my elephant. All I remember is him screaming, and flames. Carl carried me up to my room and locked the door. Later they told me I'd pushed him into the fire and he had died from terrible burns on the way to the hospital. After that, I don't think my mother spoke more than half a dozen words to me.' She took a deep breath. 'And ever since then, I've been afraid that some day I'd lose my temper and hurt someone else. I almost did with Jeff.'

His arms were still tightly around her and she heard him say softly, 'So that's it. I knew there was something.'

She pulled back and looked up at him. 'I've never told anyone about it. And I still have nightmares . . .'

'Joanna, marry me,' he said.

'What?'

'You heard. Let's get married.'

'How can you ask me, after knowing what I did? Suppose Jeff had been you? It could happen again.'

'Nonsense! You'd never hurt me. Am I really the only person you've told about it?'

'Yes. Please, Ben, promise me you won't talk about it to

178

anyone else. I couldn't bear people to know.'

'Christ, it happened years ago! You were a baby. But if that's how you feel, we'll never mention it again. I want you to marry me, Jo, and there mustn't be any more secrets between us. Promise?'

She leant against him and the tension in her body drained away. Although she knew she could never forget what she had done, he had suddenly made the future seem more important than the past. For that, her gratitude to him would remain throughout their life together.

A month later, they were married.

As Ben's fame grew, and he was increasingly in demand as a portrait-painter, able to pick and choose his subjects, so the media's interest in the young Absaloms increased.

Their pictures appeared in glossy magazines, and newspaper gossip columns. Jo was photographed by Vogue and called one of London's most glamorous women. They were seen at private views, at Glyndebourne, Covent Garden, Ascot, Annabel's, the Caprice. Ben bought a maisonette in a luxury development in Islington and when the house next door was redeveloped, he bought the top two floors of that, too. He cut through the walls and built himself a studio that extended across the two houses. They hired one of the most fashionable decorators of the moment and he spent the entire proceeds of an exhibition on furnishing the apartment.

They were two of London's Beautiful People. They had looks, money, and he was one of the world's most talented and successful young artists.

Marama Maitland was a dress-designer who had burst on the fashion world with a show of clothes that had writers reaching for their superlatives and caused her rich, doting husband to celebrate her fame by requesting Ben to paint her portrait.

Her face was more intriguing than beautiful, round and

179

flat like a Japanese doll, with large dark eyes and a small mouth. She wore her hair coiled in a bun at the back of her head and her body was skinny and flexible as a bamboo pole.

Because he found her interesting, Ben accepted the commission.

Jo rarely went near the studio when he was painting, but one afternoon she arrived back early from a visit to her mother-in-law's cottage and went upstairs to let him know she was home.

She knocked and opened the studio door. Ben was lying on the couch which had once been her bed. Marama was arched over him like a bow-string. Clothes were scattered on the floor.

A rage such as she had not known since her encounter with Jeff swept over Jo but this time her self-control did not desert her. She stood poised for a moment as their movements ceased and their shocked faces turned towards her, then she walked deliberately across the room, grasped Marama's bun of hair, hauled her off Ben and thumped her onto the floor.

She turned to the easel on which the half-finished canvas stood, picked up a brush and defaced the painting with a swirl of muddy colour.

Then she left the room.

When Ben emerged, she was in their bedroom, packing. She looked up and said, 'Tomorrow I'm leaving you.'

'No. I can't live without you.'

The simple words were her undoing. She started to cry. As when Anna had discovered his theft, he made no excuses. He simply put his arms around her and told her that he had not had the strength of mind to resist Marama's advances, though he did not even find her attractive. She would not be returning. The portrait had been cancelled. Such a thing would never happen again.

Jo believed him, and unpacked her suitcase.

That was the first, but not the last of his infidelities, and most of them were brought to her attention in one way or another. Whenever she faced him with her knowledge, he repeated that other women meant nothing to him, they were passing fancies, but without her, he would not want to live.

Eventually, after some agonizing soul-searching, she realized that since, for her, too, life without him would be intolerable, she would simply have to accept that he was incapable of being faithful to one woman, and believe that he needed her and would always come back to her.

But his behaviour caused a thickening of the carapace she had built around her emotions, to the point when her apparent tranquillity in all circumstances was virtually impregnable. Throughout his affairs, she remained in love with him, although there were times when she didn't like him much.

She also hid her disenchantment with their glittering life-style. No matter how hard she tried, she never felt at ease with his worldly, sophisticated friends. Though she became an efficient hostess, and could organize a dinner-party for twenty people at a moment's notice, she did not enjoy crowds. Neither did she like being on show and having to dress always to attract the admiring attention Ben loved.

Sometimes, when he was away, she would give their live-in maid the day off and put on the old jeans and sloppy shirt which survived from her days in the Home. She would wash every trace of make-up from her face, switch on the telephone-answering machine, and read for hours, stretched out on the sofa, bare-footed. She would make herself grilled cheese on toast for lunch, which Ben hated, and when the printed pages began to blur before her eyes, would put on flip-flops and a head-scarf and go for a walk. Even her neighbours sometimes didn't recognize her.

An alternative pleasure when London life palled was to visit Anna's quiet cottage, and listen to her talk about Martin, Tommy and her son.

Ben was unfailingly generous to her and also gave Anna a substantial allowance. He never seemed to be short of money, spent huge sums on his own wardrobe as well as hers and on lavish entertaining. He ordered vintage champagne in van-loads. He always travelled first-class to New York or Paris or Berlin for portrait sittings, and he stayed in the world's best hotels. He rarely suggested that she should accompany him.

When she worried about his extravagance, he would say: 'Plenty more where that came from, love . . .' and list the eminent men and women who were begging him to paint them. He also embarked on a series of landscapes whose value increased with every one he finished.

On the second anniversary of their marriage, he told her that he had a surprise for her: a celebratory vacation in the South of France.

They drove down and arrived in the evening at a white villa on a hillside where there was a party in progress, with crowds milling about on the terraces and around a kidney-shaped pool.

Inside, they were met by many of the same people who might have attended a similar party in London. Wearily, Jo realized that the 'vacation' was to be the mixture as before. Only the locale had been changed.

Their luggage was whisked away by a maid and she spent the first hour wondering who their host and hostess were.

She found out when Ben called for silence and raised his champagne-glass.

'This is a toast!' he said. 'To my wife, Joanna, with my love and thanks for having put up with me for exactly two years – and the hope that she will do the same for the next twenty-two, at least.' There was laughter, shouts of 'To Jo,' and everyone drank, as she stood, smiling, and wondering how long it would be before she could go to bed.

Ben had not finished: 'What some of you know, but she doesn't, is that I have a present for her.' He drew her towards the sliding doors that led into the house. There he handed her a large envelope with an elaborate wax seal. 'The papers that prove you are now the owner of the Villa Mimosa, my darling. Again, with my love.' In a lower voice, he added: 'You can close your mouth. It's true. The villa is yours.' Then, to applause, he lifted her over the threshold.

During the following year, he had to spend much of his time in Los Angeles, where he had three portrait commissions. As usual, there was no suggestion that Jo should go with him.

Instead, she went down to the villa, which was still virtually unfurnished, apart from a few beds and chairs which he had taken over from the previous owners.

He had told her to spare no expense, so she set about making the kind of home of which she had always dreamed, with none of the decorator-formality of the Islington apartment. She had walls removed to create a huge living-room-kitchen, scattered comfortable, chintz-covered chairs and sofas in groups to make the most of the view from the windows, and the warmth of a winter fire. The colour-scheme was sunny yellow and green. She turned a smaller room into a private sitting-room to use when she and Ben were alone, with cane furniture from Thailand upholstered in cool shades of grey and turquoise. All the rooms had doors leading onto terraces or lawns, and she shielded them from the hot summer sun with striped awnings. She scoured the local potteries for Provençal tiles and plates to decorate the walls and hung her favourites among those paintings of Ben's which she had persuaded him not to sell. She used a different colour scheme in every bedroom and added an en suite tiled bathroom to each.

In the evenings, she studied her Linguaphone tapes, and her schoolgirl French improved rapidly.

She realized that she had rarely enjoyed herself so much, and was never lonely.

Among the local people who dropped in to make themselves known, either from curiosity or genuine kindliness, two of the earliest were Amyas and Ona Mahr.

Jo was amused by the big, flamboyant man's transparent disappointment when he discovered that Ben was not in residence. She offered them a glass of wine, which he accepted without consulting his wife, and drank as he peered around the half-finished living-room with undisguised curiosity.

'It is a privilege to be permitted to enter the house of Benedict Absalom,' he said. 'Your husband, my dear, is a master of twentieth-century portraiture. There is no one to touch him. That is my judgement, and since I also inhabit the world of art, I know what I'm talking about.'

'What exactly do you do, Mr Mahr?'

'I have a circle of dear American friends who come to me when they want to extend their collections. I search out paintings and give them news of promising young artists who are working here on the Coast.'

'Ah, you're a dealer,' Jo said, not without malice.

'Hardly that, my dear. More an adviser.'

'Do you also paint?'

'Alas, no. But my lovely wife . . .' He gestured towards the silent, dowdy woman who was sitting in his shadow. She was wearing a curious, floating, khaki-coloured garment, sandals, and a scarf around her grey-mouse hair.

'You paint, Mrs Mahr?'

'A few local scenes. I'm not very good.' Her voice was low and whispery.

'She's too modest,' Mahr boomed. 'Her little pictures are charming. Many of my friends like to take one away to remind them of their visit. And some souvenir shops in St-Tropez show her work. She has a gift for catching the ambience, if you understand what I mean.'

Jo did. He might have been describing the output of any

of the coast's less talented painters whose water-colours of village and port scenes were produced by the hundred for tourists. She wondered if he was aware of the damnation of his faint praise, and decided that he probably was.

The reserve of the native inhabitants of La Belette, who were slow to accept strangers, struck a chord in her. She made no obvious attempt to cultivate them, but patronized the local shop and was unfailingly courteous to everyone. By the time Ben reappeared, she already felt herself part of the place.

Inevitably, the Mahrs arrived at the door before he had even had time to unpack. For once, he was not beguiled by the flattery and extravagant admiration with which Amyas showered him.

'Who is that idiot?' he demanded after they had gone.

'A kind of art-dealer. He and Ona bought their house a few years ago. I'm told that he lived in Cannes and Ste-Maxime before that. Nobody seems to know much else about them, except that they sell pictures to American tourists. Peter Garnier, who owns the Lion d'Or, told me that Amyas writes endless letters to the *Paris Herald-Tribune* and *Nice Matin*, giving his opinions on the state of art and artists in France.'

'He knows fuck all about art! He informed me that the Annigoni portrait of the Queen is greater than any Holbein. Jesus!'

'I suppose he gets a commission from his deals. He claims to have been one of Picasso's best friends, and told me the Master actually presented him with one of his early works.' She imitated Amyas's voice, lowered to a booming whisper. '"Impossible to calculate today's value, my dear . . ."'

'I'll believe that when I see it.'

Conscious of the necessity to be neighbourly, Jo would occasionally invite the Mahrs to the villa, but Ben did his best to avoid them.

She loved La Belette, and after that first year, she found it increasingly hard to settle back into London life.

2

One disappointment in their marriage was Jo's inability to conceive a child. They underwent sperm tests, timed their intercourse to coincide with her most fertile periods, and she was dosed with various pills. No medical reason for her barrenness could be established, but before it had any serious effect on their relationship, Lisa arrived.

The moment Jo saw the small, frightened girl clutching Ben's hand as they walked through the airport after their ordeal in Prague, she loved her. When she heard her story, the rapport was strengthened: she and Lisa had both lost their families by violence, both had been rescued by Ben.

He had been badly affected by his experiences. For the first few weeks after his return, he refused invitations and was content simply to stay at home. At night, he clung to Jo, and she would often wake to find him lying beside her, heavy-eyed after sleepless hours. Once he said, with a kind of desperation: 'You must never leave me. I couldn't exist without knowing you were here.'

He refused to discuss what had happened to his friends, Lisa's parents, and would not see the reporters who besieged the apartment, wanting more details of the escape. During the day, he played with the child, took her for walks, and liked to have her in the studio with him while he worked. She adored him, but it was to Jo she turned for comfort during the nights when she woke up, sobbing for her dead mother.

After a few weeks, Ben recovered his normal ebullience. The child, too, settled down and no longer asked when her parents would be coming to fetch her.

Six months later, Ben flew to New York, where a show of his recent work had been organized. Jo took Lisa down to the villa.

While they were there, she bought a copy of the *New York Times* in Nice, which she thought might have a review of the exhibition. It did, and there was also a photograph of him at the opening, his arm around the shoulders of an exceptionally beautiful young woman. The caption described her as a Texan heiress. She was long-legged, svelte, and there was an unmistakable air of possession in the eyes smiling up at Ben.

Jo looked at the photograph for a long time, then at Lisa, happily building a castle in her sand-pit beside the pool. The sun was shining, the child was brown and healthy. She had already enchanted the people of La Belette and even those who had still treated Jo with reserve now greeted them both.

She realized that she did not want to return to London, to face the humiliation of Ben's new liaison. If the usual form was followed, this woman would fly back with him and take up residence at the Savoy or the Dorchester. He would visit her several times a week, until he tired of her, while Jo kept up the pretence of knowing nothing about it.

The next morning, she wrote and told him that she would like to move permanently to the Villa Mimosa. 'It would be so much better for Lisa, and you know how I love the place. Also, I do worry sometimes in bureaucratic England that there might be an attempt to take her away from us. You say it isn't necessary for us to adopt her, but I'm not sure that the Social Services, if they were to find out about our unofficial arrangement, might not interfere. In France, she is simply accepted as our adopted daughter.

'Moving here shouldn't mean that you and I would see much less of each other than we already do. I would hope that you would also regard this as our home . . . we could build on a studio. The flat could remain our London base. Would you think about it?'

He returned an instant letter of agreement, and she suspected that he welcomed the freedom the arrangement would give him, though he assured her he would spend as much time as possible in France with her and Lisa.

So began another phase of her life.

In many ways, the longer separations improved their relationship. Away from London and its distractions he was gentler and more attentive, and, with the villa to themselves, they made love with renewed passion.

But it was never long before he was restless, and sent out urgent invitations to friends to come down and relieve his boredom. Their house-parties became legendary, and Jo had to face the fact that sometimes her husband's latest mistress would be among her guests. What made the situation more bearable was that she knew it would not be long before everyone flew off and she and Lisa would once more be left in peace.

The little girl flourished in the Mediterranean sunshine and grew up speaking French and English with equal facility. She went to school, first in the village, and later to a lycée in Cannes, as a weekly boarder.

Their closest friends were the widower, Nick Garnier, and his son, Nicholas. From their first meeting, when Lisa was five and Nick was eight, she adored him, and was his constant companion. They each regarded the other's house as a second home, and Nick looked upon Jo as a substitute for the American mother who had died a few years before.

The two children became, for several years, Ben's favourite subjects, and his paintings of them, together and separately, were regarded by many critics as his finest.

To Jo, Peter was a friend who could always be called upon in need when Ben was away. They fell into the habit of dropping in on each other two or three times a week, to sit chatting over a glass of wine, or Peter would invite her and Lisa for dinner at the Lion d'Or. When Ben was home, he effaced himself, though he appeared to enjoy any party at the villa to which he was bidden, and the two men got along well enough. Ben was too sure of Jo to regard him as a rival.

When Lisa was ten, Ben bought a new car, a sleek, low-slung Maserati, and drove it down through France. He invited half-a-dozen friends to stay, in order to show it off.

The two children were fascinated by it, especially Nick. Ben took them for a ride, and spent a happy half hour explaining how to drive it and showing them the gears.

That evening, when the house-party was at dinner – Peter was among the guests – the car drew Nick back like a magnet. Later Lisa was to tell Jo what happened then.

'Get in and we'll pretend to go for a drive,' he said. He slid behind the wheel, and she climbed in beside him.

'I bet we *could* drive it,' she said. 'Go on, why don't you? You just turn the key and put your foot on that pedal . . .'

'I know how to drive, thank you. My father lets me drive his car from the house down to the road. Driving's easy.'

'Go on, then. Just to the gate. I'll drive back. I remember exactly what Ben said.'

He caressed the steering-wheel longingly. 'Should we?'

'No one will know.'

But the Maserati was a very different vehicle from his father's Citroën. Although he made the same movements that Ben had explained, the car suddenly took off like a bullet and shot down the drive. He clung to the wheel, too petrified to think clearly.

'Put your foot on the brake!' Lisa shrieked.

As they careered through the gate, he achieved a perfect emergency stop that nearly sent them both through the wind-screen. He grabbed the hand-brake and the car pulled up in the middle of the road, fortunately empty of traffic. The engine stalled.

'My turn!' She was intoxicated by the speed and the excitement.

189

'No! It's not as easy as it looks.'

'Ben's my father. It's almost my car! I'm going to drive it back.'

After a brief argument, he gave in. 'Only be careful. Put her into neutral, start her, then into first gear, and keep your foot . . .'

'I *know* what to do.'

She started the car and let off the hand-brake. She began to fiddle with the lever and, with a grinding noise, it slipped into gear. The car jerked alarmingly, shot forward and fetched up against the iron railings at the side of the gate.

Ten minutes later, they were standing, trembling, with Jo, Ben, Peter, and the rest of the guests, surveying the damage. The car's offside head-lamp and right front wing were smashed.

'Who did this?' Ben's voice was soft, but cold.

Nick stepped forward. 'I did,' he said shakily. 'I'm awfully sorry . . . we just went for a ride . . .'

'No . . .' Lisa began, but Peter interrupted her, furiously addressing his son: 'How dare you do such a thing! How many times have I told you never even to touch the controls of a car? Do you understand what you've done . . . ?' He turned to Ben and spread his hands in a hopeless, Gallic gesture. 'How can I apologize? I'll deal with him when we get home, and I'll pay in full for the repairs. Ben, I'm sorry!'

'But it wasn't . . .' Lisa said.

'Be quiet, you're just as much to blame as he is.' Ben spoke with surprising mildness and only Jo guessed that this was because there was, among their guests, an attractive, blonde television producer. A new friend, he had called her. 'It'll teach you both a lesson. The damage is easily fixed. Don't let's spoil the party.'

As he led the way back to the house, the blonde at his side, Jo heard her murmur admiringly: 'My God, I've never seen anyone so cool . . .'

190

When she went to say goodnight to Lisa a little later, she found her sitting up in bed, crying.

'What's the matter? Are you worrying about the car? Ben was pretty nice about it, I thought.'

'It isn't that. You know how he says families shouldn't have any secrets from each other . . . ?'

'Yes.' Do as I say, don't do as I do, she thought grimly.

'Well, it was me who ran into the fence, not Nick. I tried to tell you, but no one listened, and Nick kept whispering to me to shut up.'

'And now you're worrying about telling Ben?'

Lisa nodded. 'I didn't actually tell a lie, because he didn't ask me if I was driving. But Peter's angry with Nick, and it isn't fair. Will I go and tell Ben now?'

Jo said carefully, 'He's with his friends. Would you like me to do it for you? I don't think we'll make too much fuss about it. I'll just tell Ben and Peter privately so they know it wasn't Nick's fault.'

As far as the children were concerned, that was the end of the matter. Ben's reaction to Lisa's confession was that she had been led astray by Nick in the first place. 'Garnier ought to learn to keep that bloody kid under control,' he grumbled. 'He's getting to be a bad influence on Lisa.'

It was not until the Miranda episode that the real rift between Ben and Nick occurred.

3

As Jo relived the years, Lisa sat alone in the living-room, trying to read, unable to concentrate as her mind went back over the events of the past couple of days, knowing that if she went to bed, she would not sleep.

It was raining again. Following the summer fires, the wet weather had confirmed a disastrous season for the market-gardeners, and hotel-owners were complaining that tourists were fleeing back to the drier autumns of Germany or England.

Finding her solitude and the steady dripping were getting on her nerves, she decided that a drink might help. The whisky and gin decanters were empty, but she remembered that in the past Ben had kept a well-stocked bar in his studio.

Switching lights on, she made her way through the empty corridors that led to the back of the house.

It was the first time she had been into the studio since her return and as she opened the door, Ben's presence was all around her. There was the scrubbed pine table she remembered, stacked with tubes of paint, brushes and other artists' impedimenta. On shelves was his collection of art-books, many of them signed by their authors; on the walls, framed posters of his exhibitions in the world's capital cities; his easel, looking curiously naked without a half-finished canvas resting on it; his big, roll-top desk.

She remembered the days she and Nick had spent posing, and listening to his stories; how she had loved to sit quietly, watching him paint.

Now there was a deadness in the atmosphere that she

had never known as a child. It was as though the room was sleeping, awaiting the presence that would bring it back to life: the big handsome man with the blue eyes that could be warm and laughing, or icy with anger, the dominating presence, the charm that he could turn on and off like a tap.

It was painfully tidy. Even his smock, hanging on a hook behind the door, had been unworn since it was last laundered and ironed. On the table, his cleaned brushes were lined up neatly, his palette was clean.

There were half-full decanters and clean glasses on a tray and she could almost see him standing there, pouring a drink, then wandering back to the easel to study his work. She shook off the fancy and picked up a decanter.

As she turned to leave, she noticed that the door of a cupboard was half-open behind his easel. Automatically, she moved to close it, but first she glanced inside. It was empty, except for three sketch-books lying on a shelf.

She picked one up and leafed through it, recalling that he had always kept what he called sketch-diaries, in which he made notes for paintings and intermittently wrote a journal. During his lifetime, the cupboard in which they were stacked had been kept locked. It had never occurred to her to be curious about them.

She took them back into the living-room and sat at the long table. Surely, over the years, he must have filled more than three books? She wondered what had happened to the rest.

At first she flicked through them quickly, pausing every now and then to look more closely at a sketch, and admire the talent that could create a portrait, not only of features, but of character, in a few lines. There were colour notes, facial details, sections of landscape, even groups of people, little more than stick-figures, but full of life. There were cruel caricatures of some of his sitters. When she reached the third volume, dated four years ago, there was a change: the lines no longer flowed, and some were shaky.

His writing, too, had become sprawling and untidy. She realized that she was seeing the onset of his arthritis.

Turning back to the first book, she began to read, at first with fascination, then with increasing distaste, for apart from his notes for paintings, the rest was a series of slanderous descriptions of his sitters, with what appeared to be verbatim reports of their private conversations.

Ben had been a good listener. When he was working on a portrait, she would often hear, from outside the studio, murmuring voices, and wonder what they were talking about.

Now she knew: the sitters, relaxed, talked about themselves, and he encouraged them, so that barriers were lowered and secrets poured out. Instead of respecting the confidences, he had recorded them, from minor royalty's testimony about his preference for beautiful men rather than beautiful women, to the High Court judge's confession that he liked to don a false moustache and pick up prostitutes in the West End of London. She read about the aging actress who paid young men to be 'guests' at nude swimming parties, and the millionaire stock-broker proud of having made his pile from insider trading. All were public figures and she knew that what she had been reading would be dynamite in the wrong hands. There was a libel action on every page and the thought of an outsider getting hold of them appalled her.

Instinctively, she glanced towards the big stone fireplace, and she understood why she had found only three volumes. Among the ashes were corners of charred paper and some slivers of red board which she recognized as the covers. Jo must have burned the rest, had possibly been interrupted before she could dispose of the last three.

She was about to close the book when an unusual note caught her eye. It was scrawled in pencil at the top of a page: the initials A.M., then, in brackets (aka A.M.!!), and an address in SW1, London. There was no explanation.

Before she could change her mind, she found matches, crumpled a few pages, and lit them. Little by little, she fed them into the fire-place, until they, too, were ashes. Art historians would be furious if it were ever discovered what she had done, but she had no regrets.

Lying in bed later, still sleepless, she found herself wondering whether Ben had ever written about matters nearer home, recording the intimate details of her own life. She felt suddenly cold as she imagined what his ruthless pen might have made of the day he had come upon her and Nick under the phoenix tree, and what had followed . . .

They had scrambled for their clothes and he had waited, his eyes averted, then shouted at Nick to get the hell out of his sight.

He had marched her back to the villa, and his cold fury had reduced her to a quivering child. Within an hour he informed her that he was taking her to London, where she would be sent to boarding-school. Jo begged him to change his mind, but he was adamant.

When Nick arrived at the gates, he was not allowed in, and Ben threatened to call the police to remove him. Peter telephoned, but Ben refused to speak to him.

The next morning, he and Lisa left for London, where he delivered her to the headmistress of a girls' school in Kensington. Their farewells were unemotional.

The school was strict and conventional. The girls were kept on a firm rein, rarely allowed out into London by themselves. She hated it.

Most of the lessons bored her, as did her fellow-students, and she resented the restrictions on her freedom. She felt ill most of the time, and put it down to the food.

The only classes she enjoyed were drama and ballet, and one slight relief in the dreary daily routine was that her acting ability won her the part of Olivia in a production of *Twelfth Night*, planned for the end of term.

Night after night, she dreamed of Nick, and cried silently. Jo wrote that he had left to go to college in California. 'It would be best, darling, if you did not try to contact him. You are both very young. There's no reason why, when you are older, you should not renew your friendship, but I have never seen Ben so angry, and he has made threats against Nick which I'm sure he's prepared to carry out. It is for Nick's sake that I ask you not to write to him.'

Two months after her arrival in England, she discovered that she was pregnant.

On a school outing she had seen advertisements beside the escalators in the Underground. In effect, they said: 'If you're happy to be pregnant, don't bother to read this. If not, phone . . .' The next time, she noted the telephone number.

She rang it, made an appointment, and one morning, she simply walked out of school. She had money, because even in the present circumstances, Ben had been generous, and she had told no one about the pound notes she had hidden in her shoe-bag.

The abortion organization had consulting rooms off Tottenham Court Road. She went up a narrow, uncarpeted staircase between a record shop and an office building, into a small waiting-room where several girls were sitting silently on hard chairs set against the wall. A receptionist with bleached hair and a thin, heavily made-up face handed her a form to fill in.

When she returned it, the woman glanced through it, looked at her narrowly, and said, 'Eighteen, dear?'

'Yes.' She knew the woman didn't believe her, but she managed to out-stare her, and eventually she shrugged, and said, 'Doctor will see you soon.'

She went back to her chair. Other girls came in. Most of them sat and stared at the ground. At least three looked even younger than she was, and she was surprised how plain most of them were. Yet some man had found each of them attractive enough to sleep with . . . at that point in her life, she had still believed that love was a necessary ingredient for intercourse. Only one of them was with a woman who appeared to be her mother. The rest, like herself, were facing, probably for the first time in their young lives, a crisis in which they were terrifyingly alone.

After an hour and a half, she was called to the doctor, a short, bored Pakistani, who examined her briefly and told her to see the receptionist on her way out.

The receptionist told her that the 'termination' would be performed at a clinic in South London in two days' time.

When she arrived back at school, the place was in turmoil. How dared she go out without asking permission? Where had she been?'

'I felt like a break,' she said calmly. 'I went for a walk in Kensington Gardens.'

The headmistress, Miss Enid Ralston, was a plump woman with grey, finger-waved hair, who wore flowered dresses and shoes that laced up. She was almost speechless with indignation. Lisa accepted her strictures calmly, and said she was sorry, but it had been too nice a day to stay indoors.

Finally Miss Ralston said: 'Because you're a foreigner and not accustomed to our ways, Lisa, I will not expel you. Nor, this time, will I tell your father what you've done. He's a busy man . . .' Her eyes briefly misted over as she remembered the charm and good looks of Benedict Absalom. 'But if anything like this happens again, you will be sent home instantly, and you will not be allowed to return. Do I make myself clear?'

'Yes, Miss Ralston.'

'Your punishment is that you will not take part in the end-of-term play, and you will be deprived of Saturday outings.'

'Yes. Thank you, Miss Ralston.'

197

Two days later, she disappeared again, and this time Ben was informed.

He was waiting for her when she returned to the school in a taxi at five o'clock. She was pale and heavy-eyed and walked with difficulty.

Tight-lipped, he said, 'Where the hell have you been?'

She looked at him, looked at the prim woman by his side, in her flowery dress and her sensible shoes, and said, 'I've had an abortion. The doctor said I should go to bed and rest now.'

They stared at her, speechless, then Miss Ralston turned scarlet and began to gabble. 'Nothing like this . . . shameless . . . never in my life as a teacher . . . you will leave at once!'

Ben whispered again, 'You bloody little whore!'

Supporting herself against the back of a chair, Lisa said conversationally: 'It was interesting. There was a bus-load of girls from Germany and we all sat in a waiting-room, all with the same little problem inside us, but none of us talked, and it was like being on an assembly-line: into the operating theatre, out, next please. They burn the foetuses, did you know? From where I was lying afterwards, I could see the flames when they opened the oven.'

And then she fainted.

When she regained consciousness, she was escorted to Ben's car and he drove her back to the apartment in Islington. Not a word was spoken.

His house-keeper greeted them, and he said: 'Look after my daughter. She isn't well. See that she goes to bed and stays there. I'm going out.'

She spent two days in bed, and he did not once look in to see her.

On the third day, she went downstairs. He was in the studio that stretched across the back of the apartment, putting the finishing touches to a portrait. He turned, put down his brushes, and looked at her expressionlessly. After a moment, he said: 'I'm taking you to your new

198

school this afternoon. It's in Hampshire. Before we leave, I want you to understand one thing: if you misbehave or make any attempt to get in touch with Garnier, I'm prepared to testify to the French police that he's been raping you since you were fourteen. I will write to his college in America with the same information.'

'You can't! It's not true!'

'I don't care whether it's true or not. I will not have my daughter behaving like a common harlot.'

'I'm not your bloody daughter!' she shouted.

'I've brought you up, spent money on you, given you everything. You're *mine*, and from now on, you do as I say. There's another thing: Joanna is not to know anything about this. It would upset her.' He turned back to the easel.

Convinced that he would carry out his threat, she had never written to Nick again. He didn't write to her, either, and she tried to persuade herself that she no longer cared. But there were times, lying awake in the early hours of the morning, when she would wonder if she would ever tell him that she had destroyed his child.

Sometimes it seemed that her whole life now was based on pretence. She pretended to be a normal schoolgirl among other normal schoolgirls, in an establishment whose curriculum enforced long working hours and fierce physical exercise, in the hope that exhausted bodies would keep exhausted minds from dwelling on such unhealthy matters as sex. She pretended, even to herself, that she was forgetting Nick.

The best times were when Jo flew in from La Belette to see her, but even then she had to pretend that she was happy, and that she and Ben had made up their differences. When he was in England, he visited her occasionally, and neither of them mentioned what had gone before.

But each knew that the other had neither forgotten nor forgiven.

Afraid that Nicholas might reappear from the United States, he refused to allow her to return to France for her holidays, so Jo came to London and, since he was often abroad, they were able to enjoy themselves in their own way. They spent much of their time at the theatre, for she had already decided that she wanted to be an actress.

The day after she returned to Islington at the end of her final term, Ben summoned her to the studio.

'Have you any thoughts about your future?'

'Yes. I'd like to go to drama school.'

He looked at her in silence, his artist's eye seeing the graceful figure, the face he had painted so many times, full of character, but now without warmth as she met his eyes, the natural elegance with which she invested even a denim skirt and loose shirt. After a moment, he nodded. 'Okay. But you live here. And you don't go back to La Belette.'

'Why should I? Nick isn't there any longer.' It was the first time she had mentioned his name, and it dropped like a stone between them. He said nothing, and she added: 'I'd thought of sharing a flat.'

'You're only eighteen. You stay here, or there will be no drama school.'

She shrugged. 'All right.'

The last years had hardened her, and she had already decided, coldly, that she would obey him for just as long as it was necessary. Then, having had the training to launch herself into the professional theatre, she would be free.

She enjoyed her drama lessons, and was recognized as an actress with unusual potential. She and Ben did not see much of each other, except that when he was in England, he expected her to act as his hostess on occasions, aware that she was decorative enough to reflect well on himself, as Joanna had. He took her shopping for the right clothes. His taste was impeccable and he never asked the price.

'I taught Joanna to dress,' he remarked. 'Before I took her in hand, Oxfam was her couturier.'

200

From the jeans-and-hamburger culture of a student, she would often return home to find the flat full of guests, a butler at the door, the kitchen taken over by caterers. She would change into a dress which Ben had chosen, and pretend to be enjoying herself with people years older than herself, with whom she had little in common.

She achieved a healthy indifference to the social eminence allegedly bestowed by titles, money or media exposure and discovered that the rich and famous were, on the whole, no more interesting than the poor and unknown. She met a renowned Italian tenor who whined about his health; a best-selling author who talked only about money; an American senator who tried to put his hand up her skirt; a millionaire industrialist who showed her photographs of his stable of Rolls Royces.

She came to understand why Jo's visits to London were infrequent, and usually timed when Ben was out of the country. She resented the women who flaunted their relationships with him and came increasingly to dislike his extravagant life-style.

Just before she was due to complete her course, she wrote to a television producer who had been a guest at the villa some years before. Unknown to them, he had watched one evening as she and Nick were satirizing, with deadly accuracy, the pretensions of the other guests. At the end of the performance, he had roared with laughter and said: 'Come and see me if you ever want to go into the business!'

He replied promptly to her letter, took her to lunch and told her that he was about to start auditions for thirteen episodes of a new soap which would go out the following year. He needed a young girl with her type of looks. Why didn't she have a go?

Ben was in New York when she auditioned, and by the time he returned to London, she had signed a contract to play Bridget in *Families*, and had moved out of the Islington flat into a bedsitter in Maida Vale.

He ridiculed her choice of a soap-opera in which to make her acting debut, scoffed at the producer's track-record and assured her that she would soon have to join the dole queue.

She knew that his irritation was because she had achieved something on her own, that he no longer had the power to control her life.

She saw even less of him. He was travelling a great deal and sometimes he did not even telephone her when he alighted in London. She kept in constant touch with her mother by letter but now Jo rarely came to England. When Ben was at the villa, her life was a round of house-guests and entertaining. When he was away, she wrote, she missed him, but she enjoyed her peaceful solitude.

The instant success of *Families* became a television legend, and Lisa enjoyed every moment of it, not least because she knew that Ben would resent the publicity she was getting. On the rare occasions they met, he never mentioned her work and as far as she knew, he did not watch a single episode of the series.

She moved from her bedsitter into a three-room flat. Her social life was full and amusing, and she embarked on a series of light-hearted affairs, some of which ended up in bed. None were important.

It was not until the second series of *Familes* had been completed, and the third was already planned, that she decided to go to America and find Nick Garnier.

Jo mentioned him occasionally in her letters, and she knew that he had dropped out of college, had moved restlessly from job to job, and had ended up in Hollywood. There he had recently worked in a film, billed second to an actor named Dirk Chavez, who had already created a sensation with two sleepers – low-budget movies which had unexpectedly become hits.

Nick's film, *The Illegals*, was set on the Mexican border and was about a semi-destitute family of illegal immigrants to the United States, their efforts to make a life for themselves, their constant fear of deportation. Chavez, himself half Mexican, played the lead, as the son of the family, and Nick was a young American who befriended him.

Jo wrote: 'I believe it's already a box-office success in the States and is likely to be nominated for an Oscar. Peter tells me Nick and Chavez have been on vacation, touring the U.S. by car, and Nick has just returned to Los Angeles.'

It was February, and London was cold and dank. Lisa had been thinking longingly of La Belette, but Ben was home and to be with him would awaken too many unpleasant memories of the last time they had been there together.

But she had three months off, and his threats against Nick were no longer valid. She would go to America, find him, and see how their years apart had affected their relationship. If they had become strangers, that would be that. At least she would have laid a ghost. If not . . . she did not allow herself to anticipate the alternative.

Now, in the silent villa, sleep overcame her before she needed to face, once again, the painful consequences of her decision.

4

The doorbell rang the next morning when Lisa was padding around the kitchen in her bare feet, wearing a light cotton robe and holding a cup of coffee. She picked up the intercom.

Nick's voice was sharp: 'Let me in, quickly.'

'It's early . . . what do you want?'

'Never mind that now. Open the gates. I have to talk to you. Hurry up!'

She released the gates. After a moment, she heard his car pull up outside the front door.

She greeted him without warmth. 'Isn't Peter with you?'

'He's gone to Cotolin to see the *avocat*. He'll be here later. Where's Jo?'

'She's still asleep. What's happened?'

'The press have arrived. As I came through the village, I saw at least half-a-dozen of them, including a tv crew. I guess the news has leaked and they'll be descending on you any minute.'

'Jo won't see them, and neither will I.'

'Then you mustn't open the gates.'

'Oh, God, it'll be no better than prison! I know what they're like. Paparazzi in the trees, questions shouted at you . . .'

'Look, I'm supposed to be flying to London this morning. If I can help, I'll put it off.'

Her face froze as she wrapped herself once more in polite antagonism. 'We will manage, thank you. There's no need for you to change any arrangements on our account.'

'Jesus, with you it's one step forward and two steps back,' he said irritably. 'I thought we'd called a truce.'

'I simply said we wouldn't need your help. Your father will be here. Sorry if I offended you.'

They stared at each other with undisguised enmity, then he shrugged. 'Okay, forget it. What I also came to tell you is that I've been asked to write a book about Ben. A biography.'

For the second time, she was shocked out of her defences. 'You? Why you, of all people?'

'Why not? I've known him all my life. I've already written one book. My publisher's in London and he wants to talk to me. It was his idea, not mine.'

'Jo will never allow it!' She waved an impatient hand. 'Not only because it's you. She won't want a book written at all. She loathes publicity.'

'You're forgetting something: Ben was public property. As far as you and Jo are concerned, he was the man you lived with, who happened to be a painter. To the rest of the world, he was among the most successful and admired artists of this century, and a larger-than-life personality. You'll have to face it: *someone* is going to produce a biography – could even be Amyas, but it might be better if it were me. I'm not likely to use anything that would hurt Jo. Believe me, I'm not planning a hatchet job.'

Her voice was bitter: 'How could anyone write about Ben without a hatchet?'

'You know he was a bastard. Secretly, Jo knows, but she loved him nevertheless. I know it, too, but his talent – hell, genius – transcends that. What you're forgetting is that for a long time, I loved Ben, and at the end, I was sorry for him. My personal dislike was sandwiched in between. That would have no part in the story.'

'What about me? I'm not crazy about the idea of telling the world I was his illegitimate daughter. Not that I regard it as a stigma, in ordinary circumstances I wouldn't give a damn. But right now, I've had it up to here—' She made a cutting gesture across her throat. '—with being gossiped about.'

'You and Jo would have a chance to vet anything I write.'

She thought for a moment, then said, 'I don't like it much, but you'll have to talk to Jo.'

He sensed a weakening. 'Of course. The project would collapse without her co-operation. All I propose to do in London is discuss the shape of the book. Then I'll do some preliminary research, look up reviews of Ben's exhibitions, critical essays, profiles, newspaper reports. Later, I'll have to go and see the places where he lived as a child and young man, talk to people who knew him, maybe follow the trail back to Czechoslovakia and see if he has any relatives still living. But that's in the future. It'll be a long project. This time, I'll only be away for a couple of days, then Jo and I can talk. I was hoping you might be able to smooth the way for me in the meantime. I'd really like to do this, Lisa.'

In spite of herself, she was infected by his enthusiasm. Nick had always been able to do that to her, she thought crossly. He could make any scheme seem not only logical, but essential. Just before the now-infamous bicycle race he had assured her, 'The village will love it. It'll liven things up.'

Now he said, 'Are you actually smiling?'

'I was remembering the day we did the market obstacle course on our bikes.'

'Fun, wasn't it? Remember the horror on all the faces as we swept through? Madame Sudre was selling two live hens. They escaped when you side-swiped the cage.'

'You knocked over Auguste's tomatoes and I skidded into a crate of rabbits . . .'

'I looked back to see what was happening and went straight into the flower-stall. Fetched up smothered in roses, and was collared by that bad-tempered *flic*.' His voice softened. 'You kicked him because you thought he was arresting me. Did I ever say thank you?'

She came back to the present, and her smile disappeared. 'If Jo doesn't want the book written, I'm on her side. But there's something . . .' She stopped.

'What?'

'Something else you might do in London.'

'Go on.'

'That woman, Alicia Freeman . . . I'm curious about why Ben should have paid her nearly ten thousand a year for so long. All we heard is that the money went into an account in Swiss Cottage. Jo didn't want to know anything about her, but now . . .'

'I won't promise anything, but if I have time I'll do what I can.'

She said, 'I noticed Ben's address book on the desk in his studio last night. Let's see if by any chance she's in it.'

He followed her into the studio and as he stood, looking around, she was thankful that she had burned the notebooks. They would be irresistible grist to any biographer's mill.

Nick said, more to himself than to her: 'He could still be here, couldn't he? Even dead, he's dominating our lives.'

She opened the leather-bound address book at 'F'. Ben had a habit of using initials rather than names in some cases but there was no Alicia Freeman, and no A.F. She flicked back the pages, recognizing celebrities' names on every one. When she reached the front of the book, she paused, and said: 'This is odd . . .'

Nick looked over her shoulder. Suddenly conscious of his nearness, she moved away.

'A.M.' she said. 'Forty-one Lupin Street, SW1. I came across that address last night . . .' She paused. 'It was on – a piece of paper. It said "A.M. aka A.M." Didn't make sense. The same thing's scribbled on this flyleaf.'

'A.M. Amyas Mahr? But why the also-known-as? Does Amyas keep a place in London?'

'Not to my knowledge.' She closed the book. 'It's probably someone else entirely. It's just . . . odd.'

As they reached the living-room, she said, 'Where will you stay?'

'Some hotel in the West End, I suppose. Any suggestions?'

'You can use my flat if you like.'

He looked at her in surprise. 'Considering the way you feel about me, that's a remarkably generous offer. Where is it?'

'Hampstead. And I'm not being generous. It's in a high-risk burglary area. It's not a good thing to leave it empty for long periods.'

He accepted gratefully, wondering if her offer was a sign that their frozen relationship was beginning to thaw.

Ten minutes after his departure with her keys and a note introducing him to the apartments' porter, she was already regretting what she'd done. She didn't want Nick in her flat, using her belongings, maybe sleeping in her bed. It would create an intimacy she wanted to avoid at all costs. But it was too late to do anything about it.

The door-bell rang as she was dressing. A woman, speaking French: 'Madame, I'm from *Nice Matin* . . .'

'Sorry, I'm not seeing anyone.'

'A few questions only . . .' She hung up.

The next caller was English. 'Independent Television News. We understand Madame Absalom has been charged with the murder of her husband.'

'That isn't true.'

'Are you Lisa Absalom? We'd appreciate an interview.'

'Neither my mother nor I will be interviewed. You're wasting your time. Goodbye.'

There were two other calls from reporters. She didn't dare not to answer the intercom in case it was Peter, but hung up as soon as they identified themselves.

Finally, she heard his voice and pressed the gate-release.

She went to the door. There were shouts from outside, and she pictured the newsmen jostling to try and get through before the gates shut. But only Peter's car came up the drive.

As he arrived, Jo appeared. Fully dressed, she was paler than usual and the skin under her eyes was dark, but her face was, as always, calm. There was no strain in her affectionate greeting.

'There's a mob of reporters and photographers outside,' he said. 'Fortunately Berenger arrived just before I did. They tried to storm the car, but he fended them off. I'm afraid you're in for a rough time.'

'I won't see any of them,' she said. 'If Berenger will make sure they don't try to scale the fence, we should be safe enough. I'm sure this will all blow over in a few days. Molinard will realize that Ben's death was an accident, and they won't be interested any longer.'

'How can you be so cool?' Lisa said. 'You've never done anything wrong in your life, but you've practically been accused of murder. Yet you look as though you've just come from a garden-party.'

She shrugged. 'Fussing doesn't help. Peter, do you have any news?'

'I've been to see Maître Gonnet. He's agreed to act for you, but you won't need to see him for the moment. We'll wait for Molinard's next move.'

He left a few minutes later, saying he'd be back during the afternoon. 'I'll phone first. Make sure you know who it is before you open the gates.'

'I will,' Jo said. 'And – thank you for everything.'

As he raised her hand to his lips, Lisa saw the longing in his face. She found herself thinking, how badly does he want her? He knew Ben often made her unhappy. What if it had become too much for him, and he had set about releasing her?

As he turned to kiss her cheek, she had to restrain herself from drawing away, then, ashamed of her reaction, returned his kiss with extra affection.

When he had gone she said, 'Nick called in to warn us about the media invasion.' She hesitated. 'He's just left for London.'

'Oh? Did he tell you why?'

'He's going to meet a publisher. He's been asked to write Ben's biography.'

A spasm seemed to pass over Jo's face. Her eyelids flickered and Lisa saw her hands clench. She whispered: 'And . . . ?'

'He wants to, but only with your permission.'

'I won't allow it, any more than I'd allow Amyas's ridiculous "memoire"!'

'Nick explained to me . . .'

Jo was leaving the room. 'It's unthinkable, people digging into our lives!' Her voice was shaking. 'I won't even discuss it.'

It was no time, Lisa decided, to tell her that Nick was already planning his research.

As she lay in a warm bath, scented with pine-oil, Jo tried to absorb this new blow.

First the police investigations, finding herself under suspicion of murder; now Nick would want to ask questions. He had worked as a journalist in America, so he had probably learnt how to uncover facts. Suppose he were to find out about Markie? And he would pry into Ben's character. Thank God she had burned his notebooks . . . the water swished as she sat up, remembering. Before she had finished, Lisa had telephoned to beg her to come to the memorial service, and in her hasty preparations to leave, she had allowed the fire to go out, and left the last three books.

She dried herself, pulled on a cotton dress, and ran to the studio.

As she stood, staring at the cupboard's empty shelves, Lisa said, from the doorway: 'I got rid of them.'

'How?'

'Burned them were you'd burned the others. Threw the ashes out.'

'Did you read them?'

'Only one. It was enough.'

'They had to be destroyed. It was like killing a part of Ben, but no outsider would have understood why he wrote about people like that.'

'Why did he? It was so cold-blooded, as though he *enjoyed* recording their – aberrations.'

Jo said, 'It wasn't that. He was fascinated by faces, and he believed that everything hidden in a person's character, every experience he has had, affects his expression, his features, lines and wrinkles, so that every face is unique. He told me once that it was finding out about his sitters than enabled him to show the whole person in his paintings, not just the outer layer.'

'I can't help wondering if he didn't have it in the back of his mind that one day he'd publish the diaries. They'd have caused the kind of sensation he would have loved.'

'Well, they're gone,' Jo said flatly. 'I hated finding out how he'd abused confidences. That wasn't the Ben I knew. Let's forget them. He was a great painter. That's all that matters.'

'But that's what I was trying to tell you earlier: Nick pointed out that because he was a great painter, *someone* is going to write a book about him eventually. With or without your permission. Have you thought about that?'

She seemed to stop breathing for a moment, then she said, 'No, I haven't. I've been too wrapped up in myself, I expect. He's right, of course. What am I going to do?' For once her guard was down, and it was a cry of despair.

Lisa looked at her in surprise. 'It's not all that serious, love. Talk to Nick when he gets back. You only need to tell him things that won't reflect badly on Ben: about Anna and Martin and Tommy, and Ben's childhood. Your marriage, his success, how he brought me back from Prague.'

211

Jo repeated Lisa's own words: 'I must think about it. I suppose Nick's book would be a possibility, but I certainly won't have anything to do with Amyas's so-called "memoire".'

'He's just latched onto an idea that might make him some money. If we don't co-operate, it probably won't get off the ground.'

Jo sighed. 'Everyone wants to get in on Ben's act. Why can't they let him rest in peace?'

'Because he was Ben – and I keep thinking that he must be thoroughly enjoying all this fuss.'

Jo said, 'Sometimes it's impossible to believe he's dead. While I was burning the diaries I kept worrying about how angry he would be.'

'Jo . . . who's A.M. with an address in London, SW1? I came across it in the book I looked at.'

'A.M.? Amyas, perhaps? But he never goes to London. Why?'

Lisa shrugged. 'Just curiosity.'

PART FIVE

1

Nick perched on the metal-framed sofa in Lisa's apartment, and wondered how anyone could choose such uncomfortable furniture. She must have changed. The Lisa he had known liked to sprawl, hitching her legs over the arms of chairs, burrowing into piles of sofa-cushions. In this monument to high-tech, it was impossible either to sprawl or burrow.

It was his first chance to study the flat. On his arrival at mid-day, he had called Jared Cowan and been summoned to lunch. They had spent the afternoon, with brief breaks while Cowan dealt with other appointments, discussing the Absalom project.

'Do it as well as you did *Road-runners*, and we have a certain seller,' Cowan said over lunch at the Dorchester. 'I'm interested in the man, even more than his work. Who *was* Ben Absalom? Give me his background, family, thoughts, motivations. I've read a bit about him. The Prague Spring episode could stand expansion. There are holes in the newspaper reports. I gather he was so upset that he refused to talk about it when he got home. Maybe his wife can fill you in. I want her background, too. She must be a remarkable woman to have stayed married to him. His affairs, by all accounts, were legion.'

'She is a remarkable woman,' Nick said. 'But it's all going to hinge on whether she'll be willing to co-operate. She's always kept out of the limelight – which is not to say that she's a nonentity. In many ways, I suspect she's a stronger character than Ben was.'

'Then there's the adopted daughter, beautiful girl,

talented actress, recently been divorced, I understand. You know her, too?'

'Yes.'

Cowan, a large, bearded man with bright brown eyes, waited for a moment. When Nick did not elaborate, his voice rattled on. 'Could turn out that the Absalom women are as important as the man himself. And there's this fantastic climax: his premature death, which we now find out might have been murder. Police questioning his wife. It's a great, great story.'

Someone had once told Nick that exaggerated enthusiasm was an American form of politeness, and it was a characteristic Cowan had, in spades. His round face, topped by a bald pate fringed with a kind of monk's tonsure of brown curls, was pink and animated as he leant forward, dangerously brandishing a forkful of rosemary-scented lamb. 'You're the one man who's able to do it justice, Nick. I want you to be as excited about it as I am.'

The Absalom women. Nick looked around the stark white sitting-room, searching for Lisa, finding her in the books pushed untidily into the metal shelves: actors' memoirs; Austen, Hardy, Trollope; dozens of paperbacks: Ian McEwan, Orwell, Milan Kundera, P.D. James; art histories; an old, leather-bound Shakespeare; plays by Chekov, Orton, Stoppard; poetry: Eliot, Dylan Thomas, Sylvia Plath, Keats, Ogden Nash – evidence of wide-ranging interests and an inquiring mind.

He found her, too, in the plants in their terracotta tubs: a graceful, six-foot *ficus benjamina* near the window, a variegated, green and yellow umbrella plant, a scarlet regal pelargonium, Busy Lizzies planted in an old brass preserving pan. Lisa had once said she could not imagine living in an apartment with no direct access to a garden. Here, she was compensating for the loss.

His suitcase was still standing, unopened, inside the front door. He picked it up and moved towards the bedrooms. There were three, and it was obvious which was Lisa's. Her bed was covered by a patchwork quilt and there were photographs on the dressing-table, several of the villa, even one of himself as a child, sitting with Ben and Joanna beside the swimming-pool. Lisa had taken it with a new camera which had been her ninth birthday present from Ben. There was a head-and-shoulders of Joanna, serenely beautiful, and another of her working in the garden, wearing shorts, a loose shirt and a wide-brimmed straw hat. There were no other pictures of himself or of Ben, but there was one of a man he did not recognize, a man with light hair and high cheek-bones; a good-looking man, staring straight into the camera as though challenging it, his eyes slightly hooded. Nick picked it up. There was a pencilled note on the cardboard backing: *To Lisa, with my love and gratitude, always. S.*

He restrained himself from turning it face-down on the table. Who was S.? Her new boyfriend? An old one? Her ex-husband? Doubtful, that. According to Peter, he had been gay and the marriage had been a disaster. She wouldn't keep a picture of him . . . but whoever it was, why the hell should he care? He swung around and left the room, closing the door behind him. It had been a mistake coming here. Her belongings were awakening long-suppressed emotions.

The other two bedrooms were less evocative: spare rooms in which there was nothing of her personality. They were decorated in white, relieved only by touches of black in the curtain tie-backs and the huge, clip-framed black and white photographic prints on the walls. He tossed his suitcase on a bed, opened it, and began to unpack. Having brought the minimum of clothing, he had stowed it away within five minutes.

It was 7.30, and he was facing a solitary evening. He had turned down Cowan's invitation to a late supper because he had wanted time alone to think over their discussion. Now he regretted his refusal. He hated eating in restaurants by himself, he knew no one in London he could telephone and didn't feel like a movie.

He watered the house-plants, then wandered into the kitchen and opened the fridge. It contained only half a pound of Dutch butter but, in a cupboard, he found an unopened packet of Scanda Crisps, a tin of sardines and a jar of instant coffee. He wondered wistfully what Cowan would be eating: smoked salmon? Richly-sauced venison? Pheasant with wild rice? Cream-filled profiteroles smothered in melted chocolate . . . ?

He looked for a can-opener in the drawers, had just discovered an electric one attached to the wall when a bell rang.

Sardine-tin in hand, he opened the front door. The man whose photograph stood in Lisa's bedroom was outside.

They studied each other for a moment, then S. held out his hand and said, 'You're Nicholas Garnier?'

'Yes.' Nick raised his eyebrows questioningly as they shook hands.

'I'm Simon Ashton. Lisa's husband. Ex, actually.'

Nick was surprised into silence.

Shifting uncomfortably under his stare, Ashton said, 'I wondered if we could talk. If you're not too busy . . .'

'How did you know I was here?'

'I read in the paper . . . about Jo. Christ, what an awful thing! I called the villa late this afternoon to see if there was any way I could help. Lisa told me you were staying in the flat.'

'Oh, yes,' Nick's expression was not encouraging.

Ashton began to stammer. 'Look, I don't want to interfere, or anything, but I liked Jo. Lisa said you could tell me what's been going on, and that you were trying to check up on a few things in London. I just thought, maybe there was something I could do . . . for them, you know.'

'You'd better come in.' It was not a warm invitation, and Ashton hesitated before following him inside.

Clearly embarrassed, he said, 'I won't stay long . . .'

then stopped abruptly at the door to the sitting-room. 'My God, what has she done?'

'Done?'

'I built this room around her! She was the only decoration. She's turned it into a designer's nightmare!'

'Looks all right to me,' Nick said coldly.

Ashton sighed, and shook his head. 'I knew this would happen if she was left on her own. She was always wanting to introduce bits of the outdoors. And books! Bloody books. I built her a cupboard in her bedroom where they could be shut away, but she still left them lying around.' He glanced at Nick and his indignation was replaced by a wry smile. 'Sorry, but I loved this flat. I'm a set designer by trade. This was the first time I'd ever had a chance to create my own set.'

Nick had the average heterosexual male's distaste for the practices of homosexuals, but he found himself curious about this man whom Lisa had married and divorced, but with whom she apparently remained on speaking terms.

'Would you like a drink?' he said. 'I suppose there's something. I haven't investigated yet.'

'I can guide you in the right direction.'

To his irritation, Ashton automatically assumed the role of host and opened a kitchen cupboard, revealing a well-stocked bar. 'Vodka? Gin? Whisky?'

'Whisky.'

He poured them each a couple of fingers of Glenmorangie.

After they had settled in two of the uncomfortable chairs in the sitting-room there was a brief silence while they studied each other. Nick could detect nothing of the homosexual in Ashton's appearance. His hand-grip had been firm. Of medium height, he was powerfully built, his voice was deep, there were no camp gestures. He was dressed in jeans and a denim bomber jacket over an open-neck shirt.

Leaning forward, Ashton broke the hiatus. 'About the

219

Absaloms. All I know is what I've read in the papers and it seemed so bloody improbable . . . Ben murdered, Jo under suspicion. What happened?'

He did not interrupt as Nick described how he had found Ben's body and the reasons for Jo's interrogation.

'So what are you looking for here?' he said. 'Lisa said you were doing some research.'

'I've been asked to write Ben's biography, and we thought I might also turn up something that could throw light on the reason why he was killed. Something out of his past.'

'Sounds a remote possibility but if there is anything I can do to help . . . I'm pretty much at a loose end at the moment.'

'Well, thanks . . . I can't think of anything. If I do I'll let you know.'

Ashton put his glass down, and rose. 'I'd better go . . .'

Nick still had reservations about him, but any company, he thought, was better than spending the rest of the evening alone. Impulsively, he said, 'Have another drink. I haven't anything special to do.'

'You sure? Well . . .'

Three drinks later, they had thoroughly discussed the Absalom affair, though both tacitly avoided any mention of Ashton's marriage to Lisa, and had moved on to inconsequential chat about acting, set designing and a comparison of life in London, New York, Los Angeles and Provence.

It was nine o'clock when Ashton said hesitantly, 'I suppose you wouldn't feel like coming out for a meal? There's a Greek restaurant where Lisa and I used to go. It's cheap, and the food's not bad.'

Nick realized that he was no longer watching the other man suspiciously for evidence of sexual deviation. He was simply a likeable companion, intelligent, sensitive and articulate. 'Why not?' he said. 'It'll be a damn sight more enjoyable than sardines and slimming biscuits.'

* * *

As they sat over a brandy after an excellent meal, Ashton said shyly, 'I read your book. Enjoyed it very much.'

'Thanks. Ah . . . did Lisa read it?'

'I wouldn't know. We'd . . . separated by then. She'd mentioned you, that's how I knew the name. And I saw a couple of reviews that compared parts of *Road-runners* with Kerouac.'

Lisa had mentioned him to Ashton? What had she said? Not a question he could ask.

'Your friend Chavez . . . I sort of had a feeling there were things you left out.'

'The publishers made me cut the original manuscript because of the possibility of libel actions. His family was . . . difficult.'

'How did you meet him?'

Nick leant his elbows on the table. It was a long time since he had talked about Dirk Chavez, but suddenly, he was there, tall, ebullient, the blue eyes shining in his dark face as they had during the rumbustious months when they had been unfettered and happy.

On the white wall opposite him, he saw reflections of the pictures in his mind as he talked.

'I was working in a bar. There was this drunk . . .'

2

The bar was in Anaheim, attached to a motel not far from Disneyland. At midnight, it was virtually empty, and he was cleaning up after a quiet night. The motel guests had retired early and it was not a bar that attracted young people. There was music, but it was geared towards an older generation – the current attraction, who had also long since gone to his bed, was a vocalist who had been big in the forties but was now reduced to playing and singing the same old songs in empty bars.

The place was so dark that it wasn't until he reached a corner table in the back of the room that he realized one customer remained: a young man wearing a Stetson, shades and a grey silk suit. He was sitting perfectly straight and composed, with an empty Bourbon glass in front of him. He took no notice as Nick removed the glass and an ashtray full of cigarette stubs, and cleaned the table.

It was only Nick's second week in the bar and he wasn't sure how to deal with a man who seemed to have been turned into a statue.

'Sir,' he said, tentatively. 'Sir, we're closing now.'

No answer.

'Time to go home, sir! Bar's closed. The manager will be locking up in a minute.'

The man looked up. 'Cup of coffee.'

'No coffee, sir. No alcohol. I'll help you to the door.'

In a reasonable voice, he said, 'Can't go home like this. Mama will kill me.' He had a marked Hispanic accent.

Nick forgot he was a barman: 'Oh, for Christ's sake!

Time for beddy-byes. Mama's waiting to tuck you in.'

'Okay. If you say so.' he put both hands on the table, raised himself, and slithered gently to the floor.

It had been a long day, and Nick was tired. He hauled the man upright. The Stetson came off, the glasses slipped down, and hung off one ear, revealing a pair of startlingly light, if foggy, blue eyes.

Nick staggered under his weight and, realizing that he was unable to stand alone, rested him back on his chair. He looked up, and smiled. White teeth flashed in a brown face. Mexican, Nick thought. But a Mexican with blue eyes? And over six feet tall?

'Coffee,' he repeated.

Exasperated, Nick said, 'I'll see if there's some left. But you'll have to make it fast.'

'Right.' He set his glasses in place and reached for his hat. 'Gotta keep my disguise.'

When Nick returned with a cup of the cloudy black dregs of coffee from the bottom of a pot, he drank obediently, draining it in one swallow.

'Is your car outside?' Nick said.

'No car. Harry brought me. Told him to take the night off.' He started to rise unsteadily. Nick slung one of his arms over his own shoulders and moved with him to the door. There was a lone taxi outside the motel. The driver, a small elderly man, looked with disfavour on the drunk. 'Where's he want to go?'

Nick shoved him into the back of the cab, shook him and said: 'What's your address?'

He mumbled something that meant little to Nick.

'Did you get that?' he said.

'I got it. But I'm not taking him. One, it's too far. Two, I don't believe it. That's where the stars live. Three, what'd I do when I got him there? He's too big for me to lift.'

Nick nudged the drunk. 'Can you pay?'

'Sure. I'm loaded.' He fumbled in a pocket and

223

displayed a wallet stuffed with bank-notes.

'So he can pay,' the cabbie said. 'That doesn't solve the other problems. You want to come too, I'll take you both, and you can deal with him. Otherwise, I don't move.'

The drunk was asleep, breathing stertorously. His hat had slipped off again, and Nick saw that he was young, probably in his early twenties. Some of his own tiredness had evaporated, and he was beginning to enjoy the situation.

'Okay . . . hang on while I get my things.'

It was a long drive, but they eventually reached a stone wall with carved wooden doors more than eight feet high.

'I told you I didn't believe it,' the driver said.

'There's a bell . . .'

Nick pressed it and, after a moment, heard a woman's voice through a microphone, heavily accented and high-pitched: 'Dirk, is you? What you doing, out so late? And where your key?'

'If Dirk is large, wears a Stetson and has blue eyes, it's Dirk, all right,' Nick said. 'He is also drunk. And I have no idea where his key is.'

'Drunk? Wait, I unlock.'

A buzzer went and the doors were released.

They drove up to a huge, sprawling, white house. The front door was open, and a woman was silhouetted against the light.

Nick and the taxi-driver withdrew Dirk from the back seat and eased him up a flight of shallow steps. As they did so, he made an effort to stand upright. When they reached the door, he blinked at the woman and said, 'Hello, Mama.'

She was small and square, and dressed entirely in black. She was also breathing heavily, and her eyes were sparkling with anger. Looking over her head, Nick saw two other women standing in the hall, younger versions of her.

She pulled her son over the threshold. The two women

224

hurried forward to support him. She looked up at Nick, with neither friendliness or gratitude. 'You go now,' she said, and closed the door.

It was not until he had been driven back to the cheap hotel where he was renting a room that he realized the driver had not been paid. The fare took every cent he possessed.

When he arrived at the bar to start work the following evening, a grey Cadillac was parked outside. As he reached the door, a man in a chauffeur's uniform called him.

'Someone wants to see you.' He jerked a thumb towards the back of the Cadillac. Nick recognized the slumped figure in the Stetson, eyes hidden by glasses. He went to the window.

'Hi! Glad to see you. Hop in.' The white smile blazed.

'Can't,' Nick said. 'I'm on my way to work.'

'I wanted to thank you. You took me home, right?'

'Right.'

'Who paid for the cab?'

'I did.'

'What do I owe you?'

Nick told him, and accepted the wad of notes without protest.

'I'm really grateful,' the man said. 'I mean, it could have been serious . . . someone might have called the cops. It was bad enough as it was, when I got home.'

'Your mother?'

He nodded. 'And my sisters.'

'You live with them?'

'They live with me. Hey, what's your name?'

'Nicholas Garnier.'

'You aren't American, are you? There's something in the way you talk . . .'

'Half-French, half-American.'

'A mongrel, like me. I'm Mex-German.' He took off his glasses and rubbed the bridge of his nose. 'I think I'll

225

come in for a beer. Many people inside?'

Nick glanced through the door at the interior gloom. 'As far as I can see, two couples.'

'That's okay then.' He put the glasses back. With them, and the Stetson pulled low over his forehead, little of his face was visible. He turned to his driver. 'Want to take a couple hours, Harry? Pick me up here.'

He made his way towards the table he had sat at the previous night.

'What can I get you?' Nick said.

'A Coors.'

As Nick put it down, he said curiously, 'Why all the cloak-and-dagger stuff? You said last night that you were in disguise. Who're you hiding from?'

The young man's head jerked up. 'You don't know who I am?'

'Sorry. No.'

'I'm Dirk Chavez.'

It rang a bell. 'The actor?'

Chavez laughed. 'Hey, man, this is the best thing that's happened to me in weeks. To get out, and meet someone who doesn't recognize me. Makes me feel like a human being again. Sit down and have a drink.'

'I'll have a beer. Thanks. But I'm not allowed to sit at the tables.'

'Then I'll come to the bar.'

They talked, interrupted by not more than half-a-dozen customers, none of whom took any notice of the man in the Stetson sitting at the end of the bar.

Nick had read how Chavez had recently become a hot property in the film world, following performances in two cheaply-made movies that had been unexpected money-spinners. Now, he said, he was about to start work in a twenty-million dollar epic about Mexican immigrants which, it was hoped, would be a new *Grapes of Wrath*.

But he was not enjoying his current status as a teen-idol. 'Dios, those kids frighten me!' he said. 'Girls grabbing any part of you they can get hold of. I can't go into a shop or a theatre without there's a crowd. I've always liked to be by myself, just to amble, you know? Do whatever I felt like. Now I only go to parties with other movie-people. The rest of the time, I stay home or I find bars like this.'

'Home didn't look too bad,' Nick remarked.

'It's okay. But my mother and the rest of the family are always around. Ten of them. I got ten people entirely dependent on me!'

Because he said it with a smile, Nick didn't take the complaint too seriously. Later, he was to discover the choking tentacles his family had wound around Chavez.

His father, the son of a German mother and a Mexican father, had left his Mexican wife when Dirk, their oldest child, was fourteen. The family had lived in a house that was little more than a shack on the outskirts of Albuquerque, New Mexico. To try to make enough money to keep them, Dirk had moved into California to pick grapes, then fetched up in Los Angeles and become a waiter in a Mexican restaurant. He kept only a few dollars from his wages, sent every spare cent back to his mother.

One night, the Hollywood dream came true. A female studio executive spotted the young waiter's extraordinary good looks: the wide-set, vivid blue eyes, strong features and tall, strong body inherited from his half-German father, the smooth, coffee-coloured skin and straight black hair of his Spanish-Indian mother.

'They put me in a picture for my looks, and found I could act,' he said, without any trace of boastfulness. 'Suddenly, I was rich, and I couldn't leave Mama like she was, could I? I told her to join me in L.A. She was on the next plane – with the rest of the family. Carlos was married and out of work, so he brought Maria and their baby. Mama wanted my youngest brother to go to college here, and one of my sisters brought her husband and their kid, who's five, and then there's my second sister. She couldn't be left behind. I had an apartment near the beach, no way we could all fit in it. Mama said they wouldn't live in L.A. without me. They were strangers, and scared what might happen to them. She found the house, and before I knew it, we were all together. One big, not-so-happy family.'

'Don't you get on?'

'Sometimes. Sometimes not. We're Mexicans. We're noisy. We fight. We love each other. Hate each other.' He paused, and added wearily, 'Must be the German blood, but I'd like a quieter life.'

'Why don't you move into a place of your own?'

'I tried once. Mama was so upset, it made her ill, and she's got a weak heart. She said if I left, it would kill her. She's had a hard life. I gotta do what I can for her.'

At the end of the evening, he dropped Nick home in the Cadillac. After that, he came to the bar two or three times a week, would sit, unrecognized, and talk. They became friends, swapping life-stories, exchanging reminiscences.

Nick learned that Chavez was a lonely, unhappy young man, terrified that his bubble would burst and he and his family might find themselves back in the shack in Albuquerque. His sisters and brothers were constantly asking for money. His mother, possessive and jealous, watched him like a hawk, cross-questioning him about every aspect of his life. Mostly, he lied, telling her only what she wanted to hear, about his successes, his meetings with the Hollywood elite.

While he enjoyed acting, he hated his life away from the cameras. He had been taken on by a tough woman agent who told him how to behave, how to dress, what invitations to accept, even what women to sleep with.

'It's a fucking prison,' he said. 'They all treat me like I'm their personal property: you do as you're told, amigo, or we'll take away all that lovely money.'

He was increasingly using alcohol and drugs to escape, and confessed that he had been introduced to coke-sniffing at a party given by a much-married actress, where it was the norm. 'It's the greatest,' he said dreamily. 'For a while, the studio, my agent, Mama, the family, none of them seem to matter. You should try it, Nick.'

Nick shook his head. 'I'll go to hell in my own way, thanks.'

One night, he came into the bar late, and said abruptly, 'You ever done any acting?'

'Not seriously. I used to play about when I was a kid, imitating people, that sort of thing. And I did a stint as ASM in summer stock on the East coast last year. Went on stage a few times as an understudy.'

'I could fix a test for you at the studio. The guy who was playing my friend in the picture has to be replaced. You're the right type. It mightn't work out, but d'you want to try it?' He added, 'It'd be nice for me to have you around.'

Nick thought about it, then nodded. He didn't like bar-work and had been going to move on anyway.

He did not find out for some time the excitement his test had caused. His lean, clean-cut face, straight nose and wide, firm mouth contrasted effectively with Chavez's Aztec features and spectacular colouring; his sophisticated charm, the laughter always lurking behind his grey eyes, set off Chavez's combination of animal sexuality and small-boy uncertainty. And Nick, like Chavez, showed himself a natural actor, fitting effortlessly into the skin of the character he was playing.

For a while, he enjoyed the novelty of studio life. He didn't mind getting up at five o'clock in the morning and working until after dark. He liked having a chauffeur-driven car at his disposal and was dazzled, at first, by the glitzy parties to which he was invited. He was happy to take advantage of the attention paid him by pretty starlets on the make and by the discovery that older, established female stars were equally eager to take him to bed. 'I feel like Charlie let loose in the chocolate factory,' he told Dirk.

But he took none of it seriously, not even when he

learned that he was being hyped as the discovery of the year – because by then, he had decided that movie-making was a bore.

The magic had lasted exactly a month, then the grind of repetitive takes, hour after hour, mouthing the same words to achieve a few seconds screen-time, began to get him down.

Signed for more money than he had ever imagined being paid, he was unaware what respect his genuine indifference to potential riches and film-stardom won him.

Unlike Dirk, he had no financial responsibilities, and his only extravagances were a little red MGB and a more comfortable hotel-room. The rest of his money went into his bank-account and he was surprised by its size on the rare occasions when he checked his balance.

He got on well enough with the people he worked with, but some of them, obsessed by ambition, were unable to understand his cavalier attitude to his superiors. Although he was never late on the set, he refused, after the first novelty had worn off, to attend any social gathering not of his own choosing. He made no secret of the fact that he thought most Hollywood parties were a drag, and would not dance to the tune of the powerful, publicity-seeking hostesses – wives of producers, company chairmen, agents, lawyers – eager to capture the latest young lion.

Dirk Chavez was his one real friend. They worked well together, and it was clear from the early rushes that the empathy between them was like an electric current, which infected the other members of the cast with extra energy.

Off the set, they didn't see much more of each other than they had before, because Dirk did not dare to emulate Nick's independence. Neither was Nick interested in the coke-sniffing, drunken evenings in which Dirk increasingly indulged when he was not meekly attending career-enhancing functions to which he had been directed by the studio or his agent.

* * *

'What're you going to do when the picture's finished?' Dirk said.

They were lounging in armchairs in Nick's room, feet propped on the bed, beer to hand.

'No more movies, that's for sure.'

'Haven't they come up with a new contract?'

'Sure. They sent a pile of screenplays, too. I sent 'em back.'

'You're not signing?'

'No. It's been fun, and I'm grateful to you for getting me the chance. But one picture's enough.'

'What about the money? You'd give that up?' His voice was unbelieving.

'I've got enough money.'

'So what *are* you going to do?'

'What I've wanted to do ever since I arrived in the U.S. I'm going to take off in the car, and drive.'

'Going where?'

'Wherever the mood takes me. North. South. East. West. Oregon. New England. Louisiana. Texas. Arizona. New Mexico. The Middle West. Montana. Why don't you come with me?'

'Me? Dios, I couldn't! I've got about a month off, then I'm scheduled to start work again.'

'Come for a month. Think of the freedom, man! No nagging family or agents or directors. Stopping where we want, exploring off the beaten track. We'd be back in the real world again.'

'Freedom?' Dirk said bitterly. 'There's something you've forgotten, amigo. We're recognizable. How can you be free when perfect strangers believe they have the right to stare at you, interrupt your meal, ask you to write your name on bits of paper, even grab your balls to make sure they're in place?'

'No problem. We grow beards. You wear your shades, like you did when we met. Dye your hair blonde, if you like.'

231

'I'd have to bleach my skin, too.' In spite of himself, there was a dawning excitement in the blue eyes. 'I wonder . . . oh, hell, I couldn't leave Mama and the family.'

'Of course you could! For Christ's sake, they've been in L.A. for nearly three years. They know their way around. Let your brothers take over for a change. How long is it since you had a real holiday?'

'I took Mama back to Albuquerque eighteen months ago.'

'You don't take your Mama on a real holiday.'

Dirk looked at the Rolex his mother had given him for his last birthday (for which he had paid). 'Gotta go. I told Harry nine o'clock. Early call tomorrow.' At the door, he turned. 'I'll think about it, only don't say anything. If Mama found out, that'd be the end.'

Two months later, they took Highway One out of Los Angeles, on the first leg of the 400-mile route to San Francisco, two young men wearing jeans and shabby windbreakers over t-shirts. Dirk's eyes were covered by sunglasses, he was unshaven and his coarse black hair had been streaked blonde like a tiger's skin. Nick had grown a heavy moustache and was wearing steel-rimmed spectacles, giving him the look of a studious bandit.

He sang happily to himself as he drove the little MG out of the sprawling city, onto the road that wound up the Pacific coast. Dirk sat silently beside him, his face dark and brooding.

After a while, Nick said, 'So how did your Mama take it?'

'I didn't tell her. I left her a note. I'm feeling bad about it.'

'Changing your mind about coming?'

'Christ, I've been looking forward to it for weeks! But I'm worried about them. I've arranged for Mama to draw as much money as she wants. But it's going to be a shock. I hope it doesn't make her ill.'

'From what I've seen of your mother, she's tougher than you think. She'll get over it.'

'I suppose. And I'll keep writing to them. I'll write tonight. Maybe I'll call them, too.' He began to look happier.

'Didn't she suspect there was something up when you stopped shaving last week?'

'I said I was taking a rest between pictures. And I didn't have my hair dyed until this morning. I sort of wish I'd told her, but if I had . . .' He shrugged. 'Anyway, it's too late now.'

Within an hour, he had cheered up, and begun to enjoy himself. That evening, he called his mother and Nick heard an hysterical quacking from the other end of the line. But Dirk, fortified by two double Scotches, dealt with her firmly. 'She's okay,' he said as he cut her off. 'As long as she's angry, I know she's in good health. And she was very angry.'

Freed of his responsibilities, Nick found that he was good company, enthusiastic and naively eager for any new experience. He had an unexpected appreciation of the magnificent scenery they passed through and seemed to know instinctively when Nick didn't feel like talking. They had decided, in rejecting their lives in Hollywood, to stop over in cheap motels, and he was uncomplaining when their accomodations turned out to be less than comfortable.

As they drove, they talked, and Nick began to understand the strain under which he lived.

One day he said, 'Hey, man, you're a mongrel, too. So what do you feel, French or American? I mean, where do you belong?'

'Wherever I am. In France I'm French. Here, I'm American.'

'You talk American better than I do. D'you have a foreign accent when you talk French?'

233

'No. At home my father and I talk French or English as the mood takes us. Always have.'

Chavez sighed. 'I don't belong anywhere. When I go home now, I don't have friends. The guys I used to hang around with only want hand-outs. And I sure don't belong here. I'm a Spic. I look different from the Angelenos, and I talk different. I only went to school for three years so most everyone knows more than me. At the studio, they treat me like I'm someone, because I'm making money, but there's nothing *real* about it. I got the feeling that one day I'll wake up and find myself back picking grapes.'

'That's a crock of shit! These people need you.'

'You really think so?' His compulsion to be reassured was almost desperate. 'I mean, Christ, what would happen to the family?'

'I'm certain of it. Try kicking 'em in the teeth and watch how they come crawling back for more.'

'Maybe I'll do just that . . . one day.'

He was insatiably curious about Nick's upbringing, and loved to listen to him talk about Peter, La Belette and the Lion d'Or. And Lisa: his indignant reaction to the story of their enforced separation warmed Nick's heart.

They drove too fast, enjoying the wind that swept over the little open car, playing loud music on the stereo, everything from Mexican folk songs to Mozart. Sometimes, they drank too much. Dirk was usually a few glasses ahead of Nick, but it was no longer the desperate escape-drinking to which he had turned in Los Angeles. He drank because he was enjoying himself and the alcohol, he said, enhanced his enjoyment. As far as Nick knew, he kept off drugs.

Occasionally they picked up girls for over-night stands, sometimes spent an extra day or so in a town if the girls were worth it.

Dirk called himself John Smith and Nick called himself Oscar Steinhammer, and nobody recognized them.

In Arizona, when Dirk was at the wheel, they were

arrested for drunken driving, but a fatherly cop dried them out in a cell for the night and let them go the next morning.

Near Barstow, they had an encounter with Hell's Angels.

The road was wide, the traffic light, and Nick was driving when they heard the thunder of mechanized cavalry overtaking them. Great black shapes swept up and hemmed them in. Heads encased in black metal turned towards them, red holes emitting incoherent shouts appeared in hairy faces, they saw their own reflections in mirror-goggles. The little red car bucked and swerved as Nick avoided the bikes. Dirk was laughing, enjoying the challenge and the danger.

After twenty minutes, they reached a gas-station and bar and the Angels signalled the car to stop.

Two large shaggy men wearing filthy singlets decorated with swastikas sauntered towards them, while the rest of the herd sat astride their bikes and watched.

'Spanner under your seat,' Nick said quietly.

Dirk pushed his glasses up onto his head. 'Haven't had a fight since I left New Me-heeco,' he murmured cheerfully.

They could smell the Angels when they were still yards away, a mixture of grease, sweat, stale alcohol and tobacco. Nick braced himself.

As the men reached them, they pulled off their helmets, letting loose bushes of unkempt hair. One of them leant against the car and said admiringly: 'Hey, man, you sure know how to drive that little bug. What is it, anyway?'

A few minutes later, they were all drinking together in the bar, where a terrified proprietor was only too anxious to give them good service and get rid of them without having his source of income wrecked.

They stayed with the Angels for two days, rampaging through small towns, even sharing some of their women, with the owners' permission.

★   ★   ★

In San Francisco, Texas, Dirk fell in love.

They had arrived during the morning and spent the afternoon exploring. They found the Alamo, where an American detachment had been wiped out by Mexicans – Dirk proudly told Nick – in the 1830s, and were amazed how small the fort was. They strolled the River Walk, which ran alongside what had once been a sewer, but had been reclaimed and was now a clean, cool, curving waterway winding through the city. They drank coffee on a terrace edged with iron lace-work, and took a trip on a flat-bottomed paddle boat past historic buildings, rocky gardens and under graceful bridges.

After dark, they went to eat at a restaurant with windows overlooking the River Walk, from which they could watch the passage of families and young couples enjoying the cool evening, under fairy lights strung between the trees.

Donna was their waitress, a small, fair-haired girl who seemed too fragile to carry anything heavier than a coffee-pot, but balanced heavy trays with no apparent effort.

At first, she looked nervous as she served them, and confessed later that she had been frightened of their rough appearance.

As she relaxed and came back to their table to chat between serving other customers, Nick noticed that Dirk hardly took his eyes off her. She had a pale, almost translucent skin, huge blue eyes under dark brows, and full pink lips. Her fine, clean hair had been dyed platinum, and Dirk, in an unusual burst of poetic eloquence, told her it looked like moonbeams.

By the time they were drinking their coffee, it was after eleven, and the place had emptied.

Donna came to clear their table, and Dirk said, 'What time d'you finish?'

'Soon as you two leave.'

'Can I walk you home?'

236

She looked at him thoughtfully for a moment, then nodded. Ten minutes later, they were strolling off down the River Walk and Nick went back alone to their motel on the edge of town.

They stayed in San Antonio for nearly a week, and Dirk seemed dazed by what had happened to him. When Donna was on duty, he insisted on spending two or three hours in the restaurant, eating, or drinking beer or coffee. Whenever she was off-duty, they were together. Sometimes Nick went with them, and she showed them her town and took them to her tiny, walk-up apartment. She told them that she had come to San Antonio from Houston, because her divorced mother had remarried and she did not get on with her step-father. Otherwise she talked little about herself.

Watching them together, Nick wondered if she and Dirk ever really communicated. They seemed content to cling together in total silence. He could recognize her attraction to Dirk, a simple soul himself, but her drawling, little-girl voice and her breathless worship of the dominant male was not to his taste. Also, he suspected that there was a tougher streak hidden under the shyness and the wide, innocent eyes.

After five days, he was getting restless, and wanted to move on, but at first he restrained himself from pressing the point.

Finally, as Dirk prepared to leave the hotel to meet Donna, he said: 'Look, d'you want to split up? If you'd like to stay here with her, that's okay. Maybe we could meet somewhere later.'

Dirk hesitated. 'I'm crazy about that girl. I'm going to marry her, you know.'

'Does she know who you are?'

'No. I don't want her to fall for Dirk Chavez. She's gotta accept John Smith. He's the real me, anyway. But I want her to have time to think about it. I did suggest she might like to come with us . . .' He saw Nick's dismay.

'It's okay. She said no. She's got her job and driving long distances makes her car-sick. I've told her that I'll send for her to come to L.A. She's crazy to go there.' He grinned and slapped Nick's shoulder, 'So let's get back on the road, man!'

At the end of a month, they were in New York, now wearing full beards and moustaches, which made other disguises unnecessary, except for the shades without which Dirk never emerged.

'I hate to mention this,' Nick said, 'but aren't you due back at the studio in a couple of days.'

'I'm not going back yet.'

'I thought you were under contract . . .'

'I don't care. I'm having the best time I've ever had in my life, and I'm not giving it up yet. We've got an awful lot of these United States still to see. I wrote to Mama that I'd be away a while longer. She can tell the studio. It's my fucking picture, anyway. They can't start without me.'

'You sure this is what you want to do?'

'You said I should kick 'em in the teeth, and that's what I'm gonna do. They *need* me, right?'

In Central Park that night, they were attacked by three teenagers who demanded money.

One of them approached Dirk, knife in hand. Before he knew what happened, he was doubled up on the ground, clutching his groin, and screaming.

Without haste, Dirk removed his dark glasses, put them in his pocket and said, 'Next, please.'

The others moved forward, crouching. Nick, who had not fought another human-being since he was five years old, in kindergarten, stood beside Dirk, fists doubled like an old-time boxer.

His presence was unnecessary. The fight was short and vicious. Kicking, gouging, slashing the youths with the side of his hands, Dirk had them both on the ground, beside their friend, in less than a minute.

Awed, Nick said later, 'I've never seen anything like it. Where did you learn to fight?'

'I was a street kid. No rules of the ring where I came from. In our gangs the idea was to win any way you could. That way you stayed alive.'

When they reached Boston, Nick said: 'I'm ready for a change. How about we book into a decent hotel for a couple of nights?'

'Like this?' Dirk looked at their clothes, the jeans that were torn at the knees and frayed around the ankles, the dusty canvas boots, the worn t-shirts and ragged jackets. They had both grown their hair, and he had tied his back into a pony-tail with a piece of string. Nick's hung lankly to his shoulders.

'We'll buy some clothes and go to a barber. Shorter hair, keep the beards, but have them tidied. No one will recognize us.'

Two hours later, wearing slacks and sports jackets over cashmere sweaters, scarves tucked into their shirts, they walked into the foyer of the Boston Sheraton. Their old clothes were packed into overnight bags and their hair and beards had been neatly trimmed. Nick had resumed his steel-rimmed spectacles. Mr Smith and Mr Steinhammer were two respectable young businessmen from Los Angles, and their only variation from the norm was that they paid for their rooms in advance, in cash, not daring to use their credit cards.

On the way in, Nick had bought a Boston *Globe*. As Dirk was writing one of his daily letters to Donna, he sat by the window overlooking the Charles River, where scullers were moving their shells smoothly over the water, and opened the paper.

Two photographs on an inner page caught his eye. His own face and Dirk's were staring at him, under the headline: 'Have you seen these men?'

There was a long caption underneath: 'Mystery

surrounds the whereabouts of Hollywood stars Dirk Chavez and Nicholas Garnier.

'Having completed Chavez's latest film, *The Illegals*, which is already being tipped for an Oscar nomination, and in which Garnier played a supporting role, nothing has been seen of either man.

'Chavez's brother, Carlos, said yesterday: "We haven't spoken to Dirk for two months. He has written several letters, each from a different town. We think that he must be touring the United States with Garnier. We appeal to him to come home, or at least to call us, because his mother is very ill."

'It is understood that Chavez is being sued by his studio for breach of contract. He was due to start work on his new film several weeks ago.'

Two hours later, Dirk was in the air, on his way back to Los Angeles.

3

'Pity it had to end like that,' Ashton said. 'What did you do?'

'I went on travelling for a while, but it wasn't the same. Everything was kind of flat, so I made my way slowly back to L.A. I got there about two months after Dirk. We hadn't been in touch, though I'd written to him a couple of times.

'We arranged to meet in our old bar in Anaheim. I've never seen a man change so much in a short time. It was as though all his muscle had melted and his skin was sticking to his bones. His face was a skull and his eyes were like blue stones set in black holes. He wasn't even bothering with the shades any more. There was no need, no one would have recognized him.'

'AIDS? I knew a guy . . .'

'That's what the newspapers said . . . it wasn't long after Rock Hudson's death and AIDS was the flavour of the month. But it wasn't AIDS, it was heroin. He started off trying to be cheerful, then I got it out of him. What he'd always been afraid of had happened. His bubble had burst, and it was my bloody fault. If I hadn't persuaded him to come away with me, then told him to kick 'em in the teeth . . .

'He'd reached home just in time to be with his mother when she died. She'd had a stroke. His family put the blame entirely on him, said his absence had made her ill. He was overwhelmed with guilt. When he was at his lowest, he called Donna and asked her to come to him. She told him sorry, her husband, who was in the Navy, was

241

home on leave. That was the second disaster. The third was that the studio was suing him. A lot of people in Hollywood regard being sued on contract grounds as a sign of their success. Not Dirk. He was terrified of what would happen, especially as his brothers and sisters had been spending his money like drunken sailors. The press was hounding him, too, asking questions about me and about our trip, suggesting that there had been something off-centre about our relationship.

'So he'd done what he always did when he was stressed: escaped into drugs and alcohol. But this time he was shooting up and the habit was advanced.

'Finally, it was all too much for him. He was found dead in his bedroom, from a mixture of heroin and straight vodka. It might not have been intentional suicide, but I suspect it was.'

Ashton was silent for a moment, then he said quietly, 'No need for you to feel guilt. Sounds as though you gave him the happiest two months of his life before he died.'

'Maybe. But if I'd flown back with him, instead of being so fucking selfish, and going my own way, I might have helped.' He took a deep breath, then shrugged. 'Too late to think of that now.'

'That was when you wrote your book?'

'After I found out what people were saying, I felt the least I could do for him was put the record straight. It was therapy for me, too. Got rid of a hell of a lot of anger. I flew to Boston and took a beach house out on the Cape. It was winter and the place was almost deserted . . . this row of wooden houses, right on the beach, all closed up, except for mine. I could step out of my door onto the sand and walk for miles without seeing anyone. I wrote it in six months and sent it to a New York publisher I'd met in Los Angeles. He bought it.'

'And now you're working on Absalom?'

'Just starting.'

Ashton glanced at his watch. 'Hell, I'll have to go or I'll

242

miss the last Tube. Listen, I've enjoyed talking to you, and don't forget, if there's anything I can do to help . . . let me give you my address and phone number.'

He scribbled on a paper table-napkin, and handed it to Nick. 'I've got what's called a "studio." One room with a kitchen in the corner, and a bathroom. But you know what they say: better an attic in SW1 than a mansion in Streatham.'

'You're in SW1?' He remembered that the mysterious *A.M. aka A.M.* had an address in SW1. 'Where's that exactly? I don't know London very well.'

'It takes in Westminster, Victoria, Belgravia, Pimlico.'

'Ever heard of Lupin Street?'

'It's about half a mile from where I live, a back street with a few miserable shops and run-down terraced houses. Why?'

'Maybe there is something you could do, if you can spare the time. Ben had an address in his book, 41 Lupin Street. And the initials A.M. Lisa found them somewhere else, too. There's a guy who lives not far from the Absaloms' villa, Amyas Mahr. He and Ben never liked each other. She was curious – oh, hell, it'd probably be a waste of time.'

'I'll check it out,' Ashton said. 'I'd feel I was doing something for her. When are you going back to France?'

'Day after tomorrow, probably.'

'I might not be able to do anything before that. Tomorrow I have to go after a job at one of the studios, but I'll get onto it then.'

He reached for his wallet but Nick took the bill. 'It's mine. I owe you for saving me from a boring evening.'

'Well, thanks.' He raised a hand in farewell. 'I'll be in touch.'

4

There was nearly a column of A. Freemans in the London telephone book, and at nine o'clock the next morning Nick settled by Lisa's phone to work his way through them.

He hit pay-dirt on his eighth call when, after he asked for Mrs Alicia Freeman, a woman's voice said: 'She doesn't live here any more. Who is this?'

'I'm a – friend. Do you have an address for her?'

'Well . . . she's still in the nursing-home, as far as I know. The St James's.'

'She's ill?'

The voice was cautious. 'You could say that. Yes.'

'Do you know how long she's been there?'

'We bought her flat eight months ago. She'd already gone then.'

'Could you tell me where the nursing-home is?'

'Swiss Cottage. Off the Finchley Road.'

'Thank you.'

'Oh, no, Mrs Freeman hasn't been here for nearly six months,' the receptionist said.

'She's gone home? Do you have an address for her?'

The woman frowned. 'Do you mind telling me who you are? Why do you want her address?'

'A friend of hers asked me to look her up. My name's Nicholas Garnier.'

'Mrs Freeman had to be moved into a public ward in St Merriam's in Paddington. We were unable to keep her here.'

244

'Why not?'

'This is a private nursing-home, Mr Garnier. We have no Government subsidy . . .' Eyebrows raised, he waited for her to go on. She shrugged. 'I'm afraid it wasn't possible for Mrs Freeman to stay after the payments stopped, and we were unable to contact her son.'

'Sorry, I don't understand. I didn't even know she had a son.'

'Your friend didn't tell you?'

He shook his head.

She was a middle-aged woman with a large, soft face and shrewd blue eyes. She studied him for a moment, then said, 'Mrs Freeman was brought here a year ago, on her doctor's recommendation. Her son paid for a bed for the first three months. We never saw him again, neither did her doctor. We kept her on for an extra month, then we had to move her to St Merriam's.'

'You mean her son never came to see her?'

'A couple of times at the beginning, that's all.'

'Could you tell what's wrong with her?'

'She has Alzheimer's Disease.'

Alzheimers. Senile decay. Madness?

'If I went to St Merriam's, would I be able to talk to her?'

She spread her hands. 'Perhaps. I wouldn't like to say. While she was here, she had lucid periods, but she could have deteriorated.'

The hospital was a red-brick building behind a high wall. A middle-aged nursing sister whose uniform rustled as she walked conducted Nick through wide corridors with shiny linoleum floors and walls painted green to waist-height and porridge-cream to the ceiling.

Like most healthy people, Nick loathed hospitals and was regretting that he had come. The smell, compounded of disinfectant and over-cooked vegetables, was making his stomach heave.

The nurse paused outside a door and said, 'I can't guarantee how Mrs Freeman will receive you, Mr . . . Garnier, was it? She's going through a difficult period. But if you like to take the chance . . .'

She opened the door and the air was filled with noise: incoherent muttering, groans, sobbing, the occasional high-pitched scream.

His scalp prickled as he looked over her shoulder. The ward was filled with women, some lying still and corpselike in bed, others in chairs. One was wandering around, flapping her hands like birds' wings. Another was leaning forward with her head resting on a table, her eyes closed. A third was huddled on the floor in a corner with tears trickling down her cheeks. A miasma of faeces and decay overwhelmed the corridor smells.

The nurse led him towards the far end, where a woman with grey hair was sitting on a hard chair, bolt upright, hands resting on her rug-covered knees, eyes unfocused.

'Here's a nice young man come to visit us, Mrs Freeman. Say hello to him, like a good girl.'

Her eyelids flickered, but she made no other sign that she was aware of their presence.

The nurse patted one of the slack hands. 'Come on, dear. It's a friend. Mr Garnier. You remember him, don't you?' She looked up at Nick, and shrugged. 'Not much use, I'm afraid. She isn't with us.'

'Can I speak to her?'

'Go ahead. I'll leave you. Maybe you can get through.'

'Please don't go! I'll only be a moment.'

Recognizing his panic, she glanced at the watch that hung on her shelflike breast. 'I can stay for five minutes. You talk to her and I'll see to some of the other patients.'

She moved off to a bed nearby, talking soothingly to its occupant as she straightened sheets and lifted her to shake the pillows.

Nick forced himself to squat in front of Alicia Freeman so their faces were level. She had thin, ragged hair and her

246

mouth hung half open so he could see that several of her teeth were missing. Her skin was the colour of dirty dishwater. Her face was broad and flat and her eyes were a milky blue.

'Mrs Freeman, do you remember Benedict Absalom?' he said.

Although he was in her direct line of vision, her focus did not change.

He repeated: 'Ben Absalom, Mrs Freeman. Ben Absalom.'

He raised his voice on the last words, and her face altered. While the eyes remained blank, she screamed. As he stumbled to his feet, a stream of words in an unrecognizable language tumbled out. He could only catch the repetition of the name: 'Absalom!'

As suddenly as she had started, she fell silent, and the nurse hurried up. 'It's all right, dear. Settle down now. No more noise.' She patted the woman's shoulder and smoothed her rug. 'I really don't think you're going to be able to have a chat, Mr Garnier. She's like this: all quiet, then something will set her off. Sometimes she goes on talking for hours, only never anything you can understand.'

Shaken, feeling sick from the smells and the sight of the pathetic women, Nick followed her to the door.

'I'm sorry if I upset her,' he said.

'It wasn't you. We can never tell what does it.' She became confidential. 'You're the first visitor she's ever had.'

'She has a son. Hasn't he come to see her?'

'Never. And we haven't been able to find out where he is.' She led the way into the passage and closed the door behind them. Her voice was grim. 'People like him . . . once they get a parent in here, it's out of sight, out of mind. They ought to be ashamed of themselves!'

Outside, breathing deeply in the fresh air, he checked over the little he had learned. He had no doubt that Alicia

Freeman was the woman Ben had been supporting. But she was in a public ward, presumably maintained by the National Health Service. So what had happened to Ben's money?

There was still no hint of the reason why he had made the allowance. She was a foreigner, but the name Freeman did not give away her origins. Ben had spent much of his life travelling. He could have picked her up anywhere.

He decided to follow one more lead and, his A to Z Street Guide to London in hand, walked to the address he had found in the phone book.

It was a basement flat. He rang the door-bell. After a moment, the door was opened, on a chain, and a woman's voice said, 'Yes?'

'I'm sorry to bother you,' he said, 'I phoned earlier about Mrs Freeman. My name's Nicholas Garnier. May I speak to you for a moment?'

He was aware of suspicious eyes studying him, then the chain was removed. The woman who stood there was small, flat-chested, with greying hair. She was wearing a striped butcher's apron over her dress, and her feet were thrust into slippers.

'Yes?' she said again.

'I've been to see Mrs Freeman. I'm afraid she wasn't able to talk to me. Could you tell me where I can get in touch with her son?'

'Is he a friend of yours, too?'

'I've never met him. Actually, I hadn't met her, either.'

'You said you knew her.'

'Someone asked me to look her up. I'm sorry I misled you, but it seemed a bit too complicated to explain on the phone.'

'Well . . . you'd better come in, not that there's much more I can tell you, only my husband and me used to worry about her sometimes, and that man, her son, he's a bad lot . . .'

He followed her into a small sitting-room furnished with

a three-piece suite in cut velvet, a heavily-patterned carpet and brown wall-paper with red roses on it. A cat was occupying each of the chairs.

'Did you know her well, Mrs . . . ?'

'Longmate. No. He'd already sent her away when we bought the flat. But she'd been ill for a long time before that. This place . . . it looked as though it hadn't ever been cleaned. Such a shame, but we saw what a nice place it could be . . . and it was cheap enough at forty-five thousand. He seemed to want to get rid of it quickly.' She stopped and looked at him nervously. 'Oh, dear, I'm talking too much, aren't I? As if you'd be interested in all this . . .'

'Do you know where I could find her son?'

'He came a few times after he left, that's how I knew about her, so I went to see her once in the nursing-home. Only I couldn't really, you know, communicate with her. She just sat and stared at me, so there didn't seem any point in going again. But my husband and me didn't like him at all. We always thought he neglected her. The neighbours said he only ever came here to see her for a few minutes about once a month.'

'What does he do? Perhaps I could contact him at work.'

There was a brief pause. 'You're sure you're not a friend? Well, actually, he never mentioned having a job.' She leant forward confidentially and lowered her voice. 'I've heard that he's been in prison. My neighbour told me he was caught breaking into a house in Highgate once, and another time he pretended to be an antique dealer and robbed a poor old woman of all her valuables.'

'He must have an address, though,' Nick said patiently.

'I suppose so, but I don't know what it is. For the first few months after we moved in he used to call for his mother's letters – or rather, one letter. That was all she ever got until a few weeks ago. One letter a month. We used to wonder about it. It was from the local NatWest

Bank. Then after a while he asked us if we'd readdress them to a Post Office box number in West One, to save him having to come to the flat. So we did. Now I think of it, there hasn't been a bank letter this month. It was always regular, end of the first week. Funny, that. There was this other one, though, a long envelope from some firm of solicitors. We sent it on. Apart from that, I'm afraid I can't help you.'

He refused her offer of tea, thanked her and left, followed by her exhortations to tell that young man, if he ever found him, to look after his poor mother.

The visit had not been a total waste of time, he decided. At least now he could make an educated guess at what had happened to Ben's money: it had gone straight into the pocket of Mrs Freeman's son.

But for the moment, finding out anything further about her would take more time than he had available. He decided to spend the rest of the day on research into Ben's background, and fly home tomorrow.

The news-agency library was on the fourth floor of one of the diminishing number of Fleet Street buildings which retained its newspaper identity.

For a fee, the librarian told him, a researcher would bring him the files he required.

After a short wait, he settled at a table hidden behind a green metal filing cabinet and spread out several large brown envelopes, each stuffed with cuttings, each dealing with a different aspect of Ben Absalom's life. There was ABSALOM, Benedict: personal; ABSALOM, Benedict: career; ABSALOM, Benedict: reviews; ABSALOM, Benedict: family – and here there were cross-references: See also, ABSALOM, Lisa; STEWART, Mark (deceased), STEWART, Joanna. The librarian had brought him these, too.

He worked his way steadily through them. The newspaper cuttings had been neatly scissored, marked with their date of publication, and source, and on each, Ben's name had been marked in fluorescent highlighter. Many were yellowed with age.

Read in sequence, they formed a record of his life: his early successes, the increasing enthusiasm of critics, his commissions to paint celebrities all over the world, his appearances on tv. There were stories about the young Absaloms, Ben and Joanna, with pictures of their luxurious London apartment and the villa in France. There were admiring profiles of Ben, a tribute to his ability to charm his interviewers. There were more recent stories, describing his illness, bewailing the possible end of an unmatched talent and, finally, the reports of his death, and obituaries.

The envelope devoted to ABSALOM, Lisa, was almost as thick as Ben's, and he sat looking at the pile of cuttings for several minutes before starting to read them.

He remembered a letter from Peter while he was in America which had reported her early success in TV and added that, according to Jo, she was not finding it easy to adjust to having become a public figure. He wondered whether she realized that here, in this dusty library, and in others across the country, her life was set out in print for anyone to investigate. As he began to read, he felt a sense of intrusion he had not suffered on behalf of Ben, who had loved publicity.

The early reports dealt with the new soap, *Families*, reviews, and profiles of the cast. There were several devoted entirely to Lisa and it was as though he was reading about a stranger, certainly not the cool, unbending young woman he had met in La Belette. This was an actress, gushingly described as 'charming,' 'ebullient,' 'outgoing,' 'effervescent,' 'vivacious,' even 'winsome.' Winsome, for God's sake! It seemed that she had rapidly learned to project the image required by her star status.

Then came reports of her 'fairy-tale' romance with film-set designer Simon Ashton and their subsequent marriage.

One paragraph in a long feature from a Sunday newspaper, illustrated by a photograph of the two of them, cheek to cheek, smiling into the camera, caught his attention: 'Simon and Lisa met when they were booked into adjoining seats in an aircraft bringing them back to London from Hollywood. She had been on vacation, visiting friends, he had been discussing designs for a forthcoming production. It was love at first sight. Now, less than two months later, they are married.'

The library was warm, but Nick felt suddenly chilled as he looked at the date on the cutting. Two months before that, Lisa had come to the house in which he was staying in Hollywood, and what she had seen had ended any possibility of renewing their friendship . . .

He remembered how he had sat, slumped over the table in his tiny apartment in Bel Air, trying to recall details of the party the previous night.

He was contemplating his mug of strong black coffee, wondering whether he could swallow it without throwing up, when his land-lady, Monica Martensen, had come into the apartment, without bothering to knock. As usual.

He looked up at her blearily. She was dressed in a floating pink garment frilled around the neckline, to hide the loose skin below her jaw, frilled around the too-short hem, revealing her aging knees. Her bright blonde hair fell in waves to her shoulders and her eyes were heavily outlined in black, the lids deeply purple. Fluorescent pink, painted over the outlines of her lips, enlarged them to a pout.

He shuddered. She looked like a marshmallow and marshmallows had always made him sick.

While she was pouring herself a cup of coffee, uninvited, he wondered, not for the first time, why he had let himself become involved in this situation.

On the set of *The Illegals*, playing his mother, Monica had seemed a reasonable enough human being, with a professional attitude towards her work. The younger members of the cast had been no more than mildly amused by her affectations and the way in which, at the end of each day, she hurried to transform herself from the drab woman she was playing, back into a semblance of the star she had been a quarter-of-a-century earlier.

Before he had left on his travels, she had told him that if he ever needed accommodation, she had an apartment over her garage which she would be delighted to rent to him.

He had remembered the offer when he returned to L.A. Tired of hotels, he had contacted her and moved in. Within a week, he found that on top of his concern for Dirk Chavez, he was having to deal with an importunate woman nearly thirty years his senior who, it became clear, had set her sights on him as at least her lover, if not her fifth husband.

She dropped into the habit of arriving in the apartment from her lush, sprawling ranch house each morning to share his breakfast. She told him how lonely she was, how many ways she knew to make a man happy, how her investments meant that her next husband would want for nothing. She tried to give him expensive presents, which he refused, but because he was sorry for her, he managed to hide his increasing distaste.

He had already decided to look for other accommodation when Dirk was found dead.

Overwhelmed with sadness and guilt, he had drunk steadily for two days. Then he went to Dirk's funeral and listened, frozen, while Dirk's sisters stood by the graveside, the coffin barely covered with earth, and screamed that the tragedy had been his fault.

When he returned home, he had been trapped by Monica before he could reach the sanctuary of his apartment. There was a party going on, and she insisted that he must make an appearance.

He began to drink again, to drown the memory of the women's accusations.

The party spread from the house into the garden. In the kaleidoscope of his hung-over memory, he saw couples entwined . . . silver spoons and white powder . . . endless champagne . . . pretty young starlets and paunchy studio executives stripping off and diving into the swimming-pool. He saw himself trying to escape Monica's implacable pursuit, missing his footing on the sun-deck and stumbling into the pool . . .

Monica's capped teeth gleamed as she settled opposite him. 'Wasn't it a lovely party, darling? And there'll be so many, many more after the wedding.'

He swallowed a mouthful of scalding coffee. 'After the what?'

Her face was hardened. 'You remember, darling. You said I was the only woman who looked after you, and you wished I'd do it forever. So I said I would.'

She leant across the table and kissed him. A heavy floral scent enveloped him.

'Monica . . . Jesus, I was drunk!'

'Oh, you certainly were, my dear! I can't imagine what your little friend from England must have thought, but we soon got rid of her, didn't we?'

'I don't know what you're talking about.'

'You've forgotten? She turned up at the door, Lisa something. Asked for you, so I took her up to the bedroom, only you didn't seem to recognize her.'

'The bedroom? I was . . . ?'

'Lying on the bed, starkers, darling, and so were those two naughty girls who had helped you upstairs after you fell in the pool. They'd taken your wet clothes off. Honestly, I don't know who brought them, but there they were, shameless, one on either side of you on the bed, all dripping wet on my lovely sheets.'

'Oh, Christ! *Did you say Lisa?*'

She giggled. 'She stood there, staring, then you told her to get her clothes off and join the party!'

His hands were shaking so he could hardly lift the mug

to his mouth. 'What . . . what did she do?'

'Didn't say a word. Went downstairs, back to her taxi. I just had time to invite her to the wedding, only I don't expect she'll come.'

Hang-over forgotten, he had pulled her to her feet, pushed her out through the door and locked it behind her.

He spent half an hour telephoning various hotels, but Lisa was not registered anywhere. Finally, he had driven to LAX and discovered that she had left for London on a TWA flight half an hour earlier. The flight on which she must have met Ashton.

He wrote to her four times over the next two months, apologizing, trying to explain his unhappiness that night. He telephoned her in London. As soon as she heard his voice, she hung up, without a word. Then he received his letters back, bundled up in brown paper, unopened.

After a blazing row with Monica, during which he told her savagely that older women had never turned him on and he would as soon marry his own grandmother as her, he left the apartment.

In revenge, she had begun to circulate vicious stories about his relationship with Dirk Chavez, which soon reached the newspapers. The Chavez family added their fuel to the fire with accusations about his malign influence over Dirk.

Even now, in the impersonal surroundings of the library, he shivered at the memory of that time.

In the peace of Cape Cod, as he was writing his epitaph to Dirk, he had eventually come to terms with the knowledge that he had little hope of any future relationship with Lisa. Thinking back on what she must have seen in that room: the naked women, flanking him on Monica's huge shell-shaped bed, he had not been surprised by her coldness when they met near the phoenix tree. But at the same time, he had been – and was still – aware of anger: at

255

least she might have given him a chance to explain.

He turned back to his cuttings, and came to the first gossip-column rumours of the Ashtons' separation and imminent divorce.

Then he was shocked by a headline: SIMON ASHTON ARRESTED.

The report described how Ashton, who was currently being divorced by *Families* star Lisa Absalom, had been charged with having had unlawful intercourse with a fifteen-year-old boy. Found guilty, he was sentenced to a brief spell in prison.

The muck-raking newspapers then had a field day, with stories hinting at orgiastic parties with young boys in the Ashtons' Hampstead flat. Most of them gleefully pointed up the contrast in the private lives of Lisa and the innocent girl she played in the tv series. One reporter traced three men who claimed that they'd had affairs with Simon during his marriage.

Two final cuttings announced Lisa's dismissal from the cast of *Families*, and Ashton's release from prison.

Nick took a deep breath and sat back in his chair. He felt a savage anger. How could Ashton have married Lisa, then dragged her into this squalid scandal? He was disgusted with himself for having been conned into actually liking the man. And how could Lisa bring herself to stay in contact with him after what had happened?

After a few moments he shrugged. His life and Lisa's had split apart too long ago for any point of contact to remain. The more he found out about her, the more he realized that she was no longer the girl he had known.

He turned with relief to the last envelopes.

The identity of STEWART, Joanna, was obvious, but who was STEWART, Mark (deceased)? He couldn't recall ever having heard Jo mention any family.

STEWART, Mark's, envelope contained only a few cuttings, reports of a tragedy in a house in Maida Vale, when Mark, aged eight, had been accidentally burned to death after falling into an unguarded fire. One story included the paragraph: 'Mark's step-father, Carl Costain, thirty-eight, could not explain the accident. He said that Mark was terrified of being burned and never went near a fire. The only other person in the room at the time was his younger sister, Joanna, five.'

Was the writer hinting that Joanna might have caused her brother's death?

There was a copy of the same story in STEWART, Joanna, plus another, dated fourteen years later, reporting the wedding of Joanna Stewart to Benedict Absalom. There was no mention of her brother.

Finally, a more recent cutting from a newspaper published in South London recorded the death of wealthy local resident Carl Costain, whose wife had died in a car accident some years previously. Again, no mention of the children.

Puzzled, Nick reread the reports. He thought back over the years he had known Jo. She never spoke of her family and had no photographs of them. He remembered hearing her once say lightly, in answer to a question from Lisa: 'I didn't have a childhood, darling. My life began when I married Ben.'

He was curious. Who were the Costains? What had happened to her between the death of her brother and her marriage to Ben? But did he have any right to pry into her past?

Telling himself defensively that her life was as important to his research as Ben's, he reread the stories for the third time. The children's mother and step-father were dead. The only other name given was that of an au pair, Sandra Ickes, nineteen, of Stoke Carrington, Devon. She had been in the house at the time of the fire, but had reached the room too late to save Mark.

What were two kids doing, unsupervised, in a room with an unguarded fire? The more he thought about it, the more questions occurred to him. His mind worried at them as he walked out into Fleet Street, picked up a taxi and returned to Hampstead.

With his investigation into the mystery of Alicia Freeman at a dead end, for the moment at least, he had another evening to fill. More for something to do than because he expected any success – God, the accident had happened nearly forty years ago! – he called directory inquiries, and discovered that there was an Ickes, R.P. still listed in Stoke Carrington.

Dialling the number, he told himself that if his inquiries revealed nothing relevant to his book, Jo need not know about them.

A woman's voice with a rounded Devonian burr informed him that she was Mrs Ickes, and, yes, Auntie Sandra was still alive, and lived on a converted barge called the *Pollyanna* on the Thames near Richmond Bridge.

A few minutes later, he was on his way to Richmond.

PART SIX

1

For a change, a weak sun shone on the Riviera. The day was warm and humid, but rain-clouds still hung over the Mediterranean. The hill behind the villa was a wall of mud. Because the ground could no longer absorb the water, it was striped with khaki-coloured streams which were carrying the mud down the hill, through the iron bars of the villa's fence and onto the grass, which was already sodden.

Jo and Lisa were taking advantage of the respite from rain to sit on the terrace by the pool, sheltered from the paparazzis' prying telephoto lenses by the high, curving wall that surrounded it.

Lisa was wearing a black and white bikini, sitting with her face upturned to the sun.

Jo had a book on her lap, but she was not reading. She stood up, and moved restlessly around the terrace, pausing to pick dead leaves off a tub of geraniums. 'I never thought I'd feel claustrophobic in this place, but it's like being under siege,' she said.

'I know. I keep wondering what's going on in the village, what the police are doing, if they've found out anything . . . but at least the press aren't ringing the bell any longer. Peter said Berenger has stopped that.'

Lisa pulled a towelling robe around her as a cloud shrouded the sun. 'More rain coming. London's sunnier than the Riviera these days. I wonder . . .' She stopped.

'You wonder what?'

'Nothing much. It was thinking of London . . . I was

wondering what arrangements Nick has made with his publisher.'

'I want to see him as soon as he gets back.'

'Have you decided about the biography?'

'I'll have to allow it, I suppose. I mean, what can I do to stop him if he's determined? At least I can trust Peter to make sure he doesn't write anything to hurt us – or Ben.'

Involuntarily, Lisa said: 'Peter's still in love with you, Jo.'

Normally, Jo retreated from any discussion that involved her own emotions, but after a moment's hesitation, she said, 'I believe he is. And I'm sorry about it.'

In for a penny, Lisa thought. 'Why? You're free now.'

'I'm – fond of him. But I'm *not* free. He asked me to marry him just before I left for London. He said, not yet, of course, but when I was ready. I told him I would never be ready.'

Again, Lisa said, 'Why? And what's this about not being free?'

'I owed Ben so much . . . I still owe him so much. I've said it before . . . it's as though he's still here, with everything I do revolving around him – around his memory, now. How could I marry Peter, feeling like this? It wouldn't be fair.'

'It's too soon to think about it, but time goes on, darling, and if I know Peter, he won't change.'

Jo's voice sharpened. 'I'd be grateful if you'd put the whole thing out of your mind. Imagine what the police would think if they suspected there was anything between Peter and me. I couldn't bear it if suspicion fell on him. We're friends and, I hope, always will be. But that's all.'

The door-bell jangled through a silence.

It was Peter. As he greeted Jo, kissing her lightly on each cheek, Lisa remembered with shame her brief suspicion of him the previous day. He was a good man, understanding, generous and perceptive. If Jo would only allow him the opportunity to wean her from her obsession with Ben . . .

Jo was looking at him questioningly. 'Any news?'

'One good thing. The gentlemen of the press have gone.'

'All of them?'

'A dam has burst north of Genoa. There are floods, people have been swept away, houses inundated. It happened a couple of hours ago. As news, we have been over-taken.'

'I'm sorry for the Genoese, but thank God for that. Will they come back?'

'Who knows? In the meantime, for a change of scene, I hope you will both come and have lunch with me at home. Jean-Louis is preparing us a picnic.'

Lisa said promptly, 'We'd love to.'

'I'm not sure I want to go through the village,' Jo said. 'Being stared at . . . knowing the speculation.'

Peter took her hand. 'Everyone is on your side, my dear. You're one of them, and they're closing ranks. None of them believe you had anything to do with Ben's death. At first, when they didn't understand what was going on, they talked to the police. Now, they won't open their doors. Georgette was locking the shop as I came past, because she saw Molinard and Demazin on their way towards her. She won't even let Pierre-Luc out to sit on his bench. She says their questions upset him.'

Lisa lay back in an upholstered lounger on the terrace overlooking Peter's olive grove. Their lunch had been leisurely, and it was already mid-afternoon. The air was warm and humid. The sun, intermittently covered by the gathering clouds, sparkled momentarily on the little river that bordered the property.

'After the past few days, this is heaven,' she sighed. 'Nobody cooks like Marie and Jean-Louis. One of their meals makes everything seem right with the world. Poissons grillés, a *Niçoise*, figs, perfect cheese. Some picnic!'

They had carefully avoided any mention of the police and even Jo was looking less strained. She was perched on the terrace wall, leaning against one of the columns that rose on each side of the shallow steps leading up from the drive. Wearing a turquoise cotton skirt, a tightly-belted white shirt and Greek sandals with thongs tied around her ankles, she looked, Lisa thought, no more than thirty. Only the deep shadows under her eyes hinted at her disquiet.

As they left the villa before lunch she had shrunk into the back of Peter's car, trying to make herself invisible.

In the event, there had been few people in the street, since it was past mid-day. There were visitors on the terrace of the Lion d'Or, sitting under the vines with glasses of wine in front of them, but the bar, as far as Lisa could see, was almost empty.

When she had commented, Peter said, 'Custom's fallen off. The men are all going straight home for lunch, avoiding the *flics*.'

'How about the restaurant?'

'That's crowded with tourists every day. Jean-Louis told me they all want to know where Ben died, and which is his house. The locals take a delight in steering them in the wrong direction. Yesterday an English couple followed the instructions they were given and ended up trudging three kilometres along the road to St-Tropez.'

Now, pouring brandies for each of them, he looked up at the sound of a car, then groaned. 'It's the Mahrs. Jo . . . would you like to avoid them? Go inside and I'll get rid of them as quickly as possible.'

She shook her head. 'I can't go on hiding. I'll have to face people sooner or later.'

As usual, Amyas left Ona to struggle out of the car unaided. He came up the steps, arms outstretched, and embraced an unresponsive Jo. 'My dear girl, what a lovely surprise! How *are* you? You look, of course, magnificent as always. No one would ever know . . .' Even he realized

264

that he was about to be less than tactful, and changed course: 'Peter, a delightful and unexpected gathering. Lisa, beautiful child . . .'

'Come and sit near me, Ona,' Jo said. 'I haven't had a chance to say thank you for the cake you brought me after Ben died. It was good of you.'

'It wasn't much. I couldn't think of anything . . .' Her voice trailed off as she sat uneasily on the wall, her legs ungracefully splayed under the chintzy dirndl skirt that sagged over her thin hips. Dangling ear-rings made of wire were an incongruous accessory.

'It was the least we could do,' Amyas boomed. 'At such a time, one needs to know one's friends.'

Lisa met Jo's eyes and saw her mouth twitch as she repeated, 'It was a kind thought.'

He took the thanks to himself with a majestic nod, settled in a chair, and leant forward: 'This is especially well met, Joanna, because I have some wonderful news for you. Dominic Partridge has decided to found a museum which will be dedicated to Ben's memory! What do you think of that? His own collection will form its nucleus, and I am to be its curator!' He paused, awaiting applause which did not come.

After a moment, Jo said politely: 'How interesting. I didn't realize Mr Partridge owned enough paintings to fill a museum.'

'Increasing the collection will be part of my work – I may say, from now on, my life's work. Dominic has given me *carte blanche* to buy as many of Ben's paintings as I can. The work of lesser artists will fill the gaps until the collection is complete.'

There was a moment's silence, then Lisa said, 'What are you proposing to call the museum?'

'Naturally, since Dominic is behind the scheme, it will bear his name.' Hurrying on, he turned back to Jo. 'My dear, I can offer you whatever price you ask, within reason, for memorabilia: Ben's easel, note-books, brushes, palettes, old tubes of paint.' His small eyes looked into a distance full of promise. 'We envisage, at the entrance, a life-size figure of Ben, of a quality equal to those in Madame Tussaud's, brushes in hand, wearing his paint-spattered smock, his shirt and trousers, even his shoes. Original, no? And that's not all . . .' There was another impressive pause. 'Dominic is prepared to make you a generous offer for the villa, for that is where he proposes to house his museum: in the home where Ben lived and worked for so many happy years.'

Under her breath, Lisa whispered: 'I don't believe this!'

Amyas did not hear, neither did he appear to be aware of Peter's appalled expression. His eyes were fixed on Jo's impassive face. 'We intend to create a shrine to Benedict Absalom!'

She rose and brushed down her skirt. 'But not, I'm afraid, in my villa. What you and Mr Partridge do elsewhere is your own business, Amyas. But the Villa Mimosa belongs to me, and I have not the slightest intention of selling it. Neither will I hand on Ben's old clothes, nor what you call "memorabilia". His reputation doesn't need any tasteless displays.'

Amyas's beard quivered. 'Ben's genius transcends family considerations. We owe it to him to create a suitable memorial!'

'Your museum seems to be intended for the glorification of Mr Partridge, not Ben, and I can assure you that would not appeal to him.'

'But I told Partridge you would be honoured . . .'

Her voice was still pleasant. 'You were wrong. Peter, I think it's time we went home.'

Peter moved briskly towards the steps. 'I'll bring the car round. Amyas, Ona . . .'

Amyas's face was thunderous as he went to his car. Jamming his great belly under the steering wheel, he started the engine without waiting to see whether Ona had followed.

As she scuttled past Jo, she whispered: 'I'm sorry . . .'

'The man's mad,' Lisa said as they drove towards La Belette. 'Can you imagine anything more ghastly than having the villa turned into the Partridge Museum, with that superannuated pop-singer acting the art-patron – and a wax figure in Ben's clothes at the front door?'

'It won't be,' Jo said. 'No one can force me to sell. Let's forget it. Amyas isn't to be taken seriously. I'm sorry for Ona. She was obviously embarrassed.'

'He must be a trial to her,' Peter said. 'Incidentally, the other day I dropped in to see old Jean Sudre, who used to own the timber-yard. He knew Amyas in Ste-Maxime years ago. Amyas was cagey about his background even then, but Jean told me that Ona's name used to be Rona. Amyas made her change it because he didn't think Rona had enough style.'

Lisa laughed. 'If he wanted style, he should have changed more than her name. I've never seen such a defeated-looking woman. Simply putting up with Amyas must use up all her energies. I must say, I'd like to know more about him . . .'

Jo interrupted her: 'There's Claudette Dorsey. Would you stop a minute, Peter?'

He pulled up beside the girl, who was walking slowly, her head down, away from the Lion d'Or. Lisa looked at her more closely than she had done when they were in the restaurant. She was wearing a tight brown dress in some cheap, shiny material that outlined her voluptuous figure, but her shoulders were drooping and her full lower lip was out-thrust sullenly.

Jo put her head out of the car window. 'Claudette, I'm sorry not to have seen you lately. I'm probably going to need some extra help in the house pretty soon. Would you . . . ?'

The girl stared at her, then spat out the words: 'I wouldn't help you if you were dying!'

She began to run, wobbling on her high heels, away

from the car along the rough packed-earth pavement.

There was silence for a moment, then Peter snapped: 'That girl has just lost her job.'

'Her job?' Jo said.

'She's been waitressing in the Lion d'Or. She told me you didn't need her anymore and she was desperate for something to do. I was sorry for her.'

'Ben made me fire her.' Jo sighed. 'I expect she was in love with him. She was very angry when I told her. She came back to see Ben on the morning of the day he died. I didn't talk to her, but I heard him shout, "We've told you! You're fired! Get the hell out of here, and don't come back."'

'Did she obey him?'

'Yes. I didn't see her again. I'm sorry for her, too.'

'She looked well able to take care of herself,' Lisa said.

'She hasn't had an easy life: her father worships her, but he still treats her like a child. He won't let her go out at night, drives off any boyfriends. She told me once that her only free time is when he's working.'

Lisa said, 'You don't think she could have followed Ben to Le Mur that day? She was angry . . .'

'Never! You heard what she said. I seem to be the one she's angry with.'

When they reached the villa, Peter said, 'I won't stay. I'm going to call in at the Dorseys' place and pay Claudette off. I don't want her in the restaurant again.'

'Peter, give her another chance,' Jo began. 'She didn't . . .'

He shook his head. 'Don't worry, my dear, I'll see she doesn't starve. I've been on the verge of firing her for some time. She's inefficient and the Mazeaus don't like her. In any case, she was only taken on temporarily.'

Lisa lingered at the car. 'Heard from Nick?' she said casually.

'I'm expecting him back today. Shall I tell him to call you?'

She shrugged. 'Don't bother. I expect he'll be in touch if he has anything to say.'

As his car moved down the drive, she pressed the button that opened the automatic gates.

Accelerating back to La Belette, Peter did not see the figure that hurried from the bushes outside, and squeezed through the opening before the gates closed.

'There's a storm coming up.' Lisa looked out at the darkening sky. 'Lovely! I haven't seen a Mediterranean storm for years.'

There was a flash of sheet lightning, followed by thunder. Heavy clouds cut the light as though curtains had been drawn, and the first drops of rain fell. Wind began to lash the trees. Within seconds, the lightning and thunder were almost continuous and the terraces were awash.

The two women stood at a window beside the front door, but the rain was so heavy that visibility was restricted to a few metres. After a minute Lisa said, 'I feel like a good old-fashioned cup of tea. How about you?'

'There's some Earl Grey in the larder.'

Jo followed her into the living-room. As she reached the archway that led from the hall, she saw a movement, a reflection in the oval mirror that hung facing the window. A man, his outlines blurred by the rain, but unmistakable, was on the terrace, peering into the room. A moment later, he melted back into the darkness.

The self-control which was a habit with her came to her aid. She moved calmly towards the kitchen area where Lisa was standing by the sink, filling the kettle.

Knowing that they were as visible as though they were on a stage, Jo said softly: 'Go on with what you're doing, and remember you're an actress. Behave normally. There's a man outside, watching us.'

Lisa's eyes widened, but she did not move. 'What do we do?'

'You go into my room. The shutters are closed and

269

there's a phone beside my bed. He won't be able to see you. Call Peter at the Lion d'Or. The *gendarmerie* is just next door. He can tell them, and he might get here more quickly than they do.'

Lisa strolled out of the room, with no sign of tension.

Jo plugged in the kettle and stood, leaning against the bar, her eyes on the mirror. Once again she caught a furtive movement. He was going around the house, possibly to check whether there was anyone else inside.

The villa was vulnerable to intruders. Once the fence was breached, the huge glass windows could be easily smashed. Years ago Ben had installed a burglar alarm which linked up to the *gendarmerie*, but since his paintings had been sold, they had become careless about setting it.

Lisa came back as steam spouted from the kettle. 'Peter's on his way. Have you seen anything else?'

'He's gone towards the studio.'

Less than five minutes passed before the entry-bell rang. Peter's car skidded to a halt on the wet drive. In the distance, they heard the wah-wah of a police-car.

As it swept in, the intruder, warned by the siren, slipped out through the opening, and made his way towards a small car which was hidden in the shelter of a stand of trees a few hundred metres below the villa. In the roar of the storm, nobody heard him start its engine and drive off towards Cotolin.

The house came to life. Peter dashed up the steps, followed by Serge Berenger, Molinard and Demazin.

There were quick questions and answers and Jo indicated the direction she had seen the dark figure taking. The men spread out through the grounds. Their flash-lights hardly penetrated the sheets of rain, but lightning flashes intermittently lit the area like floodlights.

Twenty minutes later, they straggled back, soaked to the skin.

'There's no sign of anyone.' Molinard took off his coat and a shower of drops fell on the tiled floor. 'You're quite sure it was a man you saw, Madame?'

'Quite sure. He was looking through the window into the hall, then he went around the house.'

'It could have been the movement of trees.'

'It wasn't.'

'We have inspected your fence. There's no sign of a ladder having been used, and the bars are so slippery from the rain that they're impossible to climb.'

'Couldn't he have got in before the rain started?'

'Do you have any idea why someone would want to break in?'

'Perhaps a newspaperman . . .'

'They have all left.' His hostility was as undisguised as it had been during her interrogation.

'Commissaire, I am not making this up. A man was on the terrace!'

'He's certainly not here now,' he said irritably. 'Demazin!'

Berenger let the senior officers reach the door, then said softly: 'He is angry, Madame, because he gets no further with his investigation. The Commissaire has a reputation to keep up – he does not like failure. I'll see them off, then I'll come back and keep watch tonight.'

'No need for that,' Peter said. 'I'll be staying.'

'No, Peter . . .' Jo began.

'Yes.' His expression forbade argument, and she fell silent.

When Berenger had gone, she started again: 'There's really no need . . .'

For the first time, he spoke to her with anger. 'I am not going to leave you here with the possibility of some stranger loose in the grounds. I doubt that we could have missed him, but if he got in once, he could do it again. If you don't want me inside, I'll spend the night in the car.'

'Don't be silly! If you insist, you must use the spare room.'

* * *

At three o'clock the next morning, Jo's nightmare returned.

Curled in a corner of her cell, she saw Markie's little body surrounded by flames, and heard her stepfather's voice: 'You murdered your brother . . .' And she heard Markie's screams.

A man was kneeling beside her bed, his arms around her, and she realized that the screams had been her own. She clung to the lean, strong body and felt the comfort flowing from him. Slowly, she relaxed, but when he drew away, she whispered, 'No, Ben,' and pulled him close.

2

Jo's body was heavy, her mind still half asleep, reluctant to accept the new day. Outside the window she saw through slitted eyes a leaden sky that was the harbinger of more rain.

She automatically felt for Ben on his side of the bed, as she always did, although they had often slept in separate rooms since the onset of his arthritis. Sometimes he did not go to bed at all, but moved about the house, seeking comfort for his aching limbs, until he might fall asleep sitting upright in a chair. Even in their double bed, he had been an untidy sleeper and would wake up with the sheet wound around him like a shroud, while she had no covering at all. Now his side was smooth, the sheet and one blanket tucked in neatly.

She remembered that she had dreamed last night, and heard Markie's screams, and her own, as the flames devoured him. And then Ben had held her, as he had done during the early years of their marriage, and she had murmured his name, and fallen peacefully asleep.

But Ben was dead.

Consciousness returned with a rush. Ben had been there, smoothing her hair, murmuring to her. She had known it was him, because no other man had been in her bed.

But Ben was dead.

The man had been Peter. He must have heard her cry out.

Fully awake, she went into the turquoise and green bathroom that adjoined her bedroom and stood under a

273

cold shower, thinking, how do you excuse yourself to a man who loves you, for calling him by another man's name?

Peter was sitting at the table in the living-room. Lisa came from the kitchen with a pot of coffee. Jo paused at the door, gathering her courage.

He was smiling at something Lisa had said and the sun-tanned face, with its deep lines, was suddenly younger, and very like his son's. He was wearing a navy blue sweat-shirt with jeans. Last night, his chest had been bare, and her breasts, covered by a fine silk nightdress, had rested against his skin. His hands had been cool and dry as they stroked her body . . . oh, God, she thought, it was a long time since she had felt the comfort of a man's affection. Ben had continued to make love to her throughout his illness, because not to would have hinted that his sexual powers were waning, and that he would never admit. But intercourse had been little more than a physical release for him, and she had been so concerned not to cause him pain that she rarely achieved satisfaction. Last night, it had been as though all the warmth he had shown during the early years had been revived.

She stepped into the room, and they looked towards her.

Keeping her voice light, she said, 'Any coffee for me?'

'Plenty.' Lisa handed her a big green bistro cup. 'No breakfast yet, though. I'm going to drive down to the shop for some fresh croissants.'

'Count me out. I'll finish my coffee, and then I must get home,' Peter said. 'I'm hoping Nick will be back some time today to give us a hand in the restaurant, but in the meantime, we have some reshuffling to do to fill Claudette's place.'

As she moved to the door Lisa said, 'There weren't any disturbances during the night, were there?'

Looking down into her cup, Jo heard him say, casually,

'Everything was peaceful. I wonder if it might not have been a stray reporter hoping to snatch an interview, and scared off by the police cars.'

When Lisa had disappeared, Jo said brightly: 'More rain on the way, I'm afraid. Do you realize that this is the wettest autumn on the coast within living memory?'

'At the same time, it's warm for October.'

'It's the humidity . . .'

'The forecast says more storms are on the way.' There was amusement in his voice. 'Jo, my dear, enough of this ridiculous conversation. How do you feel this morning?'

'I'm fine. Peter, all I can say is thank you for being there last night. And I'm sorry . . .'

'For what?'

'For not realizing who you were.'

'I'd have been a great deal more concerned if you'd called me by some other name. As it is, I'm able to presume that you shared your bed only with your husband. Since I've been jealous of him for years, nothing has changed.'

His Gallic frankness banished embarrassment, and she laughed. 'You're a good friend.'

'Friendship does not exactly describe my feelings for you.' He saw her stiffen and added hastily, 'But we won't go into that. Tell me about your nightmare. It must have been pretty frightening.'

She picked up her cup in both hands and drank the hot, black coffee. 'It's about a fire. It happened quite often when I was younger, but it's only come back since Ben died.'

'Who is Markie?'

The sudden shock in her eyes startled him. 'Markie? Why do you say that?'

'Before you screamed, you called his name.'

'It . . . I don't know. Nobody. It was just a name in the dream.' He was watching her narrowly, and she suspected that he had guessed she was not telling the truth.

He stood up, and said, 'I'll come back tonight.'

'No! Thank you, but there's no need. I'd – really rather you didn't.'

After a moment, he said quietly, 'If that's how you feel . . .'

'Peter, please don't think I'm not grateful. It's just that . . .' She tried to smile. 'I can't face any more complications in my life at the moment.'

He put his hands on her shoulders and kissed her lightly on each cheek. 'I understand, my dear. I'll get Berenger to come up and check your fence during the day in case there's an overhanging branch we might have missed.'

'Whoever he was, I'm sure he won't come back. I'm even beginning to wonder whether Molinard was right, and I only saw shadows.'

'I hope so. But if anything worries you, you know you only have to call me. Any time.'

After he had left she occupied herself setting breakfast things on the table, still warmed by the memory of the previous night, at the same time frightened by how nearly she had given herself away.

At dusk that evening, she and Lisa were in the living-room. Jo had just poured them each a sherry when the door-bell rang.

Lisa picked up the intercom. As she listened, her eyes widened.

She put her hand over the receiver. 'It's a man who calls himself Olaf Freeman. He says he's Alicia Freeman's son. He wants to see you.'

Jo's reponse was instant: 'No!'

Into the phone, Lisa said, 'Sorry. Mrs Absalom isn't available . . .'

Again she turned: 'He has a story about Ben that he wants you to hear before he takes it to the newspapers. Jo, you must see him!'

They instantly recognized Freeman. He had been at

Ben's memorial service, unsuitably dressed in denims, a short, dark, squarely-built man in his early thirties. At close quarters, they could see he had acne-pitted skin and there was a deep cleft in his chin, under which fleshy folds sagged into his open-neck shirt. His arms below the short sleeves were thick, covered in black hair.

Jo had turned on the lights and the room was cheerful despite the thickening darkness outside. He paused in the doorway and looked around at the comfortable, elegant furniture, the expensively-equipped kitchen, with its colourful Provençal china.

'Hello, Mrs Absalom, nice little place you got here.' His smile was impudent and now Jo recognized the nasal voice, too: he had telephoned Lisa's flat as they were leaving for the airport, and she had assumed that he was a newspaperman. His small eyes studied them. 'And you're Lisa, I know you from the telly. Saw you both at the memorial service, didn't I?'

'May I ask what you want?' Jo said.

'That's not a very warm welcome, is it? If you'd offer me a little something like you're having yourselves, I wouldn't say no. Seeing this is a special occasion, meeting you after all these years.'

Tight-lipped, Lisa poured him a glass of sherry.

He raised it to Jo in a mocking toast. 'Got lots of things to talk about. Mind if I take a seat?' He pulled a chair out from the long refectory table and sat down. 'Right then. You know your husband's been giving my Mum a nice allowance for the last twenty years?'

'Yes.'

'You know why?'

'No. It was my husband's business, not mine.'

'It's yours now, Mrs Absalom. That's if you want her to keep quiet.'

'Keep quiet?'

'About what happened in Prague that day when you . . .' He pointed his glass at Lisa, '. . . lost your mother.'

277

'There's no reason for anything to be kept quiet. Everyone knows how my husband rescued Lisa.'

'Ah, but you *don't* know the true story,' he said with satisfaction. 'You know his version. Only my Mum and me know the real one. We were there.'

'Where?'

'In my auntie's apartment in Prague. We saw it all.'

Jo sat down abruptly at the head of the table. 'I don't understand. You're Czech, with a name like Freeman?'

'Changed it when we came to England. My Mum was pleased to be here and said from now on her little son – me – would be a free man. Mum always had a sense of drama. So we called ourselves Freeman, see?'

'Get on with it!' Lisa said.

'In my own time. Good sherry, this. Pity you called the cops last night, Mrs Absalom. We might have had a nice dinner together.'

'That was you, outside the window?'

He nodded. 'Came in when some friend of yours drove out. Wanted to see the lie of the land. Who was around, like. Went out the same way when the cops arrived.'

Through gritted teeth, Jo said: 'Will you kindly tell me why you are here, and then leave.'

'All right, all right . . . You ever been to Prague?'

She shook her head.

'You'll remember what happened in 1968, though, when the Russians chucked out Dubcek and marched in because there was too much freedom of speech going on . . .'

Having recalled the events for Lisa so recently, they were still clear in Jo's mind: how, on August the twenty-first, Russian tanks which had been lurking outside the city, rumbled in, crewed by young Soviet soldiers who had been assured that they would be welcomed as saviours by Party members. Instead, they had found thousands of angry citizens cramming the streets, shouting abuse and pelting them with stones. Even loyal Communists, it seemed, were prepared to fight to retain the modicum of liberty they had achieved.

'Gotta give you some background about us first,' he said. 'Won't take long, then we'll get to the nitty-gritty. We – my Mum and me – were sharing an apartment with her cousin, Eva, and Eva's husband, Ludvik, and old Anna Absalom – and you, Lisa. Of course, I thought then that you were Eva and Ludvik's daughter.

'The whole apartment wasn't any bigger than this room, but my Mum says we were lucky to be there because there was a housing shortage, even though she and Eva never got on that well.

'My Mum was more light-hearted than Eva, if you know what I mean. My dad had left not long after I was born, and she kept us going by dancing in night-clubs and being a sort of – hostess. She had to be out at night a lot, so Eva and Ludvik looked after me as well as Lisa. Ludvik treated Lisa as though she was his own daughter. She was old Anna's pet, too. I always thought she was a pest.'

He grinned at Lisa, who was watching him with a distaste she made no effort to conceal.

'Second cousins, aren't we? We'll have to get to know each other. Anyhow, Auntie Eva – I always called her that – was a very serious-minded, dedicated lady, all for the freedom bit. She and Ludvik both worked for the radio in Prague and they thought it was great when things started to loosen up and they could say what they liked about the Government.

'When the Russian tanks arrived to stop all that, they went underground. The Russians shut down the radio and tv stations, but some of the Czechs had already organized hidden transmitters. Eva and Ludvik worked with the dissidents, broadcasting news that the Russians wanted to hide.'

'I was only a kid, so I didn't know much about what was going on, only that it was exciting. The tanks were great, and all the soldiers had guns and some of the Praguers went around chucking Molotov cocktails at them.

'Anna had died just before the invasion, and Eva had been too busy to let Ben know. He turned up in the middle of it all, wanting to take Anna back to England.

'My Mum was out when he arrived. She was having a pretty good time, actually, because she was entertaining the Russian officers. I mean, they had to have some relaxation, didn't they? Auntie Eva didn't like it at all, and they'd had a couple of rows.

'Well, Ben came in like a visitor from Mars. Ludvik was at the radio station, but Eva and me were home and Lisa was having a sleep in the other room. I remember to this day how Eva looked when she saw him at the door: staggered back, and nearly passed out. She had to ask him in, of course, and she told him they'd buried Anna the day before. He was a bit upset. They talked, and she gave him a box of Anna's old family photographs. He was just going when you came into the room, Lisa. She'd never told him about you, but I reckon he suspected right away that you were his, because he looked at you for a long time, then started shooting questions at her about when you were born and how long she'd been married to Ludvik, and all that. In the end, she told him the truth.

'My Mum came back while this was going on. I couldn't understand English then, but Mum could, and she told me all about it later. Seems he wanted to take you back to England with him, but Eva said she wouldn't let you go. He was pretty nasty about how you were being brought up, in a Commie country, with an invasion going on, and us crowded in the apartment like rabbits in a hutch. All the time there was shouting from the crowds in the street, and sometimes explosions.

'Mum was sitting on a window seat, looking out while she listened, and just when Eva and Ben were going at it hammer and tongs, she yelled that Ludvik was there, in a crowd that was throwing things at a Russian tank.

'We got to the window just in time to see one of its crew in the turret shoot Ludvik with a machine pistol. There was blood everywhere. Even I could tell that he was dead.

'Auntie Eva ran out and down the stairs. The last thing she said to Ben was, "I'll never let you have her!"

'As she left, he tried to grab you, Lisa, but you got away and chased after Eva. He was furious.

'Outside I could see Ludvik lying in the gutter. People were screaming and the Russians were waving their guns.

'Then Ben came to the window and shoved me aside. He opened it and as Eva was rushing towards Ludvik, he pointed at her and shouted to the Russians. I don't suppose they knew what he was saying, but they were young boys, excited and scared, because someone had just slung a grenade at the tank, only it hadn't gone off, and there was this woman racing towards them and a man shouting what sounded like a warning. So the same chap who'd killed Ludvik shot Eva, and she was lying on the ground, too, as Lisa trotted out crying for her Mummy.

'It all went quiet, with people standing around looking at the bodies and up at the Russians. Then Ben dashed down the stairs, out onto the pavement, and picked Lisa up. He carried her off somewhere, and that was the last we saw of him.'

Seeing Jo's stricken face, Lisa put her arm around her shoulders. 'How do we know this is true?'

'Could I make up a story like that, love? No way I can prove it. But that won't matter. I've seen all the stuff about Ben Absalom in the newspapers. Suspicion that he was murdered, what a hero he'd been in '68. They're going to love this. A new angle, isn't it, on the great Benedict Absalom? Mum and me might even write a book about him.'

'So why have you come here?'

'I thought I'd give Mrs Absalom a chance first. Like *she* could buy the story instead of the papers.'

'Was that why Ben paid your mother all those

years? She'd been blackmailing him?'

'Not a word I like. But that's about it. What happened was, when everything in Prague calmed down, my mother was in a bit of a mess. A lot of the people didn't like it that she'd been entertaining the invaders. They made nasty remarks in the streets and one woman said she should have her head shaved like they did with French collaborators after the war. She was scared, and she decided that we'd better leave.

'She'd always wanted to come to England, so she got her cash together, and sold Eva's furniture. Everything was confused at the time and we didn't have any trouble getting over the border into Austria.'

'Didn't you care what had happened to Lisa?' Jo said.

'Why should we? She was with her father. She'd have been a nuisance. We got to Paris by train and stayed there for a few days, then came on to London.

'Not long after we got here, Mum saw a piece in one of the papers about Ben Absalom and the poor little orphan he'd rescued. Very touching. Except that all it said was that her parents had been murdered by the Russians. Nothing about how it was Ben who'd caused Eva's death, as sure as if he'd shot her himself.

'Mum's a shrewd old thing, and she thought about it for a while, then she wrote Ben a letter, telling him we'd arrived.

'We'd taken a room in a boarding-house in Ealing, and he came to see us. He was an arrogant bastard, but he was no fool. He knew what Mum wanted. He said that if she'd shut up about what had really happened in Prague, he'd buy us a flat and give her a regular allowance. Said it was really for Eva's sake. Only we knew it was for his own. She said okay. It worked well all those years. When inflation hit us, he'd add a few quid, which showed how scared he was of the truth coming out. Wouldn't have done much for his image, would it? And I wouldn't be surprised if the powers-that-be might not have decided he was no fit guardian for Lisa.'

Jo had slumped in her chair, as though her spine was no longer able to hold her upright.

'The trouble is,' he went on, 'Ben's dead, the money's stopped, and my poor old Mum's health isn't too good. So I thought, I have to do something for her. Newspapers pay for stories like this. Then I thought, Mrs Absalom's a rich lady, maybe she'll agree to take on her late husband's burden, like, and continue the allowance. Eight hundred a month. Just enough to keep Mum in comfort. Nothing luxurious like this, of course.' He rose. 'Well then, I'm off now. Mrs Absalom, I'm gonna give you twenty-four hours to think it over. Then Mum and me'll offer the story to the *News of the World*. I've heard they pay the best. Who knows? We might even put it up for auction.'

At the door, he turned. 'I'm staying in Cotolin. Nice little pub called La Reserve. You can call me there if you make up your mind before I get in touch.'

For the first time in my life, Lisa thought, I want to kill someone. Jo was sitting, her eyes fixed on him, but seemingly incapable of speech.

'Ciao, then, as they say.' He flipped a stubby hand and was gone.

They sat in silence for a moment, then Lisa burst out, 'God, what a legacy Ben's left us! That man's right: he killed Eva as surely as if he'd pulled the trigger.'

'No!' Jo's voice was agonized. 'He never meant to! When he came back from Prague, he almost had a breakdown.' She was talking quickly, eagerly, as though she needed to convince herself as well as Lisa. 'Everyone thought it was because he had seen his friends die. He wouldn't talk about it then, nor for the rest of his life. You remember how impulsive he was? He reacted to a situation first, then thought afterwards. Freeman said he was furious because Eva wouldn't give you up. He must have shouted out of the window in anger, with no thought of

283

the consequences. He never intended her to be killed. His guilt afterwards must have been almost unbearable.'

'He killed Eva, and you're still finding excuses for him!'

'I won't have that story published! I won't have Ben's name dragged through the mud. I'll pay that man off somehow, if I have to sell the villa.'

Ben's shadow seemed to overhang the room like a risen phoenix. Lisa could sense, as clearly as though she could see him, his arrogant complacence in the knowledge that Jo was bound to him as tightly as she had been during his life, prepared to lose even her home rather than allow his reputation to suffer.

'For God's sake!' she said. 'What will it take to make you realize he wasn't worth it?'

'I owe him more than I can ever repay.'

'Jo, he's dead! And whatever you might have owed him, you repaid him a hundred times while he was alive.'

'You don't understand,' Jo said flatly. 'He gave me a new life.'

'Okay, I don't understand, particularly not why you're prepared to ruin what's left of that life for a dead man!'

'To me, he'll never be dead.'

Lisa felt a chill as the shadow shook its wings in triumph. Poor Peter, she thought, what chance does he have?

It was market-day in Cotolin and the palm-fringed square was filled with stalls selling everything from olive-wood pepper grinders to pepperoni. A couple of gendarmes leant against a tree, keeping a sharp eye on a group of young British tourists who had arrived on motorbikes, wearing their leather gear. A girl with a portfolio under her arm was moving along the terraces that overlooked the square, trying to interest customers in her water-colours.

Olaf Freeman was sitting at a table on the terrace outside La Reserve, his feet up on another chair, coffee and a plate of croissants in front of him. He looked at peace with the world, Lisa thought, no doubt contemplating a rosy future maintained by Joanna.

He made no attempt to rise when she reached him.

'Well, well, little Cousin Lisa! Come with a message from Mrs A.? We got our agreement?'

Without preamble, she said: 'I'll give you ten thousand pounds to leave us alone and keep quiet about that story you told us. Not because I care what you do, but my mother does.'

He laughed. 'Ten thousand, love? Forget it! That'd hardly keep Mum and me for a year.'

'It's all we can afford.'

'Come on! With a house like that? Mrs A. must be loaded.'

'She's probably going to have to sell the house.'

'Good idea. She'd make a bomb. Very des. res. No, ten thousand's not on. Make it twenty, and I'll think about it.'

'That isn't possible!'

He smeared butter and jam onto a croissant. 'Too bad. Doesn't really matter to me. I'll be off to Fleet Street.'

'No newspaper's going to pay you anything like that.'

'Maybe not, but I'll have the satisfaction, won't I? And like I said, Mum and me might even write a book about old Ben . . . and his "adopted" child, of course. That's what they call you in the papers. Seems to me you must have kept it dark that you're his illegitimate daughter. Nice, spicy story that'd make, with your recent divorce, and all.'

Afraid that another minute looking at his grinning face would cause her to do him violence, she spun around and hurried away.

His voice followed her: 'You've got until tonight, love.'

There were tears of anger in her eyes when she pulled up outside the Garniers' house. No one was about and she rang the bell.

Nick opened the door. He was wearing a dressing-gown, and his hair was tousled, his eyes heavy with sleep.

He stared at her for a moment, then said, 'Oh . . . hi! I was going to get in touch with you this morning.'

'Where's Peter?'

'He's gone up to the villa. Didn't you see him?'

'I've been out. Oh, damn . . . !'

He looked at her more closely. 'Hey, you've been crying. What's upset you?'

She glared at him and snapped, 'I'm angry. I never cry when I'm upset, only when I'm angry.'

'So you do. I remember. Who are you angry with?'

'Ben. And Olaf Freeman.'

Fully awake, he said, 'Olaf – Freeman?'

'Alicia Freeman's son. He's trying to blackmail us.'

He stood aside. 'Come on in. Does my father know about this?'

'No. And Jo said I wasn't to tell him, but there isn't anyone else . . .'

'Did she say you weren't to tell me?'

'She didn't mention you.'

'So you tell me about it, and I'll tell him. Okay?'

As she subsided into a chair she said, 'Do you always sleep this late?'

'I got back from London yesterday afternoon and went straight to work in the restaurant. We had some late stayers and didn't finish clearing up until after two. Now what's this about Freeman?'

'He turned up at the villa last night . . .' Having started to talk, it was a relief to spill out the story. Her actress's memory for lines enabled her to reproduce Freeman's words verbatim. As she did so, her voice almost unconsciously coarsened and she slipped into his manner of speech, with its glottal stops and sentences that ended with a question. Nick was so fascinated by the transformation that for the first few moments he was hardly aware of what she was saying.

'. . . and after he'd gone, I had a row with Jo,' she

ended. 'I said she should let him do his worst, but she wouldn't. She was going to see a lawyer in St-Tropez this morning about selling the villa. So I went to Cotolin and told Freeman I'd pay him ten thousand to leave us alone, and he laughed at me. But I know Jo hasn't more than a couple of thousand and that's all I've got. I thought that Peter might help. She'll be furious with me, but I had to come.'

'He'd give Jo his last centime, but maybe that won't be necessary,' he said thoughtfully.

'What d'you mean?'

'Give me a minute to put some clothes on . . .'

He was back in a few seconds, unshaven, dressed in slacks and a sweat-shirt.

He grasped her arm and ran her to the car. 'Get in. I'll drive. We're going back to Cotolin.'

Freeman was still sitting at his table, smoking a cigar.

'Mind if I join you?' Nick said.

'Don't know you, do I? Oh, it's Cousin Lisa again. That was quick. You upping the offer? Who's this, then?'

'My name's Garnier. I'm a friend of the Absaloms.' Nick paused, then said casually. 'I've just come back from London. Saw your mother in the hospital.'

Freeman's smile slipped. 'Did you, indeed? How was she? Poor old thing, she's been a bit under the weather.'

'I imagine she's no better than she was when you saw her last. What you might not know is that she has been moved to a public ward in a mental hospital because you stopped paying the nursing-home's fees.'

'Ah, well, you see, I've been a bit strapped. I'm depending on Mrs Absalom to put things right.' His eyes slid away uneasily.

'What happened to the money Ben sent her? That would have covered her bill.'

'She's a bit dotty, you know. I been looking after it for her. Anyhow, no point in keeping her in a private place.

Most of the time she doesn't know where she is. You must have seen that.'

'You sold her flat. What happened to the proceeds?'

'That's none of your damn business, mate!'

'The Longmates paid forty-five thousand for it. That would have kept her in the nursing-home for a good many years.'

Freeman's voice rose. 'Who the hell are you to interfere in my family matters? You been asking questions about us?'

'I have, and the answers were interesting. You've been stealing from your mother for a long time.'

'Now, look here . . .'

Nick leant forward. 'No. You look. There's more. I know you have a police record. You've been in prison at least twice. You're a convicted thief. Now you're trying to blackmail Mrs Absalom. The courts don't let third-time offenders off lightly.'

'You can't threaten me!'

'Theft. Extortion. Fraud. Blackmail.' Nick ticked them off on his fingers. 'They'll all add up. One phone call to Scotland Yard and they'll be waiting for you when you get back to London.'

Freeman's dark beard was a dirty patch against his pasty skin. 'You'd never . . .'

'Oh, yes, we would, unless you forget about selling that story about Ben. You can't prove it, anyway.'

'I wouldn't need to. The sleaze-sheets don't mind whether things are true or not.'

Nick said, 'Mrs Absalom could apply for a court injunction preventing them from publishing. And then she would probably sue for the return of her husband's money. If you've managed to keep any of it, you'd lose the lot.' He added thoughtfully: 'And I wouldn't be above giving *your* story to the newspapers: "Ex-con steals from invalid mother. Refuses to pay hospital bills." *News of the World* would love it.'

A variety of expressions pursued each other over Freeman's face: defiance, anger, fear and, finally, resignation. 'Tell you what then, I don't want to make things difficult for Mrs Absalom. I'm prepared to forget the whole thing, if she is.'

'No newspapers? No book?'

'No police? Back to square one, right? I was only doing it for Mum, after all.'

Nick and Lisa rose. 'The best thing you can do for her is to go and see her,' he said. 'Buy her a bit of physical comfort. God knows, she hasn't got anything else.'

'I'll do it, I'll do it . . .'

Jo and Peter were standing by his car outside the villa.

'I've been waiting for you,' she said to Lisa. 'Peter was going to drive me into St-Tropez, but I'll take the car instead. Where have you been?'

'You don't need to go to St-Tropez.' Jo shot her a warning glance. 'It's okay, we can tell Peter now.'

'I don't understand . . .'

'Nor do I,' Peter said grimly. 'What's this "business" you had on, anyway?'

'Come inside,' Lisa said. 'Nick has something to tell you.'

When he had finished, Jo's face had lightened, but his father's was angry as he turned to her. 'You weren't going to tell me, were you?' he said bitterly. '*Merde*, Jo, you were going to sell the villa without saying a word. I thought we were friends!'

'That was why I didn't want you to know. You'd have offered me money, I'd have refused it, and we'd have had an argument.'

'It's all over,' Lisa said peaceably. 'Don't start arguing now.'

Jo smiled at Peter, then turned to Nick. 'I can't thank you enough. Could I really have taken out an injunction or sued for the return of Ben's money?'

'I haven't the faintest idea,' he said cheerfully. 'But it convinced him.'

As the Garniers were leaving, Nick touched Lisa's arm: 'I've got more to tell you. How about we take a run up to Ramatuelle and have a beer?'

She looked at him warily for a moment, then shrugged. 'Okay. If we aren't too long.'

They sat at a table in an outdoor cafe under trees in the little hill-top village. From its square, winding alleys led between the old houses, which were built of stone, weathered into soft shades of grey, their backs forming a kind of town wall. Most of the foreign tourists who crammed the place in summer had fled the bad weather. Half a dozen men were playing boules on the far side of the square.

They talked about her flat for a few minutes, keeping the conversation impersonal, then Nick said: 'I met your husband in London.'

She kept her eyes fixed on the boules players. 'He telephoned. I said you'd be able to tell him what was going on. He was worried about Jo.'

'We had a meal together. Later, I wished we hadn't.'

'Why?'

'I found out what he'd done.'

Her head jerked towards him. 'He told you?'

'No. I spent an afternoon in a newsagency library, reading the cuttings. For God's sake, Lisa, how could you have anything to do with him now? And why the hell did you marry him in the first place? You must have known what he was.'

She repeated Freeman's words, no less angrily: 'That's none of your damn business! And how dare you pry into my life? You're supposed to be writing a book about Ben.'

Feeling his own anger rise, he said, 'So it's all right for me to uncover nasty little episodes in *his* past, but yours is sacrosanct, is that it? Well, let me tell you, it's all tucked into a brown envelope in that library for anyone to see. And from the amount of stuff there is, I must be one of the few people who didn't already know the whole story.'

She stood up. 'I'm going back now.'

He paid for their beers and followed her to the car. Their brief truce, it seemed, was over.

As she got behind the wheel, he said, 'Lisa, look, I didn't set out to . . . I mean, oh, shit, I only brought it up because . . .'

'Because?'

'Because I simply don't understand you any more!'

Her hostility did not waver. 'You don't have to understand me. My life has nothing to do with you. Nothing!'

They drove back to La Belette in silence.

3

The letter from Simon Ashton arrived the next morning and Nick, still raw from his clash with Lisa, regarded it with distaste. Only curiosity prevented him from discarding it unopened.

The envelope contained several sheets, closely written in a small, neat hand, and as he read, his interest in the contents made him forget his antipathy for the writer.

The letter began without salutation:

'I'm not sure whether all this will be of any help to Joanna and Lisa, but you've certainly given me an unusual experience. I've just got back from Lupin Street. I'm slightly drunk on Guinness and words, and I want to put it down while it's fresh in my mind. Since I don't know what might be relevant to your inquiries, I'll give you the lot.

'Number forty-one, in between a rubber-shop and a Greek fruiterers, turned out to be a junk-shop – and, Jesus, what junk! The sign above the door said Murphy's Antiques. It was a single dusty window with an adjacent door. Outside there was a rickety table with boxes of books on it, most of them defaced by dirty finger-marks, spilled coffee and gobbets of food.

'On the pavement under the table were a couple of ancient black-and-white tv sets and a thirties bakelite radio which I was sorely tempted to buy for its kitsch value.

'The door had a "closed . . . back soon" sign on it, so I decided to wait. The window was filled with the detritus of God knows how many lives: water-colours that looked as though they'd been done by somebody's aunt, boxes of tarnished cutlery, a couple of broken bentwood chairs, a typewriter with half the keys missing, a pile of warped seventy-eights, rolls of old carpeting . . . you name any object that nobody in his right mind would want to buy, and it was there.

'I hung about for twenty minutes. The proprietor of the rubber-shop called me a couple of times to come on in, my boy, no need to be shy.

'I was just about to leave when the Murphys arrived. Bridget, who owns the shop, is a skinny old crone, with black-dyed hair straggling around a face that looks like crumpled brown paper. She's about five feet nothing and was wearing a rusty black dress that reached to her ankles. Her feet were encased in high-heeled red ankle-strap sandals, forties-style. Her son, Eamonn, is in his early fifties, I'd guess, a big, shambling chap with shrewd little eyes and all the delicate charm of King Kong.

'"Come in, sor," said Bridget, thinking I was a potential customer – and from now on I won't attempt to write in dialect. You must imagine an Irish accent so thick that at first I wondered what language she was talking.

'As soon as I mentioned your "A.M.", Eamonn turned purple, grabbed my shoulders and shouted: "We have nothing to do with that spawn of the devil! Denied his family, he did, and broke his old mother's heart. Look at her now, crying her eyes out at the mere mention of his name." I looked, and indeed, she was.

'They were surrounded by an alcoholic haze that made me realize the pair of them had just come from the pub, so before he could throw me out, I suggested that they might like another drink and we could have a chat.

'Bridget cheered up and Eamonn let me loose. I gave him some money and she sent him around the corner to the off-licence for a few bottles of Guinness.

'She and I picked our way through to the back of the shop, where there were some rickety wooden chairs around an ancient kitchen table covered with stained oil-cloth.

293

'I'm going to try to put what they told me into some kind of sequence. We had a peripatetic conversation, first sitting in that awful shop, which stank of dust and old clothes, then in the public bar of the Tar and Feathers, where we were constantly interrupted by boozy Irishmen, and finally in their flat above the shop which was, if anything, dirtier and more cluttered with junk than it was downstairs. Bridget and Eamonn took it in turns to talk, and sometimes she dissolved into alcoholic tears.

'So to "A.M.", who turns out to be Bridget's older son, Alfred.

'He was born in Ireland. Bridget and her deceased husband, Kevin ("'Twas the drink that done him in"), brought him and Eamonn to London a few years later and used a small inheritance from Bridget's parents to start their "antique" shop.

'Alfred showed an ambition way beyond that of his parents. "He always loved to travel, sir," Bridget told me. "Many's the time he'd be away for hours and come back to say he'd spent the time going round and round on the Underground. He covered all the lines, changing from one to the other so he only had to pay for one journey, and he could recite all the stations from Cockfosters to Hounslow West, so he could."

'It seems that from an early age he was determined to better himself. He also had an interest in art and went to the free museums and galleries in London, bewildering Bridget and Kevin by talking about gentlemen with outlandish names like Picasso and Cézanne and Matisse. "That Mr Picasso, sir, an artist, he was, and he was Alfie's hero."

'As he grew older, he went round with his father to buy stock for the shop. They would knock at doors and offer to remove any unwanted furniture, pictures and bric-a-brac. As they never paid more than a few pence for anything, they could usually turn a small profit on reselling.

'Bridget said that among the things people in those days

294

wanted to get rid of were old paintings passed down from their parents and grandparents. The Murphys usually ripped out the picture and put the frames up for sale (oh, Sotheby's, what treasures you might have missed!).

'Alfie was sure something more could be done with them, so when he was fourteen, he bought a book called *Teach Yourself Oil Painting* and some tubes of paint.

'He chose a picture called *Cattle in the Glen* for his first experiment – Bridget remembers its title to this day. First he cleaned it with soap and water, then he brightened up the colours. Finally, he renewed the frame with gold paint from Woolworth's.

'"Just lovely, it was," Bridget said. "Our Alfie propped it up outside the shop with a sign on it: 'Original oil painting. Hand-done. £5.' A terrible price, you'd think, sir, considering we'd only paid a shilling for it. But it went inside half-an-hour, to a young couple who'd moved into one of the new council flats and needed something on the wall to brighten it up."

'After that, there was no holding Alfie. He "restored" one painting after another, and had difficulty keeping up with the demand.

'The only argument he had with his parents was when he told them he intended to keep half the selling price of each for himself. They agreed when he threatened to leave home and set up in business for himself.

'He'd never lost his urge to travel, and after establishing the right to his fifty per cent, he saved until he had enough money to buy himself an old banger and go to France for a touring holiday. He was seventeen and it was the first time any Murphy had ventured beyond the British Isles. Bridget was very proud of him. Kevin, I think, had already been taken by the drink.

'Little did she know that she would never see him again, for when he reached the Riviera, Alfred realized he had found his promised land. He liked the sun, the way of life, the girls, and he was sure he was going to make his fortune there, so he stayed.

'He wrote home quite often during the early years, and Bridget and Eamonn were able to follow his career.

'He noticed how many young painters were carrying their portfolios around the bars and cafes, trying to flog their work, and he discovered that many of them would be happy to let him take over the selling, in return for a commission.

'So he started up in business and because he had the gift of the blarney, he did well enough to be able, after a while, to open his own little gallery.

'He began to cultivate Americans – not, I gather, those expatriate residents who were knowledgeable about art, but a Transatlantic version of his junk-shop customers, who wanted something hand-done to put on their walls back home. He'd spin them a yarn about how this or that young painter was a so-far-undiscovered genius whom a few experts, including himself, expected to develop into a new Cézanne or Matisse or Picasso. Many of them swallowed it.

'He also, according to Bridget, actually became a good friend of Mr Picasso.

'What annoyed Eamonn was that although his letters were full of his successes, he never contributed a penny to his family's welfare, which had suffered by his departure.

'When he was about twenty-five, he met a rich widow named Betty Lou Riegler. She came from a small town in Texas and had consoled herself for the recent death of her husband by renting a villa for six months in the hills behind Cannes. She was twice Alfie's age, and lonely. She bought pictures from him and eventually she invited him to move in with her.

'A steady stream of her chums from Texas came over. They were rich, and they liked to spend their money. She introduced Alfie as an expert on modern French painting, who could seek out original works guaranteed to impress their friends and increase in value.

'According to his mother, he was living like a lord. Betty Lou denied him nothing, and bought a house in St Paul de Vence as their love-nest.

'This idyll lasted until Betty Lou died unexpectedly, possibly of a surfeit of Alfie. (This is my suggestion, not Bridget's).

'Unfortunately, she had omitted to make him a beneficiary in her will and everything went to her daughter and two sons. The villa was sold, and he found himself out on the street, with only his income as an "adviser on art" to live on.

'There's a gap now, because, with the downward plunge in his fortunes, his letters became fewer and eventually stopped altogether.

'About eight years ago Eamonn decided to go to the South of France to look for him. "'Twas killing our poor mam, not knowing whether he was dead or alive," he told me, and Bridget, on her eighth Guinness, burst into tears again.

'Before his letters ceased, he was about to move from Ste-Maxime, where he had been living, to a village called La Belette, so Eamonn flew to Nice, then took a bus to St-Tropez, and another to La Belette.

'He asked around for Alfred Murphy, of whom nobody had ever heard.

'He was about to leave when he saw his brother drive in, with a lady beside him – who turned out to be his wife. Eamonn gave a glad cry and rushed over to them, expecting open arms, and an invitation to be their house-guest.

'Instead, Alfie told him he had no business to come chasing him, that he'd built up a new life in which there was no room for his family. What outraged Eamonn most was the discovery that he had changed his name to Amyas Mahr – which I will call him from now on – as being more suited to his present life-style than Alfie Murphy. After a few angry exchanges, he drove away,

297

his wife having spoken not a word.

'Eamonn was so angry that he found out where they lived, and went after them.

'I won't bore you with the row they had, though Eamonn re-enacted every detail at such a pitch that the neighbours in the next-door flat banged on the wall. The upshot was that Amyas's wife produced enough money to reimburse Eamonn for the cost of his journey, and he left, having given his brother a black eye for luck.

'He was thirsty by the time he had plodded back to La Belette, so he went into the bar.

'There was only one other customer. He turned out to be English, and bought Eamonn a drink, which became several drinks. Eamonn was so pleased to find a friend that he told the kind gentleman ("Big and fair-haired, he was, with the look of the rich about him. And he said I was to call him Ben.") the whole story of his brother's background, his adoption of a new name, and his rejection of his family. The gentleman was sympathetic, and he wrote down the Murphys' address, saying that he would look them up if he was ever in London.

'They never heard from him, though, and neither have they ever heard again from Amyas.

'I left Bridget sobbing into her stout and Eamonn so angered by his recollection of his brother's perfidy that he decided to return to the Tar and Feathers and pick a fight with someone.

'I'll post this letter now – the walk to the post office might help to clear the Guinness fumes from my head.

'It was good meeting you, Nick, and many thanks for the dinner. Maybe one day you'll let me return it.'

Peter was checking the Lion d'Or accounts in his office when Nick tossed the sheaf of papers on his desk. 'Can you spare a few minutes to read this? You'll find it illuminating.'

When he had finished it, Peter's voice was awed. 'My

God, you have to admire Amyas. He's fooled the lot of us: the tragic childhood, lost lands in Hungary, or wherever, the suggestion of aristocratic forebears. I've always wondered about that accent of his. Never thought of Irish. I can't see how it has any relevance to Ben's death, though, can you?'

'I've been thinking about that. Could he have attacked Ben because of what he knew about him?'

'Seems unlikely. Ashton says that Ben found out several years ago. Wouldn't Amyas have done something about it then?'

'Ben could have kept it to himself, then suddenly decided to torment him with his knowledge, for some reason. I suspect Amyas's temper has a short fuse. Do we tell the *flics*?'

'Let's see Jo first. She might know whether Ben had ever talked about it. I don't like pointing a finger at a man without some evidence.'

'Ben never mentioned this to me.' Jo hesitated, then shot a glance at Lisa. 'He liked – knowing about people. It gave him insights into their character that he was able to use in his painting. He wouldn't have been cruel enough to use what Eamonn told him to torment Amyas.'

Lisa's mouth tightened. How long would she go on fooling herself about Ben?

'Did he ever paint Amyas?' Nick asked.

'He started a portrait not long after we came down here, but it was never finished. He couldn't stand being in the same room as Amyas for any length of time. But there was no real animosity in their relationship. If anything it marginally improved after Amyas introduced him to Dominic Partridge.'

'Should we pass this on to Molinard?' Peter said.

She shook her head. 'The police have already established that Amyas was in St-Tropez when Ben died. The fact that his real name is Alfred Murphy is irrelevant.'

'That's my feeling, but I hope we're right. There's a chance that telling Molinard might take the heat off you.'

'It wouldn't be fair to Amyas. I wonder if Ona knew before Eamonn came down?'

Peter looked thoughtful. 'In some ways, she's as mysterious a figure as he is – or was. She's English, of course, but she doesn't talk about her background either. Her accent – on the rare occasions when she speaks – is middle-class. She paints those awful little water-colours, which help to keep them. But nobody seems to know anything else about her, where she came from, or how she met Amyas.'

'Or why she stays with him,' Nick said. 'He treats her like dirt. Does he get much work from art-collectors these days?'

Peter said, 'I doubt it. People are a hell of a lot more sophisticated about painting than they were when he was Alfie Murphy. It must be harder to pass off mediocre painters as future Picassos. That's probably why he's so obsessed with Partridge and his museum. It's his last chance to get into the big time.'

4

'It's as though we're living in a vacuum,' Jo said. 'For two weeks now, nothing's happened. We're no nearer finding out the truth about Ben's death, but no one seems to be *doing* anything. I'm grateful for the respite from Molinard, but it's rather like waiting for a storm to break.'

The weather was dry and cloudy. She was dead-heading geraniums and Lisa was listlessly clearing fallen leaves from the pool. As she scooped up the last of them, she said, 'I'm going stir-crazy. Let's walk down to the village and pick up some pâté and tomatoes for lunch.'

'Would you like to go to the Lion d'Or for a change?'

'No, thanks.'

'Because Nick's working there? I wish I knew what the trouble is between you two.'

'We've outgrown each other, that's all.' Her frown forbade further discussion.

Jo sighed. 'I hoped that coming home and meeting him again would give you a chance to – what was it you said in London? – put your life together. It's been just the opposite. I should never have asked you to come.'

Lisa stood the scoop up against the wall. 'You're talking nonsense. Nick doesn't mean anything to me, one way or the other. I'd have come home anyway, as soon as I heard what was happening. Let's go. Georgette will be delighted to see you. She keeps asking about you, and muttering about those *flic*-pigs upsetting the entire village.'

Pierre-Luc was sitting on his usual bench, his mother having permitted him to return there when the newsmen departed. His big head was nodding up and down and his binoculars were around his neck. The vacant eyes under tousled hair looked up at them without recognition, but his loose lips, as always, were smiling.

'*Bon jour, Pierre-Luc. Ça va?*' Jo said.

The nodding stopped briefly, his smile widened, then his head resumed its metronomic movement.

Georgette appeared from the back of the shop as soon as she heard its bell, set off when the door opened.

There were exercise books and pencils scattered on the glass counter, and sheets of paper covered in writing. Under them was a shelf containing sausages, cheeses and half-empty terrines of pâté – the previous day's leftovers from the Lion d'Or, which the Mazeaus handed on each evening for Georgette to sell.

The shop had not changed in all the years Jo had lived in La Bellette. Sometimes she suspected that the fly-blown patisserie set out on plates had not changed, either. But there were racks of big, roughly-shaped, juicy tomatoes and fresh lettuces with the good black earth still clinging to their roots, newly-baked *baguettes* and *croissants*, and jars of tiny vegetables preserved in jewel-like layers: baby sweet-corn, beans, carrots, artichoke hearts.

It was the first time she had been into the shop since Ben's death and Georgette greeted her with kisses and a flurry of words. 'Ah, Joanna, it is so good to see you! You have had such nonsense to cope with. Those bloody *flics*! To think that you, of all people were questioned . . . it is an absurdity! And they even tried to interrogate my poor Pierre-Luc. He was on the hill that day, did you know? But he was seen by several people, nowhere near Le Mur. Everyone knows that what happened to Monsieur Absalom was an accident. My poor Joanna!'

Her voice flowed on: 'I have been so upset I haven't even been able to write. Not a poem! Not a word about my beloved Bonaparte! I take up my pencil every day, but the words won't come. Who knows when I will write again?

Inspiration needs peace to flower, my dears, and our peace has gone . . . No one even dares to talk any more, in case *they* should overhear.' She leant over the counter and the towering bee-hive of black hair wobbled alarmingly. Although there was no one within earshot, she whispered, 'Have you heard about André Dorsey and Claudette? Such a quarrel last night! André shouting, Claudette crying. The whole village heard it.'

'What was it about?' Lisa said.

'We couldn't make it out, I happened to be passing the house and you couldn't miss the noise, but the words weren't clear. Louise and Gustave Sebeille were outside, and Roger Caccia and Madame Polak. We were afraid there was going to be violence. Then André opened the front door and shouted at us, so we left. Louise said the noise went on for hours. There's your pâté, my dears, and the tomatoes, beautiful they are, firm and ripe and sweet. We can all make a pretty good guess what the row was about, can't we? I mean, everyone knows Claudette's habits. There isn't a man in the village . . .' She stopped abruptly and shot an embarrassed glance at Jo. 'She's lost her job in the restaurant, you know. I expect that's what set André off.'

She took a deep breath, but before she could go on, Jo led Lisa purposefully towards the door.

She followed them, and declaimed, 'Remember, my darling, do not lose heart! Keep faith and say to yourself, as our dear Bonaparte did, "The bullet that is to kill me has not yet been moulded!"'

Their shared laughter as they walked back to the villa was the first spontaneous amusement Jo had experienced for weeks.

As they unlocked the gates, she cleared the mail-box, which contained the morning's delivery of letters. She handed one, with a London post-mark, to Lisa.

5

Nick had come home for a couple of hours' rest between clearing up after the lunch-time rush at the Lion d'Or and returning to prepare for dinner. He was helping out full-time in the restaurant until Marie's niece, who had agreed to take Claudette's place as waitress, arrived from Strasbourg. Peter had gone to the villa to see Jo, and he was alone in the house.

Stretched out on the terrace, with his eyes closed, his mind was working on plans for his book. Jo had agreed, in principle, to the project, but had said that she was not prepared to discuss it until the matter of Ben's death had been cleared up.

The more he thought about it, the more difficult it promised to be, not because of any lack of material, but because so much significant detail might have to be left out. There was the episode in her childhood that he had discovered by accident in London. As well as shaping her character, it could have been an important element in her relationship with Ben. But it was a secret she had kept for forty years. Did he have the right to ask her to let him make use of it? So far, he had not even told his father what he had discovered. Would she stick to her determination never to reveal publicly the truth about the Prague episode, or Alicia Freeman's place in her husband's life, or Lisa's background?

Without such material, there was a danger that he would produce another bromide, shedding no new light on Ben's turbulent, contradictory character.

His musings were interrupted by footsteps clicking up

the steps. He opened his eyes, and blinked.

Claudette Dorsey, in mid-afternoon, was dressed for a night on the town. She was wearing a black satin skirt, black lace tights, high-heeled shoes and a pink cotton blouse, its top buttons undone to reveal the furrow between her breasts and an inch of black bra.

Her eyelashes were heavily mascaraed, the lids shadowed navy blue, and her lipstick was a silvery maroon. Her hair was ineptly folded into a French pleat, from which loosened strands straggled around her face. Under the heavy make-up, he could see that the left side of her face was bruised and swollen. She was carrying a shabby brown suitcase.

As he stood up, she said, 'I didn't expect . . . I want to see your father.'

'Sorry, he's not here.'

'Where is he? When will he be back?' There was an edge of panic in her voice.

'No idea. Maybe not until late this evening. He's up at the Villa Mimosa.'

'But I have to talk to him *now!*'

He looked at her curiously. 'Anything I can do?'

Her eyes became calculating. She put her suitcase down and stepped closer, so that he smelt her cheap scent, mixed with under-arm odour. 'I'm in trouble, Nicholas. Your father may be the only person who can help me.' She paused. 'Unless you . . .?'

'What's your problem?'

'I'm pregnant.' Her tone was a mixture of bravado and desperation.

Involuntarily, he glanced down at her body: the slim hips, the sturdy, well-shaped legs and aggressive breasts. Under the tight skirt her stomach had a distinct mound, and he wondered how far the pregnancy was advanced.

He caught a small smile curving her mouth as she followed the direction of his eyes. 'Why come here?' he said. 'I don't see how my father can help you.'

305

'I have to go away, and I'm never coming back. I know a place where I can get rid of it, but I don't have any money.'

'Surely you have relations you could turn to?'

She shook her head. 'No one.'

'Does your father know?'

'I've been sick in the mornings. Last night, he made me tell him.' She touched her cheek. 'He hit me. I thought he was going to kill me. I had to lock myself in my room and this morning he wouldn't speak to me. It was as though I wasn't there. He won't help me, and there isn't anyone else. I have to get away before he comes home.'

There was no doubt that her fear was genuine. Although he didn't like the girl and was reluctant to get involved in her problems, he was sorry for her.

'I'm not sure that my father would encourage you to leave home . . .' he began.

She clutched his arm, and the calculating look was back. 'I think he would. It's his child.'

Momentarily speechless, he stared at her. 'That's not possible!'

Her voice became shrill, and her face, still childishly unformed under the layers of cosmetics, was spiteful. 'It's true. What d'you think he's been doing for a woman all these years? I used to come here while my father was at work. There was no one in the house except Peter and me.' She used the Christian name with emphasis, her head tipped on one side, eyes slanted up at him, watching for his reaction.

When he did not reply, she said slyly, 'The only other person I could go to is Madame Absalom. I'd have to tell her the truth, and I thought Peter would prefer . . .'

His father and this little tart?

But Peter was a virile man. Claudette was young, pretty, and available. It was a squalid situation, and it was unthinkable that Jo should be loaded with it, as well as everything else. He felt an uncharacteristic surge of anger against his father.

'How much will you need?' he said abruptly.

'At least two thousand francs.'

He went inside and fetched all the money he had.

'I don't have that much in francs, but here are some American dollars . You can change them in any bank.'

She grasped the wad of notes, riffling them greedily. 'Nicholas, you are saving my life! I hate this place. When – when it's over, I'm going to find a job in a city. I'm going on the stage.'

He was not interested in her ambitions. 'When are you leaving?'

'The bus goes from the shop in twenty minutes, and I can make the connection from Cotolin to Nice.' Her eyelashes fluttered and a pink tongue licked her lips. 'I must thank you properly . . .'

She launched herself at him and before he could dodge, one of her arms went around his neck. Her other hand moved down towards his thigh, as she pressed her lips against his. Her body was soft and yielding.

She did not attract him, but he had not been with a woman since his return from America. Her tongue forced itself between his teeth and he found himself returning her kiss. Almost instantaneously, he was overcome with revulsion. He tried to back off, but her limbs were twined around him like tentacles.

A movement near the steps caught his eye, and he looked up. Lisa was standing there.

After a frozen moment, she turned and ran back along the drive, her feet, in rope-soled espadrilles, making no sound.

He flung Claudette away so roughly that she almost lost her balance.

Straightening her clothes, she picked up her suitcase and flounced off in the same direction Lisa had taken, stumbling occasionally on her high heels.

★ ★ ★

He caught up with Lisa in the village and fell into step beside her, saying nothing, awaiting her reaction.

When it came, it was not what he had expected. Her voice was indifferent: 'Sorry I interrupted.'

'Look, Claudette was thanking me for some money I'd given her.'

'Do you have to pay them now? You must be slipping.'

'Are you going to let me explain?'

Her shrug was theatrical. 'Why should you feel you have to explain? Your affairs are nothing to do with me.'

At that, he lost his temper. 'I'm sick to bloody death of your acting! You haven't behaved naturally since you got back. Okay, my affairs aren't anything to do with you, but this time, you're going to listen to me.' He tried to grasp her arm, but she jerked it away and walked on, without looking at him. 'I hardly know that wretched girl. She came to the house to ask for money so she could leave home. Apparently her father beat her up last night, and she's terrified of him. So I gave her some cash. She was grateful.'

'She must know you pretty well to have come to you.'

'She was looking for my father. I happened to be there.'

They had reached the outskirts of the village. She stopped, and faced him. 'Is that true?'

He made a cross on his chest with a forefinger, then licked it and held it up. When they were children, it had been their way of confirming the truth. 'So help me, God.' (Okay, God, it isn't the whole truth, but what there is, is true.)

Their eyes met, and held, then she walked on and said: 'I'm sorry. But I thought . . . you can't blame me, the way you were.'

'You might have given me the benefit of the doubt. She's not my type.'

A picture appeared on her mind's screen. Before she could stop herself, she said, 'I suppose those women I found you in bed with in Los Angeles were your type?'

'I'd like to tell you about that. Not making excuses. There aren't any, I guess. But maybe there are extenuating circumstances.'

She turned away from him, towards the valley, and a gust of wind swept her cotton skirt upwards so he saw the length of her slim brown legs. Automatically, she had turned onto the path that led to Le Mur. There, under the phoenix tree, he had known her whole body. His sexual instincts, deliberately kept dormant for several weeks, had already been aroused by Claudette. Suddenly, he wanted Lisa so badly that it was like a physical pain. He wanted to stroke the shining brown hair, the smooth skin, kiss the clean face which had no need of cosmetics to enhance its beauty, feel her arms around him.

He became aware of what she was saying: 'I had a letter from Simon today. That's why I wanted to see you.'

Her husband's name was like a draught of cold water. 'Oh, yes?'

'It was about Dirk Chavez's death. I gather you told him about it over dinner and he'd put some dates together. He thinks that the day I came to that house, you must have been to Chavez's funeral.'

'I had.'

'That was why you were so drunk?'

He shrugged. 'I'd been drunk for a while.'

'That woman, Monica Martensen . . . you were – engaged?'

'Christ, no! That was her fantasy. She was a star when I was still in rompers. I rented an apartment above her garage, and I left the day after that party.' He allowed himself a moment of impatience. 'I wrote, trying to apologize for what happened. You didn't even open the letters. Don't you think you might have given me the benefit of the doubt then, too, and at least read them?'

'There was no doubt what I'd seen.'

'No. Now you know the reason, does it make any difference?'

309

They had almost reached the tree. She turned and faced him. 'I'd gone to LA because I hadn't stopped missing you. I'd never thought of you with other women. It was always you and me, and even after Ben separated us, I believed we'd get together again eventually.' She added bitterly, 'I was very young. I hated you, and I made myself go on hating you. It was the only way I could cope with – with what I'd seen.'

'I didn't know it was you at the door until the next day. You were a blurred female shape, standing there with that perverted old bitch, Monica. The next day, when she told me, I wanted to die. I called all the hotels I could think of, but you hadn't booked into any of them. Then I drove to the airport and discovered that you'd already flown out.'

'I'd stayed in the airport hotel that night. I took the first flight I could get.'

He took a deep breath. 'I realize that you probably still regard me as a drunken, fornicating slob, but is there any chance that we might start all over again? A long way back. On that day, here, before Ben so rudely interrupted us?'

She was watching him steadily and now there was no hostility in her eyes, though they were still wary. 'We'd have to start further back than that. We need to get to know each other again.'

'But we can try?'

The corners of her mouth twitched and a younger Lisa, the girl he remembered, looked up at him. 'I don't see why not.'

He put out a finger and tipped up her chin. As he bent his head to kiss her, he said, 'Is this allowed among friends?'

6

As Nick stood with his Sabatier knife poised over the fresh chickens he was dismembering for the following day's *coq au riesling*, he was aware of a lightness of heart he had not experienced for a long time. He felt again the kiss that had started gently and escalated into passion. Lisa had fitted into his arms as though it was her natural place and it was only by exercising all his self-control that he had released her when she had shown signs of resisting his urgency.

They had stood, looking at each other, breathing quickly, then she had stepped back and said, 'That's enough for a first date.'

'How many dates will it take for – something more?'

'You'll know when the time comes. If it does.'

His euphoria only faded when, at 7.15, his father arrived in the restaurant. Early diners were settling to their meals. The bar was full and the young barman, Lucien, was scurrying to keep up with the orders. Most of the customers were men from the timber-yard.

Nick found himself looking at Peter with new eyes. It was difficult to visualize him with Claudette Dorsey. This gentle, fastidious man, with a girl nearly forty years his junior, reputedly the village whore?

He remembered his own mother only dimly, but the impression that remained was of a slender, laughing woman, speaking French with a strong American accent, intelligent, humorous, unrestrained in her affection for her husband and son. A woman unlike Claudette in every respect.

He realized that, of all people, he had no right to feel

311

revulsion because Peter had made use of a willing bed-mate. Nevertheless, he wished he had not found out about the affair.

Jean-Louis interrupted his thoughts with a brisk tap on the shoulder. 'Leave that, Nick. I need you to serve the dessert. Marie wants two *nonnepferezlas* and one *gâteau de chocolat. Tout de suite, copain!*'

In the Lion d'Or Jean-Louis was the master, unimpressed by Nick's success in other fields or the fact that he was the boss's son. As Nick shook the little golden fritters in a paper bag with sugar, then set them on plates, he grinned at the thought of what Hollywood's studio executives would think if they could see their former star now: red-faced, sweating in the heat of the kitchen, his blue and white striped apron spattered with flour and fat. They would never understand how he could be happier here than he had been in their glittering world.

He carried the desserts to the hatch for Marie to collect, and was on his way back to his chickens when he became aware of a disturbance in the bar.

Peter, who had been making his first nightly patrol to greet friends among the clientele, appeared at the door and called urgently: 'Nick, I need you. You, too, Jean-Louis!'

They followed as he ran back through the restaurant, past diners whose knives and forks were upraised, food forgotten in the drama.

Peter paused in the archway that divided the bar from the restaurant and Nick looked over his shoulder. Silence had fallen, and the customers had apparently been turned to stone. Some had glasses to their lips, but were not drinking, others were leaning on the bar, mouths open, as though interrupted in the middle of a sentence. Behind the bar, Lucien had a brandy-bottle in one hand, a glass in the other. His eyes were glazed with fear.

Everyone was looking towards a man who was standing in the doorway, a raised shotgun resting against his shoulder.

312

It was Claudette's father, André Dorsey, and his heavy, peasant's face was twisted with fury.

He was a huge man, more than six feet tall, with wide hunched shoulders and a deep chest. His head was weaving from side to side like a fighting bull, and white foam had formed at one corner of his mouth. His staring eyes were rimmed with red.

His gun was moving from one man to another, and he was muttering incoherently.

Peter walked forward slowly, talking in a low, soothing voice. Jean-Louis followed him.

Hoping he was sufficiently hidden behind the other men not to attract Dorsey's attention, Nick stepped back into the dining-room.

Marie was standing at the hatch, paralysed. He pulled her into the kitchen and whispered, 'Get Berenger! Hurry!'

As she scurried towards the gendarmerie, he dashed outside, around the building, onto the terrace. The door leading into the bar was propped open and Dorsey was standing just inside. His attention– and the gun– seemed to have focused on Lucien. His finger was on the trigger.

Nick launched himself through the doorway and knocked the shot-gun up as it went off. He grabbed Dorsey's hair and jerked his head backwards. His other arm went around the barrel chest. Pellets spattered the ceiling and the two men lost their balance and fell in a heap onto the floor.

Dorsey, on top, came to his feet first and whirled around, reaching for Nick's throat. The veined eyes were insane and his breath reeked of brandy. He wanted to kill someone; anyone would do. Peter and Jean-Louis tried to drag him away.

Nick felt his face begin to bulge as the thick, strong hands squeezed. He fought for breath, his arms flailing.

There were black spots in front of his eyes and Dorsey's face was a wavering, featureless mass as Nick summoned

313

the last of his strength and brought his right knee up into the man's groin. There was a howl of pain and the fingers fell away from his throat.

By the time he regained his feet, Dorsey was in the firm grasp of two policemen. He was still struggling, but much of his strength had gone, and Berenger was able to handcuff him. Gradually, he became still and stood, moaning slightly and blinking as though uncertain where he was. Supported by a policeman on each arm, he was led off to the *gendarmerie*.

Having made sure Nick had suffered no serious damage, Peter turned to the crowd of diners and drinkers who had gathered. 'Show's over, my friends,' he said. 'I hope you will all accept a glass of wine on the house, with my apologies for the disturbance.'

He was less nonchalant when they returned to the kitchen, where Nick was peering at himself in the mirror, gingerly touching the angry red marks that were already showing on his throat.

'You sure you're okay?' he said.

'I'm fine, except I feel as though a rock is stuck in my windpipe.'

'I don't know what brought that on, but I intend to find out,' Peter said. 'Jean-Louis, can you spare us for a while?'

'We can manage until the rush starts.'

Nick followed his father into the bar, where the talk was loud and excited as the men relived the past few minutes.

Peter beckoned to his relief barman, off-duty tonight, who was standing with a group of cronies. 'Ricky, take over for a while, will you? Lucien, I want to see you in my office.' He glanced around, and called one of the men from the timber-yard. 'Réné, can you spare a minute?'

They followed him into the little office which led off the bar, and he perched on the corner of his desk, facing them.

'You first, Lucien. What happened?'

The boy was still pale and shaking. 'M'sieu, he came to

the door, pointed the shot-gun, and said he was going to kill everyone. He's a maniac!'

'There had to be some reason . . .'

Réné Raymond interrupted. A roly-poly man in his middle forties, he had a round cheerful face and was among the most popular personalities in the village. He had never been heard to say a bad word about anyone. Even the toughest men in the timber-yard regarded him as a kind of universal uncle.

'M'sieu Peter, I think I know what caused it. Dorsey never drinks, he is against all alcohol, but today I have been watching him in the yard. He had a bottle of brandy. It was full this morning; by mid-day, it was empty.'

'What started him off?'

'Last night, he and Claudette quarrelled. He hit her. When he was drunk this afternoon, I took him to my home, and he told me about it.' He hesitated. 'I have to say this, m'sieu, she is not a good girl, that Claudette, and it seems that André has just found out what the rest of us have known for a long time.'

'Get on with it, man! What have you known?'

Nick frowned. Of all people, Peter must have been aware of the girl's behaviour. He began to wonder how well he really knew his father.

'She has been with – many men.' Nick saw Lucien's eyes drop, and he moved uncomfortably. 'André didn't know, but last night in anger, she actually boasted about it. Said she could get any man she wanted. She also told him that she was pregnant. He worships that girl, but always he has been too strict with her. Now he has learned what she really is . . .' He raised his shoulders and spread his hands. 'He has gone a little mad, I think.'

Peter turned to Lucien. 'The pregnancy . . . Was that why he was aiming at you?'

'It could have been almost any man in the bar tonight! I went out with her for a while. Then a couple of months ago she said she didn't want to see me any more. There was someone else.'

'Who?'

Was there an extra sharpness in Peter's question?

'I wouldn't know, m'sieu,' Lucien said sulkily.

'So why did Dorsey focus on you?'

'I suppose because he saw us together once. We used to meet when he was at the yard, and I had time off. He caught us walking back to my place one afternoon. He thought she was too good for the likes of anyone in the village.'

How would he have reacted if he had known about Peter? Nick wondered. Would the shot-gun have been aimed at him, or would he have been proud that his daughter had captured the rich man to whom everyone looked up? The fact that Peter had been screwing Claudette had been hard enough to take. Now his bland pretence of ignorance about the girl was painful to watch.

If he could cover up this affair so expertly, what else might he have hidden? Someone had killed Ben Absalom. Peter was in love with Jo. Was it possible that he had seized an opportunity to free her? Or even caused Ben's death accidentally, and decided not to admit it? Never! the word exploded in his mind. It wasn't possible. Not his father.

'I won't press any charges,' Peter was saying. 'Berenger can dry him out overnight, then he can go home. I'll see if there's anything I can do to help him with his family problem.' He stood up. 'Thanks, René. I'm grateful for the information. Nick, you take the night off. Go home and rest that throat.'

René and Lucien left. Peter ran a hand through his hair, and sighed. 'Lord, I'm sorry for that poor wretch. I had no idea the girl was as bad as that, although Marie did hint . . .'

Disgusted by the prevarication, Nick interrupted him in mid-sentence. 'I'm off. See you tomorrow.' With a brief nod, he walked out of the office.

7

'There's something wrong. What is it?' Lisa said.

'Nothing.'

She and Nick were strolling in the villa's grounds, a brief excursion into the open air before the rain started again. There had been two or three days respite, but the clouds had gathered and storms were forecast. The Massif was like a great sponge that could absorb no more water. Even Jo, who had found outdoor work a solace during this time of uncertainty, had given up trying to clear the fire-blackened twigs and branches that had been carried by the mud down the slope at the back of the house and were lodged between the fence's iron railings.

It was nearly a week since Dorsey had invaded the bar; nearly a week since Nick had discovered his father's duplicity. He had not been able to bring himself to tell Peter about his meeting with Claudette and his knowledge of their affair, and he bitterly resented the web of half-truths and evasions in which he had been caught.

Now everyone was talking about her disappearance.

Dorsey, allowed home after a night in the *gendarmerie's* only cell, had emerged from his front door, wildly calling her name. Then he had stumbled around the village, asking everyone he met where she was. It was Georgette Ponelle who informed him that she had seen the girl boarding the bus for Cotolin the previous day, carrying a suitcase.

In Cotolin, he was told that she had transferred to the coach that ran to Nice. On two consecutive days, he drove into the city, had cross-questioned everyone who had known her during her school-days, but could find no trace of her.

Nick was able to excuse himself for remaining silent because he knew no more than André now did about her movements. Nothing would be gained by admitting that he had given her money and he had no wish to be obliged to explain why.

Peter had tried to visit Dorsey, but the front door remained locked against him. The man had become a sodden wreck. He didn't go to work at the timber-yard, he emerged from his house only to buy bottles of brandy from Georgette. Réné Raymond, the one person whom he allowed in, reported that he sat all day staring at a photograph of his daughter.

'I know there's something wrong,' Lisa insisted. 'Is it to do with Ben's death?' Her voice sharpened. 'Have you heard anything?'

'No. It isn't anything. Really.'

'You're lying.' She had always had an uncanny ability to judge his moods.

The worst thing about the week had been his alienation from his father. Whenever possible, he had avoided contact, getting up too late for them to have breakfast together, hurrying off to the restaurant with little more than a brief good morning, going to bed immediately he reached home at night. No matter how hard he tried to dismiss it, there remained at the back of his mind the fear that Peter might in some way have been involved in Ben's death.

The bright spot of each day came between lunch and dinner, when he and Lisa had dropped into the habit of meeting, walking and talking, catching up on the years they had been separated. But although they appeared to be relaxed, the tension between them had not entirely evaporated. Both were aware that there were no-go areas in their own lives that they were not yet ready to share.

Whenever Nick thought of Simon Ashton, and her

318

marriage, he experienced the same bafflement, the same inability to understand their relationship, and knew that he could not be fully at ease with her until it was explained. She rarely mentioned Simon, but when she did, he felt the same pang of irritation– which he refused to admit, even to himself, was jealousy.

Inevitably, she had mentioned the affair at the Lion d'Or and questioned him again about his part in Claudette's disappearance. He had simply repeated that having heard about the beating her father had given her, he had been sorry for the girl, and contributed getaway money. He had asked her not to mention it to Jo or Peter. 'They have enough on their plates without getting involved in the Dorseys' affairs.'

Now she said, 'Did something happen that day that you haven't told me about?'

'Oh, for God's sake! No! If I'm distrait, I'm – I'm thinking about Ben's biography, that's all.'

'So why don't I shut up and mind my own business? Okay. What will we talk about?'

He relaxed. 'Have you heard anything from Amyas lately?'

'No, thank God. I hope Jo convinced him that she wouldn't sell the villa.'

'I'd be surprised if he has given up so easily. I'd say he's a pretty determined character – especially when his own future is involved.'

'Jo is determined, too.'

'Is she still talking of taking in paying guests when this is all over?'

'Maybe. And farming in a small way.' She added, 'I'm thinking of staying on and going into partnership with her.'

'Are you indeed? Is this a recent decision?'

'I doubt if I'd have had the guts to give up my lovely tv money. Now tv's given me up, so the decision has been taken out of my hands. I suppose I could get other jobs,

319

but I've only realized since I got back how much I love living here – even in the present circumstances.'

'Maybe we should start our own little theatre,' he said idly. 'Plenty of room at the villa. There's a natural amphitheatre, too. And a ready-made audience of English-speaking tourists panting for entertainment.'

She stared at him. 'Are you serious?'

'I don't suppose so. It was just a thought.'

'Then hang onto it – only you'd be too busy writing, wouldn't you?'

With dawning interest, he said, 'I would't mind combining writing with something else. But could we stand working together?'

'Too soon to say,' she said cautiously. 'Let's think about it.'

They turned back towards the villa, and each was aware of a new excitement.

Large drops of rain had started to fall and within seconds there was a downpour. He grabbed her hand and they ran for the house.

Jo and Peter stood on the terrace, watching them. They were laughing and Lisa's head was tilted back as she enjoyed the rain on her face. Her white silk shirt was clinging around her small, high breasts. Her hair was streaming down her back. Nick, a head taller, was having to shorten his stride so she could keep up. They saw him stop, heave her up in his arms and run on with her.

'At least one thing seems to be working out for the best,' Jo said wryly.

'Yes. Nick hasn't said anything – for some reason he's been out of sorts lately – but maybe they're solving their problems. It always seemed to me that they were meant for each other: two halves of a whole.'

Her voice was low. 'They've escaped from Ben. He'd hate that.'

'Joanna, you can't let yourself explore Ben's reactions

for the rest of your life!' There was an unusual note of asperity in his tone.

'I can't explain it, even to myself, but Ben is still around, Peter. A – a *presence*. Lisa's aware of it, too. He affected so many people's lives. Maybe, if we were to find out the truth about his death, he'd – leave us alone. But I'm beginning to wonder if we ever will.'

Have you seen the Commissaire this week?'

She shook her head. 'It's a relief, but worrying at the same time. Serge Berenger said he never gives up. What can he be doing?'

'I expect we'll find out in good time.' His face was suddenly desolate. 'Oh, my dear, I do wish . . .'

'Wish what?'

'That this bloody situation was resolved and we could get back to controlling our own lives, not having them controlled by Ben!'

'You see, you're doing it, too,' she said. 'Talking about him as though he's still alive.'

PART SEVEN

1

The previous day's promise of storms had been fulfilled, and the night had been punctuated by thunder and lightning, accompanied by rain. There was a cooler smell of early autumn in the air.

Even the luxury yachts tied up in the port of St-Tropez looked dispirited. The Beautiful People, who came out, like mesembryanthemums, when the sun was shining, had kept to their beds. The damp grey promenade was deserted apart from a group of British tourists who wandered along, complaining that, weatherwise, they would have been better off taking their late vacations in Brighton.

It was Saturday, one of the town's two weekly market-days, and Nick had called Lisa early in the morning, inviting her to accompany him on a shopping expedition for Marie.

The gloomy skies did not discourage the market-traders in the Place des Lices, who were doing brisk business.

Nick bought six chickens and several dozen eggs from Marie's supplier, a brown-faced farm-woman who wrung the chickens' necks while they waited. At the cheese-stall, they collected a round of Brie de Meaux, which he had poked and tested knowledgeably for ripeness, a Fromage au Marc de Raisin, rolled in its black crust of grape pulp, a crumbly, white Roquefort mottled with greenish flecks, and several goat cheeses.

Finally, because the Mazeaus loved bread, and believed their customers should have more choice than the ubiquitous *baguette*, he bought a selection of breads, all shapes and sizes: *Tourte d'Auvergne, Pain Alsatien, Pain au Levain, Main Provençale.*

Lisa bought fruit and vegetables for Jo, dried figs and bananas, bottles of walnut and olive oil, tarragon-flavoured vinegar, dried herbs and a light, custardy Tarte Tropezienne.

When everything had been packed into Nick's car, they walked along the narrow streets that led from the market-square, peering into expensive boutiques, reading menus outside the restaurants.

Senequier's, in high season the most fashionable and crowded of the terraces that faced the port, had few customers.

'This is the only time of the year when this town is bearable,' Lisa said. 'You know what? Not a single person has recognized either of us.'

Nick was suddenly reminded painfully of Dirk, and the pleasure he had taken in being unrecognized when they had met in the bar in Anaheim. At the time he had wondered whether it had been an affectation. His own notoriety had made him appreciate the luxury of anonymity.

But Lisa had spoken too soon. 'Don't look now,' he said. 'I suspect one of your fans is about to descend on us.'

'Oh, shit!' She brought her cup up to hide her face, but it was too late. She felt a tap on her shoulder, heard a voice: 'Lisa Absalom! I've been going to get in touch.'

She said, without enthusiasm. 'Hello, Mr Partridge. I'd forgotten you were staying here.'

He gestured towards the largest of the yachts which were tied to the moorings that edged the promenade. 'Got back from London a few days ago. That's mine. Any chance of a private chat?'

'What about?'

'About your late father, what else?' He glanced at Nick, who was observing him with fascination.

He was wearing pants that were a copy of the local

fishermen's working trousers, cut so tightly that every line of his sagging buttocks was visible. On top was a black shirt, its buttons undone, showing a chest covered with black hair and gold chains. His feet were encased in sandals with straps tied around the ankles and on his head was a Royal Navy officer's cap, its peak encrusted with gold.

Reluctantly, Lisa gestured towards a chair, but he shook his head. 'Not here. Too public. People, you know, recognize me. Fans, like. Can't turn them away.'

'Poor you.' He looked at her suspiciously, but her face was bland. 'Where, then?'

'Come aboard. We'll have a drink. Your friend, too.'

She introduced the two men and Nick shook a limp hand.

'Seen you somewhere, haven't I?' Partridge said. 'You in the business?'

'What business?'

'Music.'

'No, not music.'

He lost interest. 'Let's go aboard. Got a few chums, but we can find a quiet spot.'

Lisa said, 'If you want to talk to me about buying the villa, it's not on.'

'Amyas said your ma wasn't keen. Have to see if we can't talk her round. I mean, like making an offer she can't refuse. I want to show you my collection, then you'll see that it needs the right setting.'

She was about to refuse the invitation, but Nick took her arm and pulled her up. She recognized the look of concentration on his face. He was storing Dominic Partridge away to reproduce later, as they both used to do with Ben's more bizarre friends when they were children. The years rolled back as she remembered how anyone had been grist to their satiric mills. We could do it again, she thought, and the idea produced so casually began to take on a positive shape.

Partridge led them along the deck of the yacht, inside and down a wide, polished staircase whose rails were upheld by a series of brass caryatids, slim, semi-draped female figures with pointed breasts, on each of which pink nipples had been painted.

The stairs led into a huge room, dazzling with gold and brass and mirrors. At one end, there was a marble-topped bar edged with brass, backed by mirror against which were set shelves of gilt goblets and decanters. There were gold ashtrays on small mirror-topped tables, gold lamp-bases and shades and gold braiding on the white leather chairs and sofas. The ceiling was covered with triangles of gilt-framed mirror.

Behind her, she heard Nick's awed whisper, 'De Mille would have died for this!'

There were people lounging on the sofas and deep arm-chairs, but they were so diminished by the surroundings as to be hardly visible.

'Not bad, hey?' Partridge said proudly. 'Bought it from an Arab who had to economize when the price of oil went down.' He pointed to the floor. 'You haven't noticed that yet.'

Lisa was standing on the lowest stair, and as she looked down, she nearly lost her balance. Directly below her was the sea, with vividly-coloured fish swimming among waving fronds of water-plants. Sea-urchins were clinging to rocks and two little sea-horses were standing upright on the sandy bottom, where crabs and a crayfish were crawling.

Partridge stepped down, and she realized that the sea was covered by a floor made of reinforced glass.

'Achmed reckoned that if Jesus Christ could walk on water, so could any good Moslem.' His laughter was loud, mechanical, the joke oft-repeated.

The effect of crossing what was, in effect, a large underfloor fish tank made Lisa feel slightly dizzy and she was pleased when she reached dry land – an area covered in deep white carpet which stretched to the bar.

'Margaritas or mimosas?' At his order, an Asian barman, wearing a black jacket over a brightly patterned sarong, mixed the drinks. 'Bring your glasses. I'll give you the tour.'

Not bothering to introduce them to his guests, he whisked them through a series of staterooms, each with its en suite bathroom. The bathroom fittings were gold, even to the soap holders and lavatory brushes. The staterooms all had gigantic, satin-covered beds, mirrored ceilings and wall-panels inlaid with gold, lapis lazuli and mother-of-pearl.

Partridge's own suite, with black walls, carpet and bedspread, even had a human decoration: stretched out on the double-king-sized bed, stark naked and asleep, was a golden-skinned girl, her black hair spread over gold cushions.

He gave them a generous moment to stare before closing the door.

In the gallery, a chef and two assistants were working in high-tech surroundings of shining stainless steel and plastic, with every conceivable convenience to hand, from microwave ovens to automatic ice-makers.

'How d'you like it?' he said as they returned to the wide corridor.

'It's overwhelming.' Lisa had the same feeling of glut she suffered after one of her rare chocolate binges.

'Great, innit?' He winked. 'Decided years ago that one day I'd have a better yacht than Onassis. Made my money work for me, right from the beginning. I'm a Monagasque citizen now, so I don't even pay taxes.'

'I'm sorry I was too young to see you on-stage,' Lisa said innocently.

A spasm of annoyance crossed his face. 'They been trying to talk me into a come-back. Fans are begging for it. Might even do it one day, when it suits me. I'll send you tickets. Now for the pièce de résistance. Ready?'

He threw open a door, and she found herself facing the portrait of herself and Nick which Jo told her had been on exhibition in Bond Street. She looked up at the two beautiful, childish faces, innocent and full of life, and tears came into her eyes. Ben had painted them both with such love, and then he had spoiled it all.

Partridge shattered the moment. 'Pity kids have to grow up.' He turned to Nick and snapped his fingers. 'Knew I'd seen you before. That's you, up there, innit?' Without waiting for an answer, he pushed them into the room. 'Have a look at the others. It's quite a collection. Worth a mint. That's why I want it to be in my museum.'

The walls were lined with off-white, padded leather, against which eight paintings were set, each with its own shaded light. There were two more portraits of Lisa as a child, one of Jo, which had hung in the villa, and another of a famous British actor.

The other three were landscapes. Ben had liked to concentrate on details from a scene which a normal person would hardly register, and enlarge them so they had their own identities. What appeared to the undiscerning eye to be an abstract was one she particularly remembered: a section of the phoenix tree's trunk, from which a frond had been roughly torn; another she recognized as a corner of the villa's swimming-pool where the walls met the water, creating a pattern of shadows and angles.

'Every one of 'em paid for by a golden disc,' Partridge said proudly. 'Remember *Love Don't Matter Any More*? That bought you, Lisa. *Fast Train to Nowhere* bought your Mum. *End My Life Soon* was the big one . . .'

She hardly heard him as she and Nick walked slowly around the walls, lost in memory.

There was one she did not recall, a curiously haunting picture in shades of grey and terracotta, showing part of a brick wall, half in sun, the rest shadowed. The sunny part was broken by another shadow which might or might not have been human hands clasped in prayer.

'I've never seen it before,' she said. 'It's beautiful.'

'Mahr found it in Switzerland. I've got it on appro. The owner will only sell it on condition Mahr doesn't reveal where it came from. He's in a financial bind and he doesn't want people to know he has to sell. Gonna cost me a bomb, and Mahr says there are two more where that came from if he can persuade the guy to part with them. Typical Absalom, late period.'

Lisa was examining the picture, leaning forward so her eyes were a few inches from the canvas. Nick watched, puzzled, as she scanned every section, from top to bottom, left to right, then went over it again.

After a few minutes, Partridge was bored. 'Tell you what, Nick, let's you and me go and have another little drinkie. Introduce you to the boys and girls. Lisa can join us when she's ready.'

Abstracted, Lisa nodded, moved back a step and continued to study the painting.

In the gold saloon, a group of men and women had gathered at the bar. Partridge waved a hand. 'This is Nick,' he said. 'Give us another Margarita, Lee.'

That was the extent of his introduction, but a small blonde girl with petulant lips and a round, Barbie-doll face needed no more. 'Nicholas Garnier!' she breathed. 'You are, aren't you?' He nodded. 'I saw the movie you made with that gorgeous Dirk Chavez. It was terrific!'

Partridge looked at him with new interest as the rest of the group drew nearer. 'What movie? You an actor, then?'

The girl had a high, baby voice and her accent was from London. 'It was called, something. I've forgotten. But, wow, brilliant! I mean, you and Chavez! And wasn't it just awful about him?'

Apart from his paintings, Partridge's horizons appeared to be limited to the world of pop-music. 'Chavez? Who the hell was he?'

'He was so beautiful,' the girl sighed. 'Dark. Like Mexican, I mean, but those wild blue eyes. Oh, God, I

331

used to dream of having his shoes under my bed. Only it wouldn't have done me any good, would it?' She giggled. 'He turned out to be gay as all get out. He o.d.'d because he had AIDS, didn't he, Nick?'

'No,' Nick said.

A faint surprise disturbed her pretty, vacant face. 'Yes, he did. Everyone said so.'

'Everyone was wrong.'

'What killed him, then?'

'Success.' He turned as Lisa came in. 'Thanks for the tour,' he said to Partridge. 'We have to go now.'

'Hey, not yet! Lisa, we gotta talk about my museum.'

For a moment, she looked at him as though she had forgotten who he was, then she said, 'There's nothing to talk about. We told Amyas. If you want to put your pictures in a museum, that's up to you, but my mother won't co-operate, and she certainly won't sell you the villa.'

Without waiting to see his reaction, she made for the stairway.

As she went down the gangway ahead of Nick, she said, 'Jo told me little girls used to have orgasms when he was on-stage in the sixties.'

'Those little girls are rising forty now. I wonder if they'll turn out for his come-back?'

'There'll be a few shattered illusions if they do.' They turned back towards the square. 'Nick . . .'

'What?'

'Ben didn't paint that picture.'

'What are you talking about? What picture?'

'*Wall with Shadows*.'

He frowned. 'Of course he did! If ever I saw a typical Absalom, that's it.'

'I know. But it isn't his.'

'What makes you think so?'

'Have you ever heard about Ben's secret mark?'

'No. What is it?'

332

'I found out about it when I was a kid, and I was posing for him . . .'

She was sitting on a dais in the studio, leaning forward so her hair was falling over her face, chin resting on her hand. She was seven years old, and she was bored. Ben had been working on her portrait for weeks. This, he had promised, would be the last sitting, but it had been a long one. It was a hot day, the sun was shining, she could hear Nick splashing in the pool . . .

'Okay, that's it!' Ben was standing back from casel, eyes narrowed as he surveyed the painting. 'Not bad. Not bad at all.' He never allowed her or Jo to see a picture until it was finished, and now he said, 'Want to look?'

She was blasé about seeing herself on canvas, but she understood that he liked approval, so she looked up, and it was like looking into a mirror. 'It's very nice,' she said politely, then: 'Why are you doing that?'

He was impressing his thumb in the still-tacky paint near his signature in the bottom right hand corner. When he had finished, he handed her a magnifying glass that was lying on his table. Through it, she could see a thumb-print, which was almost invisible to the naked eye.

'That's my way of making sure no one ever fakes an Absalom,' he said. 'Remember that, kitten. All you have to do is look at my pictures through a glass, and you'll know they're genuine if you find the print. It'll be there somewhere.'

'What's faking?'

'It's when dishonest people paint pictures in the style of artists whose work fetches big money, and pretend they're genuine. Chap named Hans van Meegeren went to prison for doing it just after the war. Otto Wacker used to turn out van Goghs by the dozen. Utrillo, Rousseau, Cézanne, Chagall – there are hundreds of fakes of their work, even in museums.' As he always did when he had finished a painting, he began cleaning his palettes and brushes.

'They won't be able to do that with mine, though.'

'You're clever, Ben.'

He laughed. 'Keep it our secret, kitten. Tony Henriques has a sheet of paper in London with my print on it, so there's something to compare. Jo knows, and now you do, but nobody else. That way, we'll be able to surprise anyone who tries to cheat the market – and me.'

Flattered to have been entrusted with so important a secret, she had not told even Nick about the finger-print. She had tucked the information away and eventually it had receded into the back of her mind.

Today, for some reason she could not define, the picture of the wall had seemed to speak to her in a voice that was not Ben's, and the memory had surfaced. Idly at first, she had begun to look for the finger-print. When the men left her alone, she had gone over and over the painting. There was no print.

'Of course, I remember,' Jo said. 'Ben pretended it was a joke, but he never failed to put the print where it would be least visible. Are you sure it wasn't there? It was often easy to miss.'

'I'm positive, but I didn't want to say anything until I'd spoken to you.'

'A section of brick wall, with shadows.' Her voice was thoughtful. 'I don't remember it, but I never saw some of the work Ben did in London after I'd moved down here. There's another way of checking, though. He kept a record of every painting he did, with a brief description. It was in a note-book . . .'

She found it in a drawer of Ben's desk, and they went through the lists. Here there was no snide gossip about sitters, no cruel caricatures. Page after page was filled with Ben's neat hand-writing, detailing work completed, the titles, the length of time each painting had taken, together with colour-notes.

There was no *Wall with Shadows*.

When she had closed the book, Jo said uneasily, 'You say that Partridge told you there are other pictures where that one came from. They could be forgeries, too. I must go and see Amyas and find out who this mysterious Swiss collector is.'

Nick looked out of the window. 'Rain's coming down like Niagara Falls. Better wait for it to ease.'

But it was as though someone had forgotten to turn off a tap in the heavens, and the rain did not cease. By mid-afternoon, the pool was overflowing, the terraces were awash, the lawns were seas of mud.

Nick, who had splashed back to his car to take his supplies to the Lion d'Or, phoned to warn her not to attempt to reach the Mahrs' little house, which was at the foot of a shallow cliff, but had to be reached from below, up a narrow, winding track. Even on the main road, he said, he had driven through lakes and the windscreen wipers had been almost useless.

That evening, flood-warnings were broadcast to low-lying areas, and people were instructed not to venture out except in emergency.

2

Nick was lounging in a chair in the living-room, a glass of wine in his hand, watching cascades of water flowing down the glass doors that led onto the terrace. He had turned up at the usual time for his evening stint at the restaurant, to find that Marie's niece, Louise, had finally arrived from Strasbourg. A tall, competent, plain-faced girl, she had no doubts about her ability to cope with her new job, so Jean-Louis had told him to take the night off. On such an evening, there would be few patrons.

Peter came in, dripping wet in the short distance from his car to the house. 'Christ, what weather! I've been to see Dorsey. He's permanently drunk these days. There's no news of the girl.' He spoke with his usual ease, having for the past week avoided questioning the strain between them, although Nick knew he must be aware of it.

He watched as Peter stripped off his rain-coat and dried his face with a handkerchief.

There's no news of the girl. Suddenly, he was sick of pretence.

'I saw Claudette the day she disappeared,' he said abruptly.

Peter, who was about to pour himself a glass of Beaujolais, swung around. 'Why didn't you say so before? Where did you see her?'

'Here.'

'Here? You brought her to the house?' He paused, and said, almost to himself, 'I'd wondered . . . it was pretty obvious that she was after you.'

Nick's wine slopped over the edge of the glass as he sat

336

upright. 'After *me*? Jesus, I hardly knew the girl. She came to see you!'

'Me? Why?'

'She wanted money for an abortion,' he said brutally. 'You weren't here, so I gave it to her.'

Carefully, Peter poured his drink and carried it to a chair, turning it so they were facing each other. 'I think you'd better start from the beginning.'

'She told me who'd made her pregnant.'

'Who?'

'Dad, she told me all about it. How you and she . . . how she came here during the afternoons when Dorsey was at the timber-yard.'

He found himself unable to look at Peter and sat, eyes fixed on his glass, listening to an elongated silence.

'She told you I was the father?' Peter's voice was strangled.

'Yes. Dorsey had beaten her up the night before, and she wanted to get away before he came home. If I hadn't given her some money, she said the only other person she could go to was Jo. I knew you wouldn't want that.'

'Nick – look at me, for Christ's sake! – that girl was lying to you. I wouldn't have touched her if she'd been the last woman in the world! I didn't know her much better than you did. She came to the restaurant when she heard we needed a waitress. She said she wanted a job. I was sorry for her, she seemed to have a pretty dreary life with that father of hers, and we took her on temporarily – much against Marie's will.'

'But she said . . .'

'Go on.'

Embarrassment made him stammer. 'She asked me what I thought – what I thought you'd done for a woman all this time, implying that you'd – made use of her . . .'

'I suppose that if I had discussed my sex-life with you before, this might not have become an issue,' Peter said frostily. 'But it never occurred to me that it was any of your business.'

'You don't have to . . .'

'I want to clear this up. It's obviously why you've hardly deigned to speak to me for the past week. Since your mother died, there have been women, of course. A physical – and, to an extent, emotional – necessity. They have lived in Cannes or St-Tropez. Never in this village. But the one woman I want, and have asked to marry me, won't even discuss it rationally.'

'Jo?'

'Of course. How you could ever believe I'd take up with a child like Claudette Dorsey, I can't imagine.'

'I did wonder what you found to talk about.' Nick was conscious of a pervading relief. 'Hell, I'm sorry. I've been a bloody fool.'

Peter walked to the drinks table and replenished their glasses. 'Thank God we've got that straightened out. Who else do you think she told those lies to?'

'Probably no one. Looking back, I'd guess she made the whole thing up on the spur of the moment. She must have realized I'd need a good reason to hand over any money. So who the hell did father that child?'

Peter was biting his lower lip thoughtfully. 'If I'd been home, maybe she'd have told the truth. From what Lucien and Réné said, it could be practically anyone. You're sure she *is* pregnant? She didn't invent that, too?'

'She said she'd been sick in the mornings and that had made Dorsey suspicious. She admitted to him that she was pregnant, but wouldn't tell him the father's name. That's obviously why he didn't know who to shoot the other night.'

'There's something unhealthy about the way he worships that girl, according to people who know him. So he found out first she was pregnant, then that she's slept with most of the men in the village. No wonder he's gone off his head. She didn't tell you where she was going?'

338

'No more than Dorsey already knows, that she was making for Nice. She said she knew where she could arrange an abortion, and that she'd never come back. She could be anywhere by now.'

'The police have already circulated her description.' He rubbed his forehead with a weary gesture. 'I don't know what's happened to this village. Ever since Ben died, there seems to have been one crisis after another . . .'

'That reminds me,' Nick said. 'Lisa and I were in St-Tropez this morning. It seems that we have another little scandal in the making. Someone's been faking Absalom's paintings . . .'

At nine o'clock the following morning, they were finishing breakfast, lingering amicably over their coffee for the first time since Claudette's departure.

The rain had fallen steadily throughout the night, and flooded the terrace so that water had begun to creep inside under the doors. Peter's house-keeper, Madame Fronval, was muttering angrily as she mopped it up. The little river that bordered the property, in which Nick had played as a child, was a rushing torrent.

Inevitably, they were discussing the subject that dominated their lives.

'Molinard's silence worries me most,' Peter said. 'He virtually created a murder out of what everyone had accepted as an accident, then just left us up in the air. I'm worried about Jo. The uncertainty is getting her down. She never complains, but sometimes, when she doesn't realize anyone is watching, I've seen her let her guard down and she looks ten years older. She's lost a hell of a lot of weight, and Lisa says she has constant nightmares.'

'And now this fake painting has turned up. She said she'd probably see Amyas about it this morning . . .'

A peremptory knocking at the door startled them.

Serge Berenger was outside, water dripping off his peaked cap, rain-drops running in rivulets off his waterproof. 'Monsieur, we have big trouble! A mud-slide has started in the hills. The houses of Madame Absalom and the Mahrs are in its path. They must get away at once.'

'Have you phoned?'

'The lines are down. After last night's storm, the road from Cotolin is blocked by water and fallen trees and there's been an accident. Four cars, one man dead, two women and a child injured. I have to go. There's nobody else . . .'

'We'll go to the villa. Can we get the car through?'

'Maybe. Or near enough. To the Mahrs will be more difficult.'

'How much time have we?'

'Who can say? The mud is flowing like lava. After the fires, there's no vegetation to hold it back. I've had a report that in places it's ten feet deep.'

'Jo and Lisa are the nearest. We'll collect them first, then the Mahrs,' Peter said. 'They can all come back here.'

A lake several inches deep had formed at the bottom of the drive. The river had burst its banks and was flowing over the road. The village street was deserted. Georgette and Pierre-Luc were the only human beings they saw, peering out of the shop's door.

Several vehicles had been abandoned by the side of the road, and Peter had to detour around a van which had been left, slewed across the centre line, up to its bumpers in water.

As they neared the villa, they caught sight of the mud-slide, an awesome brown wall, rolling slowly and inexorably down the hill.

Peter put his foot down and the car shot forward onto a sheet of water.

Suddenly it was aquaplaning out of control, and skidding left and right. He wrestled the wheel, turning into the skid, remembering not to brake, but his speed had been too great and the car went on sliding.

Nick was clinging to the dashboard. As the car slewed

340

sideways, its left hand wheels slid into a ditch and he found himself on top of Peter, held by his seat-belt. The engine cut.

He managed to heave the passenger door open so he could climb out.

As Peter pulled himself upright, the movement of his weight caused the car to subside further into the ditch and come to rest on its side. He climbed up over the passenger's seat and joined Nick in the road.

There was no chance of righting the vehicle.

They looked up at the mud, which was like thick, melting chocolate and was speckled with fire-blackened branches, rocks and debris.

They began to run.

The villa's iron gates were locked, as usual, and Nick kept his finger on the button. Lisa's calm voice answered: 'Who is it?'

'Me! Open up. You have to get out.'

'What on earth are you talking about?'

'Haven't you looked up at the hill? There's a mud-slide.'

He heard her gasp, then the gates swung open.

She was waiting for them at the front door, clutching a mackintosh around her shoulders.

'Where's Jo?' Peter snapped.

'She left half an hour ago, to see the Mahrs.'

'Oh, my God! In the car?' Lisa nodded. 'We've got to get down there. If they haven't seen what's happening, they won't have a chance.'

'We'll have to go in your car. Where is it?'

'In a ditch. I was counting on using Jo's.'

She thought for a moment. 'There's a short cut across the side of the hill, beyond Le Mur.'

'Lets's go!'

'The house . . .'

'Nothing we can do except make sure all the doors and windows are shut.'

When the villa was tight, she led the way towards the phoenix tree. As they ran, their eyes turned every few minutes to the great wall of mud, which seemed to be gathering height as it descended.

The ground was slippery, obstacles were half-hidden by running, khaki-coloured water. After they had passed the tree, and the spot where Ben had fallen, they struck off down a steep slope.

The mud seemed to be moving faster and by the time they reached the Mahrs' pink cottage it was not more than five hundred metres away. It was terrifyingly silent, a relentless wave as high as a roof-top.

The cottage was set on a flat shelf a few yards in front of the cliff-face. Below it, the land fell away in a steep slope and Jo's Renault was parked a few hundred yards down the hill, beside a wooden shed in which the Mahrs kept their car.

The house had survived the summer fires, sheltered by the cliff, which had halted the flames. Now the position was a death-trap because the mud would spill directly onto its roof.

They climbed a low, dry-stone wall and ran to the back door, which was closed. Peter, who was leading the way, flung it open without bothering to knock. He had never been to the Mahrs' house before – almost no one in the village had – and found himself in a shabby kitchen. Its sink was piled high with unwashed dishes and three people were standing around a table which was covered with brown oil-cloth.

They turned towards him, all movement suspended. Over Peter's shoulder, Nick saw the scene as though it was a frozen frame on a screen.

Amyas Mahr was leaning forward, supporting himself with both hands flat on the table, facing Jo. His colour, under the wiry hair, was high and his small eyes were narrowed and angry. Jo's fists, by her sides, were clenched, and her body was rigid. Between them, Ona stood nervously at the end of the table, skinny and shrunken in an oversized grey shirt and flowery, ankle-length skirt. The hiatus could not have lasted more than a couple of seconds, though to the three new arrivals it seemed longer, then Lisa pushed past the men, and said, 'There's a mud-slide. You must get out!'

'A mud slide?'

'Look out there!' Peter waved at the open door.

Jo said, 'My God! The villa!'

'We've closed it up. It's on the edge of the slide. This place is in more danger. We'll use your car. Amyas, where's yours?'

'In the shed. I must fetch . . .' He was moving towards the stairs.

'There's no time. Get moving!'

The landslide had reached the top of the declivity and water was already pouring down its face behind the cottage. Rocks began to crash against the walls. At the top, they could see the mud mounting higher, like a wave about to break over them.

'Leave everything!' Peter said.

Nick grabbed Lisa's hand and they followed Peter and Jo through the house and out of the front door. After they had gone a few yards, Nick looked back and saw that neither Ona nor Amyas had emerged.

'Jesus! Don't they bloody understand what's going to happen?' He shouted to Peter: 'You go on. I'll get them.'

'No!' Lisa said.

'Don't argue! I'll be all right. The mud hasn't collapsed yet.' He gave her a push which nearly sent her sprawling, and raced back to the cottage.

Ona was still in the kitchen, her face white and frightened. 'For Christ's sake, come on!' he said. 'Where's Amyas?'

She pointed to the narrow staircase. Clutching her sticklike arm, pulling her towards the door, Nick looked up. Amyas was on the landing, mounted on a chair,

343

reaching into a cavity in the ceiling. 'We'll follow you,' he said, 'I have some valuables . . . Ona, get up here and help me!'

Ona whimpered.

'You idiot!' Nick snapped. 'If you want to be killed, that's okay, but Ona's coming with me!'

As he spoke, there was a roar, and the mud-wave crashed into the narrow space between the cottage and the hillside. The rooms darkened as it rose, covering the windows, sweeping in through the back door. The roof groaned under its weight.

Ona, in a trance of terror, seemed unable to move. He swept her up in his arms and ran outside. Somehow he managed to stay upright as the mud, pouring through the house, swirled around him. He waded on, feeling it rise above his ankles . . . his knees. Tumbling rocks and stones battered his legs. His boots filled up and were sucked off his feet.

Ona's arms were wrapped around his neck, her face buried in his shoulder. Fortunately, she was so light that he was hardly aware of her weight.

A rock hit him behind the knee. He fell and sank below the surface. His nose and mouth filled with stinking, suffocating mud. He managed to haul himself upright. Ona, still clinging to him, tried to brush the mud away from his eyes. All he could see of her was a brown, caked face and a pair of eyes wide with terror.

He went on, scarcely aware of where he was going, except that he was moving downhill. He was aware of pain as his unprotected feet stumbled over razor-edged stones. The mud had reached his waist and was carrying him forward, faster and faster. He couldn't stop and he knew that if he fell again, it would be impossible to rise.

Then he felt hands grab his arms. The mud sucked at him as Peter and Lisa pulled him steadily out of the main flow. The level fell to his knees, and then he was almost out of it, standing on a flat rise near the Mahrs' shed. Peter

344

detached Ona and he looked around dazedly. Most of the mud was pouring into gullies on either side of them. His legs felt like rubber hosing, but Lisa's arm was around his waist, supporting him.

Then Ona screamed. She had sunk to her knees on the ground and was looking up the hill towards the cottage.

A grotesque figure, like a great brown bear, was standing in front of it. It stumbled a few paces, threw up its arms and collapsed.

His exhaustion forgotten, Nick followed his father back up the path. The main swell of mud had moved on down the hill, and now it was about a foot deep where before it had reached his waist.

Amyas was lying face down, with the last of the landslide, more water than earth, washing over him. They heaved him up, Nick grasping his shoulders and Peter his feet. His face looked like a gargoyle carved in stone on a medieval church. No flesh showed through the caked mud. His wiry halo of hair was flattened by it and his beard hung in limp strands. His mouth was open, but neither tooth nor tongue was visible: it was plugged with mud. His eyes, too, were open, but without life.

Nick and Peter carried him down to the shed, where they turned him over and, though knowing it was hopeless, tried to pump the muck from his lungs.

Ona watched them, tears making tracks down her filthy face.

3

It was to be weeks before the village fully recovered from the catastrophe. Apart from Amyas Mahr, three people lost their lives: a farmer who was caught by the landslide as he tried to lead his small herd of cows to safety, a man and a woman in road accidents. The mud had wrecked fields, destroyed market-garden crops and killed animals, to say nothing of changing the face of the Massif which loomed over La Belette.

For Jo and Lisa, it had one benefit, in focusing their attention away from their own problems.

The Villa Mimosa had missed the slide's main force. Substantially built of stone, with well-fitting doors and windows, its interior was undamaged. The pool had been partially protected by walls, but Jo's beloved geraniums and shrubs were destroyed. What had once been lawns and terraces were quagmires.

They took Ona in and gave her clothes to wear. Showing unexpected stoicism in the face of tragedy, she tearlessly arranged for Amyas's burial.

In the house, she was quiet, and determined not to be a nuisance, which had the opposite effect, creating tension as Lisa and Jo felt they had to make an extra effort to convince her that she was welcome. She did not appear to be particularly unhappy, nor brood about Amyas's death. In fact, she seemed to enjoy the unaccustomed luxury of her surroundings, and once or twice Jo caught her studying the furnishings of the villa with unnatural attention, even fingering the fabrics. 'Almost as though she's pricing everything,' she said to Lisa.

346

The day after Amyas's funeral, she announced her intention of going to the cottage.

'Not yet!' Jo said. 'It's too soon.'

'I must decide whether I'll live there again, or move somewhere else.'

'You know you're welcome to stay here for as long as you like.'

'You've been so kind, Jo, only I can't go on imposing. And I want to see whether there's anything worth salvaging.'

'If you're determined, I'll come with you.'

'There's no need for that. I'll be perfectly all right.'

But Jo, with the memory of Amyas's dreadful collapse, refused to let her go alone, and eventually she gave in.

As though the Almighty was prepared to make up for the appalling weather He had inflicted on the Riviera, everything had changed the day after the mud-slide. Innocent blue skies had appeared, with soft autumn sunshine and a light breeze. And so it remained as they drove up to the cottage.

Jo's immediate reaction was that it was good for nothing but demolition. Half the roof had caved in, windows were broken and the front door was hanging off its hinges. There was a stink of rotting debris.

Ona picked her way past the spot where Amyas had collapsed, without looking down, and Jo followed her through the doorway.

Rain water had washed away much of the mud, but it was clear from the brown stains on the interior walls that it had filled the ground floor almost to ceiling height. The stairs were slimy with it, and it had poured into the upper floor through the roof.

Jo had a vision of Amyas, trying to collect whatever belongings he was determined to save. Belatedly realizing the extent of the danger he was in, he must have attempted to get downstairs, fallen into the rising tide and sunk below the surface. Fighting against the suffocating mud filling his lungs and nostrils, he could already have been feeling the hammer-blow of his bursting heart.

The floor was still inches deep in filthy water. The unwashed dishes which remained in the sink were jagged shards, covered in a greenish slime. Ona looked around expressionlessly for a moment, then made her way upstairs.

Jo had started to follow her when her foot touched something soft. She felt sick as she saw that she had trodden on a drowned rabbit. Other small, furry bodies were already rotting in the stagnant water, contributing to the stench. She hurried out into the fresh air.

Ona was away for nearly fifteen minutes, and there were sounds of furniture being moved. When she returned, she was carrying some rolled-up canvases, an old-fashioned silver salver and a plastic bag containing a few pieces of jewellery. 'I've seen enough,' she said. 'I won't live here again. I didn't like the place, anyway. I suppose someone might buy the land.' She offered no explanation of the canvases and Jo assumed that one was Amyas's precious Picasso.

Lisa was cleaning the swimming-pool when they got back, sweeping a thick layer of sediment towards the sump.

She hoisted out her long-handled broom thankfully, and joined Jo in the living-room.

'It'll be weeks before we get this clean,' she said. 'How was the cottage?'

Ona had disappeared with her belongings, and Jo sank into a chair. 'The place is a wreck – and the smell! She'll never live there again.'

'What will she do?'

'She hasn't said. She can stay here until she decides, of course.'

'I wonder what her financial position is?'

'I don't know, but I've always had the feeling they

348

lived on the edge of poverty.'

'Did you get a chance to talk to her about the faked painting?'

'No. She hasn't mentioned it, and I haven't wanted to bother her. I'll have to soon, though. The other day Amyas accused me of setting out to ruin his reputation when I told him about the missing thumb-print. He insisted that the painting was genuine, that Ben must have forgotten to put his print on it. Anyhow, I've decided to ask Partridge to get Anthony Henriques down to examine it.'

A voice from the doorway said, 'You won't need Mr Henriques, Joanna. I'll tell you about the picture.'

Ona was still carrying her canvases. She put them on the long table and unrolled them. One was an early Picasso, a beautiful Circus Period painting of a harlequin and a slender girl, naked to the waist, stepping into a blue costume, against rose-coloured draperies.

The other two were Absaloms. One was a section of sandstone, striated in delicate fawns and yellows. The other was a ragged, fire-blackened tree-stump standing against a section of burned-out landscape.

Jo gasped. 'I've never seen either of these before. That tree-stump . . . Ben must have done it years ago, after the last fires. But I don't remember . . .'

She fell silent, staring down at the paintings.

Although there were water stains on the back of the canvases, they had suffered no serious damage.

'They were in a box between the ceiling and the roof,' Ona said. 'Amyas must have been trying to get them when part of the roof caved in. It was just luck that they weren't destroyed.'

Her matter-of-factness broke the spell. Lisa bent to examine them as she had examined the one in Partridge's yacht.

After a few moments, she straightened. 'They're not Ben's.'

'No. I painted them. The Picasso, too,' Ona said.

'It isn't possible!' Jo whispered.

'It's true.' She took a deep breath. 'Amyas and Ben are both dead, and since you know about *Wall with Shadows*, I'd better tell you everything. And then we'll come to an arrangement, Jo.'

She sat, straight-backed, on the edge of a cane chair, a prim, plain little woman who seemed even drabber in Lisa's bright Marimekko cotton sun-dress. As she talked, hesitantly at first, Jo realized it was the first time she had ever heard her utter more than two or three consecutive sentences.

'I went to art classes in London when I was young, you see, but I wasn't much good,' she began. 'They said my work didn't have any spark, and that I couldn't seem to find a style of my own. Actually, the thing I liked best was going to galleries and copying the Old Masters. People used to talk to me, and often they'd say they couldn't tell any difference from the original.'

Their attention seemed to give her confidence. Now the words came fluently.

'I lived with my father in Winchester. My mother was dead, so I looked after him until he died. He left me enough so that I could afford to come down here and paint. It was what I'd always wanted to do. I worked out that the money would last for quite a long time if I was careful.

'I was a bit lonely at first. I've never been good at making friends, and everyone in St-Tropez seemed to be so glamorous.

'Then one day this man – Amyas – started talking to me in the Musée de l'Annonciade. I was copying a Utrillo, and he admired it. He took me out to dinner. It was the first time in my life I'd had a real date with a man.

'He told me all about himself, how he'd been brought up in Hungary, though his mother was English, and how they'd lost all their money and the family estates after the war, and how he had been in love with an American woman who had just died. He cried, and I was terribly sorry for him. I'd never seen a man cry.

'He was living in a cheap hotel in Ste-Maxime, and a month later I moved there, too. He sold pictures for young painters, on commission, and sometimes American tourists used to contact him for advice, but he hardly made enough money to live on.

'In those days, he was kind to me, and I couldn't believe my luck when he asked me to marry him. I found out later that he thought I was richer than I was.

'After we were married, we bought our house. I paid for it.

'We were happy for a while – at least, I was. Only Amyas didn't make enough to cover our expenses, so my money was spent much sooner than I'd expected. Then he suggested that I should start painting pictures to sell to tourists. I copied the best work of the artists he was selling, changing them just a little, the same way I'd copied paintings in the galleries. I actually know quite a lot about technique.

'Of course, we couldn't charge much, and we had to be careful where we sold. One painter recognized a picture I'd done from one of his and threatened to sue us.

'It was more than a year after we were married that I saw Amyas's passport one day, and found out almost everything he had told me about himself was a lie. He was Irish, not Hungarian, and he'd been brought up in London. Amyas Mahr wasn't even his real name. He wouldn't ever talk about his family, but years later his brother turned up here, wanting money. They had a row, and in the end we had to give him a few hundred francs to get rid of him.

'One day Amyas said that I should try something more ambitious than pretty-pretty souvenirs. He suggested trying a Picasso that wasn't exactly a copy, but a – an adaptation. He said we might be able to ask more for it than the other pictures.

351

'I didn't think there was anything wrong with it. I mean, I was going to sign it with my own name. But then Amyas told me he was going to pass if off as a genuine Picasso, and sell it for a lot of money. It was pretty good, but I knew it wasn't good enough to fool an expert and it would have been easy to trace it back to us. We argued and I actually threatened to leave him – I wouldn't have, of course. I'd already decided it was better to live even with a man I didn't much like than to be alone again.'

The last sentence came out in a rush, and she looked at them as though challenging them to argue.

'Anyhow, I persuaded him not to sell it. He rolled it up and put it away. Much later, when we came to one of your parties, Jo, I heard him boasting about owning a genuine Picasso and I found out that he'd told all sorts of people, including Ben, the same thing. He claimed he'd known Picasso, but he hadn't even met him.

'Did you know that Ben found out about Amyas's background from his brother? They met in a bar after the row, and Eamonn – that was his name – must have told Ben everything.

'He teased Amyas about it once, and Amyas was afraid he would tell other people. Ben said he wouldn't, but we never knew if he did, and it always worried Amyas.'

'He didn't,' Jo said. 'Not even me.'

'I expect he was just amusing himself. He was like that, wasn't he?' When she mentioned Ben there was a softness in her expression that Jo had seen on the faces of many women.

'Well, then Amyas met Dominic Partridge. He was collecting Absaloms and when he heard Amyas knew Ben he said he'd give him a commission to buy whatever paintings he could find. Amyas went to Ben to see if he had any. It was a long time since Ben had been able to paint, of course, but he found a couple in his studio . . .'

'On our walls,' Jo said grimly.

'Oh? Well, he said he didn't have any more. Next thing,

Amyas told me to try a painting in Ben's style. I didn't want to until I found out it had actually been Ben's suggestion. You see, he knew about my copies. Amyas had boasted about his "Picasso", and hadn't been able to resist showing it to him. It was a mistake, because Ben knew too much about painting to be taken in. But he thought it was a very good fake. My "Absalom" started as a joke, but I found that the landscapes were easy to adapt. Ben used to come in sometimes during his afternoon walks and watch me. I think he enjoyed it. He even gave me tips – you know "a touch of sienna here", "bolder treatment there."

'I did two landscapes and when they were finished, it stopped being a joke. I did a third one, and then he said he would allow Amyas to sell them as his work. He explained that he had some temporary financial problems and the money would sort them out. He wanted seventy-five percent of the price. I thought that was too much – I mean, I painted them – and we finally agreed to go fifty-fifty.'

A new, harder Ona was peering at them through cracks in the meek façade and Jo found herself wondering whether, for all these years, she had been sheltering behind an assumed personality as carefully calculated as Amyas's, awaiting such an opportunity as this. She had gone along with his deceptions, apparently without protest. She'd had no qualms about making use of other artists' work, nor carrying out this fraud – was it even possible that hers had actually been the subtle mind behind the plot?

She went on: 'Amyas contacted Partridge and told him he'd found an Absalom called *Wall with Shadows*, – it was the first one I did – in Switzerland. This wasn't long before Ben died. Amyas agreed to let Partridge have it on approval for a while, and told him that he knew where there were two more. The Swiss owner would sell each painting for five hundred thousand dollars.

'Partridge said he'd almost certainly buy them all – he

thought they were a bargain – and he took *Wall with Shadows* to his yacht, so he could live with it before he made a final decision.

'When Ben died, we decided there was no reason to change the arrangement. A few days before the landslide, Partridge agreed to the price. He said he'd give us a cheque this week, and that he wanted to see the other two. I'm going to take them to the yacht tomorrow.'

She looked at Jo. 'It isn't wrong, you know. I mean, it was Ben's idea. I don't mind people thinking the pictures are his. It's a compliment. And I was pleased to be able to do something for him. It was awful that he couldn't paint any more, and I admired him so much. When we met, he used to be charming . . . he made even me believe that I was attractive. I always envied you, being married to a man like that.

'He made us promise not to tell you anything about it, only now you've found out – it was a bit mean of him not to tell us about the finger-print – I've decided you must have your share of the money.' She paused. 'There's no reason why anyone but the three of us should ever know the paintings aren't Ben's. I think you and I could make quite a lot of money, Jo. I could do others, too.'

There was a stunned silence as they stared at her bland, innocent face, and absorbed the extent of the projected fraud.

Then Jo said, 'Ona, if you attempt to sell those pictures, I will go to the police – and to Dominic Partridge. I want *Wall with Shadows* back, and the three of them destroyed.'

Ona's mouth and eyes formed three amazed circles. 'You can't mean that! Ben *wanted* people to think the pictures were his. Anyhow, they belong to me. I can do what I like with them.'

'If you sell them as your own work, signed by you, that's your business. If you pass them off as Ben's, it's mine, and you'll have to take the consequences.'

'But no one would pay for my name, and I need the money . . .'

'You have your land to sell.'

'What will that bring?' she said bitterly. 'The house is a wreck. Here you sit, in this – this *mansion*, and you want to deprive me of everything!'

'It's fraud. Don't you understand?'

Her pallid face went scarlet as years of pent-up envy burst forth. 'I'm not harming anyone! You people, with your big cars and your houses and servants . . . you wouldn't know what it's like to be poor. This is my chance to be comfortable for the first time since my father died!'

Implacably, Jo said, 'If you destroy the three pictures, it will be the end of the matter. If not, Partridge and the police will be told.'

'I'll tell everyone that Ben Absalom was in on it.'

'You really think they'd believe that, especially if I denied it? And don't forget, there's no thumb-print.'

'I wish I'd never told you! I'd have been a long way away before anyone found out . . .'

She hurried out of the room, her face a mask of resentment.

There was a silence, then Lisa expelled her breath in a long sigh. 'I could almost accept the other things Ben did because I thought that at least he'd kept his integrity as an artist. Now that's gone, too.'

Slowly, Jo said, 'I have to believe that he was doing it for my sake as much as for his own. He'd known for years that he'd never paint again. He was broke, and too proud to let me know. It was a last resort. Can you imagine the desperation that drove him to it?'

Lisa looked at her disgustedly. 'So you'll even forgive him for major fraud! What happens now?'

'I'll wait and see what Ona decides. I just hope that she doesn't make me go to the police. The last thing I want at the moment is more contact with Commissaire Molinard.'

355

She attempted a smile, but Lisa did not return it.

Less than an hour later, Ona emerged from her room and climbed the stairs which led to the roof terrace, where Jo was sitting, looking out across the landscape.

'I'll get that picture back from Partridge,' she said sullenly. 'I haven't any choice, have I? I'll tell him the Swiss has changed his mind about selling.'

Jo took a breath of relief. 'Thank you, Ona. I'll do all I can to help you to sell your land for a good price. Ben knew a lot of people who talked about building down here. I'll get in touch with them, if you like.'

She nodded indifferently, almost as though the matter no longer concerned her. 'I'll drive into St-Tropez now. The other two paintings are on the table. You can do what you like with them. They're no good to me.'

As she left, Jo looked after her curiously, wondering at the dramatic change in her mood, but not prepared to question her.

Feeling that she needed exercise and solitude, she went outside, unlocked the back gate and climbed the hill, where the ground was already almost dry. No blade of grass was showing, and the devastated land was studded with rocks and blackened stumps. When she reached the brow of the hill, she sat on a fallen log and looked down at the red pantiles of her home. Within a few months, if the winter was kind, the grass would have grown and the pots would be filled with geraniums ready to burst into scarlet bloom in summer.

Would she be here to see them? Even if she were cleared of suspicion, could she afford to keep the villa going? She'd never be able to make enough to live on out of farming alone, and would paying guests find attractive a house where the owner had been suspected of her husband's murder?

She heard a call. Lisa was climbing the hill towards her.

The irritation she had not attempted to hide in the living-room had evaporated.

'I saw Ona driving out,' she said. 'Where's she gone?'

'To St-Tropez. She's going to get back the painting.'

'She caved in quickly. I suppose she had to. Her mistake was to assume that you and Ben shared the same weaknesses.'

'Let's not talk about it any more,' Jo said. 'I'm just glad it's one problem solved.'

'I really came to talk about something else. Do you know where Amyas was the day Ben was killed?'

'I understand the police asked him that. He told them he had gone into St-Tropez to see Partridge.'

'Could he have met Ben on Le Mur first? Isn't it possible that they argued, fought even, and he caused Ben's fall, then went on into St-Tropez.'

'We know now that they were partners. Why would they argue?'

'About sharing the profts. With Ben dead, Amyas and Ona could have kept all the money. I'm sure she only offered to share it with you to keep us quiet. If we hadn't seen *Wall with Shadows*, I'll bet she'd have gone ahead by herself. She's a lot tougher than we ever thought.'

Jo looked unseeingly over the landscape. Retaining the money Partridge had agreed to pay would have bought Amyas and Ona the sort of luxury of which young Alfie Murphy had dreamed. Ona would be there to paint, secretly, another 'Absalom' when the need arose. And another. And another. 'If you're right, I can't see how we'll ever learn the truth,' she said.

And I'll be under suspicion for the rest of my life.

Ona returned from St-Tropez late that evening, and put *Wall with Shadows* on the table.

Refusing a drink or supper, she went to her room, and did not emerge again.

When Jo and Lisa got up the next morning, she had

gone. Her bed had been stripped, the linen neatly folded. The wardrobe and drawers were empty. Her car was no longer in the drive.

A little later, feeling like vandals, they burned her three paintings in the outdoor incinerator.

4

The morning post had included a parcel of fan-letters for Nick, forwarded by the Los Angeles agent he had shared with Dirk Chavez. He glanced at one or two then tossed them all into the waste-basket.

'Still no yearning for your name in the bright lights?' Peter said.

'I like it here. Especially now.'

'I don't want to pry, but things between you and Lisa seem to be progressing nicely. Am I right?'

'Maybe.' He hesitated, then said, 'Mind if I ask you an impertinent question?'

'Go ahead. Finer feelings have never stopped you before.'

'Lisa told me you haven't been to see Jo for nearly a week. Something wrong?'

A shadow came over his father's face, then he said quietly, 'I can't spend the rest of my life living in Ben Absalom's shadow and I don't believe Jo will ever escape him. I finally realized that when Lisa told me she tried to convince her that he'd taken part in Mahr's fraud for her sake. Ben never did a bloody thing for anyone but himself. She's obsessed by him. I'm afraid she always will be.'

'Time passes. Memories fade.'

'Let's skip the clichés. I'm too old to hang around like a love-sick teenager. There's something else I've been wanting to say to you: I don't feel like staying here, being the "good friend" for the rest of my life. I'm going to look for a place in Grasse. Might even go back into the perfume business.'

'You can't mean it! You love La Belette. The Lion d'Or couldn't survive without you.'

'It has occurred to me that if you felt like staying on, you might think about taking it over. But we don't need to talk any more about it yet. I won't be moving until this business of Ben's death is sorted out, and Jo's been cleared. I have called her this week, by the way. I don't propose to drop out of touch altogether. She still needs all our support.'

'Has there been any word from Ona?'

'Nothing. Jo and Lisa went up to the cottage again, and found she'd cleared out a few more things, but she's left the area. I don't suppose we'll hear anything more until her property goes on the market.'

'Maybe she has more money than we thought. I have a feeling that little grey mouse can look after herself.'

'I'm sure you're right.'

'Another person who has dropped out of touch is Molinard. Has Berenger heard anything?'

'Nothing. But he's sure there's something going on. He doesn't believe Molinard has given up.'

A little later, Peter left for the restaurant. He was spending more and more time there, but he seemed to have lost much of his former vigor and enthusiasm. Nick guessed that he was finding it more difficult than he would admit to come to terms with giving up his hopes of a future with Jo.

The telephone rang as Nick was contemplating calling Lisa to suggest a drive to St Paul de Vence and lunch at La Colombe d'Or.

The girl's voice was a frantic whisper. 'It's Claudette. Please help me.'

It took him a moment to adjust to the shock, then he said, 'Your father's been going crazy! Where the hell are you?'

'In a bar in Cassis.' Her voice broke. 'Oh, please . . . I'm so ill . . .'

The connection was cut.

He dialled the Lion d'Or. When his father answered he repeated the girl's words, and ended, 'What do we do about her?'

'We don't say anything to Dorsey, that's for sure. Jean-Louis has just told me he was already drunk at nine o'clock when he went to Georgette for another bottle of brandy. Cassis? She didn't say which bar?'

'She didn't have time. We were cut off.'

'I'll pick you up in ten minutes. If she stays put, we'll be able to find her. Cassis is small enough.'

Like every other town on the Riviera, Cassis had expanded during the eight years Nick had been in America, but its fishing-port was still picturesque, lined with cafe-bars and restaurants.

In the third place they visited, business was quiet and the proprietor, a square man with a veined nose that told of years-long indulgence in the *apéritif*, was reading *Nice Matin* and sipping a glass of Pernod.

He looked at them suspiciously when they described Claudette. 'Why would you want her? You *flics*?'

'No. Friends. She telephoned. Sounded as though she was in trouble.'

'She was here. She made a call but she hung up when two other "friends . . ."' He emphasized the word. ' . . . came in. They took her away.'

'Away where?' Peter said.

'Better for you if you don't know, m'sieur. I've seen them before. That girl keeps rough company.'

'Never mind that. Where did they go?'

He looked at them narrowly, and shrugged. 'It's your choice. I reckon they've gone to Marseilles. That's where they come from. I'm only telling you this because I felt sorry for the kid. She didn't look good.'

'You know their names?' Nick said.

'Pepe and Yan. That's all. Pepe's an Algerian.'

'And they live in Marseilles? Any idea where?'

'No. But I have a friend runs a bar on the Vieux Port. He might know. You want me to call him?'

They could not hear his conversation, but when he came back he was carrying a slip of paper on which he had scribbled notes.

'How well d'you know Marseilles?'

'Give us the directions. We'll find the place.'

'If that little girl's a friend of yours, you should get after her quickly. Those two run a nasty business.'

'What sort of business?'

'If it's not white slavery, it's damn nearly. They send girls to Morocco, Tangiers, Tunisia, to dance in clubs. What they don't tell them is that dancing is only part of the job.'

'Did she go with them willingly?' Peter asked.

'Hard to tell. She didn't seem to have any strength, you know? White as a sheet. They practically carried her out to their car. When she'd gone there were drops of blood on the floor where she'd been standing. I had to clean it up.'

'Jesus! Why didn't you stop them?' Nick said.

'Because I don't mess with people like that. They work out of Marseilles and Nice and they're through here about once a week. I serve their drinks and take their money, and that's all.'

Five minutes later, they were on their way to Marseilles, which was twenty-three kilometres west of Cassis.

The city was noisier and more crowded than Nick remembered. They drove past the Vieux Port, with its fishing-boats, yachts and light-house. Above them, the great tower of Notre-Dame de la Garde dominated the scene from a five hundred foot limestone spur. He remembered an expedition with his parents to the little chapel below it, where model ships, ranging from Arab dhows to modern motor launches, hung from the roof, put up by people who believed that, in one way or another, a Higher Power had saved them from death during their travels.

On its rock in the harbour, he could see the white walls of the Château d'If. When he and Lisa were children, Ben had taken them there, and told them the story of how it had once been a notorious prison, immortalized by Dumas in *The Count of Monte Cristo*. On their return to La Belette, they had devoured the book, reading it in turns to each other.

But there was no time for nostalgia. Checking the directions they had been given, they moved on foot into the network of streets behind the port.

At first, the pavements were lined with shops, restaurants and stalls, then they turned into a narrow side street, and the scene changed. It was darkened by high buildings. The gutters were noisome with litter, and there was a pervading smell of urine. Blank, weather-stained walls were broken by closed doors from which the paint was peeling, and filthy windows, some with broken panes covered by cardboard.

A few men lounged in doorways. Many of them were dark-skinned North Africans, unshaven, wearing shabby cotton trousers, collarless shirts open at the neck, round caps on their heads.

The Garniers were conscious of hostile stares pressing against their shoulder-blades. It was eerily silent, their own footsteps the only sound.

Nick was checking numbers on the buildings. 'Thirty-nine. This is it.'

There was a brass name-plate beside the door. Under the dirt that caked it, they could make out the name Weiss, and the simple description, *Agent*.

Watched by prostitutes who were lounging in the doorways, and a group of rough-looking men, they banged on the door.

As they waited, Nick realized that the men were drawing nearer, step by step.

'I don't like this,' Peter muttered. 'Ending my life with a knife in my back in a Marseilles alley was never part of my scheme of things.'

The door opened. A woman stood there. She was wearing a man's dressing-gown gaping over a greyish nylon petticoat. Her feet were bare and dirty. Last night's mascara was smudged around her eyes and her face was the colour of curd cheese. She looked about forty. Her breasts had sagged and her uncorseted stomach bulged the thin fabric.

Observing that distaste had rendered his father momentarily silent, Nick said: 'Madame, we're looking for a girl named Claudette Dorsey.'

'Never heard of her.'

'Are Pepe and Yan here?'

She looked at them more closely. 'They've gone. You know them?'

He lied easily. 'Sure. They brought Claudette in this morning. Told us to come and fetch her. There's a job going in Tangiers.'

There was a brief snort of laughter. 'You won't get any work out of that one today. She's on her back.'

'On her . . .?'

'Not the way you mean. She passed out. She's going to be more nuisance than she's worth. Looks to me as though she's not going to last long.'

'She's ill?'

'Didn't they tell you? She had an abortion in Nice. Something must have gone wrong. She's bleeding. Those shits left her here, told me to look after her, and split.'

'Where is she?'

Her eyes became suspicious slits as she stood, barring the door. 'Who the hell are you? You haven't come about any work. They'd have told me. You cops? I never saw her before. I took her in out of the goodness of my heart, that's all.' Her voice was cigarette-hoarse.

The men who had followed them were standing in a silent row a few yards behind them.

Nick said rapidly: 'We aren't police. We only want to relieve you of the girl. Let us in and I'll explain.'

She looked from one to the other, then moved out of the doorway. They went into the house and she bolted the door behind them. 'What's your interest in her?'

Peter said, 'We're friends. We live in the same village. She called us from Cassis. We've come to take her home.'

'She's got a home? Family?'

'A father. He's worried sick about her.'

She yawned, showing yellowed teeth, several of which were missing. Her washed-out eyes remained fixed on them. 'Most of 'em don't have anyone who cares what they do. Look, I want to get rid of her, but I don't want any problems afterwards. No police, right?'

'Absolutely not.'

'And some compensation? For the trouble she's been.'

Peter pulled a wad of notes from his pocket. 'That's all I've got.'

She riffled through them. 'Five hundred? Not much, is it? I suppose it'll have to do.' She seemed to relax. 'I don't know why I should trust you, but if she dies on me, I'm in real trouble.'

'She's as bad as that?'

'Oh, yes,' she said casually. 'See for yourselves.'

She led them up a narrow, carpetless stairway, trailed by a smell of stale scent, Gaulloises and sweat. Through open doors, they saw women's clothes scattered on floors, and unmade beds, one or two humped by sleeping bodies.

When they reached the second-floor landing, she stopped outside a door, and turned. Peter thought he detected a softening behind the hard eyes.

'She's a silly little bitch, and she needs looking after,' she said abruptly. 'She's not going to be any use to us, the state she's in. I told Yan that, but she's a pretty kid, and he didn't want to believe me.'

As she reached for the door-handle, Nick said: 'How did they get in touch with her?'

Having decided to trust them, she was inclined to be chatty. She took a pack of Gaulloises from her pocket and lit one. 'Yan's sister, Lucille, was a nurse. Now she does abortions in Nice. She passed the girl on to Yan when she said she wanted to go on the stage. He's a – theatrical agent. On the way here, she started to bleed and complain of pains, so they dumped her on me. Since then she's got worse.'

Claudette was lying on a narrow bed, covered by a sheet. Her eyes were closed and there were brown shadows, like bruises, around them. Her hair was matted, her face pallid and shiny with sweat. Her breathing was a series of long, gasping moans.

The two men looked down at her, appalled.

'Hospital! You find a taxi,' Nick told his father. 'I'll get her to the door.'

As Peter made for the stairs, the woman stopped him. 'Yan's friends are out front. They don't like strangers. I'll show you the back door.'

Left alone, Nick bent over the girl. She opened her eyes and looked at him blankly.

He put a hand on her forehead, which felt as though a fire was burning under the skin. He wrapped her in a blanket and picked her up. The bed was blood-stained where she had been lying.

The woman came in. '*Merde*! What a mess! Come on. Your friend should be back any minute.' As she spoke, there was hammering at the front door, and a shout. 'That's Yan. They must've told him you're here. He won't want to let her go.'

The back stairs were steeper than the front and he had to support himself by leaning against the wall as he edged down. Claudette, unconscious, was a dead weight.

He reached a dark passage, scarcely three feet wide, separating two buildings. A taxi pulled up at the end.

Peter ran towards them. Together, they manoeuvred the girl onto the back seat, ignoring the driver's protests.

Nick turned to the woman, who was leaning against the wall, unconcernedly smoking. The shouts from the front of the house were loud and angry.

'What about you?' he said. 'Will he . . .?'

'Don't worry. I can handle Yan. He's my old man.'

As he climbed into the front seat of the taxi she called after them: 'Hey, I hope the kid's okay . . .'

5

Demazin arrived at the villa at four o'clock in the afternoon.

His bull-like head was thrust forward belligerently as he said: 'Madame Absalom is to accompany us to Cotolin. Orders from the Commissaire.'

'What for?' Lisa was standing protectively in front of Jo. Two other policemen were sitting in the back of a police-car that was parked in the drive.

'He has questions,' Demazin said stolidly. 'You are to bring what you will need for an overnight stay, Madame. Tomorrow you are to be interviewed by the examining magistrate.'

Jo's stomach lurched. The examining magistrate was brought in when the *police judiciare* believed there was a case to be answered.

'Jo, you mustn't go!' Lisa said. 'I'll call Peter . . . a lawyer . . .'

'No need for that,' Demazin said. 'There are no charges. Yet.'

'Jo . . .'

'I must go with them. But, please, call Peter and tell him.'

Molinard was sitting behind a desk in a bare, tidy office in the *gendarmerie*. He shook hands with her and motioned her to a chair opposite him. Light from the window was falling directly onto her face.

He sat for a moment, studying her, then he said softly: 'Tell me about your brother Mark, Madame.'

She was unable to speak. She began to shiver uncontrollably.

'Tell me.'

'How do you know about my brother?'

'Did you think I had given up? I have been to London. I know what happened. If you won't tell me about Mark, I'll tell you: in a fit of anger, you pushed him into a fire, and he died from his burns.'

'I was five years old.'

'A child with an uncontrollable temper becomes an adult with an uncontrollable temper. You were enraged with your husband, and you pushed him over the cliff.'

Her nerves had steadied. 'I loved my husband. I did not push him.'

'You had reason to be angry with him. He had been having an affair with a girl in the village, Claudette Dorsey. Many people knew about it.'

'I suspected that. We never discussed it.'

'There had been other women in his life. But for you, this was one too many. A pretty girl, more than twenty years younger than you. You were jealous. She had been working for you. You dismissed her. And you killed him.'

'I did not!'

'It will be easier for you if you admit it. A crime of passion. In France we understand such crimes.'

'No! My husband made me dismiss Claudette. He had probably tired of her. I did not kill him. Have you been able to talk to her?'

'Unfortunately, she has disappeared. We will find her.'

Molinard had worked hard in London. He listed women, some names strange to her, who he said had been Ben's mistresses.

Again and again, he invited her to admit her crime, because if she did, if she explained the emotional agony she must have suffered, the judge would not be hard on her.

Monotonously, she repeated, 'I did not kill my husband.'

369

As it had before, in her home, the interrogation went on and on. He did not give up until eight o'clock, when he motioned Demazin to conduct her to the room in which she would spend the night.

As she reached the door, his voice, soft and ominous, followed her. 'Your time future is indeed contained in your time past, no? Now I intend to peel away the layers of your life until I reach the truth.'

Looking into the light, implacable eyes, she understood that, as far as he was concerned, there was no escape for her.

6

Claudette died four hours after she had entered the hospital.

Nick and Peter had waited for news in a nearby bar and it was nine o'clock before they were able to leave Marseilles. Peter had called Berenger to ask him to break the news of the tragedy to her father, and arranged for her body to be returned to La Belette for burial.

As they drove home, he said, 'I used to think I'd have liked a daughter as well as a son. Now I'm not so sure. I can't get the sight of that child lying there, alone, dying, out of my mind.'

They didn't talk much during the rest of the journey. The roads were dark and empty. Few lights were showing in the villas that spread along the coast, many of which had already been locked and shuttered for the winter.

Once Nick, who was driving, said: 'I wonder whether things would have been different if I hadn't given her that money?'

But Peter was dozing and offered no reassurance.

He woke as they came into La Belette. Nothing stirred. The only visible light was outside André Dorsey's house, a single-storey stone cottage with a cracked cement terrace in front. It was illuminated by an electric lamp hanging from its thatched canopy. A wooden table and a couple of old kitchen chairs stood outside the door, which was half open. There was a faint glow inside.

As they pulled up, Georgette Ponelle hurried out of the house.

'How is he?' Peter said.

'Bad. Oh, very bad, poor man. He hasn't spoken since he heard. It's been a terrible evening. Please tell me about that poor little one.'

Peter repeated the story he had told the hospital in Marseilles, about Claudette's call and how they had come from La Belette to find her collapsed in a lodging-house.

When he had finished, he said. 'What can we do for Dorsey?'

'There's nothing anyone can do. After you telephoned, Serge Berenger asked me to come here with him while we broke the news. André just sat there, like a grey statue. I told Serge to go, and tried to talk to him, but still he said nothing. Then he went to his room. After a while, I followed him. He was kneeling beside his bed, with his head in his hands, praying. And that's where he's been ever since. I took him some food, but he wouldn't eat.'

Her kind, brown face was tired and the pile of black hair had tilted to one side, strands escaping from their pins.

Although her voice had hardly risen above a whisper, it was loud in the night silence.

Peter said, 'Georgette, we'll take you home.'

'I can't leave him alone.'

'I'll stay with him,' Nick said.

'No, no, it has to be me. He'll need me . . .'

When they reached the house Peter, half-stunned with fatigue, went to his room. Nick glanced automatically at the message pad by the telephone and saw that Madame Fronval had left a note, carefully written in block capitals: 'Please call Mlle Absalom.'

It was past midnight. Too late to call. Tomorrow would do. He went to bed.

He was awakened by the telephone the following morning and was conscious of the kind of depression that normally accompanied a severe hang-over. But the previous day he had drunk only a couple of glasses of wine. The depression was his memory of Claudette's lonely death.

He heard his father's voice, then the receiver being replaced, and feet taking the stairs two at a time. Peter flung open the door without knocking. 'That was Lisa. The police have taken Jo to Cotolin. She's probably going to be charged with Ben's murder.'

Nick sat up. 'Shit! They must be crazy! What's caused that?'

'I don't know. Molinard sent Demazin to pick her up yesterday. Lisa tried to get hold of us. She went to Cotolin last night, but they wouldn't let her see Jo or Molinard.'

'There must be a reason . . .'

'That's what I'm going to find out. Lisa's already on her way.'

'I'll come, too.'

As they passed André Dorsey's little house, they saw that the front door had been closed.

The entrance to the shop, on the other hand, was open, and Pierre-Luc was shambling towards his bench. Georgette was at an upstairs window. When she saw them, she waved urgently.

Peter braked. 'How's Dorsey?' he called.

She leant out of the window. 'He prayed until four in the morning. Then he came out and said I must go home. M'sieu Peter, is it true what Réné Raymond has just told me, that Joanna has been arrested?'

'She's been taken to Cotolin,' Peter said cautiously. 'We're on our way there now.'

'Please wait for a minute!' She withdrew her head and closed the shutters.

Peter tapped his fingers impatiently on the steering-wheel.

She emerged and herded Pierre-Luc towards her old Citroën Dyane, which stood outside the shop. She had forgotten to take off the floral overall she wore in the shop.

'We're going to the *gendarmerie*, Georgette.'

'I will follow you. I have to talk to them.'

'You know something?'

She nodded unhappily. 'I should have spoken before, but I couldn't believe they would be such idiots as to suspect Joanna. When Molinard seemed to give up, I thought there would be no need. Now I must, whatever they think.'

Peter curbed his impatience. 'Won't you tell me what it is?'

'Pierre-Luc saw M. Absalom fall down the cliff.'

They stared at her speechlessly.

Distractedly, she poked a couple of hairpins back into the bee-hive. 'I couldn't bear the thought of them bullying my poor boy. I remember the last time, when they accused him of – of watching people, and put him in a cell and he took pneumonia. But now I must . . .'

'Georgette, what exactly did he see?'

'He was up in the hills that day with his binoculars, watching birds. He looked across the valley and saw M. Absalom falling. Another man was there. He ran away past the palm tree.'

'Who was it?' Nick said.

Her eyes slid away from his, towards Pierre-Luc. 'He couldn't see who it was. But it was a man. Definitely a man. Not Joanna. He didn't tell me when he came home, because he didn't understand what he'd seen. But when he heard that there had been an accident, he remembered. People don't believe me, but he understands a lot more than any one thinks, and he does talk to me. Will the police believe us?'

They looked at Pierre-Luc's big, vacant, smiling face, the loose lips and faraway eyes, the nodding head. It would be difficult even for a sympathetic police officer to accept evidence from him. And Molinard was not sympathetic.

Driving fast, Peter led the way into Cotolin and parked outside the *gendarmerie*. A few seconds later, Georgette pulled up behind him. Lisa's car was already there.

The one good thing resulting from the hours of question-ing was that Jo had been exhausted when she lay on her narrow cot. She slept until she was awakened by Demazin, bringing her a mug of coffee.

It was ironic, she thought, that she had not even been disturbed by the nightmare of herself crouching in a windowless, airless cell, since it was nearer to becoming reality than it had ever been.

She faced the day with a kind of fatalism. There would be more questions. Then – she reviewed what little she knew of French law – she would have to face the examining magistrate. The evidence so far collected would be placed before a prosecutor. It could be months before the case finally came to court. She didn't allow herself to think beyond that.

Her interrogation began again at nine, and Molinard hammered away at the old themes. He made her retell the story of Markie's death, and go over every movement she had made in the days before Ben had been killed. She was to see the examining magistrate at mid-day, and she guessed that he was desperate for a confession by then.

Once the telephone rang, and he excused himself. When he returned, his face was grimmer than before, but he gave no indication of the reason. Again and again he empha-sized the crime of passion angle, again and again she refused to be coerced into any admission.

As Nick and Peter had suspected, Molinard, summoned from the interview room, treated Georgette's story with contempt.

'You are suggesting, Madame, that this . . . that your son could give evidence that would impress a court? It isn't possible.'

'M. le Commissaire, what I tell you is the truth. M. Garnier will confirm that I do not lie, and neither does Pierre-Luc.'

'What you tell me is hearsay only. Does your son never speak?'

'Only to me. Strangers frighten him.'

'You say he saw a man with M. Absalom. He can't identify the man. He was a long way away, across the valley. If he saw anyone, it could as easily have been a woman. Madame, you are wasting my time!'

Georgette lost her temper. 'You are a fool! If Pierre-Luc says he saw a man, there was a man. It is an absurdity to suspect Madame Absalom of killing her husband.'

Molinard stood up, his face hard. 'That's enough of this charade! There's a conspiracy in your village to hide the truth. This is a fabrication made up by a disturbed mind!'

As he turned to leave the room he said to Peter: 'Go back to La Belette, M'sieu. Madame Absalom will be required here indefinitely.'

'We're staying,' Peter said flatly. 'I wish to see the examining magistrate and talk to Madame Absalom.'

Molinard shrugged. 'You'll have a long wait. But it's up to you.'

When he had gone, Georgette sat limply, her head in her hands. 'It was no good, was it? That pig has made up his mind. And he is wrong!'

Peter put his hand on her shoulder. 'Georgette, you've done your best. Now go home.'

'I think you don't believe Pierre-Luc either,' she said bitterly. 'But I know what he said is true.'

'I do believe him. But without knowing who the other man was, there's no more you can do. And I think that probably André Dorsey will need you today.'

She stood up. 'Will you tell Joanna I'm sorry. I tried.'

As the door closed behind her, Lisa looked at Peter. 'Do you believe that?'

He spread his hands. 'I believe she *thinks* that Pierre-Luc saw someone. Who can possibly say whether he really did? I'm afraid Molinard's right, there's no way he could be produced as a witness.'

376

'I don't think she's telling us everything,' Nick said slowly. 'I have a feeling she knows who the man was.'

It was mid-morning when Molinard received a second telephone call, which had a dramatic effect on him. He stiffened and parallel lines appeared between his brows. He swivelled his chair so his back was to Jo, and put a hand over the mouthpiece, though he appeared to listen more than he spoke.

When he hung up, he rose. 'Madame, it is necessary that I go out. You will remain here until I return, but I will permit you to see your daughter and your friends.'

A few moments after he had gone, the door opened, and Lisa rushed to embrace her. Then Peter came forward and put out his hands. For a moment, she relaxed against him.

'How long have you been here? They never told me . . .'

'More than an hour,' he said. 'Has he been giving you a rough time?'

'He's been trying to persuade me to confess. I've refused.'

Lisa said, 'What's this all about? Is there anything new?'

She looked from one to the other, then she took a deep breath and said, 'He has discovered that when I was five years old, I was responsible for my brother's death.'

She expected to see shock and revulsion on their faces. Instead, there was only love and pity in Peter's expression. Lisa's eyes had widened, but she showed no sign of recoil. Nick appeared unsurprised, a fact that, for the moment, she hardly registered.

She said, 'I'd like to tell you about it.'

There was a sofa covered with worn brown leather standing against a wall. Peter put his arm around her shoulders and led her to it.

'Darling, you don't have to . . .' Lisa began.

'I want to. Ben is the only person I've ever told. Soon, I

suppose, anyone who can read a newspaper will know. I'd rather you heard it from me . . .'

And then she re-entered the nightmare.

' . . . They couldn't do anything to me, because I was only five, but until my mother died, I was never allowed to forget it. She hated me so much that she hardly spoke to me again, and my step-father used to tell me never to forget that I had killed my brother. I never did.'

She heard Peter say, under his breath, 'Oh, my dear . . .'

'The worst thing was not remembering, knowing that when I lost control of my temper I simply didn't know what I was doing. It nearly happened again, when I was eighteen and a man tried to rape me. Molinard said that a child with an uncontrollable temper becomes an adult with an uncontrollable temper. That's why he's convinced that I killed Ben.'

Peter's arm tightened around her, but it was Nick who spoke: 'How about the rest of the story, Jo?'

'You mean what happened afterwards? Six months later my mother died and my step-father put me into care. I grew up in a children's home. When I left it, I met Ben. He never blamed me for what I had done, and he gave me a whole new life. That's the rest.'

Nick said, 'Okay, you've told us what you believed as a child and what Molinard found out. Now let's have the *real* story.'

'That is the real story. I don't understand . . .'

She felt the force of his grey eyes intent on her. Then he said: 'You don't know. You really don't know? When I was in London, I went to see Sandra Ickes.' He waited for her to respond, but she shook her head in bewilderment.

'She was your au pair when your brother was killed.'

'Sandra! I haven't thought of her for years. She left us after the fire. Nick, how did you . . .?'

'I read about Mark's death in a newsagency library when I was doing some research into Ben's background.

Your name was there. I got in touch with Sandra Ickes to find out a little more.' He hesitated. 'Afterwards I was sort of ashamed of myself, digging into something that was none of my business. I realized it must still be a pretty painful memory for you, so I decided not to mention it, even to Peter, and certainly not to use it in the book.' He paused. 'It never occurred to me that you didn't know the truth . . .'

7

He had found the barge *Pollyanna* moored with several other converted barges and house-boats on the Twickenham side of Richmond Bridge. In the dim light of a street-lamp it was a dark shape with living quarters at one end of the long deck. There were outlines of washing strung on a line, and a few straggling plants in half-barrels. Light glowed behind the drawn curtains of a porthole.

A narrow gang-plank with an iron railing on one side connected it with the shore. Below it, the water was dark and oily.

The barge rocked slightly as he crossed onto the deck. He moved towards a door which led into the cabin and called Sandra Ickes' name. There was no response, but when he called again, he heard heavy footsteps. A door opened and a dog bounded out, snarling. As he backed away, it followed him.

In the light that flooded from the cabin, he could see the lips drawn back from its teeth, the powerful, half-open jaws. At least part of its ancestry was Doberman.

He came up against the deck-railing and stood like a herded sheep, the dog in front of him. Its snarl became a low, menacing growl.

Nick was not normally afraid of dogs, but once, as a child in St-Tropez, he had been cornered by two Dobermans who had escaped from their compound. He had been rescued by their owner, but the terror he had felt then still had its echoes.

Then the light was blocked by a woman's figure filling the doorway. A voice with the same rounded Devonian vowels he had heard from her niece on the telephone, said, 'Who is it? What do you want?'

'Are you Miss Ickes? My name's Nicholas Garnier. I'd like to talk to you.'

'What about? Is it the knitting?'

'The . . .? No. It's . . . business.'

As he had walked from Richmond tube station he had rehearsed various ways to approach her. If she had been in charge of the children, it was surprising that no blame had been attached to her for leaving them unattended. He had finally decided he would have to play it by ear.

The beam from a powerful torch focused on him.

'What kind of business?' she said.

As their voices floated over the water, he was aware of movement on one or two of the other boats, of a deck-light turned on. Keeping a wary eye on the Doberman, he said, 'If you'll call off your dog, I'll explain. I assure you, I don't mean you any harm.'

If less gracious than most women under the impact of his smile, she was not entirely immune to it. She reached for the dog's collar. 'You can come in. But remember, Fritz was given to me by the Lord to smite mine enemies.'

She gestured him to go ahead of her down a short companionway.

At the bottom, he found himself in a long, narrow cabin from which all traces of its working past had been erased.

It was furnished like a suburban parlour, with an old upright piano and a three-piece suite with worn chintz covers. An open Bible lay on the sofa.

There were small tables everywhere. Apart from one, which supported a television set, they were crowded with knick-knacks: souvenirs of Southend and Blackpool and Brighton; dusty glass animals, pottery cottages and Toby jugs, dolls dressed as Beefeaters, Spanish dancers, kilted Scotsmen. A print of Tretchikoff's green-faced Burmese girl hung on one wall. Next to it was a framed pen and ink drawing, on linen, of the head of Christ. As he moved, its

381

open eyes seemed to follow him.

There were other evidences of a religious inclination. A collection of post-card pictures of churches and cathedrals were attached to a pin-board. A large colour photograph of a good-looking man with a mane of puffed-out grey hair stood on the piano. His hands were raised in benediction. It was autographed, 'Yours in the Service of the Lord, Gerald.'

Against the other wall was a long narrow table on which stood three machines that at first glance might have been the keyboards of some esoteric musical instrument. Then he saw stripes of woollen fabric suspended from them, with multi-coloured strands of wool threaded into antennae-like wires, and deduced that they were knitting machines.

He turned as the woman stumped down the stairs, still holding the dog. She appeared to be in her early sixties and might once have been pretty in an over-blown, bucolic way. Now rounded curves had collapsed into fat, her hair was more grey than fair, cut short and none too clean. Her features had coarsened and there was a fluff of moustache on her upper lip. She was wearing a turquoise knitted dress that clung to every roll of flesh.

Suspicious eyes studied him. 'Well, what do you want, then?'

'Miss Ickes, I'd like to ask you about Mark and Joanna Stewart.'

Her face became expressionless. 'I don't know what you're talking about.'

'I believe you worked for Mr and Mrs Costain when Mark died in a fire.'

'Who told you that?'

'I read it in the newspapers of the time. I'm a writer, and I'm researching a book about the man Joanna married. He was a famous painter. I'm trying to find out all I can about her background.'

'I don't have to talk to you. The Lord has permitted me to bury my past.'

382

'Miss Ickes . . .'

'Go away! Get off my boat!' She took a step forward, and the dog growled.

Remembering Ashton and the Murphys, he said quickly. 'I'm prepared to offer you something for any information.'

She said nothing, but her eyelids flickered and he sensed that avarice was about to do battle with her reluctance.

'Offer what?' she said.

'Twenty pounds?'

There was a long pause as she fought her private war. Then she intoned, 'The love of money is the root of all evil, but . . .' She gestured towards the knitting-machines, 'Rich women buy from me, but I am poor. Blessed is he that considereth the poor. I don't like talking about that time, but if there is some way it can help me to increase my contribution to the Lord's work . . .'

He took two ten pound notes out of his pocket and put them on the piano.

'Thou shalt have treasure in Heaven, young man. Sit down.' She ordered the dog under the piano, where it settled, without taking its eyes off Nick. 'I used to see pictures of little Joanna in the papers. You say you're going to write about them? Has the Lord instructed you so to do?'

He decided to humour her. 'I believe so. After I'd read the newspaper stories about Mark's death in the fire, I had a feeling that a lot had been left out.'

She snorted contemptuously as she settled her bulk in a chair. 'They didn't know anything. What they said wasn't how it happened at all. We kept it dark, Mr Costain and me. Not even Mrs Costain ever knew . . .' She stopped, and her suspicion revived. 'I don't want to be in your book. You're not to mention my name, mind. I have atoned already.'

'I'm only interested in Joanna.'

'It's a long time ago, but I remember it like it happened yesterday. I've only been free to talk about it since he died.'

'He?'

'Mr Costain. He gave me money to keep quiet. I accepted it, because it was before the Lord had taught me the difference between right and wrong.'

Half-repelled, half-amused, he watched her. Now that the Lord, in his wisdom, had apparently sanctioned her to break silence, she seemed to be enjoying the opportunity to reminisce. Her voice was rough and scratchy , as though little used, but it became cosily confidential, punctuated by an occasional Biblical sonority.

'I'd answered the Costains' advertisement for an au pair in *The Lady* when I came up from Devon.' A coy smile plastered itself unsuitably on her heavy features. 'It was Mr Costain persuaded his wife to take me on. I was a foolish girl then, corrupted by the pleasures of the flesh, and I knew right away that he was interested in me.

'Mrs Costain was skinny and sick-looking. He was her second husband. Her first, the children's father, had been much older than her and he'd died and left her a rich woman. That was why Mr Costain married her. He was ever so handsome, he could have had anyone. A big man, like you, only with more flesh, and crinkly dark hair with a bit of grey in it. His face always looked smooth and clean, as though he'd just shaved.

'It was a good job. I quite liked the children, only Markie was never nice to Joanna. She was a pretty little thing, very gentle, on the whole, but he bullied and teased her something terrible, and that used to make her furious. You never heard children quarrel so much. It used to drive Mr Costain mad, especially not being his, if you see what I mean.

'After I'd been there for a few weeks he, Mr Costain, began to make, well, advances. He came to my room. When his wife was out, we used to have a really nice time.

She wasn't interested in that side of being married, but he was a man who needed it often. We had to keep it secret, of course. He said the least she'd do if she found out was fire me, and I didn't want that. The money wasn't bad and I had a lovely room and a wireless of my own. Apart from their fighting, the kids weren't much trouble.'

The words were flowing easily now, and Nick found himself wondering how long it had been since anyone had been interested in what she had to say.

'Mr Costain even said he might marry me if Mrs Costain died – she was always getting things wrong with her – but I'm not sure I would have, even if he'd asked. I'd found out that he could be quite cruel. He used to hit the children. Neither of them liked him. The only person he was gentle with was Mrs Costain, because of the money. But I enjoyed our times together. I could tell you a few things . . .'

He said hastily, 'Tell me about the fire.'

For the first time, she looked uneasy. Her eyes slid away from his and fixed on a piece of knitting. 'It wasn't my fault, you know. I want you to understand that. The Lord knows the truth.'

'I understand.'

'Well, then. Mrs Costain was out. The children had been fighting because Markie had hidden some silly toy that had been given to Joanna. She was very angry, so I sent him to play in his own room and after a while she settled down with a book in the nursery.

'Mr Costain was waiting for me in the little sitting-room where there was a lovely big fire, and he was in one of those moods – we hadn't been together for more than a week. He closed the door, didn't even wait to lock it.

'We were lying on the sofa when he suddenly pushed me away. Markie was standing in the doorway, watching us. He was no fool, he knew what it was all about. He was eight, and boys talk about it at that age, don't they?

'He said, "I'm going to tell my mother!" He was

swinging Joanna's toy elephant by its trunk, I remember.

'Mr Costain grabbed him, but he managed to get away and dodged around the room. I hid behind the door because I wasn't very . . . decent. Then Mr Costain fetched him a clout on the side of the head and he fell into the fire. His hair and clothes caught alight and straight-away there were flames everywhere.

'He started to scream, and Joanna came in. She told the police later that she was looking for her elephant. Mr Costain and me . . . it was as though we were paralyzed. Joanna ran forward. I suppose she was going to try to help Markie, only she tripped and hit her head on the fender. I had to drag her away or she'd have been burned, too.

'Mr Costain picked up the hearth-rug and tried to smother the flames, but Markie's clothes were all burnt, and his hands and his face. It was like there was no skin left. Even his eyes . . . they were just holes, with no eyelids . . . I'll never forget his screaming. Then it just stopped, and he went all limp.' Her fat cheeks shook as she shuddered. 'The elephant was burnt, too, and we had to put out little fires from sparks on the chairs and curtains. Markie died on the way to the hospital.

'I was so frightened, even though it hadn't been my fault. But while we were waiting for the ambulance, Mr Costain told me I was to say that Joanna and Mark were fighting about that elephant and she lost her temper and pushed him into the fire. He said that if I didn't, he'd say that it was all my fault. Well, I knew, of course, they'd believe him, not me.'

'So you blamed the child?' Nick made no attempt to conceal his contempt.

'I had to. I was afraid of Mr Costain, and they might have put me in prison. Anyhow, he explained that nothing would happen to Joanna, she was too little to be arrested. If I did it right, he said he'd give me some money.

'That's how I was able to start up my knitting business, and buy this barge. All the time Mr Costain was alive, I never said a word about him being the one who killed Markie, not Joanna. Only it was always on my mind, like.'

'Didn't you ever wonder what effect it might have had on Joanna?'

'Like I told the other gentleman, she was a baby. She didn't even know what was happening, and having hit her head, and all, and been angry with Mark, she actually thought it had been her fault. It was only later when I found the Lord that I began to realize what I'd done, and atoned.' She folded her hands on her lap, a sanctimonious expression on her face.

'Who was the "other gentleman" you told about this?'

'It was Joanna's husband. After I'd found the Lord.'

'I don't quite understand . . .'

Her breath wheezed in a sigh. 'Twenty-fifth of September, 1980. That's when I found Him. I'd seen a poster about this man who was coming to a meeting in Twickenham. An American, he was, and he'd died on the operating table, only he'd met the Lord while he was dead and the Lord had brought him back to life on condition that he would work for Him on earth. I went to the meeting, and at the end of it, I was Saved. Me and some other people told everyone about our sins, and the Lord's servant –' She pointed to the photograph of 'Gerald' and bowed her head as though in worship. ' – said that if we atoned for our sins we would be born again, too.'

'Miss Ickes, what has this got to do with Joanna's husband?'

'The worst things I'd done were to yield to Mr Costain's wicked temptations and the lie I told about the fire. I found Joanna's address in the telephone book and I went to see her, to confess. I wanted to make things right so I could be born again. And Mr Costain was dead by then, so he couldn't do anything to me. But she was in France and this man said he was her husband. He was very nice to me. When I said I wanted to tell the truth about Markie's death, he said I could tell him and he'd give

387

her the message. I told him everything, just like I've told you. I confessed, and I was shriven!'

Throughout the recital, Jo had not moved.

When Nick finished speaking, there was a long silence, which Lisa broke. 'Jo . . . all these years, you've believed that you killed your brother? Ben didn't tell you about this?'

'All these years. The nightmares . . . Before my mother was killed, Carl kept reminding me about it and saying I should be sent to prison. Oh, God . . .' She put her head in her hands.

After a moment, she looked up at Nick. 'Did you believe that woman? Ben knew the truth and he didn't tell me?'

'There was no reason for her to lie.'

More to herself than to them, she said, 'And he let me go on, knowing about the nightmares, that I'd never stopped feeling guilty, that I was always terrified of what I might do if I lost my temper again. He never mentioned Sandra, never once.' This was a Joanna none of them had seen before. Her eyes were blazing with anger.

'Jo . . .' Peter put his hand out to her.

'Leave me alone! I need to be by myself!' She ran to the door, past the guard who was sitting outside, back to the room in which she had slept.

She had been there for an hour when Molinard came back.

She said, 'Have they told you?'

'Told me what, Madame?'

'That I didn't kill my brother.'

He waved a hand impatiently. 'That is no longer important. You are free to go.'

She stared at him. 'Free?'

'Let your friends tell you.' His voice was bitter.

'M. le Commissaire . . .'

He snapped: 'They are waiting, Madame. And I have work to do.'

He was already marching away from her along the corridor, his back stiff, unable to bear for a moment longer the sight of this second English woman who had been responsible for his humiliation.

They were still in his office. As Jo went in, Peter said quietly, 'It's over. They know who killed Ben.'

'Who was it?' Her tone was curiously indifferent, as though the shock had had little impact after what she had already learned.

'André Dorsey. When Georgette went to see him after she got back from here this morning, she found him dead. He'd shot himself. He left a letter addressed to her.'

There was no weakening of her frozen self-possession as she said, 'Why did he do it.'

'Molinard gave us a copy of the letter. Will you read it?'

She took the single sheet of paper, covered on both sides with spiky hand-writing, and suddenly her legs weakened and she stumbled to a chair.

The words were unequivocal: 'To Madame Georgette Ponelle. You will know what to do with this. I was responsible for the death of Monsieur Absalom. He had defiled my daughter. When I returned home from the timber-yard for lunch that day, I found her crying. I forced her to tell me why. He had seduced her, and now he had discarded her. I was on my way to his house when I saw him standing near the palm-tree at the top of Le Mur. The sight of him, the thought of him with my daughter, sickened me. I believed then that before him, she had been a clean girl. I know better now, but I blame the men, not her.

'When I reached him, I told him what I knew. He asked me what I expected him to do, and said that Claudette was no better than a whore. Then he offered me money to keep quiet, for his wife's sake. When I refused it, he said I was the only person in the village who didn't already know what Claudette was. I knocked him down, and he hit his head on a rock. He managed to get up and tried to attack me, but he had dropped his stick, so he was very slow. I hit him again. We were nearer to the edge of the cliff than I realized. He staggered back, and fell. I went home.

'When I heard he was dead, my only feeling was that it was just retribution for what he had done to my daughter. Then I discovered that she was pregnant and we quarrelled. She told me Monsieur Absalom had not been the only man who had violated her. She seemed to enjoy tormenting me, naming all those who could have fathered her child. I am sorry that I cannot visit the same punishment on them as I did on Monsieur Absalom.

'I cannot live without her.'

PART EIGHT

1

La Belette was trying to settle back into normality. The Mahrs' cottage was still deserted, nothing had been heard of Ona. André and Claudette Dorsey had been buried.

The publication of Dorsey's confession had briefly revived media interest in the village, and the newsmen had been and gone.

But life, as Peter Garnier had predicted, was not, and might never be, the same. Too many secrets had been revealed, too many lives affected by the manner and consequences of Ben Absalom's death.

Some men, sitting silently over *déjeuner* with their wives, or standing at the bar of the Lion d'Or, mourned Claudette, remembering the brief exhilaration of their encounters. One wife left her husband when she found him weeping over a scrap of scarlet satin and lace, Claudette's panties, left with him as a favour.

The glamour cast by Ben's famous presence had gone, a doused light which left the people of La Belette poorer and duller.

Many women missed the sight of his handsome, limping figure, twisted hands resting on his stick as he walked slowly through the village, missed the automatic charm with which he had greeted them.

The person apparently most affected by the tragedies was Georgette Ponelle. After the Dorseys' deaths, she closed her shop and did not reopen it for several days.

Jo had been like a ghost, eating little, speaking only when she was spoken to, spending hours in her room. There were days when she did not bother to dress, and drifted through the house in a dressing-gown, her hair unbrushed. The postman brought letters from friends and acquaintances who had been shocked anew at the manner of Ben's death. She would not read them, nor answer the telephone. Peter called daily, but she wouldn't speak to him.

Only Nick realized the unhappiness this caused him.

It was mid-morning more than a week after the funerals when Lisa heard movement in the back of the house.

She found Jo in Ben's studio, kneeling in front of his desk, wearing a scarlet track-suit. She had washed her hair and it was curling around her face, which she had lightly touched with make-up.

The desk drawers were open and she was piling papers, paints, palettes and brushes into a basket.

She looked up. Her smile was unforced and the dark shadows had disappeared from under her eyes.

'Want to help me?'

'What are you doing?'

'I'm exorcizing Ben.'

Lisa blinked. 'Exorcizing Ben?'

'Exorcizing the Ben I never knew until after he died.' She sat back on her heels. 'I've given you a hard time, love, but I've had to come to terms with the future – and the past. Last night, I slept well for the first time in weeks, and when I woke up it was as though I'd shed a skin, like a snake. You understand?'

'No.'

'There's a new skin underneath the snake's old one. I've got a new life.' She stood up, and moved to the window, looking out onto the muddy hills which were now showing a flush of green under the autumn sunshine. Lisa leant against the door, watching her.

'Part of me will always love him,' she said slowly, 'I could understand the women, and the lies about what happened in Prague, and even the fraud. But what I can't

394

forgive is that he didn't tell me when he found out the truth about Markie's death.' She smiled wryly. 'I'll surprise you by not making excuses for him this time. I suppose I could say that maybe it was unimportant to him that he simply forgot to pass the information on. But I don't believe that. I believe he thought that if he told me the real story, his hold over me might have been weakened. He wanted me to go on for ever being grateful to him for having married me in spite of what I'd done.'

'He loved you, Jo.'

'Ben only liked people who were of use to him. I don't believe he really *loved* anyone . . .'

'That's nonsense!'

'No. He needed me, which is not the same thing. When I was young, I used to wonder why he married me, an unsophisticated, badly-dressed little girl out of a children's home. Then I realized that it was because he loved the idea of playing Professor Higgins. He *created* me. And because I was so grateful to him, my life revolved entirely around him and he could concentrate on his work, have affairs, come back when he felt like it. No way was he going to jeopardize that by destroying the most important reason for my gratitude. He needed to dominate people he was close to, you know . . .'

'I know,' Lisa said grimly.

'You had the strength of mind to get away from him, and so did Anna, eventually. Now it's my turn. I did love him and I don't regret our marriage. I'm glad I was useful to him. I only regret what I've found out about him. Maybe one day I'll forget the bad things and only remember how generous and charming and affectionate he could be. In the meantime, I'm ready to take charge of my own life.'

Lisa said, 'What about Peter?'

'What about him?'

She decided to break a confidence. 'He told Nick that

he can't face living here in Ben's shadow. He's thinking of moving back to Grasse.'

Jo said, 'Ben's not casting a shadow any longer. Let's see if Peter and Nick will meet us for dinner at the Lion d'Or this evening.'

Jean-Louis greeted them with kisses and led them to a table in a secluded alcove.

Peter had ordered champagne and Marie's niece, Louise, served them with cheerful efficiency. He raised his glass and, looking directly at Jo, said: 'It's in poor taste to call this a celebration, with the Dorseys scarcely settled in their graves, so let's call it a thanksgiving. To you, Jo, and your future.'

'I couldn't have survived all this without you. To *our* futures, Peter.'

As they drank, barriers were swept away. With no further words, the thanksgiving did become a celebration.

Two days later, Georgette trudged up the drive to the villa.

Lisa took her into the little sitting-room, where Jo was poring over bank-statements and tapping her calculator, trying to make sense of the figures.

She glanced up. 'If we were to let eight rooms on a bed and breakfast basis throughout the summer, we could just about break even . . .' She saw Georgette, and stopped.

'Joanna, may I talk to you?'

'Of course. Come in. Is Pierre-Luc with you?'

'I left him with Réné Raymond. There is something I have to say . . .' She glanced at Lisa, who tactfully excused herself.

Jo gestured towards a chair. 'Is there anything wrong?'

Georgette twisted her hands in her lap. 'I have come to say I'm sorry. I've been a coward, Joanna. I should have come before, but after the funeral . . . it has been a hard time.'

'But you don't have to apologize! Peter said you were

396

worried because you hadn't told Molinard earlier that Pierre-Luc had seen a man with Ben. I don't think it would have helped if you had. Molinard was convinced it was me.'

'It wasn't only that. Pierre-Luc knew who the man was.'

'He knew it was Dorsey?'

Georgette nodded. 'I couldn't tell the police . . . though I would have, I really would, if they had arrested you. But I hoped, I prayed that they would decide it had been an accident and I needn't say anything.'

Remembering the weeks of uncertainty, the agonizing hours of interrogation, there was anger in Jo's voice. 'Georgette . . . why?'

'It was because of André and me . . .'

'You and André?' Oh, God, she thought wearily, another worm crawling out of the can opened by Ben's death? She looked at Georgette's unhappy face and her anger faded. 'Tell me about it,' she said gently.

'You wouldn't have a cigarette, would you? No. Well, never mind. It all happened so long ago. Thirty years.

'I never had a husband, you know. I was born a Ponelle, and a Ponelle I have remained.

'I met André not long after I came over from Corsica. We were both living in Toulon. He was a good man. No tobacco, no alcohol. No women, either. He was a virgin at twenty-two. I was not a virgin at nineteen.

'He lived with his parents, but he used to come and see me at the shop where I worked. Then I invited him to my room, and one night . . . that was the beginning. It was a genuine affair of the heart for me. All happiness. Not for André. Ah, he hated it! I mean, he enjoyed the sex. When he had discovered it, he could not get enough. But to him, making love to someone not his wife was wrong. Only he would not ask me to marry him, because he believed that I was a loose woman, not the wife he had dreamed of.

'Then I found myself pregnant. For André, this was a dilemma. He did not want his child to be a bastard, so he said that we would marry. I had more pride than sense. I knew he didn't really love me. He didn't even respect me. So I refused him.

'Pierre-Luc was born. My poor Pierre-Luc, with his damaged brain – though he understands more than you think.' It was her ritual assurance. 'André thought that he was a punishment for his own sins and I believe that was what made him change from a boy into the – difficult man he became.

'He couldn't stand even to see Pierre-Luc, so he left Toulon.

'A few years later, I came into some money from my father. I heard that the shop in La Belette was for sale and I bought it. I truly didn't know that André was working here.

'He was angry because he thought I had come to be a nuisance to him. It wasn't true, and I never told anyone about us.' She sighed. 'Ever since he died, I've been wondering how different things might have been if we had married. Instead, he married Marianne. I think you hardly knew her.'

'I remember she was rather pretty, fair-haired, small.'

'And innocent. The kind of woman he had always wanted. He couldn't bear her ever to go out without him, or even talk to another man, and he adored the little girl she gave him. When she died, all his love for her was transferred to Claudette.

'It wasn't a normal life for a child, never allowed out by herself, kept away from the other village children because he was afraid of what the boys might do to her.

'She did escape when she went to school in Nice and lived with Marianne's sister, Nina, in an ordinary, cheerful house with several other children. My God, how she hated coming back here!

'André and I made friends again after Marianne died. He was able to talk to me and I was still fond of him.

'Claudette used to talk to me, too. She became a

naughty girl, but I liked her. She had a hard time with her father. I'm sure he would have kept her locked up if he could. He made her hate him, and to spite him, she went with any man who looked sideways at her.' She leant forward. 'Joanna, do you understand why I couldn't tell the police it was him? I always felt that what he became was partly my fault. Can you forgive me?'

Jo nodded slowly, then she said: 'Claudette came here the morning before Ben was killed. She wanted to talk to him, but he sent her away. Georgette, was Ben the father of her child?'

'I don't know! I swear to you, I don't know.' As she went towards the door, she paused and said, 'We never will know, Joanna. Better we don't.'

2

It was Georgette, almost returned to her former ebullient self, again reading her poems and extracts from her book to anyone who would listen, who passed on the news that the Mahrs' land had been sold.

Nick and Lisa were strolling through the village when she followed Pierre-Luc out of the shop, fussily adjusting his clothing as he shambled off towards the hills, his binoculars around his neck. Of all the inhabitants of La Belette, he was probably the only one who had remained untouched by the events of the past weeks.

'My dears, have you heard?' she called. 'We're to have another celebrity among us. Dominic Partridge has bought the Mahrs' place and he's going to build himself a palace!'

Having given her the pleasure of exclamations of surprise, and contributed what they knew about Partridge, they went on, their footsteps turning automatically towards the phoenix tree.

'That's bringing him rather too close for comfort,' Lisa said uneasily. 'You don't think he might be planning to open his museum there, do you?'

'Not much we could do to stop him, if he is. But I doubt it. Now Amyas is dead he doesn't have a ready-made curator and Jo has made it clear that she'll have nothing to do with the project. I suspect that Amyas was the moving spirit behind it. He probably talked Partridge into his dreams of glory.'

'I hope you're right. I wonder what Ben would have thought of having him as a neighbour?'

'Fortunately, what Ben would have thought isn't important any more.'

Surprised by his sudden asperity, she was silent for a moment, then she said with unusual meekness, 'I'm sorry, but you must accept the fact that I can't cut him out overnight. For better or worse, he shaped my life.'

'I know. I shouldn't have snapped. I won't forget him, either. But let's agree that from now on, it's our opinions that are important.'

She slipped her arm through his. 'Okay. I agree.'

'You said we had to get to know each other again. Now you've found out what a short-tempered sod I can be.'

'You could be a fairly cross little boy on occasions, so that comes as no surprise.'

They walked on in the soft afternoon sunlight, and came to the phoenix tree which had stood, unchanging throughout the weeks of uncertainty and threat, undamaged by the storms.

From the top of Le Mur they looked down in silence at the place where Ben had died. The land-slip had changed its contours, so that now, instead of a ledge, there was a continuation of the slope, built up by piles of mud and rocks brought down from the hill.

'In a few years, there'll be nothing to remind us,' he said. 'There'll be new growth: grass, bushes . . .'

'There's still the tree.'

'We could have it chopped down.'

She shook her head. 'I like it. It was always ours, more than Ben's.'

She was wearing the jeans and sweat-shirt she had worn when they first met after her return from England, the same kind of clothes that had been scattered on the ground when Ben had come upon them eight years ago. Her skin fresh and glowing, her hair loose, she looked little older than she had then.

Since their first embrace, they had kissed, sometimes with passion, sometimes casually, but he had made no attempt to carry the love-making any further.

Now, with a sense of déjà vu, he saw her smile, then sink onto her knees, part the palm fronds and slide into their shelter. He followed her, aware of a fluttering in his chest.

The space was neither large nor comfortable, and spikey, dead fronds hung to the ground around them. But the light was dim and green and there was a fresh smell of damp earth. The fronds they had pushed aside revealed a view across the valley to the slopes opposite.

When he joined her, she had already removed her shirt. Not looking at him, she spread it on the ground and lay back on it. She wore no bra.

As she began to undo her jeans, he said, 'No, let me,' and felt the soft flesh of her belly as he pulled off the trousers. Under them, she was wearing lacy bikini pants. He sat on his heels and looked at her, aware of increasing pressure in his crotch. 'I see women dressed – undressed – like you on every beach along the coast, but they don't affect me like this,' he remarked.

'Good thing. They'd arrest you for indecency.' Then she caught her breath. 'Hurry, Nick! It's been so long . . .'

This time there was no interruption, and neither of them spared a thought for Ben Absalom.

Much later, satiated and peaceful, they were leaning their backs against the tree-trunk when Nick caught a flash of reflected sunlight from the hill opposite.

'Jesus! Someone has binoculars . . .'

'That'll be Pierre-Luc,' she said calmly. 'Let's not deny him his pleasures.'

He pulled her to her feet. 'I'm getting a little tired of starring in skin-flicks. From now on, how about we make love in our own king-size bed in a shuttered room?'

'Is that a proposal or a proposition?'

'Coyness does not become you. It's what you want it to be.'

The moments before she answered seemed endless. Maybe he'd blown it, and she wasn't ready. Maybe she never would be. Maybe his light-hearted approach had offended her. Maybe he, not Peter, would have to move to Grasse, for he knew now that to continue to live in La Belette without her was unthinkable.

'Dammit, you can delete the proposition!' he burst out. 'It's a proposal!'

'That's all I wanted to hear. We've wasted enough time. How soon can we organize the ceremony?'

As they walked slowly back towards the villa, he said, 'I've got something else to ask you. But I don't want you to run out on me again.'

'It's about Simon, isn't it?'

He nodded. 'I need to know why you married him.'

She kept her eyes straight ahead. 'It was your fault. We met on the flight back from L.A. after . . . that night. I was upset. He was kind and sympathetic. We liked each other.'

'Did you know he was gay?'

'Not then. Simon hated being gay. Not so much now, he's come to terms with it. But then. What you have to understand is that we were always able to talk to each other, about anything. We were – always will be, whether you like it or not – friends. He told me about himself. When he was a kid, at boarding-school, the boys played about, but they talked about queers and fairies and pansies as though they were some kind of joke. It made him sick when he realized that he was one of them. All he wanted to do was conform.

'He read Psychology at University and went through analysis, to try and find out if there was any "cure."'

'How the hell could he have married you, knowing what he was?'

'I asked him to,' she said calmly. 'He was the only man I'd ever met, after you, that I thought I could live with. After Los Angeles, I was angry and humiliated. I needed someone who cared for me, and he did.'

'When did you find out he was gay?'

'He told me. But he'd had one or two affairs with women, trying to be what everyone called normal. We thought that maybe we could make it work. We both wanted to belong to someone. Am I making sense?'

'Sort of.'

'We got married and apart from a few men who knew about Simon, everyone thought it was an ideal match.'

'I read the reports.'

'So you did. It was never a bad marriage, we enjoyed each other's company enormously. But there was one thing missing.'

'Sex?'

She nodded. 'He tried, but it was no good. Something – repelled him. He explained that it wasn't me, it was any woman. He just couldn't make it.'

'Jesus . . . must have been terrible for both of you.'

'We kept up the façade for ages, but eventually there was a kind of coldness. I felt inadequate because I'd really thought that he'd change with me. I was pretty naive. He felt guilty because he knew he shouldn't have married me. Then one night we got drunk on two bottles of wine and cried together and agreed to a divorce.'

'Had he been having it off with other men?'

'Never, while we were living together, whatever was suggested in the newspapers.'

'But eventually he did.'

She went on steadily. 'There'd been publicity about the divorce. He'd moved out of the flat and we weren't seeing each other. He was lonely and one night he went into a gay pub in the West End. He was picked up by this boy, Chris. I saw him once, he was very beautiful, face like an angel, blonde hair. He told Simon he was nineteen and he was excited when he heard that he was connected with films because he wanted to be an actor. That was the start of their affair. He stuck to Simon like a leech and soon they were seeing each other every night.

'But Chris was only fifteen, and his father suspected what was going on. He and the police caught the two of them in bed together. Simon was prosecuted and sent to prison. That's all.'

Nick put his arm around her shoulders and said quietly, 'I'm sorry. For both of you.'

'He was shattered by the publicity. I went to the prison once, but he wouldn't let me go again. So I kept writing, and in his last letter – the one about you – he said that my letters had kept him alive.'

'Why would he write to you about me?'

'I told you, we used to talk about everything.' She stopped suddenly, remembering the night she had told Simon about her abortion, her distress at the memory, his compassion, and wondered whether she could ever bring herself to tell Nick. Maybe some day. But not now. It was too soon. 'I'd talked about you,' she said. 'He couldn't resist going to see you at the flat when I told him you were there.' She smiled. 'He wanted to check you out.'

With a touch of resentment, he said, 'I suppose he gave you his verdict?'

'It was favourable. He wrote and told me what had happened to you in L.A. and said I should at least talk to you about it. So I did.'

'And here we are. One day I'll apologize to him for what I've thought about him. He's a nice guy.'

'Yes. He's happier, too. Apparently he's formed a relationship with a decent man and they're going to set up house together.' The corners of her mouth twitched. 'It's his probation officer, actually, so prison wasn't a total disaster.'

3

The enormous invitation cards were delivered in the morning post. They were embossed in gold: 'Dominic Partridge invites you to a reception aboard his yacht, POPSTAR II, in St-Tropez, November 18, 9pm.'

There was one for Mlle Absalom, another for M. Nicholas Garnier.

Scribbled on each, also in gold, were the words. 'To show you the latest addition to my collection.'

On the telephone to Nick, Lisa said, 'Jo thinks we should go. She's worried in case Ona might have kept another forgery from us, and sold it to Partridge.'

It was a fine night, and the yacht was outlined by strings of coloured lights. Two burly guards stood at the bottom of the gangway, checking invitation cards and preventing sight-seers from coming too close.

When Nick and Lisa arrived, the deck was already a kaleidoscope of movement and colour, women competing for attention in designer dresses, a few of the men in dinner jackets, representatives of the pop world in combinations of beads, sequins, kaftans, rainbow coloured satin pants.

Dominic Partridge was alternately greeting his guests at the head of the gangway and drinking champagne directly from a bottle. He was wearing a black satin suit, the jacket lapels and wide trouser hems embroidered in gold. He wore no shirt and his black chest hairs peered through a breast-plate of gold and silver chains. The hand that was not lifting the champagne bottle was resting on the white silk bottom of a dark-haired girl who might or might not have been the one they had seen asleep on his bed.

He greeted Lisa and Nick extravagantly. 'Duckies, you look sensational! Go into the saloon. Drinks and eats first, then the unveiling.'

'Another Absalom?' Lisa said.

He winked. 'Wait and see. The Partridge Collection grows bigger and better all the time. I guarantee you'll be surprised.'

'I hear you've bought the Mahrs' land,' Nick said.

'Bought and sold it, dear, at a very, very nice profit. Had an offer through a lawyer in St-Trop'. Tied it up today.'

A new group of guests arrived, and they moved on.

'I'm delighted he's not going to be our new neighbour,' Lisa said. 'But I hope the alternative won't be worse. I don't fancy the idea of a shopping development, or a mess of ticky-tacky villas on our doorstep.'

'There won't be.'

'How do you know?'

'I was going to tell you later. Peter bought the land.'

'Peter? But why?'

'I have a feeling that he might be planning to build a house for his next bride. There's no way he's going to move into Ben's villa and our place is too full of memories of my mother.'

'Has he said anything to her yet? You know, she's going ahead with plans to run a kind of guest-house.'

Nick laughed. 'They're not likely to get far. He had a distinctly purposeful look in his eye when he went up to see her this evening . . .'

They made their way down the gilded staircase to the bar. It was crowded, but there was a brief falling-away of conversation as heads turned towards them. Narrowed eyes assessed them, estimating their interest-value, the cost of their clothes, their position in the celebrity hierarchy.

'You're wanted on set, Miss Absalom,' Nick muttered.

'You, too, Mr Garnier.'

Nick threw himself into a role he hadn't played since he left Los Angeles: the star, indifferent to (but never unaware of) being the focus of attention. When Lisa paused effectively on the staircase and looked up at him, her eyes alight with amusement, he knew that once again they were inside each other's minds. An admiring whistle from the bar signified that she, at least, had been awarded maximum points.

He concurred with the thought behind the whistle: there wasn't a woman who outshone her, although many might have paid more for their Oldfields and Chanels and Versaces, their jewels from Boucheron and Tiffany.

Lisa's only jewellery was a pair of long silver ear-rings which had, she'd told him, cost her a few pounds in an Indian shop in London. Their restrained shimmer exactly matched the full skirt of stiff silver-grey silk which was cinched into her tiny waist with a cummer-bund. Her blouse was transparently fine white cotton with floating sleeves and a boat neckline which fell off one tanned shoulder. Her hair was swept up and held by two silver roses made from the same silk as her skirt. Her only make-up was silvery eye-shadow and light pink lipstick.

Nick had dressed to create a background for her, in a black velvet Armani dinner jacket which was a relic from his Hollywood days, a white shirt with silver-edged frills, silver-grey satin cummerbund and bow tie which set off his dark good looks and emphasized the grey eyes that had made many a strong woman melt.

Posing, arm in arm, for just the right length of time, they were mischievously aware of the effect they created, of eyes envious and admiring.

They reached the glassy surface of the under-floor pool,

which was now illuminated and moved by artificial currents which were causing the water plants to dip and sway and the fish to swim in frantic circles.

As they crossed to the bar, they serenely ignored the *cognoscenti* identifying them to those less knowledgeable.

There they became the centre of a group eager to claim recognition by the evening's most spectacular couple, worth knowing as much for their titillating connection with various scandals as for their achievements.

Sarong-clad waiters circulated with champagne and trays of food: tiny *blinis* stuffed with caviare, smoked salmon, quails' eggs, miniature truffled omelettes, *pâté de foie gras*, *langoustines*, thumb-sized artichokes.

Their fellow-guests were a mixture of rich Riviera expatriates, pop musicians, singers and composers, entrepreneurs, journalists, television personalities, painters and art-dealers.

The decibels rose as the champagne flowed. When a tape of Partridge's former hits was turned on, with their insistent beat and his raucous vocal, it became virtually impossible to conduct a conversation below screaming-point.

At eleven o'clock, swaying slightly, he called everyone to order, and led the way to his art-gallery.

As he passed Lisa, he grasped her arm and said loudly, 'Here's the girl who's gonna appreciate this. The rest of you ignorant buggers wouldn't know a painting from a pagoda.'

Nick was on her other side as he opened the gallery door and ushered them in. The only difference in the exhibition from the previous visit was that *Wall with Shadows* was missing and an easel was standing in the centre of the room, draped in a length of gold silk.

'Right,' he shouted. 'Everyone ready? Wait for it!'

A drunken guest behind them was peeering owlishly at the covered easel. 'Magnificent,' he muttered. 'Brilliant. T'riffic. Work of genius, right?'

Partridge grasped the drape. 'What d'you think of this, then?'

He whipped it off and there, on the easel, was Ona's 'Picasso.'

'Great, innit?' he said to Lisa. 'Not so bad losing my Absaloms when Ona came up with this. Circus period. Painted 1905. Amyas had owned it for years.'

'Ona sold you *that*?'

'Cried because she had to let it go, but she needed the money. I had to sell a couple of other pictures to pay for it. What d'you think of it, then?'

'It's . . . interesting.'

'Worth every penny. I don't go for the later Picassos, but these . . . they're something. Not many in private collections. I've decided to spread my patronage, see? Now Amyas is no longer with us, and your Mum won't sell me the villa, and that Swiss bastard has decided to keep his Absaloms . . .'

'Have you checked its provenance, by any chance?' Lisa's voice was choked.

'Nah, don't need to. Ona explained. It isn't listed anywhere because Picasso gave it to Amyas, right out of his studio. They were old friends, you know. No mistaking it, is there? I mean, I'm a bit of an expert, too . . .'

'Amyas must have been one of the great con-men of all time!' Nick's voice was awed.

'Never mind Amyas . . . what about Ona?' Lisa was lying back in the car, exhausted from laughing. 'I bet she's enjoying herself in Acapulco or Palm Beach, with a new name and a new identity. We'll never hear of her again. So what do we do about it?'

He thought for a moment, then said decisively, 'Nothing. Partridge loves showing off his collection. The world is littered with art-historians who have recorded practically every brush-stroke Picasso made. Sooner or later, probably sooner, they're going to query that painting. Let *them* have the fun of telling him he's paid millions for a fake.'

EPILOGUE

NEW THEATRE OPENS
ON CÔTE D'AZUR

A glittering audience attended last night's opening of the Côte d'Azur's Phoenix Theatre in the village of La Belette.

The theatre is housed in the Villa Mimosa, former home of world-famous painter, Benedict Absalom. Performances, alternately in French and English, will be given in a natural amphitheatre in the villa's grounds. They will range from Shakespeare to modern revue.

Joint directors are M. Absalom's daughter, Lisa, a well-known English tv star, and her husband, actor/writer Nicholas Garnier, who is also preparing an authorized biography of M. Absalom.

The villa is the former home of M. Absalom's widow, who is now the wife of restaurateur M. Peter Garnier.

THE END

MADELEINE
by Elvi Rhodes

Although Madeleine Bates and Sophia Parkinson were both eighteen years old, the contrast between their two lives could not have been greater.

Sophia, spoilt pretty daughter of Helsdon's richest mill owner, lived a life of petted indulgence at Mount Royd, the Parkinson home.

Madeleine – daughter of a tyrannical and bigoted father who worked in the Parkinson mill – spent her time either at chapel, or working a fourteen hour day as housemaid at Mount Royd, a victim of Sophia's whims and occasional spitefulness.

But Madeleine – who beneath her obedient and dutiful exterior was volatile, strong-willed, and rebellious – was not the kind of young woman you could overlook, and when Leon Bonneau – younger son of a French wool baron – came to stay at Mount Royd he was, against his own inclinations, startled into noticing the dignity and beauty of the young housemaid.

From that moment on the lives of everyone at Mount Royd began to change, and Madeleine stepped forward into a new and challenging future.

0 552 13309 4

SUMMER VISITORS

by Susan Sallis

Madge was four years old when she first saw the Cornish sea and fell in love with it, and it was there that her family grew and suffered and loved. It was there she and her mother went to recover from a heartrending family tragedy – there she was forced reluctantly into marriage – there she fell into a wild and passionate wartime love.

And it was there she saw her children grow and love and cope with the secret legacies the years had left them, until finally they became more than just summer visitors.

The magnificent story of a family and the woman who held them together.

0 552 13346 9

SHAKE DOWN THE STARS

by Frances Donnelly

There were three of them, three bright pretty girls –
though Beattie was beautiful rather than merely pretty –
who all came from the same village and who couldn't wait
to throw themselves into the golden future.

Virginia was shrewish, bitchy, and biting. Even though
the family estates were mortgaged up the hilt she was still
the squire's daughter and she didn't let anyone forget it.
She just knew that when she 'came out' and turned into a
real London debutante, everything was going to be O.K.

Beattie was only the gardener's daughter – and Virginia
didn't let Beattie forget that either – but as well as being
beautiful, Beattie was bright. Beattie had won a place in a
teacher-training college and nothing was going to stop her
putting the village and everything in it right behind her.

Lucy was – well – just thoroughly nice. Used by everyone
– and especially by Virginia – all she really wanted was to
marry nice middle-class Hugh, with whom she was wildly
in love, and carry on living a nice middle-class life.

What none of them had reckoned with was that it was
1939. The three pretty girls were about to be thrown
headlong into the turmoil of the war.

'I warmed to *Shake Down the Stars* and I think it will be
tremendously successful'
Susan Hill

0 552 12887 2

A SELECTED LIST OF FINE NOVELS
AVAILABLE FROM CORGI BOOKS

☐	13498 8	MOTHS	Rosalind Ashe £2.99
☐	13289 6	MOVING AWAY	Louise Brindley £2.99
☐	13230 6	AN EQUAL CHANCE	Brenda Clarke £3.99
☐	12887 2	SHAKE DOWN THE STARS	Frances Donnelly £3.99
☐	12387 0	COPPER KINGDOM	Iris Gower £3.50
☐	12637 3	PROUD MARY	Iris Gower £3.99
☐	12638 1	SPINNER'S WHARF	Iris Gower £3.99
☐	13138 5	MORGAN'S WOMAN	Iris Gower £3.99
☐	13315 9	FIDDLER'S FERRY	Iris Gower £3.50
☐	13316 7	BLACK GOLD	Iris Gower £3.99
☐	13631 X	THE LOVES OF CAITRIN	Iris Gower £3.99
☐	13384 1	A WHISPER TO THE LIVING	Ruth Hamilton £3.50
☐	13616 6	WITH LOVE FROM MA MAGUIRE	Ruth Hamilton £3.99
☐	10249 0	BRIDE OF TANCRED	Diane Pearson £2.99
☐	10375 6	CSARDAS	Diane Pearson £4.99
☐	10271 7	THE MARIGOLD FIELD	Diane Pearson £2.99
☐	09140 5	SARAH WHITMAN	Diane Pearson £3.50
☐	12641 1	THE SUMMER OF THE BARSHINSKEYS	Diane Pearson £4.99
☐	12607 1	DOCTOR ROSE	Elvi Rhodes £2.99
☐	13185 7	THE GOLDEN GIRLS	Elvi Rhodes £3.99
☐	13481 3	THE HOUSE OF BONNEAU	Elvi Rhodes £3.99
☐	13309 4	MADELEINE	Elvi Rhodes £3.99
☐	12367 6	OPAL	Elvi Rhodes £3.99
☐	12803 1	RUTH APPLEBY	Elvi Rhodes £4.99
☐	12375 7	A SCATTERING OF DAISIES	Susan Sallis £3.99
☐	12579 2	THE DAFFODILS OF NEWENT	Susan Sallis £3.99
☐	12880 5	BLUEBELL WINDOWS	Susan Sallis £3.50
☐	13136 9	ROSEMARY FOR REMEMBRANCE	Susan Sallis £3.99
☐	13346 9	SUMMER VISITORS	Susan Sallis £3.99
☐	13543 3	BY SUN AND CANDLELIGHT	Susan Sallis £3.99